FIRST COUNTRY

Tinged with Rose

Previous Legends

HEARTLAND
On the Side of Angels

EMPIRE FOR LIBERTY
Dangerous Lullaby

FIRST COUNTRY

Tinged with Rose

TERRI SEDMAK

THE
LIBERTY & PROPERTY
LEGENDS

This novel is a work of fiction.

Visit www.terrisedmak.com
Official website of THE LIBERTY & PROPERTY LEGENDS
A Saga of The West & Gilded Age America

Credits: *The Interlude/The Student's Tale, Fragments, The Light of Stars, Emma & Eginhard* by Henry Wadsworth Longfellow; *We Will Not Be Slaves*, Sons of Liberty Traditional; *I Ride an Old Paint* and *Git Along Little Dogies*, Cowboy Traditional; *Pike's Peakers of 1859* by Lawrence N. Greenleaf; *Love's Philosophy* by Percy Bysshe Shelley; *Emma* by Jane Austen; *Les Miserables* by Victor Hugo.

Cover & Seal Graphics by Blow-Up Pty Ltd

Published by VIVID Publishing
P.O. Box 948, Fremantle
Western Australia, 6959
www.vividpublishing.com.au

National Library of Australia Cataloguing-in-Publication entry:
Sedmak, Terri
First country : tinged with rose
ISBN: 9781925086195 (pbk.)
Series: The Liberty & Property Legends
A823.4

Before the world as we know it,
before there were countries, before cities,
towns, villages or hamlets, there were families.
They have been the powerhouse of humanity
for hundreds upon hundreds of millennia.
Before language, before fire, before the
reach of history we were family.
This is dedicated to families.
And to your family.
Peace.

I have a tale to tell... a tale that throws
A softer light, more tinged with rose,
Than your grim apparition cast
Upon the darkness of the past.

―❦―

Henry Wadsworth Longfellow
Interlude, The Student's Tale

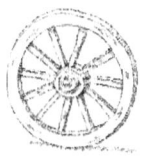

THE STORY SO FAR...

From Luke Taylor's journal, dated March 2nd, 1885...

When Mart was murdered by Wilson Cutter in March of '84, I know part of me died right along with him; his blood and my wretchedness went down into the snow of that Missouri forest and I carried the dead part of both us out of it, not knowing what good there was in existing.

Wasn't till I met Jennifer in Cheyenne that I realized that some part of me still believed in that good. She and she alone lifted me out of that bloodied snow. Gave me a glimpse of what life could be.

Ed Parsons was responsible for all the misery up till then; he hired Cutter to terrorize us – the Alliance – and kill Mart; and if that wasn't unspeakable enough, he arranged for Maverick to shoot K dead in broad daylight. I'm unable to put into words how that feels. I dream about K often, and about that moment when I heard the shot and pushed through the crowd to find her dead on the sidewalk.

The Alliance it seemed to me was like a thin sheet of damp paper, the edges ripped and not much to stop it from coming away into pieces. Only Adam, Mart and Tressa's baby boy, seemed to hold those pieces together.

I saw Cutter hanged for his crime, for killing Mart. I'd done what I had to do to get justice for Mart, only to have this achievement blown away by K's death. K had fought so valiantly to bring Parsons to trial; she gave everything to see it done. All she wanted was to do right by Mart.

For Mart's part in all this, I can only say my mind is not at rest about it. He did what he thought was right. He tried to protect the Alliance from a terror that was beyond one man's capability.

With Parsons incarcerated and Wilson Cutter hanged, we were so ready for the taste of victory. It was not to be.

I had no fight left in me to help find K's assassin.

I couldn't stay in Cheyenne, or on the ranch. I left for San Francisco, I left Jennifer. And I regretted it. But missing Jennifer more than words can say did something to me, it gave me cause. I decided to go back to her, and K deserved justice so I was going to get it for her.

There in San Francisco, Jennifer came for me, and gave me something else - hope. And I was confident I could know that damn secret of hers and bear it well. But the secret broke my heart. Her father, Dermot, cruelly mistreated her as a child, and disinherited her when she was eighteen years old. Darling Jennifer. My anger towards him consumed me. It damaged us, and she left me.

When I got back to Cheyenne, tailing her, I found another secret waiting for me – a betrayal. I had sketched businessman Loren Bodecker's likeness in my file back before Mart died, not knowing who he was, but then Cam and Cliff had withheld from me who Bodecker was and his suspected involvement in K's murder. If I had known of their suspicions I could have protected her, like I'd sworn I would always protect her.

Bodecker's business associate was a man called Donnelly. He operated the secret assassin group called Maverick, created to terrorize the small ranchers and sheep farmers and whoever else got in the way of his plans. One of these snipers was K's murderer; his name is Swinton Carter.

In one last-ditched effort to be rid of the Alliance, Donnelly and his Mavericks tried to wipe us out by placing snipers at the Diamond-T and at the Keatons' and across our valley. Without the assistance of reporter Emmaline Roberts, Sheriff Dave Ransford, and Deputy Chase Deloight, we'd all be dead. Ransford was mortally wounded for our cause; we owe him and will never forget him. Deputy Crogan was killed by a sniper before he could raise a single shot in defense of us.

Emmaline arrived in Cheyenne when I was in San Francisco; Charlie Quaid, editor of The Tribune, hired her to investigate what he thought was a cover-up by Cam and Cliff of K's murder. In the process of investigating, she became a target of the Mavericks and was nearly killed - twice. Cliff and Emmaline kind of fell for one another, although as fine a woman as Emmaline is, she's the ambitious kind and she doesn't like sheriffs much, so Cliff has his work cut out for him.

I'd be dead, too, if it weren't for Cliff. He rescued me from the clutches of Donnelly's drug-pedaling scientist, Louis Porterfield, and brought me home in time to fight off the last of the mavericks, saving Ethan and my cousin, Ben Taylor, from certain death. Now Cliff and I are in trouble with the law. Somehow we'll have to convince the Judge I didn't do those things Sheriff Walker in Lincoln County charged me with, murder and assault the worst of them; and Cliff, for helping me escape.

Less said about my time in Porterfield's basement of hell the better; visions and nightmares torment me and sometimes I get confused about which reality I live in, this or that. Ethan says I should write down what curses me, that it might take it from my mind and confine it to the page where it cannot harm me. He is too often right to ignore, but the day when I can feel comfortable about doing this has not yet come.

So much has happened I could fill a whole book, and who knows, one day I might just do that. But the brevity of this journal will have to do for now… and Caroline's courage, Emmaline's tenacity and Cliff's nobility will be briefly recorded here until then.

In three days' time the Alliance will be heading back to Cheyenne. It will be the anniversary of Mart's death and I can't think of a better way of marking it than in a united act of defiance.

We have lived to fight another day. And we *will* fight. And we *will* grow strong. And we *will* protect our liberty, all that we have a right to, and all we hold dear.

> The birthright we hold, shall never be sold,
> But sacred maintained to our graves,
> And before we'll comply, we'll gallantly die,
> For we must not, we will not be slaves, brave boys,
> For we must not, we will not be slaves.
>
> ~ The Sons of Liberty

L.T., 2nd March 1885

Ethan...

Diamond Bend Ranch,
Texas, September 1864

"What in tarnation is that in the goddamn middle of no place fit for nothin' but a white bone carcass and turkey buzzards?"

Ethan finishes his mutterings and reins the pinto to a stop; he squints against the afternoon sun's slanting rays trying to make it out... a long brown-colored object in the shade of a small tree some fifty feet away. The last three years away in the war might have taken a lot away from him but his power of observation ain't one of them.

After several moments of squinting and moving his head this way and that, he still can't make it out. Can't be sure it ain't a steer laying there... there are two turkey buzzards a-circlin' high above in a blue sky with nothing else it in but heat. The Rangers have been about their work lately... and the thought gives him a chill. There was talk a couple of weeks ago that they had a partic'lar Comanche band in their sights and...

Last thing he wanted was to get caught in their cross hairs, out on the range like this, miles from the home ranch and...

No, he admits to himself, that ain't the only thing. He still ain't got used to not having to look over his shoulder every second for a sniperin' blue belly. Just cause he got himself out of the war at last don't mean the war went and got itself out of his head.

Nope. That ain't happenin' anytime soon. Sure they ain't been home near long enough to feel any real comfort or peace of mind, more like relief. Just a few weeks is all. He and Morgan give each other that look from time to time... they're home and nobody's gonna make 'em leave again for some damn fool cause. But it ain't the same. The ranch is in bad shape. Sara is peaked and nervous all the time; Katrine and Luke are quiet and slowly coming out of themselves with their Pa; Morgan is doing the best he can with 'em. Somehow they're gonna have to make it better, or different. You can't go back and look for something that don't exist no more.

In the baking heat, the object of his attention moves...

What the heck would be lolling around out here of its own free will? Mabbe not *what*; mabbe it's a *who*...

He looks around; removes his hat and wipes his forehead on his sleeve. Hot and desolate, ain't no other way to describe it. There's no relief from this kind of heat out here. Even the cattle have given up on the place till summer loses its grip.

Well, whatever or whoever it is, it don't look to be going nowhere soon, and he can't see no Rangers for him to get caught up in the middle of their raiding shenanigans... he fixes his hat back on his head and urges the pinto forward.

Ethan dismounts and reins his pinto to a nearby bush. Then he approaches the shivering bundle beneath the tree. His breath gets caught in his chest at the sight he sees there.

She's a woman... a Comanche woman by the look of her. Young and small, quivering and helpless. Like an orphaned baby critter. His heart lurches with pity inside of his chest, and emotion pours out and he has to swallow over and over...

She's hurt, somewhere, he guesses, or sick. She's dirty, her face shines with sweat, her black hair is coming loose and sticking out of its long braids and weaving, matting around the edges.

In a frail voice she's mumbling something over and over, like she's delirious.

"Ma'am..." he says. "Ma'am..."

Her eyes fly open and fear seizes her features like he'd slapped her or something.

"Ma'am..."

A frenzy of words pours from her mouth. He doesn't have to understand Comanche to know she's pleading for her life.

2

He changes his tone, which ain't hard since what he's feeling right now is a whole parcel of pity.

"I ain't a Ranger, Ma'am, don't fear now."

If he was, forget about pity, there wouldn't even be mercy; he'd have shot her dead by now.

"I won't hurt you. I promise."

He reaches out his hand slowly. She whimpers and squeezes her eyes shut.

"I'm Ethan," he says, bringing his hand to rest on her shoulder. "You got no call to be scared."

He goes back to the pinto and retrieves his canteen. To the young woman, he says, "Water, Ma'am?"

She opens her eyes and sees the canteen he's holding out to her. Shivering but understanding, she nods. It seems like she's trying to get upright but she's that weak she can't do it.

"Let me help," he says.

When she nods her agreement, he puts one hand behind her head and lifts it so she can drink from the canteen.

"I bet you're starvin' too," he murmurs, looking at the slender nature of her buckskin-clad body.

The more she drinks the more revived she looks. He leaves her sitting up with the canteen and this time grabs a blanket from the pinto. This he puts around her trembling shoulders, although knowing as he does all kinds of Indian customs, it might not be the wisest thing to do. She might take it the wrong way. She looks up into his face with her feverish black eyes.

Beneath the dust and dirt he glimpses an elegant beauty and strength, or the promise of them, and again he feels something move inside of him, but this time it ain't pity. He notices a lot more about her now. She's wearing an extravagant beaded necklace, and her buckskin dress is of the finest quality. Stacked bracelets adorn both her wrists and – worn out as the soles are – her boots are fringed and decorated with fine beads. She is no ordinary Comanche squaw; that much he can tell.

The soulful black eyes seem to be noticing things about him as well. He ain't much to look at, but he reckons he's right more presentable than her at the moment. The thought brings a smile to

3

his face; her eyes react at once, watching his mouth smiling at her and then meeting his gaze again.

She seems to droop all of a sudden and he catches her, stops her from falling into the dust under the tree and hurting herself.

He holds her gently against his chest, saying, "Come on, you'll be okay. I'm gonna help you. Food, rest and a safe place away from those Rangers and I reckon you'll be as right as rain..."

After another mouthful of water she bucks up again. She looks up into his face with those soft, feverish black eyes and he thinks maybe he's gone a little stir crazy from riding all day in the sun and the heat.

"I'm Ethan..." he murmurs. "What's your name?"

Her eyes get a bright look to them, like she understands him and she's not scared of him.

She places a small hand on her chest and says in a gentle voice, "Eka Tomoobi."

ONE

Is it the tender star of love?
The star of love and dreams?
Oh no! from that blue tent above
A hero's armour gleams.

Henry Wadsworth Longfellow
The Light of Stars

Emmaline

St John the Baptist Church
Cheyenne, Wyoming Territory
March 1885

"Bless me, Father, for I have sinned."

"And?"

"Oh… and it has been three months since my last confession… possibly… I think. It could be more, but I've been busy."

Emmaline hastily remembers to make the sign of the cross... even if Father Nugent doesn't notice on his side of the small grate nailed to the dark window of the Confessional, likely God will.

"I see. Proceed."

"Father, I…"

"Yes…"

"I… I missed Mass."

"Happens a great deal in these parts. For obvious reasons."

"I won't go to hell?"

"God will forgive. That's why you are here. Now then, was there anything else?"

"Well…"

"Yes, go ahead." Father Nugent's voice is oiled with practiced patience.

"Father, I want a man I can't have," she blurts out. And then breathes. There. She's said it.

"Does this man know how you feel, my child?"

"Is that important, Father?"

"It could be. What precludes you, daughter?"

7

"Precludes? Er... Well, he... he's not Catholic, Father."

"Yes, I see... Mm, a challenge, yes."

"And... and he works in a job I want nothing to do with."

"Is it illegal?"

"No, nothing like that... It's a very legal job in fact..."

"But, there are good qualities in this man you find yourself drawn to?"

"Yes. He has many admirable qualities..." Far too many. "...but I can't think about those."

"Search your heart. Are you in love with this man?"

"Does God really need to know that, Father?"

"God already knows."

"Oh... yes, of course..."

Father Nugent clears his throat. "However, you might like to get it off your chest..."

"No, my chest is fine."

Emmie, for God's sake, he's a priest.

Celie, may I please attend Confession in peace... you, my sins, the priest and God all at once is too much even for me.

"God forgives unconditionally, my daughter, but the balm of Confession only truly works if you are prepared to place yourself humbly in the hands of God. And right now I am hard pressed to see what sin you have committed, except of course if you have acted sinfully upon your feelings and now must confess it."

"No, I haven't done anything like that, Father."

"But you have thought about it?"

Emmaline clears her throat.

"Well, my child?"

She bites her bottom lip. Everything was *fine* until *he* returned from Bright River seventeen days ago.

Her progress she deemed fair.

And then he came to see her at the Tribune to pay her his share of the purchase of her mink hat and muff.

So shocked was she that all her so-called progress disintegrated at the sight of him, she accepted the money, put her head down and pretended to keep writing her copy.

He made a gentle grunt and said, "That was too easy."

8

"We had an agreement."

"Ah," he murmured, "penance for my sins."

"If you say so," she muttered.

"I would like to see how my investment looks on you."

Her pencil slipped. "Not possible at the moment."

"Well, I can see it right there on the desk..."

"So it is." She reached for the hat, planted it on her head, picked up her pencil and continued writing her copy.

All he said was, "Glad to see you looking so well, Emma."

And then he left.

Meanwhile, her stomach had collapsed.

It was only then did she realize the enormity of the task before her. And she reapplied her efforts. True, she had to see him often, since their paths crossed through work, but she didn't have to speak to him, did she, engage him socially?

That is, until they met twice in four days in the only decent bookstore in town, which like most good bookstores holds more books than it has shelves and more shelves than is comfortable to accommodate; so while hiding in the reference section was tempting and feasible, it was not meeting the problem head on and fixing it. Accusing him of following her into the store was not viable since he was already there when she walked in, both times.

On the first occasion she was polite but showed no interest in him or his books. She purchased her book and left, before him in fact. On the second occasion she charged across the store in her lunch break, towards the history section, only to run into him.

He smiled and said, "New consignment of history books."

"I know," she replied.

He stood back. "You first."

"You were here before me."

"I insist."

"Very well." She ran her gaze along the spines.

"There's something inviting about the smell of new books..." he remarked.

After spying a book on the topic that interested her – the French Revolution, in fact – she had to stretch to reach it.

"Allow me," he said and pulled down the book.

9

She thanked him, took her book and stepped back to decide if it was worth her hard-earned money. Her curiosity for what he would choose burned too hot to ignore this time and from the corner of her eye she watched him take a book entitled *History of the Fourth Estate in America*. He flipped through it, stopping here and there to read the text, something she should've been doing with her selection. After forcing herself to do so, she found that by and large the book was very uninterestingly written; she sighed and snapped it shut.

"No good?" he said gently; by now he had his book under one arm and was selecting another.

"No. I prefer history books that make you feel as though you're right there when it's happening…"

"I agree."

"Would you mind placing this back for me? I must return to work. Thank you kindly."

Once he'd taken the book from her, she mumbled goodbye and left.

From then onwards she chose a different time of day to haunt the bookstore.

She knew she would succeed eventually; she just needed time and more effort. She saw him a great deal; in the street, at the courthouse, at the jail… wherever. She poured so much effort into her goal that it became a living breathing entity of its own, ready to overtake her life, and keeping the problem very much before her.

She had to try something new.

Don't try quite so hard, she told herself. Focus on work, on reading, on writing. On other people.

She liked Pat McNamara a lot. And her little twin daughters, Lucy and Lola; trying to tell them apart was the ultimate diversion.

And she found that Meg Faraday, somewhat confined by her condition of being in the family way, was always pleased to see her.

Father Nugent welcomed all helpers in the parish, particularly when it came time for the food and clothing hampers for the poor needed to be packed and distributed.

But even this wasn't simple.

She was assigned to the food hampers, enjoying both the task and the camaraderie of her fellow-packers; when the men came to

10

take the hampers for distribution, she employed every effort to lift her hamper only to find the strong pair of hands relieving her of it belonged to *him*.

Their fingers mingled at the moment of exchange. A delicious charge of something forbidden wriggled up her arms and struck her heart. They seemed to stare at one another in some kind of *Love's Philosophy* trance for uncountable moments, during which she found herself compelled to admit, amongst other things, that her nursed and harbored resentment from their argument at the Diamond-T had evaporated completely, as if it never happened. She'd forgiven him? She was over it?

Oh dear...

This was not good.

The only barricade left standing had fallen.

"I... thank you," she mumbled.

"You're welcome," he replied with a smile. And left.

And then one evening they found themselves walking home at the same time, along 19th Street. She heard footsteps behind her, and turned to see; she stopped, knowing they would have to talk because she couldn't out stride him. He halted by her side and they looked at one another by the light of a perfect wintry dusk.

"Allow me to carry your satchel," he said.

"Not necessary," she said.

"It looks heavy."

"I can manage."

But he took it from her. "Let's go."

And he walked on with her towards Nan Morris' front gate.

"I received a wire from Luke today," he said. "He'll soon be returning to Cheyenne."

"And he's well?"

"I'm not sure to be honest. I mean, I believe he's physically recovered, but..."

"There's a long road ahead."

"Mm. The mind is complex, and Luke's mind more than most."

"I believe I know what you mean."

"I heard on the grapevine that you called on Cora Daniels."

"What else did the grapevine say?"

"Not enough."

"What I spoke about with Mr Quaid's infamous ex-secretary is none of your concern."

He laughed gently. "Forgive my curiosity, but oh, to have been a fly on the wall…"

"Very well, I shall tell you. Cora is very happy where she is; she said Mr Quaid was a good boss, but his crooked tie bothered her daily. She believes his accusation of her desertion to the Bugle is an over-reaction, and Mr Quaid forgets people are human beings, not machines."

"They have feelings, emotions and like to think for themselves."

"I believe I said I would tell you what Cora spoke about, not discuss it; and it is confidential, so I don't expect to hear it doing the rounds."

"Discretion is my middle name."

"What *is* your middle name?"

"Curious?"

"You know mine."

"So I do."

And he didn't tell her.

He merely smiled.

Locked eyes with her.

And handed over her satchel.

"Good night, Emma."

He took himself off. His tall striding figure disappeared into the dusk and her heart was paralyzed by abysmal clichés… gone from racing like a train to sinking like a stone. She was forced to admit that the friendship and nothing more she demanded of him, she was unable to command of herself. And it occurred to her that she would have to learn to live with this for as long as she stayed in Cheyenne, until she could put hundreds of miles between them and start over again, and it would all dissolve into a distant memory.

She needed more help.

Emmie, pay attention to the priest…

"But you have thought about it?" Father Nugent repeats.

She blinks. "No, I've been fighting it."

"Ah."

"Father, I... I just want to get him out of my head."

"Constant prayer, fervor for your goal, will win out in the end, child, but you must be persistent. Unless..."

"Unless what, Father?"

"Unless you are too scared to confront these feelings as something genuine and worth considering. Have you truly examined them, rationally, carefully?"

She swallows and feels her insides squirming. "Father, why are you counseling me this way?"

"Because you may be running away from something God wants for you. And that would be serious indeed."

"God doesn't want this for me, Father. He wants what my mother wants, believe me."

Again, Father Nugent clears his throat. "All right then. I want you to pray, my child, and ask for guidance – heaven knows, in this day and age we could all use a little. Now... was there anything else..."

Anything else? How much help does he think she needs?

Jennifer

St Louis, Missouri,
March 1885

Petrie Avenue stretches out ahead, lined with ornamental plum trees that are patiently waiting for the end of winter so they can bloom. When that happens there will be pink everywhere, on the trees, in the air, along the sidewalk.

As if to give hope to such a fervent wish, the sun emerges. All at once there are reflections bouncing off everything, while the dark trunks of the plum trees stand to attention. The comfortable homes adorning both sides of the street come to life as the sunshine illuminates them, like peacocks opening their extravagant tails and showing off their gorgeous plumage.

The whole prospect is admittedly a little overdone, and yet somehow irresistible.

"I love the street where we live, George," Ariel declares. A prospect even more irresistible to a shy and whimsical little girl who recently turned seven. "It's lovely."

"Even in winter," Jennifer agrees. "And don't call me, George."

"You'd let me if you weren't in such a big hurry."

"No, I would not."

"But ain't… "

"Aren't."

"Aren't you going to even stop and admire the trees?"

"They'll be worth admiring in another month or so. Right now, they are waiting with as much anticipation as we are for the touch of a truly warm day."

"You think they're boring, don't you?"

"Long suffering. Now, if we hang about any longer you'll be late home for your piano lesson, and your mother will have my guts for garters."

Ariel bursts into soft laughter. "You're not supposed to say those things like guts for garters in front of me. I ain't..."

"Uh..." Jennifer prompts.

"*I'm* not supposed to know stuff like that."

"There's worse stuff you could know, believe me."

"I believe you, AJ."

They look at one another and giggle.

"Just stop for a second, AJ, and let's look," Ariel continues to coax. "You won't regret it. It'll do you good."

Jennifer capitulates. "One minute, that is all. Which tree is your favorite again?"

Ariel breaks away immediately and runs. "This one, up here," she shouts over her shoulder, almost slipping on the wet sidewalk. "Hurry, or I'll be late for my lesson."

"I'm not running in the street, even for you, Ariel Sullivan."

She arrives at the tree. Ariel is twirling around like a top with her arms in the air, breathing in so hard she wonders her little niece doesn't pass out.

"It's just magic, AJ. Breathe, go on."

"My lungs are cold enough already thanks."

"When you look up, all you can see are the branches reaching up like long skinny arms holding giant lumps of snow. I imagine them pink. I love pink."

"That I know." Jennifer raises her eyes to the spectacle of snow-laden boughs above their heads.

"Are you imagining it pink, AJ? Pink. Pink. Pink."

"I'm trying," she says and closes her eyes to satisfy Ariel.

"Ain't it beautiful?"

A breeze springs up.

"Ooh, it's so cold..." Ariel breathes. "Not good for pink."

Jennifer opens her eyes to snowflakes scurrying all around them. Ariel's expressions of delight intensify as the white dusting falls on Ariel's bouncy, blonde curls and her own dark ones.

"Snowflakes are so beautiful in your hair, AJ. With your chestnut hair and the snowflakes, you look like this plum tree!"

"Chestnut?"

"Papa says your hair is chestnut."

"Papa is very kind," Jennifer says dryly and Ariel giggles.

"This breeze is kind of gentle, ain't... isn't it, AJ?"

She allows herself a moment to feel the breeze from Ariel's perspective. "Yes, I suppose it is."

"It feels like something... um... I know, after Papa's kissed me goodnight, I feel his breath, all softy on my cheek. That's it."

"I'm sure Papa's kiss isn't quite as chilly, Ariel."

"You know what I mean, AJ."

"I guess. I think we'd better go, Ari."

"It's angel breath."

She stops as she's reaching for Ariel's hand. "Angel breath?"

"God sending his breath down from heaven to earth. Like God's kiss, AJ."

She looks up at the tree again. "A kiss?"

"God can't kiss everyone himself. That's why he has angels to help out."

"What would an angel be doing here with us?"

"Looking after us. And giving us a special kiss. You see, AJ, if you don't stop and look at the plum trees and nature, you might miss the angel's breath."

"Oh..." she says, wishing she wasn't so impressed. She glances up and down the street, thereby spotting Ariel's piano tutor striding up the front path. "Oh my, Mr Gladtidings is on his way."

"Mama said you shouldn't call him that," Ariel giggles.

"I know. It's wicked. Now, you'd better run."

Ariel starts moving. "I ain't allowed to run in the street," she shouts over her shoulder again. Ariel likes to do most things on the run or back to front. She stops suddenly and turns around. "You won't be sad again, because of the angel breathing on us, will you, AJ?"

She feels like someone poured cement in her shoes.

"No, Ari."

Ariel grins and takes off again. The agile youngster skids past the austere (*grumpy-britches*) Mr Adams on the doorstep, almost knocking his music satchel out of his hand. With that heart-warming sight concluding with the thump of the door, she raises her eyes again to the crown of snow above her. There's no chance her sadness will return because it has never left.

Why won't they write her? Why do they leave her in the dark?

You ran away, the plum tree sighs above her. *Jennifer, you ran away.*

Luke

Judge Callaghan smacks his gavel and brings proceedings to order.

"Now, Mr Taylor, you are aware, I trust, that this hearing is to determine whether you should be expedited to North Platte, Nebraska, where you have been charged with murder, assaulting a deputy and escaping custody."

"Your Honor, if I may…"

"You know the procedure, Mr Faraday, wait your turn."

"Yes, Your Honor."

"And, Mr Ryan, this hearing is also to determine whether you should be expedited to said place for concealing a prisoner – Mr Taylor – and enabling his escape. Present your case, Mr Walker."

Sheriff Ralph 'Iron pants' Walker gets to his feet. "Your Honor, Mr Taylor was found hunched over the body of the prostitute Cadie McClements; she had just been murdered. Her neck was broken. Witnesses say his hands were on her neck. I arrested him immediately. He claimed he was innocent and that he saw who did it. A man named Donnelly. He asked me to contact Cheyenne, said that Sheriff Ryan would vouch for him.

"It was Sunday evening, Your Honor, I said he'd have to wait till morning. He was mighty agitated, like he couldn't wait. Next thing I hear, the deputy in charge of jailing him has been bashed and Mr Taylor's got away. I searched high and low throughout Lincoln County and I could not find him. Mr Ryan arrived in North

18

Platte disguising himself as a reporter investigating Mr Taylor's disappearance, locates him and then steals him away.

"If Mr Taylor was innocent of the charges, why didn't Mr Ryan front up at my office? Mr Ryan relinquished his position as the elected law enforcement officer of Laramie County, stole into my jurisdiction and helped himself to my prisoner. Mr Taylor here walks free and easy around Cheyenne as if he's done nothing wrong, Judge, right under the nose of US Marshal Dan Hummer. But I haven't dropped those charges because I have found no evidence that makes me believe I should. Mr Taylor is still my prisoner."

Ralph Walker sits.

"Thank you, Mr Walker. Mr Faraday, I'll hear from you now."

Cam is quickly on his feet. "Firstly, Your Honor, Mr Taylor is no murderer and there are scores of people who will testify to that. He was wrongly accused and Mr Walker knows this. Mr Taylor was found over the body of Miss McClements because he'd just witnessed her neck being snapped at the hands of Mr Donnelly and was checking her carotid pulse.

"Your Honor, the witnesses on the train substituted hysteria for clear thinking and common sense, which was beyond Mr Taylor's control. Mr Walker arrested him, questioned him, and enjoyed dismissing Mr Taylor's request for assistance from Cheyenne. As Mr Taylor was being jailed, his jailer was assaulted by another party, who then kidnapped Mr Taylor and smuggled him away to a crazed scientist by the name of Louis Porterfield.

"Doctor Porterfield drugged and poisoned Mr Taylor so that he could not escape. By this time Mr Walker's tactics for recapturing Mr Taylor had become resolute; if Mr Taylor escaped, then he was guilty of the crime. Mr Taylor was beyond help and he very likely would have died if not for the efforts of Sheriff Ryan.

"Your Honor, Mr Ryan's extrication of Mr Taylor from the clutches of Louis Porterfield was carried out because Mr Taylor is the key witness in a complex and ongoing case against Mr Donnelly and his associate whom I cannot name at this time.

"When it was discovered that Mr Taylor had gone missing in North Platte, everyone here knew that it was not in Mr Taylor's character to assault a deputy and run away. We deduced, and reasonably so, that he had been kidnapped by Mr Donnelly. We all feared for his safety.

"Your Honor, the train that was bearing Mr Taylor back to Cheyenne before the murder also bore another key person. A witness who is protected by this court and its officers and whom I cannot name. This witness returned to Cheyenne with information that is crucial to this impending case against Mr Donnelly and his unnamed associate. Mr Taylor shared his information with this person precisely because he feared something could happen to either one of them.

"Your Honor, the information is extremely sensitive and the witnesses have to be protected at all costs. Such was Mr Ryan's motivation for extricating Mr Taylor from North Platte without alerting Sheriff Iron... er, Ralph Walker.

"Your Honor, Mr Ryan acted the way any citizen of this territory or Nebraska would want their sheriff to act – decisively, compassionately, with their welfare in mind and in the interest of justice. And the only damage appears to be to Mr Walker's ego. Mr Ryan did what he could not – find Mr Taylor."

Ralph Walker objects bitterly and Judge Callaghan hammers his bench.

"Your Honor!" Walker exclaims.

"Sour grapes, Mr Walker?" the Judge asks, his eyebrow arched.

"Your Honor, this is a matter of law. Mr Ryan acted outside his jurisdiction and concealed his intention and his actions. I had to find out from Marshal Hummer what Mr Ryan had done. He should step down as Sheriff immediately."

Cam clears his throat and says calmly, "Your Honor, no two men exhibit and uphold the duties of the diligent citizen and the office of law enforcement more than Mr Taylor and Mr Ryan. They are proven and irrefutable.

"When the upcoming case against Mr Donnelly is underway it will become clear why Mr Ryan and Mr Taylor acted the way they did. In fact, all will be revealed and the case itself will remove any doubt regarding the two men.

"Therefore, I urge Your Honor to dismiss these extradition

proceedings; extradition and subsequent trials will achieve nothing except delay and jeopardize this important case against Mr Donnelly which is coming before the court in less than two weeks, and for which both Mr Ryan and Mr Taylor are vital components."

Judge Callaghan thoughtfully rubs his chin. Luke forms the impression that although Cam's arguments are by far the most persuasive, the Judge is not yet prepared to let the matter go.

"Mr Ryan," he barks. "What was your intention when you boarded the train to Laramie on the Monday morning after Mr Taylor went missing?"

Before Cliff can open his mouth, Cam is back on his feet. "Your Honor, it is extremely important that Mr Ryan not be forced to…"

Judge Callaghan interrupts with a sharp tap of his gavel. They all jump. "Mr Faraday, this is a closed courtroom. There are no reporters, no spectators and no hangers-on of any kind."

"I understand that, Your Honor, but Sheriff Walker…"

The Judge grunts. "If the Lincoln County Sheriff divulges any of these proceedings to anyone outside of my courtroom, I'll have him charged with contempt and he'll be the one stepping down from his position and staring at the inside walls of prison." He peers across at Walker. "For a long time. Is that clear, Mr Walker?"

Iron Pants gulps, "Yes, Your Honor."

"Good. Now let's get along. Answer my question, Mr Ryan?"

"My intention, Your Honor, was to deliver information to Sheriff Dave Ransford concerning an imminent attack on the Alliance by Mr Donnelly and his team of mavericks."

"Did you intend to return and look for Mr Taylor after delivering this information?"

"I could have, but at the time I believed Mr Taylor wanted me to take care of his family and the Keatons. If this had been my course of action, I would not have left unless Dave Ransford could have convinced me he didn't need my help.

"In hindsight, a delay of this size would have been disastrous for Mr Taylor, in terms of his health and well-being, since his life was at stake, and although I would have been on hand to protect his family, it is more than likely that Mr Faraday and I would no longer have our key witness in the upcoming trial against Mr Donnelly and his associate. And that is a matter of justice that transcends Mr Walker and his petty grudge against me."

"Your Honor!" Walker exclaims.

The Judge stops Walker's tirade with a sharp motion of his hand and stares hard at Cliff during the following intense silence.

"In hindsight, Mr Ryan, is it possible Dave Ransford and Jim Crogan would still be alive today if you had gone to Laramie and not to North Platte?"

"Anything's possible, Your Honor," Cliff replies, "once you change the variables."

"I see," the Judge muses. He sits back in his chair.

"Your Honor, I feel the loss of Ransford and Crogan as keenly as anyone. More so, since I understand the occupation of..."

"Yes, I realize that, Mr Ryan. Now, I understand that you had the opportunity to change your mind once you got on the train to Laramie. You were agonizing over your dilemma: you needed to fetch Mr Taylor here back from a dangerous situation in North Platte, and you needed to go to Laramie with extremely delicate information regarding the safety of the Alliance. You couldn't send anyone else – you had to go yourself. Didn't you reckon on Mr Ransford needing you, and Mr Taylor expecting you to help protect the Alliance?"

"Yes," Cliff says very quietly.

"You changed your mind. You seized that opportunity. What made you do that, Mr Ryan?"

"It wasn't an impulse, Your Honor. Yes, I did have to make the decision quickly, but I did weigh it up."

"You gave the delicate information regarding the safety of the Alliance to someone on the train who was also going to Laramie."

"Yes, Your Honor."

"Miss Emmaline Roberts, of the Tribune, I believe."

"Yes, Your Honor."

Judge Callaghan once again leans forward in his chair. "You gave this delicate information to a reporter, Mr Ryan."

Cliff doesn't respond.

"I'm curious, Mr Ryan, as to why Miss Roberts was still in town after you both told me she was leaving."

Cam stands up. "If I may, Your Honor…"

"No, you mayn't. Mr Ryan?"

Cliff clears his throat. "Miss Roberts is herself a witness in the case against Mr Donnelly, since she is a victim of two attempts by Maverick to kill her. After the second attempt, as a matter of law she couldn't leave as we had the maverick in custody. When I found her on the train going to Laramie on assignment for her newspaper, she already knew a great deal about what was going on; I told her more and she surmised the rest…"

"Why did you do that, Mr Ryan?"

"Because she was determined to go to Laramie to investigate Donnelly and I couldn't stop her. I believed that knowledge would arm her. She was walking into a dangerous situation."

"And she picked up on your dilemma," the Judge assumes.

"Your Honor, Mr Ryan cannot answer that in place of Miss Roberts," Cam interjects.

The Judge grunts. "Bailiff, go fetch Miss Roberts from the Tribune and make sure she understands that if she doesn't appear before me now I'll find her in contempt as well as have her facing charges of aiding and abetting Mr Ryan here."

As the bailiff hurries from the courtroom, the Judge jabs his finger on his bench and snaps, "Thick as thieves!"

"Your Honor?" Cliff almost squawks.

"You and that reporter," the Judge rasps.

"I object!" Cliff exclaims.

"Oh, you do, do you?"

"That comment is downright inflammatory," Cliff retorts.

The Judge looks censored. Begrudgingly, he says, "Strike it from the record."

The court reporter follows orders. The Judge elbows his bench and then rests his cheek on his unturned fist. And they wait.

Emmaline

Emmaline enters the courtroom to the familiar smell of polished wood and cherished sight of law books. But the bailiff urges her forward – past Mr Faraday seated at his table and another man wearing a sheriff's star seated at the opposing table – to where Cliff and Luke stand several feet away from Judge Callaghan seated behind his bench. Now what has she walked into?

The Judge nods brusquely. "Swear Miss Roberts in, bailiff."

"Do you swear to tell the truth, the whole truth and nothing but the truth, so help you God?"

"I swear."

The Judge indicates, with an impatient gesture, she is to stand beside Cliff.

"Thank you for coming so promptly, Miss Roberts."

"Well, I believe you gave me no option, Your Honor."

The Judge blinks. "A caution, young lady…"

"Yes, Your Honor?"

"I am in no mood for games. Every man in this courtroom will testify to that!"

"Yes, Your Honor."

"Do you know why I have summoned you here?"

"I would prefer Your Honor enlightened me."

"Very wise. This is, in part, a hearing to determine whether Mr Ryan should face charges of deserting his duty as Sheriff of Laramie County in favor of rescuing our friend Mr Taylor here right out from under Sheriff Walker's nose."

"Is it not the solemn duty of the Sheriff of Laramie County to protect the life of a key witness in an upcoming trial, and indeed to protect the evidence itself?"

The Judge whacks his gavel. "I ask the questions, young lady."

"Yes, Your Honor. I only thought that…"

"Miss Roberts, I am not going to debate the legalities of the situation with you, I simply want you to answer my questions."

"Yes, Your Honor."

"In what way did you influence Mr Ryan's decision to give you the job of taking the extremely delicate information regarding the maverick assault on the Alliance to Sheriff Ransford in Laramie?"

"He had a dilemma and I was convinced I could help. My job is to convey information after all."

"Answer the question, Miss Roberts," the Judge replies.

Think I'm in trouble, Celie.

You're so good at it, Emmie.

"Your Honor, I gave Mr Ryan a realistic option of finding Mr Taylor. I told him he could trust me without question, that I could take the information safely to Mr Ransford, and that I knew Maverick's moves as well as he did."

"Did you expect to fight once you delivered this information?"

"Fight, Your Honor?"

"Yes. Take Mr Ryan's place with Mr Ransford in fighting the mavericks. Guns and shooting, Miss Roberts."

"No. But I did help. I assure you I wasn't useless, Your Honor. My experience of Maverick helped Mr Ransford plan his…"

"Sheriff Dave Ransford and his deputy Jim Crogan died at the hands of the mavericks, did they not?"

The Judge's insensitivity towards what she considers one of the darkest days of her life has her swallowing hard. "Is Your Honor insinuating some of the blame for their deaths rests with me?"

"You convinced Mr Ryan that you could do his job," the Judge argues.

"Meaning no disrespect, Your Honor, but you are drawing a very long bow. I know I can be convincing when I set my mind to it, but Mr Ryan is not a man who is easily persuaded. I am aware that he would have been an asset to Sheriff Ransford's campaign, but on the train it was my impression that, one, the information was more important, and two, Mr Ransford was extremely capable and would see the job done. If Mr Ryan didn't himself think so, clearly he would have resigned himself to proceeding to Laramie and leaving Mr Taylor for dead."

Silence. The Judge stares at her.

She keeps her mouth tightly shut and her eyes fixed on the Judge, waiting for his next question. However, his gaze shifts to Cliff.

"Loyalty is an admirable quality, Mr Ryan. Yours was divided, it seems."

The Judge expects an answer; Cliff is deliberate in offering one. Eventually, he says, rather heatedly, "When I found Luke, he was poisoned, blind, half-frozen and lying in his own filth. From that moment if I had any lingering doubt about what I had chosen to do, they were completely erased. I know Luke's family; he is the cornerstone of it, and finding him *was* protecting them."

The Judge blinks and says nothing.

Cliff continues. "And Mr Walker might like to know there is such a thing as reckless endangerment..."

Mr Walker storms to his feet. "Now what is Mr Ryan getting at?"

"Your Honor, Mr Walker refused Luke help when it was possible, after Luke had explained the critical danger Mr Donnelly presented to him and his family, then he put Luke in a position whereby Donnelly himself snatched Luke from under Mr Walker's nose and placed him in the hands of a madman who only had to wait for Donnelly's order to kill him. Mr Walker will be very lucky if Luke's mother and Ethan Benchley don't have him charged with reckless endangerment and ask for damages in civil court!"

"Your Honor, this is outrageous!"

Emmaline winces as the Judge repeatedly hammers his gavel, shouting *Order!* She looks over her shoulder to espy Mr Faraday's reaction to Cliff's outburst; the man slides his hands into his pockets and looks down, hiding a very large grin.

"You have nothing to say, Mr Faraday?" the Judge barks.

Mr Faraday straightens immediately. "It is being said, Your Honor."

The Judge grunts. "Thank you for that diversion, Mr Ryan. You made your point. Now…" His eyes dart back and forth between her and Cliff at her side. "Miss Roberts, I become very uneasy when the law enforcement in town and an investigative reporter develop a rapport."

"Excuse me, Your Honor?" she replies.

"Doing deals for information and stories in exchange for…"

"Your Honor!" But before Emmaline can protest any further, someone else does and much louder.

"That's bull…balderdash… and I object!"

She glances up at Cliff's face. He's furious, his jaw is clenched with forced restraint.

The Judge squirms. "Mr Ryan, you'll watch your language in my court…"

"I thought I did!"

"Your law background is really starting to get on my nerves."

"And mine," Mr Walker exclaims.

"Mr Ryan," the Judge continues, "you would've had to have known your actions would have repercussions?"

Emmaline says, "Your Honor, I operate from the highest ethical and professional standards. I do *not* do deals for information. And I protest this *most* vehemently."

"Miss Roberts, you cannot interrupt."

Suddenly, Mr Faraday appears at Emmaline's side. "Your Honor, if I may be allowed to simplify matters. Mr Ryan has been a deputy and sheriff in this county for five years. Never once has his integrity been called into question. There are hundreds of people in town who will testify to his good character and his dedication to his job. This cannot be ignored."

"I am not ignoring it, Mr Faraday. I am wondering why he would risk it!"

The Judge and Cliff are eyeing one another. Emmaline fears what will happen next; Cliff will not permit an attempt to discredit his integrity from any quarter, including the Judge.

"Miss Roberts," the Judge barks. "Why did you help Mr Ryan?"

Her heart is literally pounding. "Because I could."

"He didn't offer you a story in exchange for your help?"

"Most certainly not, Your Honor."

"Mr Ryan?" he barks again. "Did you offer a story in exchange for Miss Robert's help?"

"No, I did not," Cliff grinds out. "Under no circumstances would I put myself or Miss Roberts in that position."

The Judge glares into Cliff's eyes.

"This is preposterous!" shouts Mr Walker. They all jump, including the Judge.

Luke, she notices, sighs hard and folds his arms.

"Something to say, Mr Taylor?" the Judge grunts.

"You do what you think needs to be done, Your Honor," Luke says, "and when you think you need to do it, but you'll have to pardon us right now if we're kinda distracted by the upcoming case against Donnelly and his associate. But I'm pleading with the court; you can charge me with whatever you want *after* the trial. I'm willing to go to North Platte and sit in Mr Walker's jail till next winter if it makes him feel better, but this thing's gotta be done and it kinda needs all of us to be doing it. I'm surprised that someone as interested in law and justice as Mr Walker don't see it that way.

"I didn't murder Miss McClements. Why would I? – if she were still alive, she would also be a witness because she saw and heard what I did. Who knows – maybe that's why Donnelly killed her. I didn't bash the deputy and I didn't escape. I was kidnapped by Donnelly and taken to Louis Porterfield's laboratory where I was drugged and starving and freezing to death. Mr Ryan found me, rescued me and brought me home. Mr Walker here would have shot me on sight without explanation. I am the key witness, Your Honor. If I died at the hands of Porterfield, or Mr Walker, the broader justice that will be served by this trial would be put in jeopardy. No one, particularly Mr Ryan, wanted that to happen."

"Your Honor," Mr Walker protests yet again.

"Silence, Mr Walker," the Judge murmurs firmly.

Minutes tick by.

"Mr Taylor," the Judge says finally, "unless the upcoming trial reveals evidence to exonerate you of the charges Mr Walker has brought against you, I order you to face those charges at the conclusion of the Donnelly trial. Until then, you are ordered to stay in Cheyenne to be Mr Faraday's key witness. You are not to leave town for any reason, is that clear?"

"Your Honor..." objects Mr Walker.

"You're getting a good deal, Mr Walker, don't push me."

"Yes, Your Honor."

Mr Walker appears mollified at last.

"Mr Taylor, is that clear?" the Judge continues.

"Yes, Your Honor."

"As for you, Mr Ryan, your good character and record in this county and in Cheyenne are your saving grace at this moment. I am not satisfied with your explanation as to your motivation for deputizing Miss Roberts and rescuing Mr Taylor. You know the law and you know the consequences of the law. I believe you disregarded both. However, your courage and skill brought about an outcome that is widely acclaimed, not least by the governor himself, and I am giving you a reprieve similar to that of Mr Taylor's in that you will answer Mr Walker's complaints at the end of the upcoming Donnelly trial. Until then, you will remain in your present position and do whatever you must to bring about justice. Mr Faraday is fretting at the prospect of losing you and that will never do. Miss Roberts?"

Emmaline can barely steady her breathing or rein back her racing heart. "Yes, Your Honor?"

"Your part in this is still my concern. Your actions, however, are upheld by the First Amendment, and although you will be called as a witness when Mr Ryan faces Mr Walker's complaints, I find no charges against you. However, at this point, you, too, cannot leave town. Ironical, wouldn't you agree?"

Emmaline is so stunned speech deserts her.

"Miss Roberts?"

"Miss Roberts agrees, Your Honor," says Mr Faraday beside her.

"Excellent. Mr Walker, go home and sit tight. This hearing is concluded. Good day, gentlemen, Miss Roberts."

The Judge steps down from his chair and removes himself from the courtroom, followed by the recorder.

Mr Walker stalks up to them and stands right in front of Cliff's face.

"I'll see you in North Platte – Sheriff."

"Why don't you make yourself useful, Walker, and find Porterfield," Cliff retorts.

Walker turns away, gives Luke a menacing glare and leaves.

Emmaline raises her eyes to brave a glance at Cliff; his blue-green gaze swings down, encompassing her in a blaze of anger made worse by the courtroom door slamming shut behind Walker. She gives a start; he turns away and strides from the courtroom.

"He's really mad," she murmurs, biting her lip.

"It's completely unfair," Luke remarks.

"It's not something he didn't expect," Mr Faraday says. "Although the Judge made a point of his displeasure and was particularly harsh."

"If I hadn't given him the option..." she laments quietly.

"I'd be dead."

She looks up into Luke's face; his blue gaze is intent upon her, dark with meaning.

"We'll be going round in circles forever, Emmaline," he says. "What's done is done. It was done with good intentions. Now let's just move on and get down to business."

"Good advice," Mr Faraday murmurs, smiling at her.

As they turn and start to walk, Luke says, "Handy for you, the First Amendment."

"Indeed," she sighs. "No, the Judge should have found me guilty of complicity at least. I've been expecting it. He's got it in for Cliff for some reason. Mr Faraday, is Watt's Landing in Laramie County or Albany?"

"Laramie County, Miss Roberts."

"What are you getting at, Emmaline?" Luke asks.

"Only a jurisdiction issue. If Watt's Landing was in Albany County then technically Cliff wasn't deserting his post as sheriff of Laramie County when he deputized me, was he?"

"Ain't he sheriff of Laramie County wherever he is?"

"Unfortunately, that's the way the Judge is viewing it," Mr Faraday offers.

"The Judge completely shut you out, didn't he, Mr Faraday?"

"He did indeed. No matter. Cliff received good practice for the excellent attorney he will be one day when he comes to his senses and stops chasing criminals and outlaws."

"You're not concerned?"

"About Cliff? He's like a cat. Always lands on his feet. He'll find his way out of this, he just doesn't know how at present. But he will."

Sheriff Ruthless... she didn't give him that name once for nothing, now, did she?

Cliff

Cliff barges through the vulture-like ring of reporters outside his building, heads straight into his office and shuts the door. He pegs his hat, strips off his coat as he paces and tosses it onto his chair. Then he picks up his coat again, throws it on the floor and sits down instead. He gets up, retrieves his coat from the floor and threads his arms into the sleeves.

Jamming his hat back on his head, he yanks open the door; after heading through the outer office, he plunges straight back outside again where the fiercely chill wind dispels some of the heat in his body. For a while he doesn't even know where he's walking to, and several people attempt to address him while others tip their hats or nod politely. He ignores all of them. If he hadn't lived and breathed this job for the past five years, he'd hand in his badge, just hand it in, get on a train and not get off till the climate changed.

He knew his actions wouldn't be without repercussions. He knew it. But the way the Judge looked at him. Questioning and accusing. Okay, so he'd told a few tactical untruths in his time, but lying under oath? Never. Making deals with reporters? Not on your life.

He pushes hard on the door of St John's; it flies open and he strides through. He rips off his hat, takes a deep breath, inhaling the candle grease and well-worked polish until his heart stops racing. Calmer now, he closes the door, leans back against it and stares straight up the aisle to the altar. Sunlight strikes the stained glass and throws light patterns across the floor and over the pews. Colors rain down from high above the altar, drenching it, while golden reflections bounce off four tall candlesticks. Everything is utterly still. Even the air. Even time itself... captured, and dilated, like a capsule of endless delay in which to find respite from the world.

He throws himself into a pew several rows from the back, elbows his arms on his knees and presses his face into his fists.

The Church has been used as sanctuary by many throughout the ages. Why?

This is the sacred and the transcendent and all people, whatever their creed, recognize it. I understand that for you, who have been raised on human justice, this is a hard concept, but one day you'll know the value of it. I believe the days are coming, Cliff, when you will need more than you've known.

"Cliff?"

He gives a start but quickly relaxes. Father Nugent.

"I saw you come tearing in here like you were on fire. Is there anything I can do?"

"I need to sit for a spell." He senses Nugent's hand hovering like a feather on the top of his head.

"A prayer," Nugent says.

Since his memory of his own father comforting him is beyond dim to almost non-existent, Cliff doesn't mind.

A moment passes, then Nugent takes his hand away and says, "I'll be about if you want someone to talk to."

It's not until the utter stillness has penetrated his rattled brain, the shaking has stopped and his mind has returned to order that he realizes Nugent's no longer there. He lifts his head from his hands and looks up.

The church appears fuzzy in the few moments before his vision clears. The light through the stained glass has shifted, its angles cast sideways and acute.

He could use a little consolation and knuckles Nugent's door.

"Coffee?" Nugent offers at once.

Cliff slides into a chair at the kitchen table. As a cup of steaming coffee is placed before him, he says, "I'm never going to make it."

Nugent surprises him with a chuckle. "You are closer than you think. Drink your coffee. The afternoon's cold."

As he's drinking, there's a knock on the front door. Nugent excuses himself to answer it. Cliff overhears the conversation.

"Good afternoon, Mr Peterson."

"Father, I'm so sorry to be bothering you, but it's my neighbor, the widow Shaw, she's that poorly the doc said you should come right away."

"Ah, Mrs Shaw, yes. I'll fetch my things, Mr Peterson."

"I have my wagon out front, Father."

"Good man."

Nugent appears at the kitchen door. "Sorry, Cliff. Finish your coffee though, that's a good lad." He gives a wink and disappears.

Nugent's house is almost as quiet as the church except for a large clock ticking over the old sideboard. On top of the sideboard rests a small golden crucifix, a candle and a prayer book. Making themselves comfortable beside these is a stack of other books and a Bible.

Here he sits at a scrubbed table with second – probably third – hand chairs. It's a simple house designed for a life of simplicity. Or is it?

Nugent needs to know and remember everyone's business. He needs to counsel them, care for them, and know both spiritual and non-spiritual details about their lives. Their corporal and spiritual concerns he makes his own.

He must know Latin like the back of his hand, be able to pray at the drop of a hat, read the Bible and understand it. And that's just the tip of the iceberg. His life isn't simple; the physical aspects are kept that way so he can pay attention to his complex job and not be distracted.

And when he has to make himself accountable, it isn't to Judge Callaghan, but a power to which Callaghan himself must answer.

... the whole truth and nothing but the truth, so help me God...

He grins into his coffee cup.

Odd where your consolation arises.

Cliff

When he gets back to his office he finds he has a visitor.

Coolly, he pegs his hat.

"Marshal Hummer."

They shake hands.

"Sheriff Ryan."

"What brings you by?"

"I heard the Judge beat you up in court earlier."

Cliff gapes at him. "Where did you... how do you... never mind."

Hummer chuckles. "Ran into Iron Pants at the depot."

"Lucky you."

"Hope you didn't let the bastard scare you none, Ryan."

"Walker? Are you kidding me?"

"Good, because I need you."

Cliff narrows his eyes. "What do you mean?"

"Hopin' you'd ask." Hummer sits in Cliff's chair and stretches out his legs. He removes his cigar, inspects it and shoves it back between his teeth. "I hate to admit it but I ain't havin' much luck findin' Bodecker. Can't find Richard Taylor neither. And no one's seen a trace of this Porterfield character. Even I can't be in three places at once."

"You must have some leads."

"I followed every one of young Taylor's clues. Bodecker has disappeared. Now Luke saw him in that hotel in Omaha that night with Donnelly. The whore conducted her business with him the same night. The hotel clerk said he checked out two days later. It's like I said: the shenanigans with Donnelly and the mavericks, and Luke and Porterfield, gave Bodecker the perfect cover..."

"For a start, I believe Donnelly decided to take matters into his own hands. He stayed out of Cheyenne just as Bodecker told him, but the man is deluded, thought he could fix things his own way."

"Makes you wonder why someone like Bodecker would take Donnelly for a partner."

"But I don't believe for an instant Bodecker would run away with his tail between his legs looking for an escape route."

"You don't?"

"No. I've seen first-hand what his intentions are."

"How?"

"A map on Ed Parsons' study wall. Remember you instructed me to go over and take a look? There's a huge map of the south-east quadrant of Wyoming. Ranches, mines, railroads, towns, you name it. At the bottom someone has scrawled the words, Empire of PDB."

Hummer whistles softly.

"Yes, I know. It gives me nightmares. You don't give that up in a hurry. The point is Bodecker can just as easily divorce himself from Donnelly as he did from Parsons. The only evidence we have to the contrary is what Luke heard in the hotel room in Omaha where the two of them were planning how to proceed."

"Sure, Ryan, but Bodecker's gotta take to the willows for a while; figure out how to deflect the heat."

"Mac's been tailing Dillon Kerr for weeks now. Kerr stands outside Bodecker's building telling shareholders and anyone else who cares that his boss has gone south for the winter with a chest complaint. Meanwhile, Mac's turned up nothing watching his mail, his telegrams, messengers..."

"That's a twenty-four hour a day job. Kerr's smart..."

"Devious."

"Smart and devious. Look, Ryan, Iron Pants ain't interested in trackin' down Porterfield, the authorities in Omaha are goin' for the south for the winter crap and won't lift a finger, so what d'you say?"

"I'm already in enough hot water with the Judge."

Hummer starts chuckling again. "Ryan, you and me are the

only ones who don't believe that Bodecker decided to fly south for the winter and care about it."

"Where's that entourage of deputy marshals from last year?"

"Chasin' bank robbers and tryin' to get one step ahead of the Pinks. You know how it is."

"Mm, in case you hadn't noticed there's a court case about to start and…"

"Aw, Faraday won't need you for a week or ten days. We could get a lot done in that time. Heck, you found young Taylor in a day."

"That was different."

"Don't think so. You had a hunch and you acted on it. I like that. So, what's your hunch about Bodecker?

"How do you know I have a hunch about Bodecker?"

Hummer gives him a long, dry look. "You'll be sworn in as a Deputy US Marshal before Judge Callaghan. How does that sit with you?"

"I get indigestion just thinking about it."

"You get a pay increase, a substantial one." Hummer moves his cigar from side to side. "No offence intended, Ryan."

Cliff expels a huge sigh. Nothing would give him a greater sense of achievement than to haul Loren Bodecker into court after wrenching him from his hiding place and throwing him off the train at Cheyenne depot for all his cronies to see.

"I made sure the Judge was free…" Hummer consults his watch. As he's easing it back into his pocket, he adds, "…right about now in fact."

"I need to talk to Mac."

"Done! Mac's enjoys a pay rise as much as the next man and when you leave town and leave him in charge that college fund for those twins girls of his just keeps on gettin' fatter and fatter."

"I need to talk to Cam."

"Already saw Faraday. He said if you and me catch Bodecker within ten days he'll make sure we get a nice fat bonus."

"I should talk to Luke."

"Ran into Taylor on my way here. He reckoned they'd name the next new street in Bright River after you if you nab Bodecker."

"Anyone else I should talk to?"

Hummer gets to his feet. "Didn't get around to the Roberts girl. You oughta do that for yourself, Ryan. You know how females can be."

Cliff stares at him, lost for words.

Hummer rearranges his cigar and grunts. "You comin'? Don't wanna be late. Callaghan's kinda outa sorts today. Wonder what made him that way…"

Cliff unpegs his hat and coat. "How well did you search for Bodecker in Omaha, Hummer?"

"You oughta know me by now, Ryan."

"That's what I figured. Well, then…"

"You got a hunch." Hummer's eyes sparkle. "Let's hear it, Deputy Marshal."

Jennifer

Home of Frank & Jeanne Sullivan
St Louis, Missouri

Unfortunately, but not wholly unexpected, the 'angel breath' surfaces during supper; Ariel even places her knife and fork correctly so that she may address her family with utmost confidence…

"AJ and I felt the angel breath this afternoon. Under the plum tree."

Baby sisters like Davina and Caroline are constantly fascinated by such goings on, and they sit bug-eyed, ready and waiting for Ariel's story to continue.

Meanwhile, Finn chokes noisily on his food; eight-and-a-half year-old boys are capable of displaying the most abysmal table manners. Conor, who at ten has perfected what Finn aspires to, is about to use his fork to catapult a pea at poor Ariel, who sees him lining up his target and closes her eyes tight.

Conor should know better by now. Jeanne has the measure of her sons.

Calmly, she says, "Conor Sullivan, you have been told not to throw food more times than it is possible to count. You will grow up to be a gentleman whether you like it or not. And if you don't it won't be because you had a mother who failed you in the attempt. Therefore, consider yourself confined to the house before and after school for the next three days and Sunday morning after church."

Conor is dumbfounded. The pea plops onto his plate. The errant young man looks at his father.

Frank says, "Apologize, Conor."

Conor looks contrite but appearances can be deceiving – he is persistently naughty and no one knows why. "I'm sorry, Mother. If only I had my own horse I know I would be better."

"Better at what?" Jeanne exclaims.

He shrugs and mumbles, "Just everything."

Jeanne rolls her eyes at him and his expression picks up.

That's the trouble with this family; they all possess far too much character, good humor and lovability, and it's always possible the sternest moment could end in someone going soft.

"Now, Ariel," Jeanne continues. "What is all this about angel's breath?"

"AJ and I were standing under my favorite plum tree this afternoon and we felt it, didn't we, AJ?"

Jeanne's eyebrows shoot up and Jennifer swallows the urge to laugh with her mashed potato.

"Angel breath," Jeanne reiterates with breezy sarcasm, which is lost on the children, but not Jennifer. "How nice."

"It *was* very nice," Ariel says. "Softy. Like when you kiss me goodnight, Papa."

Frank frowns and turns his puzzled gaze on Jennifer. "Angel's breath?"

"I've felt it before," Ariel persists.

Frank glances at his daughter.

"Ariel, I'm speaking to your aunt," he reminds her gently.

"Sorry, Papa."

Jennifer holds her brother's concerned gaze while she thinks of what to say that will ease his mind without destroying Ariel's feelings.

But Jeanne breaks the silence. "It amazes me that you, a doctor, and in your case, my darling Jennifer, a person – and notice that I did say person, not woman – of extraordinary intelligence and education, could be remotely interested in angels, let alone their breath."

Conor and Finn dissolve into uproarious laughter. Ariel and her sisters endeavor to shush them.

"Right!" said Frank and they all jump. "If you don't all be quiet and let AJ speak, no one gets dessert. Not one crumb, not a sniff, not even a look at it."

"I've already seen it, Papa," Davina says, her five-year-old innocence melting the expression on Frank's face. "It's chocolate cake with walnuts on top. I asked Cook not to put walnuts on top. Cherries are better. I don't like walnuts. Neither does Caro, do you Caro?"

Caroline shakes her adorable three-year-old curls and says, in a manner rather advanced for her age, "Hush, Davie, I want to hear about the angel."

Davina turns her expectant face towards Jennifer. In fact, all seven faces are looking upon her, brimming with anticipation. This is Ariel's story, why are they looking at her? "I'm afraid I don't know anything about angel's breath. When it comes to angels, Ari is the knowledgeable one."

"Aw, Ari don't know a thing," Finn moans.

The table erupts.

Walnuts or cherries, no one eats chocolate cake; dessert is abandoned.

Cliff

Cheyenne

As the working day is coming to an end, Cam calls a meeting in his office. Josh Bridger sits at Cam's elbow with an endless stream of file folders and notebooks at the ready. Just as Cliff finds a seat, Luke arrives. He draws a chair next to Cliff's but seems aloof.

"What's up?" Cliff asks.

Before Luke can answer, Cam, sitting behind his desk, calls the meeting to order.

"As we all know, Cliff is now a Deputy US Marshal and will be accompanying Dan Hummer on a mission to find Loren Bodecker."

"I should be going with him," Luke declares.

Cam shuffles some papers, his ever-patient demeanor cracking a little. "The Judge is not about to reverse his ruling and let you out of Cheyenne for any reason. You'll have to stay put."

Not one of Luke's best attributes, staying put – even as Cliff is thinking it, Luke gets out of his chair and starts prowling around the room.

"You could try focusing on the trial," Cam suggests.

Cliff studies Luke's face. If anyone knows that face better than him, he'd like to meet them. Luke clenches and unclenches his hands constantly as he walks. What occurs to Cliff at that moment bothers him so deeply that he opens his mouth to comment on Cam's suggestion. And then closes it.

"Are you all right, Luke?" he asks instead.

Luke glances sharply in his direction. "I don't know. And if you go gallivantin' who's left to know if I really *am* all right."

"Ethan will know," he says calmly.

With a touch of desperation in his eyes, and a tone of voice to match, Luke says, "Oh, I hope so. But I'm never gonna know, am I? I'll always need someone to tell me."

"It's only been a few weeks. You're just unsure; Doc Kincaid said it would take a while – even Porterfield acknowledged that."

"What if I go loco being cooped up and go breaking the law? – I'll never be with… see…"

"Cam's is good advice. Focus on the trial. On Donnelly and the mavericks. On remembering every detail of what you heard between Bodecker and Donnelly in that hotel room in Omaha. On looking after Caroline…"

He starts to nod, calmer. "I think Caroline is looking after *me*."

Cam says, "Caroline has a great propensity for mothering. In some people it is how they feel most useful and they often are. Caroline saved Meg from going out of her mind with worry about you when we didn't know what had happened to you."

Luke looks across at Cam as he speaks. Cliff wonders what's going through his mind; where Luke is concerned, Cam's credibility concerning his welfare is almost irretrievable. Maybe the two of them working together again, with Cliff out of town, something of their splintered friendship may be salvaged. A hopeful prospect which could begin from this moment.

Cliff leans forward enthusiastically. "So Cam, let's begin. Reviewing all the facts in evidence, are we?"

"That's correct," Cam confirms and they leave Luke to find his seat. "One…"

"Yeah, *one*," says Luke testily. "The sketch of Loren Bodecker in my file."

Cliff catches Cam's sidelong glance.

Josh says, "That's purely circumstantial."

Luke shifts in his seat, looks up at the ceiling and blows a huge sigh. An objective viewpoint on this is not what he wants to hear.

Cam continues, "As I was saying, one…"

"But you realize without the sketch," Luke interrupts again, "I would not have been able to identify Bodecker in Omaha in the hotel. I snuck into the hotel room and hid purely on this. It wasn't random; it was calculated. It was knowing about Bodecker from you two that alerted me to Caroline's problem, and to the partnership between Donnelly and Bodecker, and between those two and Richard Taylor. And you both made the connection between Bodecker and all the trouble in the first place because of his sketch in my file. Circumstantial in the first instance perhaps, but *I'm* inclined to hold it in *high* regard."

In the pause that follows, Cliff studies Luke's tormented expression. Despite the volcanic proportions of his present frustration, Luke seems quite capable of logical and convincing argument.

Cam clears his throat softly. "Very well. One: the sketch of Loren Bodecker in Luke's file. Despite the circumstantial nature of this evidence, it remains the catalyst for all subsequent investigation and..."

"Ethan will testify to seeing Bodecker with Ed Parsons that day. He was there; he came home and gave me the description, which I sketched. The only circumstance I can see here is that Ethan was in the right place at the right time, same as I was in Omaha."

Cliff scratches his eyebrow as Cam shoots him a defeated expression.

Luke continues, "You think it circumstantial because of the way *you* came across the evidence, flicking through my file. In retrospect, it's probably one of the most important pieces of evidence we have. After K was shot, where would you two have gone? We had no idea who did it then and you needed a place to start. And Bodecker's sketch in my file is where you started, right? And if I had known that face was as important as you..." He stops, his expression melting into emotion. He slides down into his chair and pushes the heels of his wrists into his eyes.

Cam loosens his collar.

Josh coughs politely, looks up from his note-taking and says, "I have all that."

Slowly, cautiously, Cam says, "One: the sketch of Bodecker in Luke's file."

Josh says, "I might point out that as valid as all this is, the indictment against Donnelly is..." and he shuffles through some papers to find what he wants, "...conspiring, organizing and operating hired guns for the purpose of murder and intimidation, murder for hire, the murder of Miss Cadie McClements, assault on a deputy sheriff, kidnapping and holding a citizen against their will... the point I'm making, gentlemen, is the indictment doesn't mention Bodecker or their dubious partnership.

"Now, I know and you know the mavericks in the lockup are a big part of this case against Donnelly, but to convince a jury of Donnelly's motivation we will have to make the case for his partnership with Bodecker. And that, if you don't find Bodecker, Sheriff, will have to be done in the courtroom and with great difficulty without the man himself."

Josh is on a roll and no one feels inclined to curtail him but very inclined to allow him to do all the work; at least Luke doesn't feel the need to interrupt him.

"Yes: Bodecker stayed in Donnelly's house in Laramie during the Parsons' trial and we have witnesses. Yes: Donnelly threatened Caroline Taylor in her home regarding Ben Taylor's journey to Bright River. He didn't want Ben to make contact and join up with Luke, who is the sworn enemy of Donnelly and Bodecker's Empire aspirations, an enemy of the "Association". Caroline Taylor will identify Donnelly in court as the man who threatened her. She will also testify she tried to get Ben to return home by sending a series of telegrams, which Ben always answered by encouraging her to be strong and saying he wasn't ready to return. Ben also urges her by telegram to investigate Donnelly because he has serious concerns about him...

"So, Ben will testify that he recognizes Donnelly as Bodecker's partner from the train. Donnelly himself told Ben he recognized him from when he was waiting for Bodecker during the meeting. Ben will testify Donnelly spoke against Luke as Ben's cousin. Donnelly's motivation at this point appears to be a well-developed dislike for Luke and the Alliance. As the usual cattle barons versus the small ranchers scenario, the jury won't have a problem. But the whys and the wherefores always speak to Bodecker and we either present a clear case of murder for hire using the mavericks' testimony, or we find Bodecker and present the lot...

"The testimony from North Platte regarding the Maverick telegrams and Larry Fulbright is pure Donnelly though. But we need Fulbright and Porterfield. Your testimony, Luke, and yours, Cliff, could be well countered by the Defense bringing Sheriff Walker to the witness box, particularly now as the Judge has held over Walker's grievances. Although Judge Callaghan does expect this evidence to be presented at trial, doesn't he? – because it will determine whether you two are extradited to Lincoln County."

Luke bursts out with, "If you leave out the maverick telegrams and Donnelly's planning and scheming, then his attack on the Keatons and the Diamond-T makes no sense."

"Donnelly may be Bodecker's partner," Cliff argues, "but Donnelly acted independently."

"But Bodecker told Donnelly in Omaha that he was making mistakes, bad ones, namely the attempts on Emmaline's life, and that he wasn't to do anything other than what he's told. Donnelly didn't like being treated that way. That's his motivation. He's supposed to be Bodecker's partner; Bodecker treated him like his second."

"With just the mavericks, Donnelly presents merely as a Maverick himself, harassing the locals," Josh prattles on. "Marshal Hummer returning without Porterfield, Richard Taylor or Bodecker himself after three weeks is extremely disappointing for our case, and, personally, I wonder what he's been doing all this time. Even while Donnelly's bank records indicate payoffs at the appropriate times to various individuals we now believe to be the various mavericks, we have yet to discover something monetary to connect him to Bodecker. They have been deliberately cautious here. And we have spent weeks investigating bank records, the buying and selling of shares, financial dealings, the lot, but there is nothing we can discover to connect them. Nothing in writing regarding their partnership..."

"Except for the map," Cliff cuts in. "The Empire of PDB."

"Significance?" Josh asks. "It's only a map..."

Cliff recalls the way the hairs on his neck prickled when he first saw it. "Their immediate stumbling block to their ultimate goal was the Alliance. Ed Parsons failed. Donnelly has failed. Without his gun for hire – his Maverick – Bodecker has been brought to heel somewhat. He has his wealth and power, his Association, and his influence with people in high places left to bring about his Empire. If we don't prove the murderous conspiracy between Donnelly and Bodecker, we could spend a long time trying to bring Bodecker down and not succeed. Even if I find Porterfield and Fulbright, or Richard Taylor, it won't be enough. Bodecker must be brought back to Cheyenne to face charges of conspiracy to murder and murder for hire. We have to bring Donnelly and Bodecker face to face and let them try to deny it."

Cam nods decisively. So does Josh.

Luke sits up suddenly, folding his arms. "How many people has Maverick murdered?"

Josh shuffles some more. "We have a copy of the portfolio from the sheriff's office in Laramie… and I've made a comprehensive list…"

Cliff frowns… Miss Keaton is on that list.

"Including Adams the sheep rancher and two cattle ranchers in Laramie County…" Josh's glance falls silently down the page. "…there are six dead and numerous attempts on people across two counties…"

"K…"

Josh lowers his papers. "Miss Keaton is on the list, of course," he murmurs and adjusts his glasses.

Luke lapses into a brooding silence. Cliff exchanges another glance with Cam. So, he doesn't intend to let either of them forget it, as if they ever could.

"Well," says Cam, "you might be interested to know that the governor is fully informed of the situation as it stands, including your new position, Cliff."

"What's that, Cam," Luke rumbles, "lawyer talk for we need absolute proof about Bodecker or else we're cooked?"

Josh, gathering his papers together, says, "Well, I firmly believe we should maintain a high level of confidence in our collective abilities to bring this whole matter to a successful conclusion."

"Here, here," Cam murmurs, sliding his hands into his pockets.

"But it won't bring them back, will it?" Luke murmurs.

"Will that be all, Cam?" Josh asks. Cam nods and Josh leaves, somewhat hastily.

As the door closes, Cam removes his hands from his pockets. "I seem to remember a man who returned from San Francisco, after a lot of soul-searching, full of determination and purpose, who said to me one of his reasons for returning was to win justice for Miss Keaton."

"I also said that you knew that Loren Bodecker was a force to be reckoned with six months ago, just like he is now, and you backed away from doing then what you are about to do now, only if you had done it six months ago, K would still be alive."

"There is not a day that goes by when I don't think of her, but you seem to be saying what I did or didn't do changes who you are. Is that true? Is that what you are saying?"

Luke glares at him. "A lot's happened. I know I am not myself. And there is a distinct possibility I may never be *that man* ever again. But if I have to wear it, then so can you."

Cam's professional demeanor seems ready to collapse.

Luke strides to the door, ramming his point home: "And if you're worried about Jennifer, don't be. I won't be turning myself loose on her any time soon."

Cam lets out an impatient sigh. "I'm not worried about Jennifer, I'm…"

Luke shoots a glance from the door he's angrily wrenched open.

"Well?" he barks.

Cam throws down his pencil. "I'm concerned about you!"

Obviously surprised, Luke stares at him. A flicker of contrition surfaces when he catches Cliff's eye. And then he's gone.

"That went well," Cam says.

Cliff blows a short laugh. "Now you know how I felt when he refused to get off the train when we got to Cheyenne. Either I dragged him off or I stayed on…"

Cam's eyes grow keen suddenly. "You've risked your job."

"I protected our witness wherever he felt the need to go."

"No wonder Judge Callaghan is suspicious of you."

"He'll get over it."

"And what about Luke? Will he be all right? Will he get over it?"

"Luke needs Jennifer."

"A bold statement."

"You know how it is when the only light in your life is a woman."

"All too well, in fact."

"Well, take that and triple it. The worse thing the Judge could have done was seal him up in town. He's just lost some confidence."

"That's not who he is."

"Not before Porterfield's basement, no."

Jennifer

Home of Frank & Jeanne Sullivan
St Louis, Missouri

After the children have gone to bed, Jennifer sits by the fire in contemplation. Frank, meanwhile, wanders into the parlor with a large piece of cake on a white china plate. Dessert abandoned? Not quite...

"This is excellent cake, George, sure you won't have some?"

"How can you eat that and not feel guilty?"

"Because I am the father and they are the children." Frank makes himself comfortable in his favorite chair and hoists his feet onto the footstool. "And this is how I remind myself of the fact."

"If you say so, Frank. Walnuts?"

"Never you mind. What's that you have there?"

"A letter from Meg."

Frank swallows a mouthful. "You've been waiting for that."

"It came this morning."

"You spent the whole day dwelling on it."

"Pretty much the whole day."

"What does Meg have to say?"

"It's the most un-Meg-like letter you could imagine, except..."

"Mm?"

"Frank, whatever you do in your life, whatever decisions you make, your actions, plans, et cetera, you always think of Jeanne?"

"I think you know the answer to that, George."

"She is a part of the process of thought and action."

"You make it sound like breathing. I guess it is. And, when you

50

come to think about it, a marriage can't be a good marriage if that isn't part of it."

"Because you love her."

"Not necessarily."

"Now I'm confused."

Frank rests his cake plate on the side table. "It is a choice. I could love Jeanne and choose to do what I think is good for me. You know the idea: what's good for the husband must be good for his wife. A different way of loving your spouse to what you described before. I know men like this; if their wives are truly happy then I've yet to see it."

"Men always think they know best, don't they?"

"Yes."

"What's best for them."

"Often the ultimate decision rests with the man. That's the way of the world."

"It would be unwise for a woman to hand a man so much power voluntarily."

"George, if that man and that woman truly love one another it is not about power, it's about trust."

Trust, she muses. It's about trust! Trust is like a destination you never reach.

"Frank, do you believe if two people are meant to be together, they will be?"

"There is no scientific basis for that."

"Well, yes, if there was you could explain it and then you wouldn't need to believe, you'd just know. There's no scientific basis for trust either."

"Although I'm able to predetermine mathematically quite a number of things, George, the concept of fate, of destiny, of kismet, is not my field of expertise."

"You certainly know a lot of words for it."

Frank takes his feet off the footstool, floors them and leans forward. "But faith and trust and all their many aspects are undeniably an integral part of human nature and the way the natural world works, and there is so much about both that remains a mystery."

She thinks quietly for a moment. "Frank, I...I ran away."

Frank's eyes catch the firelight. "You were scared."

"Not as prepared as I thought I was."

"Your expectations?"

"Probably. But it doesn't change the fact that I ran away. I told myself it was about being fair and understanding, but... well, I wasn't being totally honest."

"And you came to this conclusion today."

"The angel in the plum tree breathed into my ear."

Frank leans back again. "You can always believe whatever happens, happens for a reason. A lot of people believe that."

She glances down at Meg's letter. "I think Meg believes that. Whatever is happening in Cheyenne, I'm being shut out. I don't know why, I may never know why, but I'm not part of that equation. That's what you get for running away."

"Possibly."

"All theories need to be tested, correct?"

"Well..."

"I believe in fate and destiny and kismet, Frank ..."

"I never knew that."

"I think I need to... to test it."

"Are you going to Provincetown?" he murmurs.

She looks up from the letter. A familiar churning begins in the pit of her stomach. "I'm trapped, Frank. Can you see it? There's nowhere to hide. East or West, therein lies the same problem..."

"Challenge."

"Challenge, then. Whichever direction, I proceed blind and unsure of what awaits me. And if *you* are uncertain of what Dermot wants of me, then I certainly have no idea."

"He's old," Frank says.

She considers this in silence. Frank never says anything for the sake of it, and although she could fathom a number of reasons for his comment and how it pertains to Dermot and herself, she cannot bring herself to articulate them either mentally or verbally. Simply, she turns the other way.

"So, *will* you go to Provincetown in response to Father's telegram?"

His father. Joseph's father. Miles' father. The father of her brothers. The man who married her mother, the woman who gave birth to her and died in the process. So the man's old… why should she care in any way whatsoever? How much does a child owe the man who planted the seed of human life inside her mother to create her?

Emmaline

As she takes the corner at the top of Ferguson Street and turns into 19th Street, Emmaline braces for the icy wind to cut across her. Her defeat of the insane chill that dogs her every move in Cheyenne is up for debate, but defeat it she must. The only glimmer of warmth is that the sidewalk is tracked in the gloom by a string of pearly street lamps. She imagines the streets probably look rather pretty in summer when the trees are all leafy and green and swinging in the breeze. Her favorite is the brave oak tree near the Congregational Church. Every day she looks up into those chilled branches for the tell-tale buds of Spring and every day brings disappointment. This world is permanently cold. The only way not to be overwhelmed is not to think about it too much.

19th Street is also *his* street – well, half a corner of it. His house shares the corner with Ransom Street; as she walks, it comes into view… and right now there is light glowing from a number of windows. She blinks in amazement. He's not usually home before most of the folks in town have put their children to bed…

So he's home. So what?

In two minds she approaches his house. She stands outside the gate… and a voice creeps into her head.

Unless you are too scared to confront these feelings...

Scared? Emmaline Roberts? Since when? Father Nugent doesn't know her that well yet.

You may be running away... Not well at all. Emmaline Roberts doesn't run away. She makes decisions based on logic and common sense. And right now, in this moment, she intends to prove it with simple concern for a friend. The Judge was particularly harsh, Mr Faraday said so. She felt Cliff's distress and witnessed his anger; she should make sure he's all right. Any friend would do as much.

She opens the gate, walks down the path by the splay light of the porch lamp, up to the door and raps on it. And then hastily steps back. They're not friends...

What is she doing here?

She turns away; with any luck he didn't hear her knocking.

The gate is within reach when she hears, "Emma!"

Darn.

She hesitates, and then decides to keep going.

"Wait..."

She has her hand on the gate when another hand intervenes.

The full impact of his presence close at her side freezes her to her spot.

"I didn't think anyone was home," she fibs.

"May we go inside? It's freezing out here."

"I just remembered I have something urgent that needs doing."

"Stop fibbing. It's a bad habit you've picked up and you need practice to be remotely convincing."

"Well, of all the..."

"I'm glad you came by. I wanted to talk to you. I was going to call at the guesthouse after supper."

He wears a pair of worn denim britches and an old comfortable shirt.

"I disturbed you."

"No. Come in, I want to show you something."

"No, I really shouldn't. I have to be going. I only wanted to see how you were after..."

"After my encounter with the Judge."

She nods.

"I was angry but I got over it."

"Then you're not..."

"Angry with you?"

55

She shrugs; a non-committal approach is best.

"When have I ever been angry with you…"

She opens her mouth to tell him the last time they conversed at some length, at the Diamond-T, they ended up fighting, and he was annoyed at the very least; that was nearly three weeks ago and since then they have pursued this odd kind of truce.

"You frustrate me sometimes, but… Emma, I'm not angry with anyone, except Walker maybe…"

"Well, then, you're fine and I can le…"

"I know you'll want to see this. Will you do me the honor of the pleasure of your company for just a few minutes?"

Of all the things… he holds out his arm for her take. And smiles.

It's like a sunny morning in June – too hard to resist.

"Very well," she says, taking his arm.

At least she made him work for it.

"Thank you."

"I can see right through this, you know."

"I know."

He closes the front door.

"May I take your cloak?"

"I really can't stay that long…"

"Please."

She removes her cloak. He takes it from her and hangs it on the coat stand by the door, on the peg beside his coat. Something new pinned to his coat catches her eye. A different kind of star. More like a shield with a star punched out in the center. Still silver, but shinier than his sheriff's star, it bears different words. She steps up to it and turns it to the light.

Deputy US Marshal.

She catches her breath. "This is what you wanted to show me?"

"This afternoon Dan Hummer asked me to help him search for Bodecker, Porterfield and Richard Taylor. Walker is uncooperative, so are the authorities in Omaha. Hummer's deputies are chasing bank robbers and guarding gold consignments."

"And there's so little to do here in town?"

"Well, you would be acquainted with how much I have to do since you and Quaid make it your business to write about my business every day."

"Yes, that's our business. Donnelly still refuses to talk?"

He nods. "He's got himself this lawyer from Omaha."

"Who insists that Mr Faraday hasn't established Donnelly's motivation for killing people."

"Hummer had me sworn in before the Judge this afternoon. Mac has everything under control, despite the fact that Bodecker's association members have closed ranks. They won't need me till the trial. I have Cam's approval."

"So why are you telling me?"

He opens his mouth and then closes it. She catches his eye and then looks away. Looks back and gets stuck. And then a bit lost. Gazing at him, into those pretty eyes of his, is like wandering in unexplored land, so much to discover, so full of wonders and...

And then she comes to her senses.

This is no way for a reporter to behave. He could be giving her a scoop. Why didn't he just say so and dispense with the attempt at charming her inside his house?

"Is it off the record?" she asks, offering a concession.

"No...yes... I... What I really wanted you to see is upstairs."

"I'm not going upstairs..."

"Emma, it's all perfectly innocent, I assure you."

"Why can't you bring it down?"

"Well, I could but I haven't quite put my hand on it yet."

He breaks away and heads for the stairs, which he bounds with an energy about him she cannot take her eyes off.

Is this to do with work or not?

"I know you're curious," he calls out from the top.

So curious her toes are squirming inside her shoes. Dang.

At the top she follows the lamplight and finds him in a large room cluttered with crates. Light from half a dozen lamps warms every recess, along with a toasting fire in the grate. Except for the lamps and green drapes covering the window, there is one wooden chair and no other furnishings whatsoever. The floor is littered with books, mainly arranged in small stacks, and old scrunched up newspapers, that clearly once padded the crates from which he is now extracting several volumes and examining the spines.

"What is this?" she breathes.

"My paternal legacy."

Looking around in a daze, she says, "Oh, my. Shouldn't they be in a library or something?"

"There's something very permanent about a library."

"You live here, don't you?"

He doesn't answer.

To fill the gap she says, "Now I understand what Mr Faraday meant."

"What did Cam say?"

"He said Judge Callaghan gave you good practice for the excellent attorney you will be one day when you come to your senses and stop chasing criminals and outlaws."

"Are you sure you're supposed to tell me that?"

"I don't rightly care."

"Fair enough."

"Have you read all of them?"

"Many of them. Certainly not all. But I suppose now would be a pertinent time to tell you I'm a bookworm."

"Yes, it would. Particularly after teasing me for being one how many times? – I should think you would be very sheepish about it."

He gives a gentle laugh.

"You're looking for a particular book?"

"One I want to show you."

"You want to show me a book? Good heavens, what for?"

"You'll see."

"You've forgotten what crate it's in?"

"Mm," he murmurs. "This is the last, wouldn't you know it...."

"Of course. Why don't you make an inventory for each crate?"

"I guess I should."

"My, how fine they are." She casts her eye over the collection.

"You can look at them... closer up."

"No. Thank you, but Nan will be expecting me for supper..."

"How many suppers has Nan kept warm for you since you started working for Quaid?"

"A couple…"

His dark eyebrow lifts, reproaching her for fibbing.

"I really have to go… I shouldn't…"

No, she shouldn't. What was she thinking? This is more like an ambush than a scoop.

She makes her exit only to hear him say, "Found it!" more to himself than her. Even so, it stops her in her tracks. Before she knows what's happening, he takes her by the arm and leads her to the solitary wooden chair…

"I *really* have to go…"

He holds the chair for her. "This won't take long."

"What won't?"

"What I have to say."

She sits. Better to get it over with.

He pulls up a crate and sits in front of her, so close that her knees fit in the space between his. He has a small, blue covered book in his hand. "Emma…"

"Yes?" she replies suspiciously.

And then he smiles at her.

She winces. And reassesses her decision to get this over with.

"I think I should go, really…"

Gently, he catches her hand. "Emma."

Warmth radiates up her arm and becomes longing in her heart, the sensation restraining her as effectively as if he cast a net over her… in his look, in the tips of his fingers, in his voice is the innate strength of his character, his spirit, his regard for her. Again she laments her lack of progress – one touch and all her efforts are gone to pieces.

"Don't go, not yet."

"What has that book got to do with you becoming a Deputy US Marshal and leaving town?"

"The book is for you."

Her heart is doing a good imitation of a racehorse by now.

"You… you went through all these crates and all these books to find *this* book for me? I can't accept it, so I'm sorry for all your trouble."

"Emma, I'm going on a mission tomorrow and there's a chance

– a slim one – that I might not see you again. If something happens to me while I'm gone, or to you and you need... I want you to have the book."

Not see him again? She swallows hard. "Cliff, you're scaring me... what are you talking about?"

"I don't mean to scare you. You know, I was thinking before. Whenever I take all these out and look at them, it's like being transported back into the past. Each cover I open is like a door. I have no fear about it, but it just seems weird. My father died when I was eighteen years old, and my mother one month after him, so guess I should feel something. Regret, loss, maybe even anger, but I don't. My grandmother would say: you turned your back on your father's memory when you became a sheriff."

"Would she be right?"

"You would say she was."

"You think so? Old people tend to lose their understanding of what it's like to be young and want to make your own decisions."

"You're defending me now?"

"I really *must* go..."

"I thought you'd like the books."

"I do like them," she says, exasperated. "Their wonderful, but... Why are you torturing me this way?"

"Every moment I spend apart from you is torture. Allow me this?"

What did he just say? She forgets to breathe.

He takes it as a sign to proceed. "My grandmother was a little like you described before but she was also wise and understood me. The book was a gift on my twenty-first birthday. It's a first edition and extremely valuable. When I give it to you, when you read my grandmother's inscription inside..."

"What is the book about?"

"You're cold," he mutters and caresses her hand.

"The book is about me being cold..."

"No," he smiles. "You're trembling, you're cold..."

"Have you felt the temperature outside? Speaking of which, I should go before it drops any lower and I arrive at Nan's as an icicle."

"I want to explain why I was so angry today."

"The Judge pressed you too hard… what has this got to do with the book and your grandmother?"

"I know you're used to controlling the interview but, Emma, if you would just hear me out."

"I'm listening."

"The Judge could see there was something I wasn't saying."

She blinks. "You lied?"

"Not under oath. Emma, you know me better than that."

"Well…"

"When he questioned my motivation for giving you the information on the train, how could I tell him I'd found the one person in my whole life who I believed in and trusted completely in you. That I knew in the deepest part of me, in my heart, you wouldn't let me down."

"Oh. Yes, put *that* way it would have sounded a little strange in court…"

"Are you listening to me, properly?"

"How could I deflect your meaning so astutely if I wasn't listening properly?"

He gives a short laugh. "Emma, weeks have gone by and has anything changed since the way we felt at the Diamond-T?"

"I was making great progress until you lured me up here with your books. I thought I was getting a scoop…"

"Avoidance is not dealing. It's just avoiding."

"But until my job is finished and I leave Cheyenne that's how it's got to be. We talked about this, we agreed."

"Well, I certainly didn't," he exclaims. "We've avoided each other with some success up till now because that's how I managed it. For a start, I wanted you to get over our fight at the Diamond-T."

"That's all it was to you? A test? I was doing what I said I would; sticking to my agreement with Mr Quaid."

"I know and it was admirable. But I haven't seen indifference in your eyes. If I had I wouldn't be doing this now. I know you want to be with me. As much as I want to be with you. You walk into my house and nothing's changed…"

"I thought I was getting a scoop…"

"...we are more curious about one another than ever. Time won't change this. As difficult as it was to do, the past couple of weeks has proved it."

"I declare, Cliff Ryan, sometimes your ruthlessness just clean takes my breath away. I have no idea what's to be done about it, none!"

"Emma, I know so much about me falls short of your expectations. I'm not Catholic. I work a job you will never approve. I have my ruthless streak. You question my honesty, and my conscience. But, Emma..."

"You think this is easy? Trying to do what's expected of me. Sticking to the course I set out on."

"No... I don't think it's easy. I admire your tenacity..."

"Well, I'm glad, because I just don't know what more I can do to convince you to..."

"It's my turn to convince you, Emma."

"Cliff, you are a good man. And you know very well I question everything, even what I understand. This is about circumstance. If it weren't for the Judge ordering me to stay in Cheyenne, I would give Mr Quaid my story and leave town. Then you would see."

"And you would see..." he says quickly, "...that a thousand miles and as many years would make no difference. We could live our whole lives apart and meet in heaven to know the same thing we know here and now." He shifts closer, still clasping her hand, looking into her face with enthralling intensity, the warmth of him seizing her, his closeness holding her spellbound.

"Heaven?" she breathes.

See the mountains kiss high heaven... and the moonbeams kiss the sea... what are all these kissings worth, if thou kiss not me?

The warmth of his smile intensifies; his eyes, all brilliant and melting into that irresistible viridescence, lock onto hers and stick.

"Emma, do you know what I see when I look at you? I see beauty and warmth, compassion, boundless spirit..."

"Just a country girl, simple Southern country girl..."

"I see intelligence and integrity, and complexities that fascinate me to the brink of utter confusion... I am completely bewitched by that Southern country girl. Emma, I'm in love with you."

In love with her... bewitched... *In love with her?*

This was supposed to be a scoop.

The blood rushes to her head and drains away... a feeling she despises and usually tries to avoid at all costs.

"Fiddlesticks!" she declares and springs to her feet, upsetting the chair, sending it backwards and crashing onto the floor.

"Fiddlesticks?" he echoes with a comical look of disbelief.

"I won't hear of such a thing." And she frowns at him, more than annoyed... strangely and pin-pricklingly confused.

"Emma..."

"Goodnight."

She takes her leave – quickly – while she has him stunned.

Cliff

He sighs. Frowns at the toppled chair. Mumbles *won't hear of such a thing* to himself. And waits for the front door to slam shut behind one irate and uncooperative female.

But a minute of buzzing confusion passes by without a sound in the house.

From the top of the stairs he spies her cloak still hanging there next to his coat.

Curiosity doesn't begin to describe what's taken hold of him.

As he enters the parlor she's there, pacing in front of the fireplace, wringing her small hands white and wearing a decidedly put-upon expression on her face.

He wanders into the middle of the room...

Her attention swings his way and she shoots him a look of such excited disgruntlement he has to bite back a smile.

"You can't pretend you didn't know," he says.

The graceful, wordless pacing continues.

"Do you plan to say something, or just make holes in my rug?"

She appears to be about to speak, then closes her mouth.

"Why didn't you leave just now?"

"Because I saw your new badge as I was about to take my cloak and it suddenly seemed... mean..."

"Like when soldiers go off to war?"

"Something like that. I reacted...badly. I'm sorry."

"Stop pacing? Be still, and listen to me, Emma?"

She turns towards him, her whole body tense. "You cannot say what you said upstairs to me again. I will not listen."

"Then please know it is important to me to have told you before I went away."

She resumes her pacing. "I don't know what you want from me. I'm just Emmaline Roberts, a reporter. That's all."

"You are much more than you realize, Emma."

"Oh, what kind of talk is that? I'm just Emmie, Celina's totally unexpected twin, named by my mother for the title character in her favorite Jane Austen novel, a name my father considered lacking in strength and insisted be Emmaline. No one calls me Emma except you."

"I…"

"You are a man of the world, anyone can see that; I am only a small town girl. I'm a reporter, that's all. I have no ambition to be anything else."

He holds his emotions in check. All of them… from the impulse to laugh out loud to the overwhelming desire to sweep her up. If someone had told him he would enjoy this situation more than having her fall into his arms and declare her reciprocation of his feelings he wouldn't have believed them.

And as for her ambition… it's no small thing.

He makes his approach, stealthily, with the book in his hand; when she turns to retrace her steps she finds herself face to face with him.

"I can see why Marshal Hummer would want you along," she mutters, her golden eyes emitting a defeated gleam.

"Thank you," he grins. "Will you read this?"

"What is it?"

He holds the book before her and draws her gaze to what he wants her to see. The facing page is filled with his grandmother's even, elegant handwriting floating across the paper in black ink.

She takes the book, and although he doesn't expect her to read it aloud, she takes a breath and his grandmother's words come to life from Emma's own lips… he marvels, speechless, at the beauty of her voice, her gentle success with the Spanish names, and mostly at witnessing the meeting of his grandmother's prophesy and the subject of it.

"To my grandson, James Ashcliff Alejandro Alvarez Ryan, if

you should be blessed to meet a woman for whom books are worth more than gold, words more valuable than money, the persuasive truth of passionate writing more stimulating than wine, then let this book be a symbol of all that you love in her and of how much you love her. If she would be the woman who would value this book more than gold and money and wine as symbol of your love for her, offer it to her. If she would accept it, then I know you are in excellent hands. Your loving Grandmother Juanita Alvarez. 18th August 1874. Live your life to make the dreams of the world come true."

When the sound of that last word is lost to silence, and only the crackle of the fire in the hearth breaks it, he rushes into speech...

"My grandmother's father was Spanish; my grandmother married an American, my grandfather, but kept her Spanish name because they were nobility..."

"Hush..." she whispers. She looks up and meets his gaze. "This is what you wanted me to see?"

"There's a little more. Turn over to the title page."

She does this without questioning, and then gasps, "Oh, my."

Emma by Jane Austen is what she sees there, looking back at her.

"I know I called you Emma from the beginning, but I didn't even recall the book until we were eating pie at Martha's."

"I recall that day..."

"You'd just blown the wax out of Dillon Kerr's moustache with that pedigree of yours. Emma, I'd fallen in love with you. Then I remembered the book..."

"I recall you went moody and played with your pie."

"That would be why."

"And have you read it?"

"Once. After *Lita*... my grandmother... gave it to me."

"What did you think of it?"

"I didn't relate to any of the characters, if that's what you mean."

"Not one?"

"All I know is that Mr Whatever-his-name-is in that book has his Emma and I have mine."

"Mr Knightly," she says.

"That's the one."

"What made your grandmother choose this?"

He shrugs gently.

"Did you never ask her?"

"I was twenty-one. I thought she was crazy."

"No, you didn't. You're curious, remember? You asked her."

"I don't remember what she said."

"A likely story. I can tell you respected your *Lita*."

"How will I ever get you to believe anything I say?"

She smiles like a secret. "And your name?"

"James, my Christian name; Ashcliff, a family name on my father's side; Alejandro, some Spanish relative's name; Alvarez, my ancestral Spanish name; and Ryan, my father's last name."

"It's very fine, all of it," she murmurs. "Ashcliff... it suits you... but it's not exactly the name of a sheriff, is it?"

He shrugs.

"What do people in your hometown call you?"

"In Chicago? Ashcliff mostly. My cousin and friends, Cliff..."

"I suppose your mother called you James."

He shakes his head. "No one did... does."

"That's a shame, as I think it reveals another side to your character. I understand what the Spanish parts would mean to your grandmother. You were her only grandchild."

"Mm."

"*Live life to make the dreams of the world come true...* Live for others. That's what you do, I think."

"I do my job, that's all."

"Was she Roman Catholic, your grandmother? With her Spanish heritage an' all?"

He gives a nod.

"But she never took you to church with her?"

"No. My parents had given religion away before I came along, before they were married. When I was six they decided to send me to Sunday school to the Methodist church around the corner to curb my wild tendencies. My grandmother was horrified naturally. She said I didn't have wild tendencies, that I just needed more activities to satisfy my curiosity. I'd stopped attending by the time I was ten. Then, after they died, *Lita* – as grief-stricken as she was – invited me to her church; religion can be comforting, she said. But I didn't need comfort and I had no conviction. As much as I loved my grandmother, my father's father had the greater influence at the time and he believed the Rule of Law was the only thing a man needed to believe in. They were often at loggerheads over what was best for me. He passed away while I was in law school. For the rest of her life, *Lita* kept her faith to herself; she practiced it all right, but all my life I never saw it alive in her." He smiles. "The only person in whom I have seen it alive, Emma, is you."

She says nothing for a few moments; her golden eyes dart over his face with beguiling curiosity but as to her thoughts he hasn't a clue. Then: "What happened to your family?"

"My father, my uncle and my grandfather were desperate characters. They lived and breathed their work and their ideologies; my mother lived for my father. He and my uncle, my mother and my aunt were on their way to a political gala and there was an accident; my father and my uncle were killed instantly, my aunt died a day later, and my mother lingered for a month before she finally went. They said her spirit was broken."

"That is devastating."

"My father was a persuasive, outspoken man, who believed the only way was his way, and my uncle was loyal to him, tempering his outspokenness to a degree, but to his own ruin. My cousin Phillip and I were left in the hands of our mutual and respective grandparents until we came of age."

"I am so sorry."

He shrugs. "Like I said, desperate characters. My mother didn't deserve what happened to her. There wasn't an ambitious bone in her body; she just loved my father."

Emma looks down at the book in her hands.

So they like to talk; they're curiosity for one another burns. But so does something else and he can't wait any longer; he takes the book from her and slides it onto the mantle next to them; then takes her face into his hands.

Emmaline

This is the scoop: her face into his warm, gentle hands. She holds her breath as she looks at him. And the inevitable? His lips and hers, finding their way back to one another. His arms and hers, relieving their lonesome existence. A connection flows between them, like an uncharted river begging to be explored. A tropical river. With the sun beaming down, glittering on the water, sunshine on them, and in them, in every cell of her body, bringing her to life, making her warm, making her want more… and he smells *so* good, like his blue coat. Ashcliff… does something to her, his scent, the essence of him.

Entertaining the notion of being in love with him seems to take over for a while. How could it not? – her arms are full of him, the distance between her and his bare skin being a worn out shirt. She knew girls at home and then at college who loved to boast how this boy or that boy: *makes me weak at the knees!* No boy ever did that to her, but this man has her so weak at the knees she can't even feel them.

And then there comes a tapping on her brain that is unmistakable. *You can't have him. You can't have him…*

She stops kissing him.

You made an agreement with Mr Quaid remember…

Catches her breath.

His gaze is alight with feeling for her.

"Emma…" Whispered tenderness.

Melting kisses on her mouth, the side of her face, her throat, send ribbons of delight shimmering through her.

Step away from the handsome, desirable sheriff, that brain-tapping voice instructs her…

With no knees?

Step away now while you still can…

It's not easy, but she wobbles back. He follows, so she puts a hand on that warm, lean chest of his and takes another step back to keep him at arm's length. A gentle smile lights up his face and makes her stomach flip. They look at one another for a long tantalizing minute before she finds her voice.

"May I have some water?"

"No."

"No?"

He gives his dark head a shake.

"Why ever not?"

"Diversionary tactics won't work. I'm onto you."

He plucks her hand from his chest and kisses it, her palm, so that her hand follows the contour of face, the tips of her fingers touch his warm skin, and the kiss goes right through her. The whole thing makes her quiver.

At that moment she dubs him the most dangerous person she knows.

"You know what I'm most curious about right now?" he asks, placing her hand back against his chest and holding it there with both of his.

She hasn't a clue.

"If you will take the book."

"Where am I supposed to keep a first edition Jane Austen secure in Nan Morris' guesthouse? I'm sure the front door key – and we all have one – fits every lock in the house as well as the chicken coop."

His eyes gleam. "Where do you keep *that* notebook? The *Love's Philosophy* one."

"I know the one to which you refer. I keep it with me. In my satchel. At all times."

"Oh, if it should fall into the wrong hands!"

"Like Judge Callaghan's for example?"

"For example."

Gently, she extracts her hand. "Well… I've really enjoyed our chat but sadly I must go…"

He starts laughing. He reaches for the book on the mantle and holds it in the space between them.

She looks at it and then looks at him. Suddenly, they are both very serious. *Lita's* words are powerful and memorable. Ashcliff is mistaken, though. She cannot be this woman; she could never command such a place in any man's life.

"We've known each other barely six weeks… I am not this woman your *Lita* wrote about. This kind of woman changes a man's life and I have no intention of changing yours."

He frowns as if confused. "You don't?"

"I have my mother as my very own example of that. She wanted my father to be something he didn't want to be. It made her miserable and eventually it meant they couldn't live together. They are still married and I believe they still have some civil regard for one another, but what good is it? He won't give up what he does for her sake, and she won't give in and accept it for his."

"That's a difficult situation…"

"I vowed that in my life I would not repeat their mistake."

"That's unlikely… for a start, you and I are not them."

"I intend to learn from it."

"Their mistakes hurt you, Emma. And you go on letting them."

"Learning from them," she corrects him.

"Do you remember, Emma, that morning after church in Nan's kitchen, we talked about finding happiness. I told you I hadn't found it yet, but I have since. I'm looking at it. It's you, Emma."

This declaration is too beautiful even for her to repulse. She lets it ring in the warmth of the moment. For his sake, she doesn't want him ever to regret saying it and yet she knows he will.

"No fiddlesticks?" he says with a lopsided smile.

She shakes her head.

"Emma, there is something I have to explain, something I need to tell you, and I need you to listen…"

Enough of the warm moment. "There is nothing more to be said. I was raised to believe that who a person is and what they do are synonymous. Their spirit and their vocation in life somehow match up. Seems to me you and sheriffing are a perfect match. You need a woman who won't mind. Because the woman that truly loves you won't, will she?"

"You won't hear me out?" he asks.

"I believe whatever else you have to say you should say it to the woman for whom it's meant, not me."

His thoughts parade mysteriously by. The intensity in his eyes softens. "I guess *Emma* by Jane Austen goes back in her crate."

Her heart rushes within her chest, pumping what feels like disappointment to every corner of her being. Dismayed by what should have been relief and is far from it, she seeks comfort in her own words.

"I will take care of *Emma* awhile."

Besides, the thought of stuffing her back into a cold and lonely crate seems so heartless and ungracious… and after such an honor.

"You will?" he says, handing over the book but sounding like he hadn't heard her properly.

"Just awhile… and, after all, you are going on a dangerous mission," she says, clutching the book.

He closes the gap between them and kisses her cheek. Her senses fill up with him; it's as though all the things in her life that should matter more than this attraction to him scatter without any loyalty whatsoever to make way for him. And something else… that familiar, peculiar tug of pain in her chest. It hadn't bothered her in the last little while, but now it has returned with a vengeance.

Leaving him. Him leaving. Their separation.

"I'll miss you, Emma."

She doesn't want him to miss her; she needs him to forget her.

"Godspeed…" she says.

She leaves at once and takes *Emma* by Jane Austen with her.

Cliff

The following morning

At the depot Ben Taylor hovers by the ticket office, his shrewd eye on the lookout. Interesting. And probably not wholly unexpected. Hummer always kept something extra up his sleeve.

"Ben," Cliff greets him. "Nice mornin'."

"Sheriff," Ben says, stepping forward.

Cliff drops his fully packed duffle bag. "You wanted to see me?"

"I'm going with you."

"In case you hadn't noticed, I'm not the sheriff and this operation is being run by Dan Hummer."

Ben nods sharply. "I noticed. And I know about Hummer. I spoke with him. He said he didn't have a problem with it and when I spoke to you, you'd know why."

Cliff knows. "Welcome aboard."

"Thanks," he says warily, because wary is this man's middle name.

"Your mother okay with this?"

"Not particularly. She eventually acknowledged if I was with you, she'd be okay with it."

"I see."

Ben smirks. "I'm not some greenhorn kid, you know."

"I know."

"I'm just not my cousin."

The only rivalry with a family member Cliff can recall is a scuffle he and Phillip had over who really was the best with their

73

slingshots, in particular, using Phillip's neighbor's spoilt cat as their favorite target, not to hit it so much as make it hiss. Cliff was better, which made it worse for Phillip who practiced on the cat a good deal more often. They were pulled apart, made to shake hands by their fathers and instructed to respect other people's possessions or suffer the consequences. They never fought otherwise, their whole lives. They liked one another, sure, but they innately understood and respected, from an early age and without a word spoken, that without each other their lives could be very lonely and insecure...

He comes out of his memory with a jolt.

"You know, we all have someone..." he mutters.

"Yeah? Listen, my mother really wants us to find my father."

"Even if he is getting what he deserves?"

"Despite what I said, if he's mixed up in this, then he needs help."

Suddenly, Dan Hummer appears in their midst, a fresh-looking cigar clamped between his teeth.

"Mornin', Ryan."

Cliff gives him a dry look. "Mornin'."

Hummer seems bent on studying him. "Get your goodbyes said, did ya?"

"Listen, Hummer, nothing about this arrangement says I have to put up with you needling me about things that are none of your business."

Hummer chomps rapidly on his cigar and then chuckles. "You're right. You're absolutely right. You just let me know when I'm crossin' the line, and I'll step right back again. Not a problem." He turns to Ben and grips his shoulder. "Well, looks like I got another young Taylor to contend with. What d'you say to that, Ryan?"

He and Ben swap glances.

"Don't call me sheriff," Cliff says to him.

"What do I call you?"

"I have a name."

Hummer chuckles out loud. "We're all gonna get along fine, just fine. Come on, boys, the train's all steamed up and rarin' to go."

Cliff looks up to see Luke standing a short distance away, also not unexpected. He excuses himself from the others and joins Luke who gives him a searching look.

"Marshal, eh?" he says with a wry smile.

"*Deputy.*"

"So Ben's going with you, instead of me. Kinda ironic, ain't it?"

"Oh, he's a puppy dog compared to you."

"An orphaned one by the look on his face."

The train-whistle sounds in the frost-laden air, descends into a tweet and then hawks like it's been strangulated. The engine driver gives up.

"I got a favor to ask you. Never thought I'd be asking it, but…"

"Emmaline?"

"I know she's a handful…"

"I'll keep an eye on her."

"I'd appreciate it. She and Tressa get along, so…"

"Do they?" He frowns as if annoyed for being so preoccupied with himself that he'd missed this. With a vague smile, he recovers and says, "Don't worry. We'll take her into the fold."

"Ryan, get your sorry ass on this here locomotive!" Hummer booms out of a nearby window.

"Did something happen?" Luke asks as they stroll towards the car.

"Yes," Cliff says simply, "and no."

"That sounds long."

"It will be."

Luke starts chuckling as Cliff, grinning in spite of himself, tosses his duffle on board. The engine driver tries the train-whistle again and cuts their conversation short.

"Good luck," Luke says.

"Thanks." Cliff boards. "Take care of yourself."

The cars begin to trundle; Cliff salutes and hangs in the doorway, watching thoughtfully as Luke's figure diminishes. Eventually, he moves along towards his seat and joins the others.

Clearly disgruntled, Hummer barks, "You plannin' to get your mind on your work sometime soon, Ryan?"

Towards Denver City let us now
propel,
Of its strange sights and startling
wonders tell.

Lawrence N. Greenleaf
Pike's Peakers of '59

Luke

Late morning, Luke walks towards Emmaline's work desk accompanied by Tressa and Adam. While Adam tries to get his attention by offering him his beloved toy horse, Luke studies Emmaline's distracted expression as she sits making squiggles with her pencil on her notepaper.

"Ain't you supposed to be writing something?" he says.

She looks up. "Pardon me?" Her weary, vacant expression takes a moment to clear. He observes her relief and then, as she sees Tressa and Adam, her gladness.

"Yes," she says and springs out of her seat.

"Emmaline," Tressa breathes.

They hug one another.

"I'm so pleased to see you," Emmaline says. "What a lovely surprise... you should come by often... come every day..."

"I'm happy to see you too, and we could see each other more often except I'm not allowed out without an escort," Tressa remarks. "And escorts seem to have a great deal else to do."

"Surely not," Emmaline grins. "Then I shall stop by your house more often." She holds out her hands towards Adam, who is determined to 'gallop' his horse over Luke's chest. "Come on, baby..." she invites.

Adam flashes his two small, white bottom teeth and stretches out towards her, horse and all, gurgling.

Emmaline takes him, her face alight with pleasure. "Yes, I've met your pony; he's very special..."

Adam babbles in reply, waving the horse excitedly, dribbling.

Emmaline talks to him in a lively way, tugging at his horse, tickling his chest, making him smile and giggle.

Does Cliff know how good this girl is with babies?

"We're here to take you to lunch," Tressa announces.

"Oh, how thoughtful," Emmaline declares. She glances at the wall where a large clock is showing it's just after eleven thirty. "A little early for lunch perhaps, but..."

"We're on Adam time. Early everything today."

"Of course. You, young man, take priority over every single thing."

Adam giggles loudly as she tickles him.

Luke recalls the look on Cliff's face as he asked him to keep an eye on her, and swallows. A girl like Emmaline ain't so easy to keep sight of. She hands Adam over and starts wrapping herself up in coats, mufflers and gloves.

"Think you'll be warm enough?" he asks.

"I'm always hopeful."

Tressa giggles.

"Let's go," Emmaline enthuses.

"Pencil," he says.

Emmaline blinks her long lashes. "Oh." She reaches for the pencil stashed behind her ear and stuffs it into a coat pocket. "I'm ready. Oh, I almost forgot..." She bends low into a desk drawer and extracts her satchel. As she's looping it around her neck and settling it on her shoulder and hip, she looks a little sheepish and says, "To put Mr Quaid at ease."

He flicks another glance at her satchel. A journalist is bound to have secrets, right? He wonders if she sleeps with them under her pillow.

Despite everyone's good intentions, however, the mood at lunch becomes subdued.

"Let's face it," Emmaline says as they finish their meal, "we are both trapped here in town on the Judge's orders and nowhere near where we want to be."

"Where do you want to be?" he asks, curious about her answer.

Her eyes flash. "Do you know how good an investigator I am?"

"*You* could find Loren Bodecker?"

"Don't sound so surprised."

Meanwhile, Tressa, wiping drool from Adam's chin, mutters, "There are different kinds of being trapped, don't you think?"

"How so?" Emmaline encourages gently.

"Well, there's physically trapped – inside a place. And there's being trapped in a situation. I suppose you two are both really, trapped in Cheyenne, trapped by the Judge's orders from the situation in which you find yourselves."

"Go on," he murmurs.

"And… and then there's me. Mart's gone forever and there's no escaping that – is there?"

He swallows hard. "No."

Tressa shrugs. "So, we are all trapped in some way. By the past, or by the present. One day, I hope I will wake up and declare I am no longer bound by the past, that everything that has gone before no longer makes me feel trapped in any way. I want to be free to come and go between past, present and future. No pain and no regrets."

"Makes me feel free just thinking of it," Emmaline murmurs.

"It all seems so far away now – all locked up behind a gate, way off in the distance and I'm walking and walking and never reach it. Yet there is something inside me that won't give up on it. As though I have a… a right to reach it and pass through it."

His eyes sting.

"Silly, I know, and probably selfish."

"No," he says, "you got the right, Tress, same as everybody."

Emmaline says quietly, "I'm sure that day will come."

After Luke has returned Tressa and Adam to the Keatons' rented house, he and Ethan take a stroll through town; it's about one o'clock and they happen upon Dillon Kerr holding court with several reporters and a mob of townsfolk outside Loren Bodecker's building. They stand apart from the crowd but close enough to hear the proceedings.

"We just want a straight answer, Kerr. Is Mr Bodecker associated with this Donnelly character in Ryan's lockup?"

Dillon Kerr, the color of his skin slinking from red to purple to yellow to white and back again, twirls his moustache with nervous fingers. "That is preposterous! Mr Bodecker doesn't associate himself with criminals."

A reporter asks, "Where is Mr Bodecker, Kerr?"

"I am asked that question every day and I am happy to answer it yet again. Mr Bodecker took ill and went to a warmer clime to recover."

The reporter bites down. "You say that, Kerr, but where's the proof?"

The crowd reacts, shouting their approval of the question, demanding an answer. Dillon Kerr holds up his hands, turning purple again. The noise subsides a little. He reaches into his breast pocket and produces a telegram paper.

"Here is the proof. Here is a telegram I received from Mr Bodecker himself only this morning. The doctor says he must stay put if he is to recover his health."

Luke murmurs, "I'd like to get my hands on that telegram."

Ethan grunts.

"Meanwhile, I repeat: Mr Bodecker's enterprises the territory over are not affected by his absence. He is aware people are concerned for his welfare..."

"Why can't you say where he is?"

"Mr Bodecker chooses to keep his place of recovery concealed from the public and has every right to privacy."

"But one word from him would place all our fears to rest," shouts a member of the crowd.

"Let me repeat – you have nothing to fear!"

"Let's see that telegram," yells another irate shareholder.

Dillon Kerr stuffs it back inside his coat. "Gentlemen, put your trust where it belongs. Loren Bodecker has never let any of you down. Sheriff Ryan, on the other hand, and his supporters over there at the Tribune, have done nothing but create fiction to taint Loren's good name. Mr Ryan not only damages Mr Bodecker's excellent reputation by these lies and innuendoes – he also places the financial health of this town and this territory at risk, and that means *you*, gentlemen!"

Luke grunts this time. "He wouldn't be saying that if Cliff was in town."

The crowd nod and comment to one another; the reporters scribble madly.

One journalist, however, seemingly appears from nowhere to ask, "Mr Kerr, isn't it true Mr Bodecker spent most of last summer, during the trial of Ed Parsons, with Mr Donnelly at his home in Laramie?"

Emmaline.

The crowd stops muttering; they look at her and then at Dillon Kerr, whose skin flames red, whether from anger or embarrassment Luke can't be sure. The man throws out his arm over the gathering, his index finger resembling the tip of a spear.

As Kerr prepares to rant at Emmaline, Luke spies the telegram paper falling from inside Kerr's coat to the ground, fluttering like a leaf onto a patch of snow. Kerr doesn't notice; he's too busy screaming.

"YOU! The worst of all, Miss Roberts!"

"If you could just answer the question..." she responds calmly.

"Yes, answer her question," someone shouts.

"Is it true?" demands another.

"Of course it is not true! Another Tribune lie! Who are you going to believe – a man who has worked his guts out for this territory to help it and yourselves prosper, or this Southern upstart who came here at Charlie Quaid's request to dig up dirt and write lies, lies and more lies?"

Luke watches as this vitriol goes straight over Emmaline's head and she prepares to challenge Kerr yet again.

Ethan murmurs, "That girl's got..." He stops and they both crank their ears.

"You were born in Virginia yourself, were you not, Mr Kerr?" Emmaline asks in a gritty tone.

The other journalists snigger and Kerr turns white.

"That has nothing to do with Mr Bodecker," he splutters.

"Then why raise place of birth as an issue of credibility?" Emmaline retorts. "Did Mr Bodecker stay with Mr Donnelly last summer during the trial of Ed Parsons?"

"An absurd question!" Kerr yells.

"If there are witnesses, what do you plan to do to them?" Emmaline persists, raising the bar considerably.

Everyone turns to stare at her. The hush is unsettling, it appears, for everyone but Emmaline; she holds Kerr's outraged glare with calm expectancy.

"This meeting is over!" Kerr rasps; he turns on his heel and disappears inside the Bodecker building.

Emmaline doesn't notice the others giving her long, departing looks because she's too busy jotting in her notebook. While everyone is so engaged, Luke breaks away from Ethan and retrieves the crumpled telegram paper from the snowy patch on the sidewalk where it fell. The paper is a little damp, but perfectly intact. Casually, he walks over to Emmaline, who looks up mid-jot.

"Where did you come from?"

"Up the back."

She looks, spots Ethan and waves. Ethan raises a hand and saunters over.

"What are you up to, Luke?" Emmaline asks.

"Why do you think I'm up to something?" he counters.

She closes her notebook. "You're always up to something."

"I could say the same for you."

"It's my job. Good day, Ethan. How lovely to see you…"

Ethan chuckles. "Emmaline. Two attempts on your life weren't enough?"

She scoffs defiantly. "After all these witnesses, let them try that again!"

"I guess," Ethan muses.

Luke opens his palm slightly and reveals the telegram paper. Emmaline's gaze flies to his face.

"It's not?"

"It is."

"But how…?"

"He dropped it."

Emmaline's light brown eyes shimmer. "Well, read it then."

"Shouldn't we do it somewhere else?" he says, closing his palm again.

She nods. "Cheyenne Hotel lobby in five minutes." She takes off. They watch her for a moment, then stride off themselves.

Ethan remarks, "She trusts you."

"Yeah, well, she knows who can be trusted, doesn't she?"

"It's a gift for sure, knowing who to trust. I feel sorry for those poor saps who trust Loren Bodecker."

A few minutes later they wander into the Cheyenne. Emmaline is waiting by a solitary parlor palm in a brass pot, looking every inch the reporter waiting for her source but trying not to.

"Well?" she says breathlessly.

Luke smoothes out the paper and reads…

"**KERR, SEND TUCKER MILE HIGH PRONTO, LOREN.**"

Emmaline catches her breath. Ethan whistles softly.

"Tucker the lawyer," Emmaline rasps.

"Assume so," Luke says. "We need to find out if he's left town yet. I'm taking this straight to Mac. You can't say anything, Emmaline."

She scowls at him. "Well, Mr Faraday might like to know, don't you think?"

"Let's find out if Tucker's left town first," Luke argues.

She nods brusquely. "I'll wander over to Tucker's building and ask some questions."

"No, they'll think we've been tipped off. Let Mac go."

"Oh, very well."

Ten minutes later, he and Ethan observe from a concealed position Mac walking into the building where Marvin Tucker has his office. They wait. The afternoon is dissolving and the cold bears down with it. Suddenly, Mac is hustled outside by an elderly man who is closing the door behind them and locking it. Mac waits until the old gentleman is on his way before indicating to Luke and Ethan with a nod that they should join him on the sidewalk across the street.

"Well?" Luke breathes.

"Tucker left this morning, but Mr Perkins said Tucker wouldn't say where he was going. He happened to mention, though, that Tucker hates trains. I'm heading down to the stage depot to question the ticket seller. You two find Emmaline and go wait at Cam's office. Tell him exactly how you came by the telegram. I'll give it to him as evidence when I join you later."

They wait half an hour in Cam's office, almost sick with anticipation. Finally, Mac bursts in, his face flushed. He takes the telegram out of his pocket and hands it to Cam. They raise their strained voices as one, "Well?"

Cliff

Cliff's brain has long ceased registering the passing view from his window. He's burrowed deep inside his thoughts of Emma. Marveling again at *Lita's* insight. Astounded the woman who fits *Lita's* description even exists, let alone that he's found her. That she walked into his life. The woman who finally makes sense of who he is. She could still reject him. In fact, he knows he hasn't won her. Not yet. But surely the impact of his grandmother's prophecy is not something even Emma can ignore. Or can she…

Or can she…. He becomes aware of the train slowing; he extricates himself from his thoughts of Emma, his heart beating strangely, and looks around to find Ben frowning at him from across the table.

"We're coming into a town," Ben tells him.

Cliff remembers they are seated for lunch, the last seating of the day, and the food is now before them, not smelling particularly appetizing, but hot and nourishing at least. And he becomes cognizant of the ringing sounds of murmuring chatter and clinking cutlery.

Dan Hummer appears. "Unscheduled stop. The porter just told me the stationmaster waved down the train."

"Let's check it out then," Cliff suggests, on his feet and moving past both of them. "Ben, stay here."

Out on the icy platform, a warmly clad man emerges from the station house.

"Deputy Marshal Ryan?"

"That's me. This is Marshal Hummer."

"Duncan Greer, stationmaster. Glad to meet you. This here telegram came through for you. Been following you along the line. Got a wire to halt the train and make sure you got it. Here it is."

Cliff takes the telegram... DEPUTY MARSHAL CLIFF RYAN. KERR ORDERED BY INTERESTED PARTY TO SEND TUCKER MILE HIGH PRONTO. TUCKER TOOK THE MORNING STAGE TODAY. INVESTIGATE AT ONCE. FARADAY.

He hands the paper to Hummer who reads it and then folds it into his coat pocket.

"Looks like your hunch was right," he mutters.

"Looks that way," Cliff says. And to the stationmaster, "Much obliged, Greer."

"Don't mention it. Always happy to help a bunch of marshals. Now, what reply do you want?"

"Urgent. Cam Faraday, Cheyenne, message received, Ryan."

"Okay. Good as done. Let's get this train moving... your meal will be getting cold. All aboard!"

"What's the discrepancy between our time of arrival and Tucker's?" Ben asks, still picking at his lunch.

Cliff studies his pale face silently while Hummer answers.

"If I remember the timetable right, we should arrive half an hour ahead. Sure it's tight. But it's hard to say. Different route to this here train. That stage-run often gets held up – not by outlaws partic'larly, though that can happen," Hummer says chattily. "Stops at lots of towns along the way, that's why it still exists. Changing horses. The drivers. Meal stops. Goes on and on, like a night in Dodge after the long drive used to and..."

"You really ought to eat that," Cliff interrupts.

"I'll eat when I'm ready," Ben snaps.

Hummer does something strange; he lights the cigar that's usually hanging unlit from his mouth, and through the plume of smoke he does what Cliff's doing – he studies Ben.

"When I was your age, Taylor, why I was skinny as a rake. I was in the war, nervous as all hell most of the time, saw my friends blown up on the battlefield, took me a while to recover once I got back home. Then I took up with the Texas Rangers for a spell. Before some of those raids I couldn't eat a jot. My superior said I weren't cut out for the Rangers because I was too weak. I took some time off Rangerin'. Worked a ranch in New Mexico. Put on some weight, some muscles. Got my nerves all together. Saw myself right. Best thing I ever did. Went to school and got some law education. My teacher reckoned I'd be helpful to the US Marshals' office and he had some contacts. I reckoned he was right, so I agreed. I got the job. I was big and strong by then. Glad to serve the President and this here United States. Justice Department never had no complaints puttin' me on. I caught a lot of bad men. And a couple of bad women…"

"Women?" Ben squawks.

Hummer chuckles deeply. "Sure. When a woman goes bad, son, they go right off. Ain't natural. That's how you can tell if a woman's really bad. Just ain't natural. They get to shootin' and killin'. There's a power in that, wieldin' a gun and such, that women are short of in the real world. Physical power, if you get my drift. They got other power, though…" and again he laughs, "…don't you know. And a bad woman uses that, too, lot more than she should. You seen a bad woman, Ryan?"

"One or two."

"Now, the saloon girl and the whore ain't so bad. They're just tryin' to make an honest livin'. That's a question of decency or morality for most folks. Once gals get to stealin' and shootin' there's no tellin'… why, the wives of some of the most notorious outlaws are decent women, takin' care of their menfolk and families."

"Everything always black and white to you, Hummer?" Ben asks.

Hummer studies him through his cigar plumes. "You weren't listenin', Taylor. I was talkin' about women."

"Women don't go bad because they feel like it," Ben argues.

Hummer taps cigar ash into a small glass dish. "Women wanna be treated right, I know. I hear what you're sayin' and it's a fair point…."

Cliff's attention wanders. Sure, he's thinking about a woman. He's thinking about a woman who walked into his office on the twenty-seventh of January and said *I believe we got off on the wrong foot. Emmaline Roberts. New investigative reporter for The Tribune.* She was pretty, so was her southern accent, and he was wary of her. When she stood up to him this peculiar feeling came over him. She had his attention and never lost it from that moment.

Where has he been heading all these years if it wasn't towards Emma?

"Ryan!"

Who has he been waiting for, if not her?

"Ryan..."

Like heaven to hold... *what are all these kissings worth, if thou kiss not me?* Oh, they are worth it.

"Ryan!"

He takes a drink of water. "Yes, Hummer?"

"What do you think?"

"About?"

"Our next move... shit, Ryan... where have you been?"

"Bad women no longer the topic of conversation?"

Hummer grunts.

"We should arrive before Tucker does, hence Cam's urgency. We stake out the stage depot and when he arrives and we follow him."

"What if he gets off at one of the towns along the way?"

"Look, it's always possible that he planned a detour, but he has no way of knowing we came by this information, so he has nothing to be suspicious about, except maybe what Bodecker wants with him. He wouldn't have paid for the whole trip if he intended to bail. I got a handle on Tucker; for a lawyer he acts like an accountant. And if he hates trains, it could well be he knows he'd get confused by a rail hub the size of Union Station. The stage, however, goes into the center of town and he walks off. But we have to spot him before he disappears into the tramway network and the city. It's big and busy."

"Okay, but what about my father?" Ben asks, frowning.

"Second on the list, son, you know that," Hummer tells him. "Gotta be Bodecker first. And who knows, Tucker might lead us to both of 'em."

"How do we even know that Bodecker will be where Tucker is headed?"

"Not for sure, that's true. But it's called a lead, son. A clue. And it fits with Ryan's hunch. So we latch onto that like a steer on a patch of spring grass. Don't let go neither, not 'til it's all chewed out. Got the analogy, son?"

Ben snorts in amusement. "Sure, Marshal. I got it."

"It's all about patience, Ben. You got the patience? I wonder."

"If my father isn't where we're going and with Bodecker, Marshal, I'm getting back on this train and heading to Omaha to look for him. That's the deal. I got the patience for that and nothing else. Understood?"

Hummer narrows his eyes. "Who runs your father's business while he's away, son?"

Ben's expression sharpens. "Me."

"Ah. And if he's not there and you're not there, who then?"

"That situation has never arisen before. But, there are two other managers who are more than capable."

"When was the last time you heard from anyone at Taylor Minin'?"

"I haven't."

"Well, when we reach our destination, I want you to send a telegram to the office, I want you to pretend you don't know your father's missin', and I want you to enquire about how things are goin' in Omaha. Got it?"

"It's been a while…"

"Exactly. You're curious, I can tell. Send it while Ryan and myself are off lookin' for Tucker, and wait for us at the stage telegraph office."

Ben sighs.

Hummer chuckles. "Told ya, lotsa patience is required."

"How far to go?" Ben asks after a moment.

"Couple of hours, give or take."

Cliff

The Mile High City
Colorado

The afternoon is dissolving into a cold deep dusk as their train trundles through the web of iron and steel that is Denver's Union Station and steams to a halt.

They alight and make their way through the depot to busy Wynkoop Street.

The depot itself is a huge and highly stylish building which is constructed out of pink stone, trimmed with sandstone, with a clock tower over a hundred feet high that soars into the darkening sky. This is the first indication and lasting impression of the wealth of this city – there are many more to come.

Leaving the steaming crisscross of humanity and machine behind them, they head out into the city streets, following Hummer's lead.

"What's that smell?" Ben inquires as they move along busy sidewalks piled up slush.

"The smelters, son. Welcome to the Mile High City!"

Before long, they come upon a rowdy Irish saloon where the stench of beer is matched only by a raucous and vulgar rendition of My Wild Irish Rose. They dodge several patrons forced to take some fresh air; one lands at Ben's feet, giving his head a bemused shake, his beer glass still in hand. Ben steps around him.

Cliff hauls the man to his feet and drapes him against the wall of the saloon.

Meanwhile, Hummer grunts and removes his cigar. "Don't

know what more we can expect of a town brought into this world in saloon halls."

"It looks like it was just dropped here," Ben remarks as they move along.

Hummer chuckles and replaces his cigar. "You ain't the first person to make that observation. Wait till ya see it in full daylight tomorrow mornin'."

A streetcar rolls by, clanging its bell, full to the brim with workers going home for the day.

"Of course, the whole town ain't all like this, son," Hummer elaborates. "The thing about this town is that it's diverse. You spend some time here and you'll see."

"I just want to find my father."

"If he's where I think he might be, then you're gonna get to see how lotsa people find that smelter pong more like perfume."

Ben doesn't respond; they are tackling the next street. "Did we have to come this way?"

"Holliday Street is the quickest."

But not the most pleasant.

Despite the fact this district contains many of the city's important businesses, banks, hotels and even the mint, it had another reputation and its notoriety is known far and wide.

Between the higher class pleasure parlors are squeezed cribs, brothels, dance halls and saloons. This is the domain of Denver's soiled doves and the bagnio madams, the city's demimonde.

In the window of one brothel there's a woman showing her wares. She's shapely and quite undressed, her pearly skin luminous in the glare of several electric lamps. Beside her is an eye-catching sign:

Men Taken In And Done For!

Further along, one of those soiled doves steps in front of Cliff, forcing him to stop. She has a velvet cape half-pulled around her, and it's likely she's not wearing much else; she flutters her eyelashes sweetly at him and her smile is fresh, but her garish face paint can't hide the fact she's barely seventeen.

He opens his coat, which she takes as a come-on until her glance falls where he's pointing – to his badge; the girl's kohl-ringed eyes pop and she slinks back into the gloom of her brothel entrance, rearranging her cape around her body.

"And they thought this place was too far from Cheyenne to ever amount to much," he remarks as he catches up to the others.

"Don't act like Omaha don't have this kind of district, Ben," Hummer is saying, "coz I seen it."

"Then you know it ain't like this exactly," Ben grumbles.

"So, you've seen it then?" Hummer laughs.

Ben gives him a look that would cut glass. Hummer only laughs louder. Even Cliff checks a laugh. That's the thing about Ben; he's not what he appears to be.

"Cheer up, boys," Hummer chuckles. "I'm pretty sure Tucker intends to show us how the other half lives."

Emmaline

Cheyenne

"Miss, I must insist you make your decision; it's closing time and my supper's on the table."

Emmaline, peering out the store window and through the gloom to the building across the street, absentmindedly lifts a book from a pile on the table and holds it out. "This one will do fine, thank you."

The sales clerk removes it from her grasp.

Still there's no movement from across the street. Dillon Kerr has to emerge sometime…

"*The Manatee: Mermaid of the Tropics*. Are you sure, Miss?"

"Pardon?"

"The Manatee…"

"Oh, no. I know all about those," she says, picking up the book beneath her hand and passing the sales clerk this as well. Across the street, the door to Kerr's building opens. Her pulse quickens; she squints, wishing she could get closer.

"You know about Manatees?"

"Mm."

"Extraordinary."

Dillon Kerr creeps onto the sidewalk from the door and starts looking about him. Ah-huh!

"This one is *Tapirs: Mating and Habitat*."

"Tapirs?"

"Yes, Miss. Do you know about *these*?"

Cliff

At the stage depot, crowded and stifling, the harried clerk is quick to point out they aren't the only ones waiting for the Cheyenne stage's arrival and would they mind exercising some patience.

"What happened to it?" Hummer asks, chomping on his unlit cigar and squinting his eyes.

The clerk huffs, pushing his spectacles up his shiny nose. "It's late, that's all I know."

"Son, that's all any of us knows."

The clerk is not impressed.

Hummer and Ben hang about the depot waiting room while Cliff takes a turn outside in the cold. It's stuffy inside anyhow; a man can't think in an atmosphere like that. Suddenly, Ben appears, burdened with their luggage.

He sides up to Cliff and mumbles, "Hummer wants me to send the telegram now."

Cliff nods and watches as he ducks next door into the telegraph office.

Not long after this, a familiar rumbling swells the noise in and around the depot. A lot of people spill out onto the sidewalk. Hummer is one of them, but then he takes cover in the gloom across the street.

Cliff observes each passenger as they alight and wait patiently for their luggage to be hoisted down from the roof. Six people disembark, none of them Tucker.

He edges around the stage, spots Hummer and whistles. Hummer looks over and shakes his head.

Cliff moves closer to the stage now. There are still three people on board.

"Stand back, folks, let the others get out now," the driver is coaxing. "Come on, stand back."

"What happened to you?" one man asks the driver.

"There was some snow up round the pass. Someone on aboard felt sick and we had to stop. Then the horses weren't ready at Beaver Creek. You want the whole list?"

The crowd laughs and resumes their meeting and greeting.

Another passenger alights – a woman, looking timid. And then a countrified youngster, tugging on his tie, his eyes agog. Finally, Tucker.

Cliff watches as Tucker, neatly dressed in starched collar, smart suit and long woolen coat, picks up his carpetbag from the stand of luggage. He takes off down the street in the direction Cliff, Hummer and Ben took from the station.

Cliff meets Hummer on the sidewalk.

"Well, it's on then," says Hummer.

"Seems so," he replies.

"Kinda goin' the long way but..."

"We'll see. Which side of the street do you want?"

"I'm happy with the one I had."

"Let's go then."

"Stick close by. I don't want this goin' south."

"It won't," Cliff assures him.

Emmaline

Dillon Kerr begins to look hard. He pushes snow around with the tip of his boot.

"Tapirs?" Emmaline mutters again.

"Yes, Miss."

Kerr sticks his hands on his hips and looks up and down the street.

"No, I don't like the sound of tapirs."

"The author is an expert and has thoroughly researched and documented extensive years of study of the creatures."

"Mm…"

Kerr locks the door to Bodecker's building and strides away into the gloom.

"I'm sorry," Emmaline says. "You are very helpful. But I'll come back tomorrow and take a better look. You have my word. Good evening."

Emmaline takes off, leaving the sales clerk with the manatee in one hand and the tapirs in the other.

Outside, the bitter evening cold bites into her cheeks. She stuffs both hands into her gloriously warm sable muff and glimpses Dillon Kerr's figure heading towards the end of the block. She hurries along, frosty air filling her lungs and making them sting.

Darn this cold climate.

Marvin Tucker

Marvin scurries downtown as fast as the cramped muscles in his legs will take him, casting about him a wary eye. He hates being summoned; never too sure what kind of reception he's going to get. Bodecker loved surprises; announcing himself as decamped to a warmer climate for health reasons and then encamping himself here, surrounded by boosters of every description who have undoubtedly closed ranks around a brother, might temporarily fool shareholders, but the proponents of Law and Order in Cheyenne make it their business not to be fooled. Still, Hummer has been on Bodecker's case for weeks and turned up nothing. They wouldn't think to look here.

Emmaline

At the end of the block Dillon Kerr has disappeared from view. Who knows where he's gone, the point is that he came out onto the sidewalk to search for something. He'd realized he'd misplaced the telegram. What he does next, whom he sees, speaks to, might all be relevant, or they might not be. Does the thought of losing the telegram fill him with concern or panic?

Emmaline gives a shiver and her stomach makes a gurgling noise; she's been cold and hungry too many times this winter to ignore the signs.

She turns to make her way home only to cannon into Luke.

Marvin Tucker

Marvin stops abruptly at the brothel, seeing what he came this way for and sorely tempted by what he sees. It ain't exactly one of Jennie Rogers' splendid establishments, but it's grand enough. A fancy sign was boasting 'all the comforts of home'. He consults his pocket watch.

"You got plenty of time, honey," says a wide-eyed beauty from the doorway. She moves towards him. She's wearing a cape over something scanty.

Marvin puts his watch away, fumbling as he drinks in her ripe, voluptuous figure. He places his finger at the nape of her neck and draws it down and across her soft, full bosom. He likes the way it makes him feel. She puckers her red lips at him playfully, takes his wandering hand and pulls him firmly towards the entrance.

Cliff

"Damn!" Cliff mutters, white clouds pouring from his mouth as he huffs and puffs his annoyance.

Hummer appears at his side. "He won't be long."

Cliff frowns. "What's that supposed to mean?"

Hummer removes his cigar and says, "What do ya think it means?"

"You're a regular clown, Hummer."

Hummer grins and puts his cigar back in.

"It's too damn cold to wait about while he gets…"

"Some much needed attention, I'll wager."

"You're just full of laughs."

"Lighten up, Ryan. It ain't comfortable stakin' out a house of ill-repute, I agree, partic'larly when that exotic gal had her eye on you first, but I find it's better if ya don't think about it too much."

Emmaline

"Great God Almighty, Luke Taylor, you scared me near half to death!"

"Emmaline, I'm sorry! Are you hurt?"

"Just had five years taken off my life is all. What are you doing sneaking around like that?"

"I could ask you the same question."

"I'm doing my job. And now I'm going home!"

"I'll walk you," he offers.

"Considering my heart just stopped, I would appreciate the company."

"You saw Kerr look for the telegram," he says as they walk.

"Yes, I saw. Did you see what became of him?"

"He disappeared down a side street and into the darkness."

"Who lives down the street? Him?"

"I don't know."

"Are you following me?"

"Making sure you and Tress and Adam got together for lunch was following you. Everything else is a coincidence."

"Why?"

"Why do you think?"

It takes all of five seconds to figure it out, but she walks on quietly before she's ready to articulate it. "Cliff asked you too."

"At the depot before he got on the train."

For a few moments she can't feel the cold. "When did he tell you?"

"About you? He didn't. I guessed."

"You guessed? How? When?"

"In North Platte, when he was telling me how he'd deputized you on the train to take Sheriff Ransford the information about Maverick. Emmaline, you're a reporter. All reporters ever do is annoy him. But he trusted you. You can understand why the Judge was bewildered."

"Bewildered, perhaps, but not doubting his character. How can anyone doubt his character?"

"Mm. I know."

They proceed to the top of her street in thoughtful silence.

She confides, "I know about you and Jennifer, too."

"How?" he asks in a low tone.

"When I first arrived here Charlie Quaid said he'd heard a rumor. Then a funny old woman called Mrs Landers told me; she seemed to know all about it, although I don't know how. And when I asked Cliff if he knew he said he did. But that was a while ago, not long after we met."

"I never told Cliff. Never told anyone..."

"He said he only had to be in the same room with the two of you to know."

Luke gives a laugh, a raw and rather sad sound. He's melancholy, anyone can see that. Even at lunch he was putting on a brave face for Tressa's sake.

"I'm sorry you can't be with her."

"Jennifer is a very complicated individual."

"I hope you introduce me one day."

He gives her a long look. "Are you trying to tell me not to give up, Emmaline?"

"Yes," she demurs. "That and the fact she and I probably have a lot in common. I'd certainly be interested to hear how she became a doctor. A female doctor is no ordinary thing. But then I can't imagine you falling for anyone who isn't something special. And lovely."

"She's definitely that..."

Quiet once more, they eventually reach the gate at Nan Morris' guesthouse.

"What are you going to do?" he asks her.

"How do you mean?"

"About you and Cliff."

If Cliff had discussed her with Luke – and she shouldn't be surprised because complex relationships often need input from a friend – then she probably should consider Luke a friend also.

"He hasn't said much," Luke elaborates as if reading her thoughts. "It's just I know how complicated things can get..."

"I'll be leaving Cheyenne one day, probably as soon as my assignment is completed and when the Judge rescinds his orders."

"And Cliff knows that?"

"Of course, he knows. But you – what are you going to do?"

He shuffles his feet on the frosty sidewalk. "Time is no longer a friend."

"My twin sister Celina says if you believe you are meant to be with a person then it will happen."

"What's it like having a twin?"

"I'm often asked that. We have a special connection and we love it, most of the time. Celina is older so she gets to play big sister."

"I had a big sister, until I was nine and she was twelve."

"Tip told me about her, when I was at the Diamond-T. There is a framed sketch of her in your mother's room. Tip said you made it."

"Yeah... I've sketched Katrine a lot over the years. That one is my mother's favorite."

"It's very good. Looking at it, I felt like I knew her."

"I didn't ever want to forget her, the way she was before the Kiowa-Apache got to her, so I drew her whenever I got a strong memory of her. Whatever she was doing, I'd draw that..."

"You have a gift, Luke."

He shifts his feet again and sighs. "Yeah, I get told that. But in the end it ain't the kind of gift that does much good for the world."

"The significance of your file at Ed Parsons' trial would defy that statement."

"Touchy subject, Emmaline."

"I know. But you have a gift for making the world see itself through the eyes of someone who is carefully watching and weighing how it behaves. You hold it accountable in a powerful way. That's important. You shouldn't hide it away or belittle it."

"Well, ain't you the philosopher..."

"Art is art..."

"Art? I draw stuff, Emmaline."

Here stood one tough nut. And standing in the cold with an empty stomach was not going to see her crack it.

She smiles and reaches for the gate latch.

He opens the gate for her and then stands back.

She steps through and says, "Will Cliff be all right?"

"He can handle himself. I just wish I was with him."

"It's hard being stuck here, I agree."

"I guess there's another way of looking at it. Cliff would've got Mac's telegram telling him about Tucker bolting on the Denver stage. We got that lead right here, so I reckon being stuck in town ain't so bad if it means..."

"That we are forced to be totally focused on obtaining clues like that one."

"Mm," he murmurs. "Dillon Kerr's first mistake, by my reckoning."

"Mine, too. Well, good night. And thank you for seeing me home. Who's going to follow me tomorrow? – little brother Tip?"

"It can be arranged."

She lets herself into the house, aware he's watching her safely inside. He didn't deserve to be heartbroken.

Nan Morris greets her, bustling about the hall. "Oh good, you're home, Miss Emmaline. Supper is five minutes from the table. Wash up now. There's a grand fire in the dining room, too."

Anywhere warm sounds grand.

Exhausted, she retires to her room early. She removes the first edition *Emma* from her satchel and sits back against her pillows. She can't deny Cliff feels close to her as she skims Juanita Alvarez's inscription. To dwell on *Lita's* words in any meaningful way is not sensible, even though she knows full well this is precisely what Cliff hopes she will do in his absence. The book itself is as perfect in aspect as you would expect from it having lived its entire life in a crate and having been opened and read but once in its existence.

She turns to Chapter One. And reads that:

Emma Woodhouse, handsome, clever, and rich, with a comfortable home and happy disposition, seemed to unite some of the best blessings of existence, and had lived nearly twenty-one years in the world with very little to distress or vex her.

Then, patiently, and carefully preserving the pages in their perfect condition, turns to one of her favorite lines, in Chapter 49:

He has imposed on me, but he has not injured me.

And dwells on that instead.

Marvin Tucker

Marvin consults his watch by the street lamp. He's going to be half an hour late, but it was worth it. He's entitled to the good things in life. Besides, anyone who knows Bodecker beyond board meetings and shareholder days knows his fondness for the girls on Holliday Street, so he should understand.

His brain still feels thick and foggy, so this long cold hike up town will clear his head. If he had gone in the other direction, the more direct route, as Dillon Kerr urged him to do, he'd have missed a good time. A professional man in his position in Cheyenne can't just walk into the local saloon there; he has to be discreet or leave town. So he wasn't about to pass up a half-dressed girl offering herself to him at the door of a classy bagnio because Dillon Kerr thought it advisable. Marvin had every intention of going back there as soon as possible.

For now, unfortunately, there's business to take care of, and Marvin draws a huge breath of cold air into his lungs.

The streets have settled down for the evening. Even the saloons have modulated into a murmuring roar as the liquor quells the collective brain of all its victims. And as Marvin moves quickly along different streets and through the downtown precinct, another side of this town emerges. The part that grew up. That found a way. Maybe it's not all that pretty to look at, but it's intent on yielding a pretty good living.

As he gets closer to his destination, his queasy stomach begins to roll and surge. Maybe the girl-whore wasn't such a good idea after all.

Cliff

Cliff gapes at the brilliant, imposing edifice that Marvin Tucker just strolled into.

"Pull your bottom lip up, Ryan," Hummer needles him. "You're from Chicago, you must've seen more than your fair share of electric lights."

"Electricity has come a long way since I lived there."

"First time for everythin' and by that I mean first time I ever seen you amazed by somethin'. Well, you're just full of wonder, ain't ya?"

"Standing here with you, Hummer, I'm full of something but it's not wonder. So, now what?"

"You better get on in there."

"What are you talking about?"

"Well, I can't go in there. I'd be recognized." He starts chomping down on his unlit cigar.

"Like your famous or something?"

"You're a funny feller, ain't ya? Don't forget, Ryan, I got no word that says 'deputy' on my badge."

"And I have no word that says 'lackey' on mine. So, are you telling me you want me to pose as a member?"

"That's what I like about you, Ryan – quick on the uptake."

"Hummer…"

"Face it, you got the looks and the brains. They'll fall for it. At the very least if you act natural and look like you belong, you can sniff around inside until you find what we're lookin' for. Just look at what you achieved in North Platte."

"I'm not sure I can take any of that as a compliment, Hummer."

Hummer snatches his cigar from his mouth, looks hurt, and then jams it back between his teeth again. "That scowl ain't becomin' on ya, Ryan."

Cliff sighs; then he cranes his neck for a better look at the place. "Give me the warrant then."

"What?"

"If I'm going in I'll need the warrant. Bodecker will want to see it."

Hummer fishes for the warrant and then reluctantly hands it to him; he stashes it inside his coat pocket.

"Thanks. I'll be back."

That's one huge club building looming up before him, with its mansard roofs, tall turrets and deep windows. From electric lamps set within glittering chandeliers, light spreads out into the dark and illuminates patches of snow. External lighting throws striking beams up the structure's high walls, bouncing off intricate moldings and other features, creating arcing patterns of shadow and light. Set back from the road with gently sloping grounds, it has a path that sweeps gracefully to the wide front stoop made of marble.

Before he enters he straightens his tie, his collar, and his coat; removes his hat and runs his fingers through his hair. His look is not that of a well-healed businessman, and traveling on a train all day and standing out in the cold for two hours won't enhance his appearance. He should have bathed, shaved, oiled his hair to black smoothness and changed his clothes.

The front desk is contained within a glittering front lobby complete with marble floor and tall stands of potted plants. It's official in its presentation, but the idea of the club being a home away from home is also projected by the leather chairs and sofas gathered on a rich woolen carpet in one corner; there are a couple of men sitting there talking together, while a wide copse, framed in ornately carved mahogany is set aside for coats and hats.

The clerk at the desk picks him in one. "So, what can I do for you, pilgrim?"

Cliff clears his cold throat. "I'm looking for an associate.

Marvin Tucker. We were supposed to meet at the stage depot but I think I missed him. We were supposed to arrive here together. He was going to introduce me to a potential backer, Loren Bodecker. I don't suppose you could tell me where I could find Tucker, could you?"

The desk clerk is a young man with a polished appearance. He doesn't seem to mind Cliff's rough look; he merely pushes a large book forward, hands Cliff an expensive looking pen that he's just dipped in ink and asks him to sign in.

Cliff writes *James Ashcliff* below the last person to make an entry. That person is Marvin Tucker.

"Oh, look," he says with an unassuming grin, "I've just missed him. Here he is. Right here!"

The desk clerk looks. "So it seems. Well, Mr Ashcliff, Mr Tucker intended to go straight up to see Mr Bodecker. I can tell you where to go if you like."

"Much obliged," he smiles.

"You go through these doors, there's a drawing room on the other side and you go across that and up the staircase on the right. There are several staircases in the building so make sure you don't take the wrong one, or you'll end up in the wrong wing. At the top of the stairs, you go right again down a long hall. Mr Bodecker's in room 2D."

"You've been a big help, thanks. I'm just going to tell the feller who gave me directions I've found who I'm looking for and be back in one moment."

The desk clerk lifts an uninterested eyebrow and turns away. Cliff crosses the marble once more and lets himself out in the cold and onto the deep front porch. While casting his gaze around for Hummer, he hears a soft whistle, and spots Hummer nonchalantly half-concealed behind a tree several yards down the path.

"Well?" he says, chomping, as Cliff joins him.

"Bodecker's in room 2D," Cliff whispers. "A wing on the right. Go across the drawing room, up the right-hand staircase and right again down a long hall."

"Got it. Don't suppose you found out if he's got minders?"

"He'll have them. Hopefully they're not friends of Donnelly."

Hummer grunts.

"Gotta go."

Cliff straightens his tie again; makes sure his badge is hidden.

Inside, he nods to the desk clerk and passes by.

The Cheyenne Club has many distinctions, but this club probably has twice as many. When the boom hit this town, it hit in a big way and kept right on going. Union Station is testament to that. But this palace rams it home to such a degree even he is impressed. The drawing room and its occupants alone would be comparable to the worth of the entire Cheyenne Club. To belong here would truly mean something. He thinks back to Eliza Vade and Wilma Young in North Platte, struggling from day to day, unsure if they would survive the winter, but so generous they would give you whatever little they have if you needed it.

Difficult to resist the grandness of wealth. The potency of its seduction. That it makes you feel important. Noticed. Influential. Powerful.

And small! While the pointed looks he receives from at least a dozen men enjoying themselves find their mark like darts in a target board, he feels every bit like the low-paid sheriff of a frontier county coming to grips with progress and the rule of law.

Then he remembers who he is, a Deputy US Marshal with federal jurisdiction.

"Are you lost, friend?" one man asks, his eyes quivering curiously.

Cliff shakes his head. "No, thanks for asking."

And he wends his way towards the right hand staircase.

Marvin Tucker

Bodecker puts a whiskey in his hand and invites him to sit down.

"Well, Marvin, how goes it in Cheyenne?"

Marvin looks longingly at his whiskey.

"Go on, take a swig," Bodecker laughs. "I was expecting you hours ago. What'd you do? Stop by Holliday on the way?"

Marvin gulps his whiskey. "The stage was held up."

Bodecker plants himself in a leather wingback opposite, his eyes boring into Marvin's. "Learn to like trains, Marvin. They're safer. Quicker. Give a man more control over his destination."

"I guess," Marvin says and sips.

"So, back to my original question. How goes it in Cheyenne?"

"As you would expect. Donnelly is in deep trouble."

"You hired that Omaha lawyer, what's his name…"

"Sturrock. Yes. He's engaged in Donnelly's defense, but Faraday has indicted Donnelly to the wall. At the moment he and Ryan are trying everything to make the connection between you and Donnelly. Charlie Quaid and that Tribune reporter Emmaline Roberts are out there every day looking for clues, anything. She knows a lot that Roberts girl. To top it off, the Alliance arrived in town two days ago and now we have Luke Taylor and his cronies snooping around."

"Let them snoop. They won't find anything."

"Dillon's out front every day fielding questions from reporters and shareholders, anyone and everyone wanting to know what's happened to you and when you're returning."

Bodecker shrugs. "My share prices haven't budged."

"Dillon's doing a sterling job."

"And the Association?"

"All holding tight. Faraday and Ryan can't break through there. The members have ironclad alibis and their records are foolproof. Donnelly's trial is set to start in two weeks. So it looks like you're safe."

"Safe?" Bodecker barks.

"Yes," Marvin says, hurt that his word should be doubted.

"What about the governor?"

"He doesn't know anything; he thinks you're sick like everyone else does. He's concerned about you, told me so himself."

"When?"

"Came by my office to ask if I'd had news of your condition."

"And there's been no shooting since this Maverick business finished?"

Marvin shakes his head. "None."

Bodecker eases himself forward in his chair and in a low voice, says, "You know, Marvin, Donnelly can't be allowed to go to trial."

"Mr Bodecker?"

"You heard, Marvin. He acts tough, but he gets uncomfortable mighty quickly and I've seen the way Faraday screws his victims."

"Not if Donnelly doesn't take the stand."

Bodecker pushes his big lips back and forth.

"Faraday doesn't need a witness stand to screw his victims."

"Donnelly is holding up well, Mr Bodecker. He doesn't say a word unless Dillon lets him."

"Maybe now, while he's protected, but once the trial starts he'll squirm. And the chances that he'll sing will soar. I can't take that chance, Marvin."

"But, Mr Bodecker…"

Bodecker moves his large head from side to side. "No, Marvin. It's got to be done. For the sake of the Empire."

"I'm not that kind of lawyer, Mr Bodecker."

Bodecker lets out a laugh. "What kind is that, Marvin?"

"I don't hire guns. Besides, won't it appear a little obvious if you have Donnelly killed? On top of that, Ryan will ruthlessly investigate his murder."

Bodecker looks thoughtful. "I know. But Donnelly will squirm, I tell you. And I can deal with Ryan."

Marvin can't speak for a while. He's not sure what to say. Ryan is not without powerful friends.

"You know, Marvin," Bodecker says, leaning back again, "I love this town. It has everything I want. I own enough gold and silver in Colorado to not want for anything. But it's not my territory. I've poured my capital and my heart and soul into south-east Wyoming like I ought to own Union Pacific outright. Cheyenne is my town. Laramie County. Albany County. Carbon County. The plains. I, and my association, own them. Their mines, their ranches, their streets. My beef feds the nation; my coal fuels the nation's industry. If they want to make that drafty transportation corridor a state someday soon, it has to be done my way. In time, they'll come to see it. Change is never easy. These foolish people came out west to be independent, find themselves, make a living their own way, so I can understand it's not easy to give all that up. Why the men who are making this here town great, even as we speak, don't dilly-dally around. They make their mark. They say how things are going to be..."

Marvin listens to all this typical grandstanding with patience. Maybe Bodecker should take a better look at this town. Get away from the mansions, the clubs and the palaces. Even while they sit here, Italians, Irish, Germans, Scots and Swedes by sheer hard work are turning their corner of it into their own private boomtown, determined to make their children a comfortable future here.

People who have risen to grandeur tend to forget that people who have fought tooth and nail for what little they have aren't about to give it up because a grandiose person says so.

Luke Taylor is a case in point. And his allies are Faraday and Ryan.

Marvin doesn't like where this is headed.

"So, you see, Marvin, I worked damn hard to get where I am and we don't stop what we're doing because things go a little awry."

A little awry?

"I'm going to give you the name of someone here in town. I

want you to go see him and tell him what I want. And then you leave. If you like you can stay in town another day. I reckon you already know what delights are out there for a man like you. Make use of them."

Marvin recalls the caped girl and takes another swig of his whiskey.

"It'll be all on me," Bodecker adds.

While visions of her body swirl through his head, Bodecker's fat hand holds a fist full of notes before him.

"That should about do it I reckon," Bodecker asserts.

Marvin looks up at Bodecker's face; the man's eyes seem to see into his very soul.

"Not enough?" Bodecker says, and as he reaches into his pockets for more notes, Marvin lowers his eyes.

He recalls the day of his graduation; his father shaking his hand vigorously. "You are going to be a great lawyer, son. This is a big country; it's going to need great lawyers. You go out there and make your mother and me proud." But the memory is tainted. He hasn't seen or written to his folks for years. He hasn't done anything to make them proud. Instead, he was proud of himself for escaping the small town that stifled him.

None of it matters anymore. This is who he is.

The memory dissolves in the bottom of his whiskey glass, and in its place there is the vision of the girl. He had felt free knowing that he was unknown in this town. He slipped something from his pocket into both their drinks while she wasn't looking. Not long after, the magic started to work. By half way up the stairs he was high and so was she. Her energy matched his; not easy to find. Something to savor, that.

He stifles a groan. With the money Bodecker's offering him, he could buy that girl and others like her for a long time, whenever he wanted.

And his supplies would never run dry.

He takes the money quickly. "It's done."

"Good," Bodecker says in a smooth tone. "You won't regret it. The name and address is in there with the money. You won't have any trouble. Just tell the Severini boy to come see me here."

As Marvin swigs the last of his drink, there's a knock on the door.

"I'm not expecting anyone else. See who that is, Marvin?"

Marvin clears his throat, not sure if he can stand up. "Certainly, Mr Bodecker." He makes it to his feet and straightens his clothes. He tries a swagger in his walk as he strides to the door.

Cliff Ryan is standing there.

"Hello, Marvin, you look a little flushed."

Suddenly, he's being pushed into the room and shoved into a chair. The drugs, the whiskey and the caped girl have dulled his senses. *What is going on?*

Bodecker is shouting, "What is the meaning of this? Where are my men?"

"They are taking a nap," Ryan says jauntily.

"What are you doing here, Ryan?" Bodecker says, not so calm now.

"I've come for you, Bodecker."

"What a joke! You can't arrest me, Sheriff!" Bodecker is moving about the room, but Ryan is one step ahead of him.

"Stay where you are, Bodecker."

"And I suppose you are going to make me."

Ryan pulls a colt from his hip. Bodecker halts mid-stride. Ryan turns back the lapel of his coat and reveals his badge.

"A promotion!" Bodecker declares. "How nice."

Ryan pulls out something else. Marvin gapes at it, feeling sick. "He has a warrant, Mr Bodecker."

"Very good, Marvin," Ryan says. "A warrant that states you must return with me to Cheyenne at once."

"Well, I simply won't go, Ryan," Bodecker informs him. "There is no reason for me to go anywhere with you."

"The warrant has been issued by the Supreme Court of the Territory of Wyoming, Bodecker. The Judge got a probable cause bee in his bonnet, figured your disappearance made you some kind of a federal fugitive, so I'm here to make the arrest. All over a thing called Maverick and a bigger thing called The Empire of PDB."

"Empire? What empire?"

"Perhaps you or Marvin might like to read the warrant."

"You can't serve me with a warrant, Ryan. Now go away. I'm busy."

Ryan starts laughing. "Make a good report, Marvin? Tell Mr Bodecker here all about Dillon's extraordinary efforts to keep things humming along. Well, things aren't humming along, Mr Bodecker. We have witnesses to your association with Donnelly."

"What are you talking about?"

"I'm not obliged to discuss the circumstances with you but since we're waiting for somebody else, I'll continue. Luke Taylor is alive and well and you might be interested to know was in the room that night in Omaha when you and Donnelly were discussing the fate of the Alliance."

Marvin cringes as Bodecker's face goes white.

"Who's going to believe that upstart?"

"A grand jury. Faraday. Me. In fact, I rescued him from your other friend, Louis Porterfield. Let me see, who else? Ah, the governor believes him, too."

Bodecker stands still and eerily silent.

Suddenly, Marshal Hummer appears in the doorway. Marvin wants to vomit.

"Good, Ryan. You finally got him lost for words. That's just how I like my prisoners. Quiet and co-operatin'."

Bodecker turns his head and glares at Marvin. "You fucking imbecile. They followed you!"

Hummer moves into the room, extracting manacles from his deep coat pocket. "Yeah, we followed him from the stage depot. Had to wait a while down in Holliday Street, but you know how that is, Bodecker, when you see a nice lookin' young gal."

Marvin is mortified. They were outside waiting while he and the girl were…

"Weren't easy, tryin' not to think about what you and that cavortin' caped creature were doin' upstairs, but we kept our heads. Ryan here had to turn her down before we got to the depot, so imagine how he felt…"

"Shut up, Hummer!" Bodecker rasps. "You always talk too much."

"Well, I didn't know you knew that much about me, Mr

Bodecker. I'm humbled." Hummer approaches him with the manacles.

"I won't wear those," Bodecker says, taking a step back.

Hummer guffaws. "Ryan here can sit on you while I do it if you like. He's got a Deputy Marshal's penchant for stuff like that, don't ya know. Comes natural."

Bodecker hisses. "Don't just sit there, Tucker, get help."

"No, that won't do. Besides, the help is all tied up. Come on, Loren, be a good boy. Hold out your wrists so I can put these on."

"I refuse to be trussed up and taken away."

"Look, Ryan and me don't want to make trouble. We just came here to do our job. We don't want to have to use Ryan's colt and wreck up the furniture and such, but you know he will do it, and the establishment won't be happy with you for makin' him."

"Where are we going?" Bodecker gasps, holding out his wrists at last.

Marvin watches, horrified, as Hummer manacles the big man's wrists.

"The sheriff's place. Hope he's got room. Hell, he'll just have to make room. There – don't that feel snug. Let's go. You, too, Tucker."

"Me? What did I do?"

"You can't hold him," Bodecker argues.

"Get up," Ryan orders him. "Marvin, you've known like everyone else we've been looking for Bodecker."

"How… how did you know where I was going?"

"Good question," Hummer says. "I like questions like that. But ya know, Tucker, we ain't gonna answer it 'cept to say we got a tip off. And Ryan here has the best hunches in the business. Never seen nothin' like it in all my years."

"That's a lot of money you have there, Marvin," Ryan says as he's winding manacles on Marvin's wrists. They're cold and heavy.

He feels so nauseous now he can feel bile burning his throat.

"Hold it down, Marvin."

Ryan removes the wad of money from Marvin's pocket and stuffs it in one of his own.

"You can't take that," Marvin protests and then bites his lip in frustration.

"You've just been paid off for something, Marvin," Ryan says. "What was it?"

Marvin holds his tongue.

Ryan gives a superior smirk. "You're wearing that Holliday scent, Marvin, did you know that?"

"Just one question, Bodecker," Hummer says, giving the man a shove towards the door. "Where is Richard Taylor?"

Cliff

They found Bodecker and Tucker a bed for the night in the holding cells in a precinct not far from Union Station. The police officer on duty didn't know what to make of it, although he knew a warrant when he saw one, and not one but two US Marshals had him on the call box to his superior *pronto*.

The deputy chief of police on night duty, Bill Cornwall, arrived ten minutes later, taking great offence at Cliff and Hummer putting Denver's esteemed guest, Loren Bodecker, in his lockup. The warrant was duly enforced, but Cornwall excused himself and went in search of a state's attorney to verify it and the extradition. Hummer shook his head, muttering that the police department in Denver couldn't lie straight in bed, and added getting Bodecker out of Denver was probably the most exacting part of the mission.

"But don't you fear, Ryan. I got their measure. Been through it before. Expect a parade…"

Meanwhile, Bodecker remained dignified and quietly alert. He knew exactly what was going on and intended to milk every advantage he had, namely, a police department endemically tied to the political bosses who enjoyed his favor.

Another of those advantages should have been the presence of his attorney, namely Tucker, but good old Marvin was losing it.

From watching him with that caped girl before the pair went inside the pleasure palace, and then finding the roll of money in Marvin's pocket, Cliff deduced Marvin's weakness. Marvin didn't seem to be in control of himself at the time of the arrest; Bodecker bedeviled him into taking the money, knowing Marvin's weakness also. Marvin liked them young, expensive and exotic. Bodecker understood it because he shared it. Something Luke witnessed with young Cadie McClements. But Marvin had another predilection Bodecker wasn't aware of, one that made all that money utterly irresistible.

Marvin sits trembling and sweaty in his cell, of no use to himself let alone Bodecker, who dispatches an expectant look at him every now and then. Marvin takes several shaky breaths as he tries to pull himself together.

Cliff takes a seat at the jailer's desk and pulls out the money. Very carefully, he separates and inspects each bill, until about half way through the wad when something extraordinary appears.

"Hello, what have we here?" he mutters.

"What? What is it?" Hummer pounces, turning his back on the jail cells.

Cliff gives Bodecker a sidelong glance, murmuring, "A name and address on a piece of paper."

Hummer takes the paper carefully between his fingers. "That Highland address ain't local. And I don't recognize that name."

"Me neither."

"Don't make any plans for that money, boys," Bodecker says, "it doesn't belong to you, and my attorney will want his retainer returned to him."

They ignore him.

"A hired gun?" Cliff murmurs so that only Hummer can hear.

His eyes bore down into Cliff's. "Who's he trying to bump off?"

"My guess – Donnelly."

Hummer nods thoughtfully. "Tucker's the go between. Hell of an assignment for an attorney."

"He's got to make it look respectable."

"A respectable attorney with a taste for exotic whores."

"No one who works for Bodecker is ever going to be all that respectable, are they? He always knows what to exploit in any man who works for him. Donnelly craved respectability; his weakness is cruelty. Loren knew exactly how to use it."

"Well, we got to go find out who lives at this address."

"I'll go. You can handle the state's attorney and the parade."

Hummer chuckles. "Yeah, I reckon I will."

Cliff stands. "I'll find Ben and send him along."

"If he had any sense he'd have gone to a hotel for the night and then return to the depot in the mornin'."

"Ben's got sense enough," Cliff says, putting on his coat. "It just gets sidetracked from time to time."

"His father."

"Mm. Good luck."

"Er…"

Cliff waits. "What?"

"Watch yourself, Ryan. I don't wanna be bringin' the Roberts girl any bad news."

He slides his colt into his belt, grinning a little. "I'm touched by your consideration, Hummer. Now walk me out. I need directions."

Fortunately, another young police officer in the outer office, Allan March, says he'll take Cliff to the address. To reach Highland at this time of night they'll need a buggy. Cliff negotiates with Allan to swing past the overland stage depot telegraph on the way.

"The telegraph office is probably closed down for the night," Allan tells him on the way out.

"I only want to be sure he's not standing on the sidewalk freezing to death."

"Sure, Deputy Marshal. This here's our transportation…"

Cliff uses the buggy ride to try and map out more of the city in his mind, not so easy at night, even with street lamps, but he's not comfortable constantly relying on other people for directions, including Hummer.

They head up Holliday Street. The place is really smoldering now. In the street, where a few men come and go, the air is abuzz with honky-tonk, loud talk and laughter. Lights from the windows are muted and shadowy and there's a thick heat simmering behind the walls infusing and melting into the cold night.

At the telegraph office there's a note tucked into the doorframe. Cliff lets the street lamp spill over it and reads: *Meet back here in the morning. Found a place to sleep for the night. Your gear is stashed at La Splendide, that brothel showing its wares. The woman at the desk has been paid to keep them safe. Ben.*

He's sure his jaw's dropped.

Allan says, "Everything okay, Deputy Marshal."

Cliff climbs into the buggy. "Drop me at La Splendide a minute, Allan."

"Back on Holliday, sure."

"And Allan..."

"Yes, Deputy Marshal?"

"Call me Cliff."

Allan nods and gives the buggy horse some encouragement.

They clop along in silence until La Splendide comes into view.

Allan pulls up. "Here you go, Dep... Cliff."

"Won't be long."

"I'll be waiting," the young police officer says in a jaunty tone. "If you're not out in five minutes, I'll come back you up."

Cliff steps down onto the sidewalk.

The show window is bare. He sighs and steps inside.

It's dim at first, shadowy, other worldly; the heavily perfumed heat strikes him first, assaulting his senses, trying to batter him with sensuousness, seduce him into thinking there is something inside here he wants; in truth, he wants it, but not with anyone in here and frankly he wishes this place hadn't reminded him.

The music from a tinkering piano strikes him next, although he can't tell where it comes from yet. His eyes water and then quickly adjust, and he sees a large comfortable parlor with statues and paintings of nude women weaving in and out of tall parlor palms. In one corner there's a bar, propped up by a rotund older gentleman with a corseted brunette draped on his shoulder. Beneath a high wooden archway a red carpeted staircase leads up. Nearby is the source of the music, a grand piano played on by a black man in a fancy vest. A blonde woman in a red corset and black stockings is dancing with a client. All three are relaxed and smiling.

Light to see all these indulgent wonders stems from a central chandelier and a dozen or so candles, and is cleverly accentuated with the help of ornate gilt mirrors; these also reflect the sensual movements of several young women wearing colorful corsets, lace undergarments and silk robes who lounge on pink velvet armchairs or chat with their clients on red circular sofas.

Even so engaged, they are eyeing him closely, sizing him up as a potential client. A number of men are giving them all the attention they could want, however, and interest in Cliff wanes amidst giggling, deep voices, outrageous flirting and bawdy behavior; one young woman has unlaced her camisole so her client can glimpse her considerable assets; the well-dressed gentleman laughs and eyeballs her with lascivious intent. She acts like she enjoys it.

Cliff turns away before he's witness to anything a man who has just declared his love to a woman (very different from these soiled doves) is better off not seeing. Although, it's more than likely Emma wouldn't see it that way; she'd likely see a story behind each and every woman here that she believed needed telling. Sometimes, without even realizing it, and in her own sweet southern way, Emma could be as ruthless as he is.

Behind a white-lacquered, gold-trimmed desk that resembles a bedroom dressing table without a mirror, presides a lavishly dressed older woman, with shrewd countenance, vivid red lips and shiny blond hair (likely a wig) arranged high on her head, and she is eyeing him closely. Behold La Splendide's Madam, he guesses...

"Good evenin', honey, somethin' I can do for ya?"

"I hope so. A friend of mine – Ben – said he stashed my gear with you."

"He said you'd have black hair and be tall. He didn't mention those pretty eyes. You'll have to take off your hat."

He wonders if Emma thinks his eyes are pretty as he removes his hat.

The woman's eyes gleam. "That's black all right. Right to the roots. Say, you're kinda classical. Did anyone ever tell ya that?"

Classical? "My gear?" he reminds her.

"You're in an awful hurry, honey. Sure ya don't wanna look around and see if ya might like somethin'. There's lots to try."

"Do you have my gear or not?"

The woman frowns. "I got it. I got it. Lan'sakes. What are ya? Police? We got that sorted already this week..."

He opens the lapel of his coat.

"Why the heck didn't ya just say so in the first place? We ain't doin' nothin' a US Marshal'd be interested in, unless of course..."

"I'm not interested in what you're doing, Ma'am. I only want my gear."

She tosses an indignant look at him and disappears into a room behind her. A moment later she returns. "It's back there all right, but you'll have to get it yourself."

Allan appears. "Five minutes. Need some help?"

"Take Hummer's bag, will you?"

The room is a tarted up office. There's a safe in one corner, which obviously keeps the substantial takings. They retrieve the bags and join the woman in the parlor.

"By any chance do you know what happened to my friend?" Cliff asks.

The woman simpers a little. "Can't say that I do."

He studies her face for several moments. The woman lowers her eyes. Some lies are more telling than the truth.

"Thanks for your help," he says and puts his hat back on.

In the buggy, Allan says, "Your friend will be fine."

They head for Highland.

Ben

Ben chose her because the moment his eye fell upon her he knew she wasn't like the others. He knew he liked her. She sat in a corner of the parlor reading a newspaper; he admired any woman for reading a newspaper. With bright blue eyes, clear skin and pretty features, she appeared natural and wore her thick dark hair and silky clothes simply, without affectation. But when their eyes met over the top of the newspaper he was surprised by a wordless awkwardness between them. She gave him a searching look, which arrested his next breath, folded up the newspaper and walked away, expecting him to follow her. He went with her to her room where, by the light of a candle, they stared at one another across the divide. As the moments ticked by, he continued to feel drawn to her and was intrigued by it. But he wasn't there to be intrigued, so he crossed the divide. Yet another odd moment followed; they stood face to face, maybe an inch apart, and he looked into her eyes – lively, intelligent eyes. She stared back at him for an age. And then promptly apologized as if someone had reminded her it was rude to stare. He told her to forget it, all the while lengthening his gaze still further. Beauty he expected, and a certain voluptuousness for sure. Yet there was strength in her bearing that again had him intrigued. She stood quiet and still. As he looked into her face and her eyes clung to his, the urge to kiss her seemed to override everything else. He put his hands on her waist and his lips against her lips; her arms came around his neck; there was a moment in which his senses registered the cool lips and hands of a stranger, followed by a flash of profound revelation. Coolness turned to warmth, a glad sense of knowing. Fireflies invaded his body, scattering delight to all corners of it. Aroused, moved beyond words, he lifted her in his arms.

Her name is Maya.

What happened is still floating in the warm air between them.

He lifts his head from her shoulder and the fall of her dark, tousled hair to look at her face by the light of the candle burning in a corner of her room; she is smiling at him, her eyes glittering. He returns the smile.

"You're not married," she concludes.

"No."

He feels just as he should. Yes, the bitter tension and dreariness has left his body. But something else is the focus of his attention, something distracting and amazing.

He puts his arms around her and draws her close. "You're very pretty, Maya."

"Thank you."

"How long have you been here?"

"A while… a month."

"Did you always live in Denver?"

"No. Why aren't you married, Ben? You're good-looking and to afford this place you must have money. You're obviously smart, well-educated, have made your way in the world, and well, you seem normal."

He gives a soft laugh. "Normal? What's normal? Are you?"

She frowns gently. "What do you think?"

"You look perfectly fine to me. Too fine for this place."

"No one here is fine. And this job makes some of the girls crazy. Some take drugs, or drink, so they can do things for men that pay a great deal of money. They become entangled in a web. And lose sight of the good and decent things the world has to offer."

"The caped girl…"

"Yes, Darla. She's the star around here. A lot of men are interested in her because she's very exotic. She's a beautiful girl, she has mixed blood, I don't know what, but she'll do anything for a lot of money."

"And you don't want a lot of money?" he asks.

"Not that way. And I'm not going to be doing this forever."

He thinks about this. "How do you plan to get out of it?"

"In a few weeks I'll have enough money to move on."

"Where will you go?"

"Back East."

"Back?"

"I was born in New York, but my father took me away when he separated from my mother ten years ago. I'm going back to find her. And I'll do whatever I can to support myself, but it won't be this; this is strictly temporary."

"Do you think you can keep a month of whoring a secret from any future prospects?"

"I can," she says with gentle firmness. "A month of whoring as you call it is an invaluable investment in a happy marriage."

"Explain that."

"I'll know how to keep any husband of mine very happy," she says.

"Who gave you that advice?" he asks.

"Miss Willona who employed me. I told her I only wanted temporary employment and she said any experience is something."

"Well, it wasn't right what she said, Maya. Some people will say anything."

"I know. But I have to do this and if that advice helps, then… Look, maybe you should get some sleep."

"And if you were to marry me, Maya?"

"You?" she exclaims softly and laughs. "Is that who you're waiting for, Ben? A soiled dove?"

"I just made love to you."

She shakes her head. "No."

"Maya, I made love to you. And you made love to me. You know it."

She frowns hard at him.

"Was here in this place the first time you'd been with a man?"

She doesn't answer. He assumes so.

"How old are you?"

"Twenty-one. You?"

"Twenty six."

Their eyes lock; it seems to him a lot of things are running through her mind and he's not allowed to know any of them.

"Why'd you do it for, Maya? You're too good, and you're not like the others, any others."

"You don't know anything about me."

"I know you gave up your virtue in a high class brothel to work your way home to your mother."

"My virtue," she mutters and wriggles out of his arms.

She turns over, her bare and beautiful back failing the attempt to shut him out... he moves up and slides his arm around her, drawing their bodies together. She stiffens but doesn't move otherwise.

"You're lovely, Maya," he murmurs, snuggles his head on her pillow and sleeps.

Cliff

"This is it," Allan says. "Lots of southern Italians live here, Cliff. Came to work on the railroad but many own these large vegetable gardens, or work for someone who does."

"I've yet to meet an Italian who couldn't grow food. Hard working and enterprising people."

Allan nods. "People here work hard and live simple; they aspire to greater things but enjoy what they have here and now."

"Glad to hear it, but this Alfredo Severini better not be aspiring to what I think he's aspiring."

"Same as before, come get you after five minutes?"

"No. Is there a back alley?"

"Reckon so."

"Good. Go and keep watch in it. This Alfredo might try to run."

"Sure. Will do."

Cliff knocks on the door of the humble brick cottage that is the Severini home and waits. From inside he hears plenty of movement; outside the occasional bark of a dog and the strains of distant music float across the night air.

He's about to knock again when a stout middle-aged woman opens the door to him. Delicious cooking smells escape and hit his nostrils.

"Buona notte, Signora." He knows a little Italian. This much at least.

131

She eyes him suspiciously as she wipes her hands on her apron. "What you want?"

Cliff shifts his weight. "I'm looking for Alfredo Severini. He lives here?"

"Si. My Alfredo live here. What you want with my Alfredo?"

"Could I talk with him, please, Signora?"

"No." And she goes to shut the door.

Cliff stops her as gently as he can. "I need to talk to Alfredo."

Her dark eyes go wide. "You polizi?"

Cliff reveals his badge. "I'm Deputy United States Marshal Cliff Ryan. It's important I speak with Alfredo."

"Alfredo a good boy. You no need speak. He do nothing." And she pushes on the door.

"Is he your son, Signora?"

"Si, my boy. Now go. Go away."

Then, from within another voice, a young man's, joins theirs, saying, "Mama?"

A flurry of Italian follows. In this exchange Cliff's limited knowledge of the language is useless. He waits.

A dark-haired young man suddenly appears at the door. "I'm Alfredo."

Cliff looks into his beetle-black eyes. The young feller shifts his feet. It's as good as a blink. "You tell me now where Alfredo is, or I will come back with a warrant for his arrest and yours and your mother's. Do you understand?"

"No."

"You think Mama will like spending the night in jail for not cooperating with a federal marshal?"

The young man practically gulps. "I am Gianni. Alfredo's brother. I get Alfredo."

"Get moving, Gianni."

Cliff holds the door wide while Gianni goes in search of his brother. Mrs Severini stands to one side her hands rolled up in her apron, fear contorting her face.

"I'm sorry, Signora," he says.

She just shakes her head.

Moments later, not only does Gianni return, but Allan as well, escorting a taller, broader, older version of Gianni at the point of his colt with a very determined look on his face.

"You were right, Deputy Marshal. He tried to run. Got as far as the back gate."

"Put him in the buggy, Allan."

Signora Severini pleads, "What you do with him? He do nothing wrong. Why you take?"

"We only want to ask him some questions, Signora. You can answer a few questions, can't you, Alfredo?"

Alfredo looks like he wants to bolt again. But he says, "Why you pick on Severini?"

"Been in trouble before, Alfredo?" Cliff asks as he's urging Alfredo into the buggy.

They pull away, with Signora Severini and Gianni standing mute on the doorstep.

Ben

Ben wakes again when the candle has burned out and only the faint glow of street lamps finds its way into Maya's room. He's on his back and Maya is tucked up against him, inside the curve of his shoulder. Once he deals with the surprise of realizing where he is and what's happened, those feelings come rushing back. He should leave and do this properly, but after what's happened between them he can't tear himself away. Her body moves slightly; that she is sleeping with him this way reveals far more than words.

"So you like me, Maya, as much as I like you," he whispers.

Again, her body stirs, so gently yet familiarly against him.

"Maya," he murmurs and kisses her forehead. "Look where I found you."

Suddenly, she wakes. She moans and pushes against him. "What... what..."

"It's all right, sweetheart," he says.

"I'm not your sweetheart," she retorts.

"You were sleeping in my arms."

"I... I normally sleep on that side of the bed."

"I want to make love to you."

"That's what you paid for."

"You're not listening to me, Maya. I want to make love to you."

"You didn't pay for that then. So, maybe you had better leave."

"Maybe, but I don't want to. I don't want to leave you. Do you really want me to go?"

She doesn't answer.

"How many men have you had in a month?"

She gives a loud sigh. "That is an unforgivable question. You can't have me, Ben. And I'm not answering any of your questions. Besides, how many brothels have you visited?"

"One. Just once," he tells her hastily. "You don't really want to be with a different man tomorrow?"

"Because of you? You flatter yourself."

"There's something between us, Maya."

"Now you're imagining things."

"That sounds like a challenge to prove it."

"Fine! How do you propose to do that?"

"Well, I have a bed and I have you. I'm sure I'll think of something."

Cliff

"Leave my mother and my brother out," Alfredo snaps.

"They're not in it," Cliff retorts. "Not for us anyway. But you, Alfredo, are putting them right in the middle. You tell us the truth about this piece of paper with your name and address on it."

"I don't know nothing about it."

"It was found in the middle of a great wad of money paid to an agent of Loren Bodecker to find you. What were you supposed to arrange for Mr Bodecker, Alfredo?"

"Who is this Bodecker?"

"Everyone's heard of him," Cliff says, pulling up a chair. "He's a very rich and powerful man. He has hundreds of people working for him, all over the place. In at least two states and one territory that I know of. You must have heard of him."

Alfredo gives his head a stubborn shake.

"What do you do for a living, Alfredo?"

"My brother and me work in gardens down by river. Is there a crime in that?"

"Who do you work for?"

"I don't have to tell you."

"Don't they pay you enough, Alfredo? You have to find other ways of supporting your young brother and your mother?"

"We do fine."

"On your wages? Anybody else in the Severini clan, Alfredo – brothers and sisters, cousins, grandparents – relying on you?"

136

Alfredo shakes his head.

"Big responsibility keeping a family fed, clothed, educated. Falls on the eldest boy. What happened to your father?"

"Papa die last year," he mumbles. He lowers his eyes. Plain to see it's a painful memory.

"I'm sorry, Alfredo," Cliff says, meaning it. Alfredo glances at him from beneath his hooded eyelids. "I don't want to take you away from your family, Alfredo, knowing how much they need you, but if you don't tell me what's going on, that's exactly what's going to happen. Now, how did you hear that Loren Bodecker was looking for a hired gun?"

"I don't have no gun," he bursts out, his eyes flashing.

"I'm going to repeat my last question, Alfredo, and I urge you to answer it honestly."

Alfredo lets out a cry of anguish. "No more questions."

"There won't be any more if you just tell us what we want to know."

"You think if I do this me and my family be safe?"

Cliff sits forward. "How do you mean?"

"I speak about such things and I will die."

"What are you mixed up in, Alfredo?"

Alfredo shakes his head.

"I'm a federal marshal, Alfredo. I have the power to protect you and your family."

"No good."

Cliff rubs his eye. He hadn't been expecting this.

"Alfredo..."

Suddenly, Signora Severini and Gianni burst in.

"Alfredo!" Signora cries.

"I'm sorry, Cliff," Allan says, coming up the rear. "They surprised me."

Signora clasps her arms around her son and he protests.

"Tell! Tell!" she sobs.

"No, Mama. Go home. Gianni, you shouldn't have come."

"Mama made me. We want you to tell the truth, Alfredo."

Signora nods furiously. "Tell. We leave. Go someplace else. Tonight."

All three exchange a rapid-fire conversation in Italian.

Signora turns her tear-filled eyes on Cliff. "Tonight we go. After Alfredo tell. You don't stop us, signore?"

"Calm yourself, Signora, please," Cliff says. "Gianni, calm your mother."

Gianni helps his mother to a chair. Meanwhile, Alfredo's pained expression appeals to Cliff's better nature.

"Allan, fetch Marshal Hummer from the cells."

"Sure, Cliff."

Cliff studies all three for some time before he stands up. "Now, one way or another we are going to get this all sorted out. When the Marshal gets here, Alfredo, you are going to tell both of us what is going on. When you have told the whole story, the truth, Alfredo, you and your family will be free to go – but only if I know you've told the truth."

"He's good at knowin' it," Hummer says from the door, announcing his arrival, his cigar swinging from his teeth. "Evenin', folks. Just pretend I ain't even here."

The Severinis stare at Hummer like he's the latest exhibit at the fair.

Alfredo's gaze returns to Cliff. "We can go after I tell?"

Ben

"Ben," she says in a drowsy whisper, so low he almost misses it. "I lied to you."

His heart skips. "What do you mean?"

"I haven't been here a month," she says, her lashes blinking sleepily at him. "I only came yesterday. There's only been one other man; he was old and drunk, he pushed me on the bed and passed out before he could do anything. I slept in that chair by the window and left my room before he woke up. The Madam here, Miss Willona, was angry with him because he'd only bought enough tokens for the evening; she made him pay extra for staying overnight."

"What... but..."

"Does it change anything?"

"You never... I am the first..." Now it all begins to make sense. She didn't act experienced; she let him lead... he thought... never mind what he thought. "You lied to me, Maya."

"I told you now... before morning comes, so you can leave, if you want."

Leave *now*? What is she *thinking*?

With her sleep-heavy eyelids fluttering to stay open she says, "And there is something else."

He waits, his heart pushing out beats like a horse breaking down its stall. "Yes?"

"I... I'm actually nineteen. And my name isn't Maya..."

His heart comes to a thudding halt and then feels like it will bolt into oblivion.

"…it's Raina."

"Raina," he croaks.

"Nothing else I said was untrue. I had to protect myself. Had no other defenses. You were here for only one night. I needed to keep you distant."

"Raina…"

She gives a small yawn. "Men come and go here all the time; not one is anything like you. If you hadn't come along when you did, I would be… miserable. But you came, Ben. I wasn't afraid…"

"Raina," he implores her, "why did you choose this life two days ago?"

"My father utterly controls my life… and I am desperate to return to my mother. Ben," she whispers. "I am yours. There truly has never been anyone else."

"Did I hurt you, Raina?"

She smiles sleepily as if she's having a particularly nice dream. "As if you could."

He can't help grinning.

"I don't know what will become of us," she murmurs, "but every word I said, every kiss, every touch, every time we… you know…"

"Lit up the universe?"

"I meant it… with all my heart." She closes her eyes.

"Raina…"

She's asleep.

"It can wait," he whispers and folds her in his arms. "Raina."

Cliff

"No one will know?" Alfredo asks.

"Loren Bodecker is down in the cells," Cliff tells him. "He doesn't know you are here. No one will tell him anything."

"Bodecker?"

"It's him you fear, right?"

"I am connected to this man Donnelly. This Maverick. You hear of him?"

Cliff frowns. Hummer swears under his breath.

Signora *tsks* and glares at him.

Hummer is contrite. "Beg pardon, Ma'am. My apologies."

"Yes, we've heard of him. Go on, Alfredo."

"I fear this Donnelly. He has people everywhere who can do his will."

Bodecker intended to send one of Donnelly's own mavericks to kill him. Cliff exchanges glances with Hummer, who looks like he's thinking the same thing.

"So you know nothing about Donnelly's association with Bodecker, Alfredo?"

"What can a man like me know?"

Frustrated, Cliff rubs his eye. "Alfredo, Donnelly has been captured and put in jail in Cheyenne, and his maverick operation is shut down. He can't hurt you or your family if you don't do what he says."

"I did not know Donnelly is captured."

"A few weeks ago, Alfredo."

"You catch him, Deputy Marshal?"

"No, a friend of mine, a good and brave sheriff in Laramie, who lost his life in the process."

Alfredo shakes his head. "Bad. Very bad. There is one paper some fellow hand out one day in the garden, it says there is job opportunity to make lot of money..."

"Just a minute, Alfredo," says Cliff, astonished, "do you still have this paper?"

Alfredo shrugs. "Maybe at home somewhere."

"All right. Please continue."

"Since Papa gone we struggle. We work in garden long hours and also we make musica for matrimoni and celebrazioni..."

"Weddin's, shindigs and such?" Hummer offers.

"What is shin dig?"

"Parties, Alfredo," Cliff says. "You're musicians as well..."

"Si. But is not enough. Mama, Gianni and me we need money to buy our own garden and not work so hard for someone else for little wages. So I go to see. A very hard man says to make lot of money I must kill a man, or even a woman, when he says. This man is Donnelly. He give me so much money straight away I can't say no. Mama go crazy at me, tell me go back, take it back. I try, Deputy Marshal, I try very hard, but too late. Donnelly says I must keep it and he will find me. So far, nothing. But before last two days, I get letter in my door saying I be needed soon and must wait for sign. I think Mama think you were sign..."

Mama Severini is nodding her head, tears streaming down her plump cheeks.

"Mama, Gianni and me – not bad people, Deputy Marshal..."

"I believe you, Alfredo. Since Donnelly has been in jail for three weeks, I'd like to know what day exactly you were contacted."

"Not yesterday, er, day before."

"Do you have the letter?"

Cliff is taken aback when Mama Severini rummages in her deep dress pocket and produces the said letter.

"Take, signore," she says. "I bring. I know."

"Grazie," he says and she blinks smilingly.

"You good young man. Bravo ragazzo. You help us."

He clears his throat. "I'll do my best, Signora."

He opens the folded note. The haughty scrawl reads, *You will be contacted soon with a job. Be ready. Maverick.* He hands it to Hummer, who is vigorously chomping on his cigar. "I'll need to keep this, Alfredo."

Alfredo nods.

"You can't have received this two days ago from Donnelly, do you understand?"

Again, he nods. They all do.

"So someone else sent it, someone who knows all about Maverick."

"Signore Bodecker," Alfredo supplies.

"How do you know that, Alfredo?"

"At my job interview, when I get money, Donnelly says we work for a rich and powerful man, we only do good work for him, we do our best."

Hummer hands the letter back to Cliff. "This handwriting would appear to be a match with the note found in Tucker's pay off."

Cliff concurs. "Book ends to a draft of criminal intent. If we could match it with Bodecker's or one of his employees…"

"Best chance in Cheyenne."

Again Cliff agrees.

"We help. We go now?" Signora suggests plaintively.

Cliff turns to Alfredo and looks him square in the eye. "Will you help us some more, Alfredo? Will you testify in court to what has happened to you? To what you just told me and Marshal Hummer."

"No, no, no…"

All hell breaks loose in the Severini family.

Hummer scratches his head. Cliff holds up his hands and they stop. "Will you give me a statement then, a sworn statement that I can present to the Judge in court?"

"No!"

"Alfredo, this is very, very important. Bodecker is a very bad man and we need people like you to be brave and come forward. You won't be in trouble yourself."

"No!" Alfredo folds his arms.

Hummer sighs and rolls his eyes.

Cliff rubs his chin thoughtfully. He looks at Mama Severini. Sincere, hard-working Signora, who has raised good sons, who is proud of her family, who came to this country to give them a better life only to lose her husband…

She catches his look and her eyes grow bright and sad.

"Alfredo," she says. "We must do this."

"What! Mama, no!"

"Alfredo," she admonishes him, "you make very bad mistake. Now you fix. Capito?

"But what about you and Gianni?"

"We stay with you. Papa would want us to fix. We fix."

"How about it, Alfredo?" Cliff asks.

Alfredo considers his mother's sad expression for a long time. Finally, he hangs his head.

"We fix it," he says. He looks up at Cliff. "I will go to court and tell the Judge about the letter and Donnelly."

"Even better than that, Alfredo. You're going to court to help us put Mr Bodecker in jail."

His eyes pop.

Cliff smiles. "You and Mama and Gianni will be well taken care of in Cheyenne."

Later, when the Severinis are safely back home, with Allan to guard them and help find the handbill that lured Alfredo into trouble, Hummer joins Cliff in the office.

"Well, how goes it with the state's attorney?" Cliff asks.

"Never showed. Not even for Bodecker. They're smart. It's night. They sleep."

"At least that's what you think they're doing…"

"And that's what we're gonna do. There's a room with a couple of bunks in it down the hall. Shuteye time, Ryan. Enough *bravo* for one day."

"If you say so, Hummer. Who's guarding Bodecker?"

"Would ya believe Cornwall? He just declared nothin' was goin' down on his watch. Say, ya must be missin' that feisty reporter of yours by now…"

Ben

The following morning

Ben's head feels thick and his body heavy, and when he reaches out for her and she's not there, he sits upright, his heading spinning, searching for her. She's standing over by the window, looking out, her slender body wrapped in her purple silk robe, her rich dark hair flowing down her back. There's a fire in the grate crackling heartily and a fine morning sun filling the room. He feels the stubble on his chin, fingers sleepiness from his eyes, pushes his fingers through his hair and swings his feet on the floor. She's all he can think about, despite what lurks like a deep black shadow in the back of his mind. She's like the sunshine filling her room; a fine and warming presence to brighten his day, his dreary world.

He goes to her; stands behind her, hesitant.

"You're still here," she says.

"I…" he clears his throat. "I… understand how difficult things can be in families. What it can make you do. What time is it?"

"Around seven o'clock. A fine morning for March, don't you think?"

"I've never known a finer morning in my life. Rain…"

"Mm," she says, fiddling with the tie of her robe.

"Come back to bed. It's still early and we have a lot to talk about."

"I expected you to be gone, and now… now I don't know what to do." Her voice thins and dies away.

"I know what to do," he tells her. He puts his hands on her shoulders and turns her to face him. He lifts her chin. "Look at me."

145

Her eyes are shut. Her lashes are dark with a distinctive curl to them.

He suppresses a laugh. "I probably don't look the best, and I need a shave, but... Rain, please look at me."

Her eyes flutter open and gaze up at him. His heart skips a hundred beats... the dazzling penetration of those clear, honest eyes. She sees into his soul, he's sure of it.

"Ben..."

"I'm listening..."

"This won't work between us. We know nothing about one another."

He puts his hands on her waist; her breathing quickens, making him smile. "For someone whose name is Rain, you sure do look like sunshine to me."

"It's Raina," she corrects him.

He pulls her close. "It sounds strong and true like the person who owns it. Come back to bed."

They gaze at one another for a long while.

His breaking awareness lags behind the dawn but he begins to understand. In this sparkling morning light they present honestly to each other a reality both unexpected and convincing. In a way it's like starting again, the dawn of something entirely new; new day, new life... with the whole truth in their hands it heightens every sensation and every touch and every thought.

"You love me, Ben," she says simply.

"Yes."

It strikes him then – he *can* love; he never thought it would happen, that he could do it, love a woman the way he loves Raina. Nothing his father created or uncreated in him has destroyed his ability to love...

"I think we are made for one another."

"Yes," she says intently. "I believe so."

It only takes one person, the right person, to make sense of your life. And give you the joy you never expected.

"I'd never have known this without you, Raina, all the things I needed to know."

And now their new life can begin...

146

Cliff

"Breakfast weren't half bad considerin'. Eight o'clock, accordin' to Cornwall's fancy-lookin' timepiece over on the wall there. Reckon Ben will show this mornin'?" Hummer prattles, slurping his coffee.

Cliff rubs his eye. "He's up to something."

"Yeah, up is right."

"Well, I guess that's probably right, Hummer."

Hummer starts laughing. "Who'd have thought..."

"I keep telling you he's not what he appears to be. He keeps things locked up inside."

"You're a doctor now, Ryan?"

Cliff arranges his colt in his belt. "Merely a student of human behavior, Hummer. I'm heading down to the telegraph office and see if he's there. If not, I'll leave another note saying where we are. He'll turn up eventually."

Ben is nowhere to be seen when Cliff stakes out the telegraph office for a while. He writes yet another note and takes it to the telegrapher.

"A young feller by the name of Ben Taylor will come by here sometime this morning. He'll probably ask if there's any word for him. Give him this, would you?"

"Sure, Deputy Marshal."

"Much obliged."

Cliff walks by La Splendide, where nothing is stirring, and then heads down on this fine March morning in Denver to Union Station for a look around.

Ben

"Well," he says, raising himself on one elbow and gazing down at that radiant face with the dark tousled hair framed by her pillow.

"Well," she grins.

Just like the morning sun.

"There are things I need to tell you, Ben."

"Same goes for me. I adore you, Raina."

"Ben," she whispers, and with a bold grin adds, "Breakfast and shave."

She's organizing him and he's beginning to like it.

She returns with a breakfast tray, and the welcoming smell of coffee and toast. He towels his freshly shaved face dry and watches as she sets the tray down on her table by the window.

"The kitchen was deserted, so it hardly took any time at all. I helped myself. Coffee?"

"Please."

"Cream? Sugar?"

"Thanks."

After placing the towel on the washstand, he puts on his shirt and, buttoning it, moves across the room to fetch his coffee. He takes it from her; she gives him a dazzling smile and then sets about fixing her own. He sips his, watching her sure, quick movements.

The sun is warming a wooden chair near the window and she sits in it.

"Not breakfast in bed then?" he asks.

"We don't talk in bed, Ben. I feel sure you must have noticed."

He smiles and places another chair close to hers. "Where would you be today if you weren't here?"

"Today I'd be in school."

"Here in town?"

"It's only a private ladies college for rich girls. My last year."

"You hate school that much?"

"I actually love it, but I can't stay in Denver any longer."

"Why?"

"My father recently divorced my mother, after their long separation. He… he met and married someone, a woman I simply can't abide, who doesn't want me around. And I miss my mother. She doesn't even know where I am. After I was taken away from her, she wrote to me, but eventually the letters stopped coming. I found out from my new stepmother that my father destroyed my mother's letters and destroyed those I wrote to her. All these years we've been apart. I have to find her."

He's not sure if Raina is aware of the tears sliding down her cheeks, but he restrains his urge to comfort her so that she'll continue.

"I've lived here since I was thirteen, with my father; he's made a good living out of this town. Before that we lived in St Louis. My father hates my mother. And I believe he has used me to punish her for the failure of their marriage. I guess I came to this place for two reasons, one to make my own money secretly so I could be independent of my father and he couldn't control me, and the other was to spite him. I … it is unpardonable, I know…"

"I'd pardon you."

"Ben, what kind of prostitute would I be? I hid behind the newspaper constantly so no one would pick me. I think they were getting ready to kick me out."

"I picked you."

"I half expected my father to come charging in at any moment and drag me out by my hair after he'd forced my best friend to tell him where I was and what I was getting up to. I'm sure it made me look even more nervous than I was already."

He starts chuckling. Raina takes a deep draft of her coffee and swallows it as though it is the most delicious treat in the world.

"You're definitely growing on me, Rain," he says.

"I live in Capitol Hill. I love to read and study and learn and know people, all kinds of people. I need coffee in the morning and I adore baked ham and French mustard sandwiches. My father is very wealthy and getting more so by the day. He intends to marry me off to further his own interests. I hate his politics. I don't like my life with him and his new wife. I want to be free of them. Live my own life. Have my own home. Have adventures. Be with my mother, who loved me and who should never have lost me."

"Who is your father?"

"Leslie Montgomery."

"And you're his only child?"

"That's right."

"You're Raina Montgomery, heiress?"

"Oh, Ben, don't hate me."

Hate her! He's out of his mind about her. And he admires her courage and her spirit to stand on her own two feet, even if the attempt was cockeyed.

"Ben?" she says searching his face.

"It's all right, Raina. You just remind me of someone."

"Who?"

He looks down at his hands, recalling a gentle face. "A girl who fell in love at first sight with a decent and brave man, and defied her tyrannical father to marry him. He was killed, leaving her expecting their child. Her father turned her out of the house and she fled to her husband's family in another territory, hundreds of miles from her home and her mother whom she loved."

"That's horrible. Who was she?"

He looks up briefly. "My sister."

"Your sister! Oh, Ben. So that means your father... You sound angry."

"Only with myself for judging her, allowing my father to do that to her when she didn't deserve it. It took me a while to understand her, but I did eventually."

"I must thank her one day."

"Why?"

"Because you don't judge me now. You don't, do you?"

"No."

"Because of her?"

"Because I'm hopelessly in love with you, and we Taylors it seems are prone to fall hopelessly in love at first sight. And, because of her."

"Ben Taylor," she murmurs.

"Raina," he says leaning forward, "I'm not... I haven't... I'm not good like you."

"Ben, look where I am, how can I be good..."

"Sure there's that kind of good, but I'm talking about the kind that sees the good in people, that is always fair and just. You trust, and don't have to decide if this person and that person deserves your kindness or not. Raina, I can tell when I look in your eyes you are good. And I know you saw into my very soul the moment you laid eyes on me. I felt it. I still feel it."

"And yet you are prepared to bare your soul to me every time."

"Yes," he admits. "I need to."

"I feel safe with you too, Ben. Do you want to know what I see when I look in *your* eyes?"

He gazes at her, loving her, with all the wonder that it brings. "What do you see?"

"A man who will love me, protect me, laugh and cry with me, understand me. Share himself with me. A man who wants desperately to be loved and trusted to love in return. And who, despite misgivings about himself, has conviction and strength."

She's incredible; he knew it, knew she would be.

"That's why I need you, Raina. No one sees what you see."

"Because you show it to me, Ben."

"Then, thank you."

"You're welcome, Ben Taylor of...?

"Omaha, Nebraska."

"Omaha? Really?"

"Is there a problem with Omaha?"

"Not at all. What is your father's name? I mean, Taylor is not an uncommon name, but..."

"Richard Taylor."

"Ben, I know him! That is, if he is a businessman... mining?"

"What? Yes, Taylor Mining."

She nods enthusiastically. "He had dinner with my father and stepmother four nights ago. I sat across the table from him. He seemed charming but I didn't pay a lot of attention to him because I was angry with my father for making me eat with them when I'd been invited to supper elsewhere…"

"Raina, what was he doing at your father's house?"

"Business, of course. Always business. They were introduced to one another by a very rich man; he's well known, you might know of him…"

"Loren Bodecker?"

"The very same."

"Now you're really growing on me, Rain. So my father is here in town?"

"I assume so. For business. Ben, don't you know where your father is?"

"I came to Denver to look for him. How did he seem to you, apart from charming? Was he well?"

"I suppose so. As I said, I didn't pay very much attention. I'm sorry."

"Rain, would your father know where my father is now?"

"He might. Ben, what is the matter? You've gone very strange."

He drags his fingers through his hair, his mind racing. "It's a very long story."

"What do you want to do now?"

"How do you mean?"

"Well, we could go home and ask my father if he knows where your father is – it seems the logical thing to do. I can't stay here anymore. I told my father I was staying a few nights at my friend's and attending several parties. And I'll have to front up sometime. I'd rather do it with you next to me, especially as discussing your father's whereabouts would distract my father's attention away from what I've been up to."

"Rain, sweetheart, this is a complicated situation. I wouldn't want to involve you in my problems."

"What is so complicated about asking my father where your father is?"

When she put it like that…

"But first I must have a bath."

Of course, she must. She's a girl.

"You know, for twenty dollars extra you are allowed a back-scrub in the bath."

"Twenty dollars!"

"Well, this is a brothel, Ben, not a bath house. What do you think men who have their backs scrubbed by exotic women get up to while they get clean?"

"You know, it's amazing how at home you are in this place."

Her eyes sparkle up at him, but she makes no comment.

"Nobody minds me taking a bath?" he asks.

"You can leave an extra twenty dollars at the desk if you feel guilty about it."

His mind wanders to thinking about the two of them in a bathroom with warm water and soap and steam and…

A blush stains her cheeks. "Eat your breakfast. I'll go first and be back soon."

He watches her every move until she disappears out the door. Likely she'll be gone for ages, so he eats the simple breakfast she's prepared for him, and then pulls out some clean clothes from his bag.

When she returns she's radiant and soft and smells good.

"My turn?" he says.

"Down the hall, fourth room on the right. Don't forget to lock the door."

"No back-scrub?"

She stops what she's doing and bites her lip. He goes to her and folds his arms around her. He kisses her cheek, then the side of her neck.

"I won't be long."

The bathroom is lavish, exotic in colors of dark pink and orange and purple. With ornate gold and brass faucets and fixtures. Floral bowls of perfumed soap and elegantly shaped bottles of colored mixtures. Sponges and large towels and brushes and face cloths are contained in a huge mahogany cupboard; there's a matching commode by the bath. There's even a velvet-upholstered sofa and a fancy porcelain privy with a golden flushing chain. And everywhere there are large gilt-framed mirrors. Compared to Rain's room, the management has spared no expense on the client's, or worker's, bath; this luxury is clearly meant to be a feature of the establishment. The building doesn't look from the outside what it's like inside anyhow, but this room is indeed a marvel in comparison. No wonder the heiress felt at home here.

And while he is scrubbing his back, and thinking of his heiress, it occurs to him what he'd asked of her – however jokingly – and how stupid he is. He'd made his first mistake.

He hurries now to get back to her. With a towel around his middle and another draped over his shoulders, rubbing his wet hair with the corner of it, he prepares to burst into her room. Somehow his brain engages and he stops himself in time.

Raina... His love, his heiress; not his... not that.

He knocks softly and after a moment her reply to enter falls on his ears. Smoothing back his hair as best he can until he can get to his comb, he enters her room. Signs of her packing are evident throughout, and she is standing in front of her full length mirror brushing her hair, still wearing her silk robe.

He discards his shoulder towel and goes to her; he puts his arms around her waist and his face in her dark, glossy hair.

"You need a comb," she says breathily. She turns herself in his arms and looks up at him; his insides are melting.

"I'm sorry about the back-scrub remark..."

"Well, it's understandable, and I forgive you."

They gaze at one another; so many things to say, to organize, to sort out...yet only one thing is necessary.

"Raina..."

"Nothing's changed, Ben."

"Just a couple of things."

He'll have to fight for her.

"I'm still the same girl as last night – the one you found behind the newspaper."

Fight damn hard.

"Yes, in my father's autocratic world there are a lot of men pursuing me, but none that I have ever wanted. I want you, Ben."

And then there's the real reason he's here.

"We'll find your father," she says.

He frowns. "What are you doing? Reading my mind?"

She nods. She puts her fingers in his hair and fiddles with it. "I think you came in here last night because you were terribly worried and burdened and needed someone." Her hands wander down to his shoulders and caress him. "I'm glad I was here. That it was I and not someone else. You chose me. You knew I was the one who could do it. And I am. And I always will be. If you want me…"

"I want you," he says, his murmured thought interrupting her.

"Nothing has changed from that moment to this, if you don't allow it."

It occurs to him, as he stands there gazing at her, that she is as determined in her way as he is in his. In this they are alike.

"I love you," he says.

"I know you do."

"Head over heels, risk everything, do anything, lie, cheat, steal for you kind of in love."

Her breathing starts to hurry.

"Do you understand what you're getting into?"

Her breasts, so firm and full, rise and fall as her emotions get the better of her. "I understand," she breathes. "It's what needed. He won't understand anything else."

"Your father?"

"Yes, yes," she says impatiently. "Otherwise he will throw you out and insist on choosing someone himself. I tell you I won't stand for it, not after you. But…"

"But?"

"If you decide to go your own way… well, I will get to my mother somehow. And I won't ever forget you, because if I ever try to feel this way again about another, I will know if what I feel is true love or not."

Watching her troubled spirit as it moves in her eyes and saddens her strengthens his resolve even further.

"Raina, I don't want to go my own way, and I can't bear the thought of you with someone else… we will find your mother, I promise." He folds his arms around her and kisses her tenderly.

"I don't even belong in this world anymore," she sighs.
"We've created a new world."
"A beautiful thought, Ben."
"We might actually fit in this one."
Her eyes spring to life, dancing with renewed brightness.

Cliff

"Ah, here's Deputy Marshal Cliff Ryan," Hummer declares. Beside him, a well-groomed, middle-aged gentleman remains fixed to his position at Cornwall's desk. "Ryan, meet assistant state attorney, Doug Clarke."

Cliff steps up. "Clarke."

"Ryan."

They shake hands.

"So, Ryan, what's your take on this?"

"Simple. We need to take Loren Bodecker back to Cheyenne."

"Hummer here insists Loren is involved with some maverick called Donnelly."

Cliff exchanges sidelong glances with Hummer. "That's right."

"The man is part-resident here. Significant in the community. Business community in particular."

"None of that is relevant. We have a warrant to take Loren Bodecker back to Cheyenne to face charges of conspiracy to murder and murder for hire. Capital offences, Clarke."

"I know, but they are false of course."

"And you would know that how exactly?"

"Because they are preposterous. Can't we do this here? I'm sure we can get it all cleared up."

"You can't impede a warrant carried by a federal marshal."

Cornwall picks up the warrant from his desk and holds it out to Clarke who promptly ignores it.

"I know that, Deputy Marshal."

"Then you know you can't keep him here."

"What evidence do you have?" he fires back.

"Evidence we can't disclose in order to protect the witnesses."

"So," Hummer jumps in, "with all that said, Clarke, I think you should let us get on with our job. We've been polite waitin' and you paid us a visit. But now that the pleasantries are over – and it's been fine meetin' ya – I think we'll take Mr Bodecker..."

"And find a train back to Cheyenne," Cliff finishes.

Hummer gives a decisive nod and chomps on his cigar for good measure.

"Cornwall," Clarke says, stiff with indignation. "Don't you let them near Mr Bodecker until I return."

"If you say so, Mr Clarke."

Before he departs, Clarke flares his nostrils at Cliff and then bestows Hummer with a filthy look. "Gentlemen."

Cliff blows a sigh.

Hummer grunts.

"What do you want to do with Tucker?" Cornwall asks. "Can't hold him here forever."

"We're not asking for forever."

Ben

Raina sits on the bed watching him dress. He tucks his shirt into his pants and winks at her. She laughs and he starts on his tie.

"Help with that?" she offers and stands up.

"Thanks."

He lets her fiddle with his tie.

"Now, you have the address in your pocket, don't you?"

"Yes."

"I'll meet you there in two hours, right?"

"That's what we arranged, Raina. Are you sure you don't need any assistance getting out of this place, monetary or otherwise?"

"None. I used a false name – Maya remember? – and dressed very different than usual to come here. My father's name is well-known but I was very careful so no one would discover my real identity. Anyway, Miss Willona will let me go without a fuss. I'm a failure at this line of work."

"That depends on…"

"Don't start that, Ben. Now, my friend's name is…"

"Mary, I know. Mary…"

"Then we go to my house. My father goes into work late these days, since he got his new wife… while she settles in apparently and produces a male heir…" She shudders. "Anyway, he should be home and we can ask him if he knows your father's whereabouts."

Her bitterness seems confined to her father and the new bride, because she sweetly finishes his tie, presses it down, smooths his jacket lapels. "You look very handsome. Your coat…"

"By the door. Where I left it last night."

Prettily, she looks into his face. "I'll miss you."

"Raina," he murmurs.

"Yes, Ben," she says.

He takes her in his arms. "I can't imagine this life without you. I adore you, Raina. I want you until I can't think straight anymore. I want to love you forever and ever. Make you feel like this every day. Share everyday with you. The good days and the not-so-good ones and the in-between. Inside me, somehow I know I'm not supposed to be alive on this earth without you. I don't know how we got that way in one night, in one instant of time, but we did. You saw into my soul, and I wasn't afraid of who I was, what I've been."

As he is speaking, tears well in her clear blue eyes.

"Can you forget where we are... this place... for just one moment?"

"All I know is that I'm with you," she says.

"Will you marry me, Raina?"

She catches her breath.

Tenderly, he says, "You didn't think I would do this to you and not want to marry you, did you? That's why I had to ask you before we left this place. We can do all the things you want and need to do, like find your mother. Only please be my wife for as long as we both shall live. Be my family and my one true love."

"Yes, Ben. The answer is yes..."

He clasps her tight and takes her down onto the bed.

"What are we doing?" she asks, breathing very fast.

"Sealing our engagement."

"That's usually done with a ring."

"It will be. Give me time."

The only time they have is the here and now. Opportunity seized as it comes: to create a whole future from an instant in time. He loves her with deep and tender emotion holding sway. And when it's done, he is ready to face whatever Raina's old world sees fit to throw at him. With trembling fingers he buttons his pants, gazing down at her as she lays there; her blue eyes blink up at him, following him as he pulls on his boots and straightens the rest of his clothing, finds his overcoat and threads himself into it.

Cliff

While Cliff is sitting with his feet up on Cornwall's desk contemplating the homeless and drifting nature of being a federal marshal, and feeling the need to take his thoughts further, Ben walks in.

If Cliff is the student of human behavior he professed to be, then he should know why Ben has a different air about him – a night in a brothel can ease the tension and the loneliness, sure, but Ben has a smile that reaches right down deep passed the physical relief to...

"Ryan," Ben says, removing his hat.

"Ben." He puts his feet on the floor. "Got my message I see."

"Yeah, thanks for that."

"Thanks for finding a safe place for stowing our gear."

"Where's Hummer?"

"Smoking off his frustration somewhere."

"So what's going on with Bodecker?" He pulls up a chair.

"We're waiting for Bodecker's many fans to say they can live without him."

His eyes go wide. "You got him?"

"Sure. I forgot. You weren't around when all the excitement took place. We followed Tucker to this town's version of the Cheyenne Club. Found him holding court in a fancy room bribing Tucker. Can't go into details right now. So – what about you?"

Ben holds his gaze with the steeliness Cliff's come to expect, but something is bubbling behind his eyes. "I got a lead on my father."

Cliff's impressed. "You did? Well, that's handy, since Bodecker's not talking…"

"I need you to trust me while I follow it up. Can you do that, Ryan? Trust me?"

"Of course. No reason not to. If you need any help…"

"Well, I might – later. In the meantime I need the rest of the day."

"Don't worry, we're not going anywhere."

"Thanks."

"Care to give me some idea of this lead?"

"I've met someone who saw my father here in town four nights ago. We think we can find out more. I realize it looks like the most incredible of coincidences…"

"Doesn't matter. In this business coincidences come with the territory. I know someone who likes to say he'd rather have a hunch crawling with coincidences than no hunch at all."

"I still can't believe it myself. It's just the way it's worked out, I guess."

Cliff nods, studying him hard. "What are you going to say to your father when you see him?"

Ben lets out a laugh. "Good question. Probably something like: Mother's fine, if you're interested, thanks to Luke."

"Bodecker bribed Tucker with a lot of money, probably more than he's ever seen in one hand. Since we've discovered Tucker's weakness…"

"His weakness? What do you mean?"

"You missed that, too. Marvin decided on a rendezvous with that caped girl outside the fancy bagnio. Staid, ordinary and respectable Marvin Tucker can't resist. More than likely Bodecker knows it too. What I'm trying to say, Ben, is that people prostitute themselves all the time. Not only women in a bordello."

"My father. It all went to his head."

"More than likely. And Bodecker is the devil."

Ben's gaze arrows straight into Cliff's mind. There's something he wants to say, but can't – not yet.

Cliff smiles. "You'd better get going. And good luck."

"Don't worry, I'll stay in touch."

When Ben has left, Cliff sighs and wishes Emma were here; investigating is more fun with her. He hoists his feet back on the desk and resigns himself to thinking about her, wondering if she's given him a second thought...

A plan is needed to win her. She likes books. And while she doesn't mind being held and kissed, or kissing him for that matter, there's more to...

"Deputy Marshal?"

Cliff frowns. He's barely got started. What could be so important? He looks up at the young police officer who took over from Allan.

"Sorry to disturb you, Deputy Marshal," he says. "Tucker says he wants to talk to you."

Cliff gets to his feet. "This better be good, Kirk."

"Tucker's shaking and sweating all over. Says he can't stay in the cell another moment."

"Have you called for a doctor?"

"Says he wants to talk to you, Deputy Marshal."

Ben

Ben steps down from the taxicab at the address Raina gave him and stares up at the Tenth Street mansion house before him. The building is enormous, with a row of four marble pillars two stories high marking the entrance, gables, balconies and all manner of arched and sashed windows. He asks the cab driver to wait. The driver tips his hat and settles back.

Ben crosses the paved sidewalk to the wintered lawn and follows the swept pathway to the house. The structure rises above him like a giant bird, ready to pick him up and swallow him whole. Omaha elites take a slightly more subtle approach, he reflects.

He knocks on the door, impatient to see Raina.

A manservant opens the door and makes inquiry about his business there.

"Mary is expecting me," he says.

An attractive young woman, richly gowned and about Raina's age, pushes herself in front of the servant. "I'll look after the gentlemen."

Ben is hastily admitted.

"She's waiting for you in the study. She described you perfectly. I knew you at once…"

They cross an entrance the size of a ballroom, with ocean-sized Oriental carpets, parlor palms that tower over him, ornately carved chairs and in the middle of all a huge marble-topped mahogany table upon which stands a classical white marble statue of two naked lovers.

Mary leads him through and they pass a sweeping staircase on his left leading to the next level, in effect a gallery which overlooks the entrance. He looks directly up at the ceiling and discovers that the center part of it is an immense sky window of colored glass.

He and Mary take a right turn and Mary opens a door.

"Here he is." Mary withdraws and shuts the door behind her, leaving him in a cavernous room of books and dark furniture, that is until he looks up…

Raina.

His breath gets caught in his chest. She stands by the window where she obviously saw him arrive. The morning light is pouring over her; she looks nothing like the girl he left behind. Her arranged hair, her satin dress, her studied figure. His slender, silk-clad girl – corseted, preened and adorned – looking like a queen. She is resplendent.

Queen Raina.

He is speechless.

She holds out her hand to him. Mesmerized, he does as she bids and goes to her. He stands before her, gazing down, stupefied. Raina steps up to him in a rush of satin.

"Kiss me, Ben," she whispers.

He really can't move.

She lets out a groan of some kind and reaches up and hugs his neck. The feel of her body pressed against his begins to impact him with some much needed familiarity. Her blue eyes gaze up at him. "Kiss me, and you'll know."

"This is what you escaped from?" he gasps.

"Well, Mary's father owns three gold mines, five silver mines, various smelters and an electric light company, and my father not quite as much, but you get the general idea."

"Raina, the morning sun pales before you."

"Ben, it's just me."

She's right. Before last night he might have seen her and admired her from afar but not dared to venture across the line. She peeled off more than her clothes last night; she peeled back the layers of her world to have a man finally see her for herself.

He kisses her, trying not to seem overawed, and whispers, "We have the rest of the day to do what we need to do."

Her bright-eyed scrutiny is relentless, and a little unnerving.

"What do you mean…?"

"Raina, on the way here…"

"Yes?"

"Rain, I have a marriage license in my pocket."

"License?"

"City Hall was on the way. Raina, we can do this."

"Before we see my father?"

"Do you see it any other way?"

"I think you sound particularly ruthless at the moment."

"I'm sorry," he says. "Just the sight of you, where we are…"

"Don't think about any of that."

But he *is* thinking about it; he has to.

"No one can control everything in their life, Ben."

He nods, acknowledging the wisdom of this, although something in her tone of voice puts him even more on his guard.

"You have to trust sometime. Trust yourself and those who love you. And as for me, I'm dying to live every minute of the future with you and for us never to be apart."

What else does he need to hear?

"Then let's make it official."

Cliff

"I don't want to talk here, Ryan," Tucker says. He seems to be in a permanent state of perspiration, which is odd because Cornwall's lockup is not the warmest place in town.

"What do you want to talk about, Marvin?"

Tucker is white knuckling his cell bars. "Not here."

Cliff sighs. "Marvin, Loren is way down the other end. We're practically whispering. He can't hear our conversation."

Marvin wipes his brow with a soiled handkerchief.

Cliff comprehends him with a hard look.

"What are you staring at?" Marvin rasps.

"You're coming down off something, Marvin."

"What are you talking about?"

"The caped girl, what did she give you? A little something she was happy to share?"

"You're talking rubbish."

"I saw her earlier in the evening; I saw it in her eyes; and you haven't stopped sweating since you got here."

"She gave me whiskey!"

"And?"

"All right. But only a small amount."

"You lie, Marvin."

"The girl had more."

"You're still lying."

"Listen, Ryan…"

"Expensive habits you have, high-class whores and drugs. You need a lot of money."

Marvin's milky, bloodshot eyes stare at him.

"Do you have your own supply, Marvin, or do you rely on the kindness of exotic strangers?"

"I... I have a supplier. I don't take it all the time, I tell you."

"Sure. Whatever. Who is your supplier, Marvin?"

"A scientific colleague of Loren's. He's discreet."

"So far, Marvin, I'm the only one who knows about the drugs. Unless Loren knows."

Marvin shakes his head.

"So he only knows about the women."

Marvin nods. "As I said, my supplier is discreet."

"Okay, it stays between us for now. Who supplies you?"

Marvin swallows hard and says, "Louis Porterfield."

Cliff's heart lurches; he can't let Tucker see how this news is affecting him. He says coolly, "Porterfield from North Platte?"

"I know what that piece of information means to you, Ryan. If I testify to what went down in the room with Loren, will you let me go? I will tell you everything I know."

"You'd better hope that's not withdrawal talking, Marvin. How do you normally come down? Not in jail. You sleep it off with whatever woman you happen to be with..."

"Yes, yes, all right."

"Maybe you gave the girl some yourself in return for all sorts of favors. I didn't find anything in your luggage and you've been searched. Did you trash it on the way here? Need another fix, Marvin?"

Marvin holds Cliff's rigid stare unsteadily. "Have we got a deal?" he asks shakily.

"So you can return to the caped girl and another fix... oh, I don't think so. You see, Marvin, people like you tend to make rash deals."

"Ryan, I swear my habit is not as bad as you're painting it. Can we make a deal?"

"I'm just the deputy marshal. You make deals with Faraday when we get back to Cheyenne."

"But I want to make a full statement," Marvin rasps. "Listen, Ryan, I know nothing about Bodecker's goings on..."

"So?"

"But he did pay me off in the room. Told me to go to that address and tell the Severini boy to come and see him in his room at the club. I don't know what it means, what Loren intends..."

"That part, Marvin, is a lie. You *do* know. And while this little tidbit of information is very tasty, Faraday won't deal until you come clean with the rest, which you seem very reluctant to do. Now I suggest you drink plenty of water and get some more sleep. You're a wreck."

"No, no, wait...you don't understand..."

Cliff understands perfectly; he turns away and heads for the office, locking the jailer's door behind him.

Ben

City Hall

"By the power vested in me by the State of Colorado, I now pronounce you husband and wife."

The joy of their sealing kiss is matched only by the expression on Raina's beautiful face, in her dancing blue eyes.

After they have signed the official papers and the marriage register, the judge hands Ben the marriage certificate, saying, "I think you'll need this, young man. *Some* people might like proof."

They leave hand in hand and take a taxicab bound for her father's house. At this moment all his other concerns are eclipsed by this one spectacular yet humble event. This feeling has to be rare, he reflects; it's a kind of elation, a profound one, infecting his whole being, his mind and heart, right to his soul. Is he pleased with himself? Well, matrimony is simple once you find the right woman to marry. Does he care what anyone else thinks? Stupid question.

Pennsylvania Street

Ben looks up at the imposing castle before him and swallows. The other, smaller mansions on Pennsylvania Street have similar features, but here is yet another giant animal preparing to devour him, this one three stories high with shooting turrets and parapets with spires on top, massive chimneys, dominant ornate stone gables, steep sloping roofs of slate, walls of stone blocks and bricks and panes of stained glass. Well, whatever lay inside, he wouldn't let it undo him. Mary's place had prepared him at least.

"It's not as drafty as it looks," Raina quips.

"Stop reading my mind."

"Come. Let's get this over with and then we can find your father."

"Mm, I have a partner now," he says, grinning at her.

"A wife, Mr Taylor, you have a wife," she reminds him, grinning back. "*And* I have a gold ring on my finger to prove it."

"A very beautiful, very desirable wife."

She groans sweetly and makes a start on the flagstone path. "This way, my husband."

She's right; inside it's not drafty at all, but it certainly isn't to his taste. An opulent, gilded mansion fit for a baron or lord.

"I call it the citadel, which thoroughly annoys my father."

As they walk across the marble entrance hall, a good-looking woman about his age steps out from a double door.

"Raina, what... where..."

"Deanna, this is Ben Taylor. Ben, I'd like you to meet my stepmother, Deanna Lewis-Montgomery."

Raina's surprisingly young stepmother stares at him.

"How do you do?" she says sharply.

He politely tells her he's happy to make her acquaintance.

"Your father expected you home early this morning, Raina."

Ben detects a note of reproach; he feels Raina stiffen as she stands close at his side.

"Where is he?"

"In his study. Shall I tell him you're home?"

"No. We'll go to him now. Thank you, Deanna."

"I hope you haven't done anything foolish, Raina."

Ben deeply resents being the insinuated object of Rain's folly. Raina steers him away to her father's study.

Mr Leslie Montgomery cuts an imposing figure. He's as tall as Ben, aged about fifty with flecks of gray in his hair, fit looking and debonair. Set amongst his books and curiosities and other paraphernalia in his huge study, he looks stately and stern.

"Raina, where have you been?" Montgomery steps forward.

"I've brought someone to meet you, Father."

She's so sweet and beautiful, clutching her baby pink wedding roses they'd bought on the way to City Hall. How is it possible the man could be so unreasonable?

"Father, this is Ben Taylor," Raina says.

"Happy to know you, sir," Ben says, his hand outstretched.

Montgomery takes it firmly, saying, "Taylor. Well, this is odd... You wouldn't be Richard Taylor's son by any chance? I'm seeing a resemblance, I believe. Taylor's not an uncommon name but..."

His slate brown eyes look straight into Ben's. The challenge is there already. Ben knows how to deal with men like this, but he doesn't want to, not in front of Raina.

You have to trust sometime. Trust yourself and those who love you.

He has no intention of disappointing her.

"Yes, Richard Taylor is my father. I'm here looking for him. We haven't heard from him for some time."

Montgomery blinks. "Why, he was here several nights ago. My wife and I entertained him. We were settling a business arrangement. Successfully, I might add. I don't think you have anything to worry about."

"You wouldn't happen to know how I could contact him?"

Montgomery moves across to the desk, lifts a cigar from a polished wooden box and twizzles it between his thumb and forefinger. "Well, he was staying at the Golden Palace. I suggested he move to the Club. Loren was going to see to it. You know Loren Bodecker of course."

"Yes, we met in Omaha."

"Cigar?"

"No, thank you."

Montgomery looks thoughtful for a moment, then says, "Well, if you go to the Club – I'll write down the address for you, if you like – and tell them I sent you, that you are looking for your father, I'm sure they'll oblige you access to see him. Of course, he'll probably be delighted to see you, eh? Nothing finer in life than a son to follow in your footsteps. Strange though, that Richard didn't mention you."

"Nothing strange about it. My father and I had a falling out of sorts a while ago, and since he is a man who brooks no challenge to his authority, it's taking a while to mend."

Montgomery laughs. "I get it, young man. You're of an age. Your father can't see it yet. Well, time heals all wounds they say. So, then, to other matters: how do you come to know my daughter?"

"Father…"

"Raina," he says, "I'm asking your friend."

"I'm not allowed to tell you my news?"

"What news, Raina?"

She opens her mouth, but instinctively Ben knows he must do this.

"Mr Montgomery, Raina and I were married half an hour ago at City Hall."

Montgomery's stately frame freezes and he gazes coolly at his daughter. "What is this nonsense?"

"It's true, Father." She snatches a breath. "Ben and I are married. These roses, my wedding bouquet…"

He throws his cigar onto the desk and sticks out his hand. "Show me the certificate."

Coolly, Ben takes it out of his breast pocket.

Montgomery wriggles his fingers.

Ben unfolds it, unhurried, and holds it up. "Your daughter is Raina Montgomery-Taylor."

"Bring it here!" Montgomery demands.

Ben holds his ground. He must not budge, blink or back down. Raina delivers it. Montgomery eyes him coldly as he snatches the certificate from Raina's dainty fingers. His eyes run rapidly along the paper. He finishes and throws it on the ground.

"I will have it annulled," he says, mauling every word.

"It's been consummated," Ben says.

"Impossible!" Montgomery shouts. "When? Where? On the seat of the taxicab?"

"Last night and this morning," Ben tells him.

"What did you do to my daughter?" Montgomery yells.

"We fell in love, we slept together and this morning we got married."

"Raina," he booms. "Come here!"

She gulps a large breath and straightens her shoulders; if Ben were her he'd want to run in the other direction, but Raina goes to her father and stands before him.

"Yes, Father?"

"Tell me this isn't true."

"I can't do that, Father, because every word is true."

Montgomery stares bitterly at her for some time and somehow she bears it. Eventually, he says through his teeth, "I'm going to give you a choice, Raina."

Raina stands fixed, her chin raised.

"Either I annul this marriage or I disinherit you. Which is it to be?"

"I... I'm sorry that it had to happen this way, Father, but you have to understand how it is between Ben and me. You cannot have this marriage annulled. We are truly husband and wife. And as for my inheritance, I don't need all the wealth you possess for a happy life; I have Ben and that is all I need. Disinheritance, the shame of it, is something you will feel, Father, not I. I know Deanna is with child or about to become that way. That's why you don't go to the office as much. I'm not blind, Father. You are trying to procreate a new heir..."

"Raina!" Montgomery barks.

"You're not exactly discreet."

"Raina, stop!"

"Enjoying yourself, Father, with a woman who is not my mother! Do you have any idea how that makes me feel?"

"How dare you!"

"My inheritance will diminish as each of Deanna's offspring comes into the world. It's what you've always wanted, a son heir. Not a daughter you think you've turned into the princess of the city. Do whatever you want, Father, but this marriage will not be annulled."

She turns away from him, back to Ben's side, while Ben keeps a poker face to conceal his pride in her courage.

"You are *promised*," Montgomery growls.

"Mm," she says, her fingers dallying with Ben's. "To the son of a business colleague. I would never have been loved by him. I would have been miserable. You know that and yet you didn't care. I went in search of my own life, Father, and I found Ben. And we both are going to find my mother."

Montgomery snorts. "Your mother…"

"Yes, my beautiful, abandoned and betrayed mother!"

Montgomery swings his gaze to Ben. "Look around you. You think you can keep my daughter in this manner?"

"I think your daughter will be very easy to keep."

Raina's hand slips into his and he squeezes it gently.

"What if I call off my business arrangement with your father? Once word gets out, it could ruin him and you…"

"Father!"

Ben finds himself amused by this. "Mr Montgomery, that is a risk I will gladly take. If the day ever comes, and pray to God it doesn't, when I put business before Raina's happiness then I will have proved myself entirely unworthy of her. But we both believe that won't happen. Mr Montgomery, I love your daughter, whole-heartedly, passionately, don't you want that for her? Love and happiness?"

Montgomery's frown is cold and bitter. Ben's seen that look before. On the face of his own father. Everything, no matter how trifling or how large, is business and money and status. Montgomery believes that these constitute happiness, so why wouldn't everyone else? Ben recalls his mother talking about things like love and happiness to his father and his father glaring at her, just like Montgomery; she would excuse him – *it is beyond his understanding*. Ben embraces now what he had been once so reluctant to embrace – he refuses to accept his mother's excuses; these men don't want to understand, and they proliferate their own shallow ideals and self-indulgent misery.

He thinks of Tressa, as she stood before their father, pleading for his compassion about Mart Keaton, her disastrous, tragic marriage and her unexpected child, how it nearly broke her, but like Raina now, Tressa wouldn't allow it to happen. Now he truly and profoundly appreciates that quiet, fierce, costly strength, and feels strengthened in return.

"My daughter's behavior…" Montgomery mutters.

"Raina is the most beautiful woman in the world," he says. "You have every reason to be proud of her. And I will love her and honor her all my life."

Montgomery gives a cold, sloping smile. "You certainly don't talk like your father."

Ben looks down at Raina by his side, deep into her clear blue eyes. His wife. His beautiful girl.

Now a scornful laugh from her father. "I should have known you'd turn out just like your mother, Raina. Unlike her, however, it seems you've found the right man for the job. So... What do you intend to do now?"

Ben faces Montgomery solemnly. "Locate my father. It's vitally important for reasons I can't tell you. Then, when Raina is ready, we're going to find her mother."

Montgomery sighs deeply and sticks his hands on his hips. "I won't stop you, Raina."

"Thank you, Father."

"But I'm not happy."

"I know you're not. I only wish it was for the right reasons, your unhappiness."

"Give me time, Raina, and the right reasons will surface. That I can promise you."

Deanna Montgomery bursts into the room. "I'm sorry, but I just can't stay out there any longer..."

"Deanna, my love. Come and meet our brand new son-in-law."

While his wife looks on flabbergasted, Montgomery issues her with instructions about ensuring they eat lunch and that Ben has everything he needs. Then he declares it was time he was at the office and marches out of the room. Deanna follows him.

"I can't believe we did it," Raina laughs. She heads for the door. "Come, help me pack. We're leaving this castle today, Ben Taylor, my courtly knight in shining armor!"

"Where are we going to go?" he says.

"Wherever you are going, of course. And don't you think for one minute that anywhere you are going to be isn't fit for me." She stops mid-stride and swings around. "My God, Ben, you found me in a brothel, don't tell me there isn't anywhere that isn't fit."

"Well, that was hardly a crib I found you in..."

"Ben!"

"Wherever I'm going you're going too, I promise."

He remembers the certificate, picks it up and returns it to his breast pocket.

Montgomery

Montgomery paces outside the study until they appear. He dismisses Raina's puzzled glance and tells her to go to her room, adding, "I want to talk to Ben."

"Very well. I'll change out of this dress. It's Mary's and I'd like to return it later."

The pair part company, Raina mounting the stairs, his son-in-law watching her. When she's out of sight, the boy unexpectedly seizes the advantage to speak first.

"What do you want, Montgomery?"

"If you leave now, leave Raina here now and go, I will have the marriage annulled before she knows what's happened to you. And, I will pay you a great deal of money."

The boy's dark, intense eyes glare at him, but there is a hint of confusion of which to take advantage. "That was all an act?"

"I am responsible for Raina's future happiness."

Before Montgomery knows what's happening, the boy is moving. He's mounting the stairs, fiercely glaring down at him.

"If you take one more step the deal is off and I'll have you thrown out instead…"

"Will you now?"

"Where are you going?" Montgomery demands.

"Where do you think?"

Montgomery stands aghast; Taylor disappears around the landing; he can hear him calling for Raina and her answer, guiding him along the upstairs corridors.

"You cannot consummate this marriage here in my house," Montgomery bellows.

Deanna appears, alarmed and pale. "Monty, what is going on? Did you just say what I think you just said?"

Montgomery takes her by the shoulders and looks into her eyes. "Deanna, I want you to go into my study and wait there for me. Stay there until I come back."

She frowns sweetly. "But Monty..."

"Deanna, I know you have Raina's welfare at heart, but this is between father and daughter and this new fellow. Will you stay in the study until I come back?"

"Yes, Monty, if you say so."

Montgomery ushers her inside, kisses her forehead and closes the door. He walks to the stairs, his insides feeling queer; he mounts them slowly, and his hands are trembling. Along the upstairs hall he strides, his feet feeling detached from his body.

There is a narrow opening to Raina's door and as he stands outside it he can hear them already engaged... He listens to Raina's light, innocent voice... to the deep intimate voice of his knave of a son-in-law...

"Raina..." he murmurs and pushes open the door.

Raina's room is long; there's a large sitting area upon entrance and the bed is contained on a raised platform at the other end of the room.

He sees her and stops; she lays across the bed, the top of her head towards him; her garments are scattered over the floor, the bedclothes have been stripped away.

Raina...

Unaware that her father is watching, all propriety is abandoned. The marriage is being consummated before his eyes.

Montgomery feels utterly dazed. He breaks into a sweat.

Raina...

Abruptly, the scoundrel glances up and catches sight of him.

The boy, his clothes half off, raises his head, and with his blue eyes aflame with glittering defiance, he glares straight into Montgomery's.

Montgomery is not sure he's breathing any longer. The boy

knew he would follow. He's been waiting for this moment. He has his wish. Montgomery has gone numb.

Excitement flares in the boy's eyes as the brazen scoundrel flaunts their conjugal intimacy; Montgomery experiences a sharp pain in his chest. Trembling violently, he covers his mouth with his hand and leaves the room. Quickly, quietly, he closes the door. He stands in the hall, blocking his ears, numbed by the weirdness gripping him; as his head begins to throb, a recollection long abandoned comes to him. Raina's mother. Lovely and full of life like Raina, she begged for his love. Tried everything to get it. He thought her frivolous and without concern for his ambition. After several years their union was doomed. In the beginning he had loved her. Later he despised her weaknesses and constant desire to be loved. He had to leave her behind, take Raina and try to mold his vivacious daughter into someone more like himself.

For years Raina has been demanding in her own way that he be the man that her mother wanted him to be. But this, too, was doomed to fail. He should have seen it coming. Raina has found what her mother could not; a man who will not only love her pre-eminently and passionately, but who will do anything to win and keep her. If nothing else, Ben Taylor has proved that. What's more, he knew he had to.

Downstairs, after he has dismissed a bemused, curious Deanna to see about the lunch, Montgomery shuts himself in his study.

Ben

Ben wakes with a start and when he opens his eyes, Raina is before him, a sparkling vision, dark silky hair tumbling over smooth shoulders, her head cradled sweetly on her hand as she looks at him, smiling.

"What time is it?" he asks.

"Don't worry, husband, you weren't asleep terribly long, but I think you needed it."

"Mm..."

"I'm going to see about lunch," she murmurs. Her eyes skip over his face with deceptive shrewdness. "Are you feeling all right?"

"'Course," he says.

"We're consummated," she whispers and leans in to kiss him.

"We are," he returns, kissing her back.

"I'm glad. I never want to be anywhere without you, Ben, ever again. Do you feel like tea?"

"Sounds good."

She smiles wider this time. And then slides away.

He follows her with his eyes until she walks out of his line of vision. He can hear her putting on clothes and then she says, "Get comfortable. I won't be long."

He raises his head; she's gone. He gets up and rushes headlong into her bathroom, frantically looking around the opulent arrangements for the lavatory; he sees the shiny white porcelain covered with dark pink roses and falls at its feet.

He retches violently.

His breakfast is well and truly digested, so there's not much to come up, but that doesn't stop his stomach. He can't stop for several minutes. It's painful, he feels flushed and Montgomery's horror-stricken face keeps swimming across his eyes. What does it say about the man and his regard for his daughter that he could stand and watch Ben do what he did?

Finally, he stands up and goes to the basin. He washes his hands with Raina's fragrant soap, and then, having doused his face with cold water, stares at his reflection in the mirror on the washstand. What does it say about Ben?

As long as they are in this house and in this town he will never tell Raina what happened. One day, when she is far, far away from her father, then he might tell her. His stomach lurches again; he forces it into submission. A man like Montgomery accepts only one thing; total victory or total defeat. Ben didn't intend to be the vanquished. Not with Raina at stake.

He traipses back to bed, puts his head on the pillows and dozes... until Raina returns with a tray of tea and dainty-looking sandwiches.

She pours his tea, sugars it and hands it to him. She organizes the tray on the bed and then settles herself beside him.

"I've arranged for the carriage to take us wherever we need to go. It'll be ready when we are." She looks as genteel as any young lady at luncheon. He drinks his tea, grinning at her. "Deanna was strange. She was seeing to Father's lunch..."

"Oh?"

"She asked me what happened. I didn't know what she meant. She said Father made her wait in the study while he was going to talk to us..."

"He must have changed his mind."

"Mm," she says. "Odd, though..." She offers him a sandwich. "Baked ham and French mustard – you'll love them!"

He takes a couple. His stomach appears to be accepting the sweet tea, and he could certainly use the food. He eats, the mustard tingling his tongue, hardly taking his eyes off her as she eats, as she drinks, and she pours more tea, offers more sandwiches...

"Raina, I'm crazy about you," he mutters.

She leans across to kiss him; there's a trace of mustard on her lips and more on her tongue.

"Raina," he whispers. "Rain…"

Almost shyly, she says, "I didn't think it could get any better, but …"

"We're still getting to know one another."

"I think we can be deeper in love."

"I think so too."

Ben gathers the cups and sandwiches back onto the tray and pushes it away; he takes her in his arms and holds her tight. She looks into his eyes, their smiling blue clarity diverting him temporarily from the sensuousness of her body pressed to his chest.

"What will we do next, Ben?" she asks.

"I guess by the end of this day we'll know. If we stay here in town another night, which is very likely, we find a hotel. We eat supper together, go to bed together, sleep together, and wake up together. And face tomorrow together."

She places her head on his shoulder and nestles even closer. He strokes her hair, plays with the glossy tips, puts them to his mouth to feather his lips. There isn't the tiniest part of her that he doesn't love more than life itself. He can't understand how that happened in less than twenty-four hours, but it did. The purpose and direction of his life is set. His joy, his life, is right here in his arms.

"There is nothing I want more," she murmurs.

"You're reading my mind."

"I can't wait to find your father and tell him. Hopefully, he won't be as morose as my father was."

He clears his throat. "Cut from the same cloth," he murmurs.

"Oh, I see."

"Rain, there's a lot I have to tell you concerning my father. I think now would be a good time."

Ben decides it would be wise to fetch Ryan to accompany them to the Club. When he asks Raina to wait in the carriage, she agrees. Ryan and Hummer are munching on their own sandwiches, huddled around a desk, talking in low voices with a man wearing a policeman's badge.

Ever vigilant, Ryan spots him at once. "Ben..."

The others look up. Ben is introduced to Cornwall, the deputy chief of police.

After a few grunts and exchanges, Ryan typically gets straight to the point.

"How's that lead shaping up?"

"It's firming. In fact, I'm hoping you can be spared..."

Ryan is on his feet at once.

Hummer chuckles. "You're an active kinda man, Ryan."

Ryan grabs his hat. "Let's go."

"The carriage is outside," says Ben.

"The carriage?"

"I'll explain. Just..."

Ryan gives him a speculative glance. "Just...?"

"Try to keep an open mind."

Cliff

Half way across town and Cliff's open mind closely resembles an overactive imagination. He watches the new Mrs Taylor from the corner of his eye; she's a lovely girl, with shiny dark hair, topaz blue eyes and a winning smile. She seems intelligent, likable, genuine and unaffected, extraordinary considering who she is; her eyes dance and sparkle, mostly with Ben in their sights, and the connection between the pair fills the carriage like a heady scent.

"So, Ben," he says at last, "your father is probably at the Club."

"Raina's father seems to think there's a good chance."

"Have you been to the Club before, Mr Ryan?" Raina asks.

"Yes, Ma'am. Once."

"Impressive, don't you think?"

"If you like that sort of thing."

"Good answer."

Cliff gives a laugh. Where Ben actually found his heiress he's not saying, and maybe the particulars are nobody's business but theirs, but Ben appears to be a little off-color. Could be due to the fact that he's about to face his father, and nothing to do with the strain of ripping an heiress away from her father. Maybe...

Politely, Cliff asks her how long she has lived in Denver.

"Since I was thirteen. Almost six years in fact. The town has made phenomenal progress since the day we arrived. So has my father. I suppose what brought him here is the same as what brought everyone else. The prospect of wealth. The rewards of greed. The place has boomed, as they say, and continues on its singular way."

"If I may say so, Ma'am, well-drawn but somewhat cynical."

"I don't know your politics, Mr Ryan, but I've seen firsthand how some obscenely wealthy men operate in a town like this one, and I don't like it, not one little bit, so yes, I guess I am cynical, even a little disgusted."

He could hardly blame her; heiresses are a commodity, often traded for lucrative alliances. "Unfortunately, it's the same wherever you go."

"Then what can be the solution?"

Smiling, he says, "Live life to make the dreams of the world come true."

Her eyes shine delightfully. "You're an altruist, Mr Ryan."

"I'm actually a sheriff. Laramie County, Wyoming."

"A politician? – of sorts, I mean."

"If you call asking people to vote for me politics. I'm a lawman. What it comes down to is whether I can do the job they want me to do or I can't. They vote accordingly."

She glances at Ben, grinning broadly. "Seems your friend is a great believer in democracy."

Ben regards him with amusement but typically says nothing.

Cliff refocuses. "So, Ben, what's your plan?"

"We go to the reception desk and ask for Richard Taylor."

"And you need me because…?"

"Because if he is still there and I get to see him, quite likely he won't believe me. Or, worse still, he won't care."

"That's possible." Any man who could callously desert his wife the way Richard Taylor did, and not question what happened to her when she disappeared, is capable of anything.

"And if he is still there and refuses to see me – which is entirely possible – I need you to convince him."

Cliff considers him thoughtfully.

"Is there a problem with that?" Ben asks.

He shakes his head. "Not at all. But there is still another possibility."

Ben scoffs lightly. "This is my father we're talking about. What other possibility is there?"

"Just one."

Ben

As Ben walks into the extravagant structure that is the hub of his father's latest existence, he tries to remember the last time they saw one another. They were talking over their meeting with Bodecker. While his father was very excited by all the prospects that lay before him, Ben was approaching madness. Escape was paramount, before it was too late. With his mother's blessing he got away and he didn't care if he never saw his father again.

Strangely, anticipation at seeing his old man has now taken hold. He's not scared or even concerned. After securing victory over Montgomery nothing else he does today seems daunting. All Ben wants to do is convince the old man he is wrong about Bodecker and to go home. Specifically, return to his mother… who still loves the man… who can't quite bring herself to believe he would deliberately abandon her. Now that's love.

He is roused by a smartly dressed man about Ryan's age behind a desk, saying, "Miss Raina Montgomery, a lovely surprise."

"Good afternoon, sir. I'm sorry I don't know your name…"

"Lamont. How may I assist you – and these friends of yours?"

"We are hoping Mr Richard Taylor would still be in residence. My father seemed to think he would be, but wasn't sure. This is his son, Ben, from Omaha, looking to visit him. And this is his friend, Mr Ryan."

Lamont gives them a good long look, particularly Ryan. Shame Ryan couldn't look less… well, just less.

This done, Lamont rings a small bell and a young lad appears, dressed in a navy jacket with gold braiding.

"Yes, sir?" the lad squawks, and then frowns at Lamont as if confused.

"Smarten up, boy. Go up to Mr Taylor's room and inform him that his son is here to see him, and that Miss Raina Montgomery is here also."

The boy straightens at once, looks eager. "Do you want me to tell Mr Bodecker, too, sir?"

"That won't be necessary; Mr Bodecker is not to be disturbed, you know that."

"Sorry, sir. I forgot." The lad tips his forehead as he departs.

"Is Mr Bodecker unwell?" Raina asks.

"Something like that."

She smiles. "I hope he feels better soon. Please pass on my regards to him."

"Perhaps, Miss Raina, you and your friends would be more comfortable waiting in the library?"

"No," she says pertly, "here in the lobby is just fine. We'll sit over there, shall we, on the lounge?"

They wait five minutes.

Ryan leans across to Ben and whispers, "I don't know what's going on, but I don't like it. I'm a little familiar with the place. I'm going around to the back entrance. Do whatever you need to see your father. I'll be close by."

Ben nods.

"Raina…"

"Yes, Mr Ryan?" she says eagerly.

"Keep doing what you're doing. Ben's going to need your influence around here."

She nods confidently. "Got it."

"Raina!" Ben half laughs, half gasps.

"Well, I'm ready," she says. "I never thought for a moment our life together was going to be dull, Ben."

Ryan wipes a grin off his face. "One more thing, take care of each other. There's something strange going on around here."

"Got it," Raina says again.

Ryan looks at him with a raised eyebrow.

"Oh, I got it all right," he says.

Ryan lets out a laugh and leaves the building by the front door. Lamont gives him a curious glance but then returns to his own business, sorting mail.

"Do you trust me, Ben?" Raina whispers to him.

The issue of trust is beginning to bite since Ben forced Montgomery to witness his daughter consummate her marriage without her knowledge. He's going to have to tell her... but then, it would be better if she never knew...

"Ben!" she rasps.

"Yes, Raina, I love you and I trust you," he whispers.

"Good. Now don't worry about me," she says and gets to her feet. "Oh, Mr Lamont," she calls, her garnet-colored brocade silk suit whispering over the rug as she approaches the man's desk.

"Yes, Miss Raina?"

"Well, it isn't Miss anymore, Mr Lamont," she says with a coy smile. "It's Mrs. I got married this morning."

Lamont blinks. "I... I didn't know."

"Well, not many people do. Ben is my husband and we really do want to tell his father of our nuptials."

Lamont regards her with interest, mindlessly shuffling letters at the same time. "I can understand that. Does Mr Bodecker know?"

She looks perplexed. "I don't think so. Does he need to know?"

Good question, Raina.

"Well, your father and Mr Bodecker being so close in business and all," Lamont explains.

"Oh, this isn't a business arrangement," she continues, "Ben and I are hopelessly and devastatingly in love."

Ben bites back a smile.

"How nice."

"Oh, it's very nice," she says. "And I'm enjoying it immensely. So do you think you can find out where that boy has got to? Ben and I are in a dreadful hurry to tell his father about us. You know how newlyweds can be. Honeymoon awaits and all that."

Her tone of voice on that remark causes Lamont to adjust his collar.

"You're probably married, Mr Lamont, you remember... you know."

When a loud thud sounds from the room behind reception, Lamont drops his mail.

"What was that?" Raina asks.

"Er, nothing. I'll see what's keeping that slack boy, shall I?"

"Oh, thank you, Mr Lamont," she smiles.

Lamont leaves via a pair of paneled oak doors on the other side of the lobby.

Raina resumes her seat.

"You're good," Ben says.

"Why do you think you love me so much?"

Ben coughs. And changes the subject. "How often have you been in here?"

"Quite a few times, but only as far as the gala hall. You know, for parties, receptions and such. There are limits for women, wives and daughters included. This is a man's world."

And Bodecker's world.

Suddenly, the lad in the blue jacket appears in front of them. He's puffing and can hardly speak.

"Oh, hello," says Raina pleasantly. "Did you find Mr Taylor?"

The lad shakes his head.

"Oh, why ever not?"

Yes, why ever not?

The lad shrugs and rushes away.

"Oh, that is so rude!" Raina declares softly.

"And suspicious."

Lamont reappears at his desk and continues to sort his mail.

Raina is on her feet. "Mr Lamont?"

"Yes, Miss Raina... Mrs Taylor, I mean."

"You were going to find Ben's father."

"No, I was to find the boy. I sent him to you. Did you not see him?"

"Yes, he spoke to us. Very briefly. And not at all satisfactorily. I demand that we see Mr Richard Taylor, at once!"

"That's not possible, Miss Raina. He's not here. The boy should have told you."

"Well, I don't believe you," she argues. "Now show me your register and I'll see for myself which room he occupies."

"I can't do that, Miss Raina."

Ben notices her making signals at him with one hand behind her back.

"You certainly can! I've seen the regular clerk do it many times... at other places, too..."

As she continuously argues her point, her signal becomes clear. As she's distracting Lamont, Ben is to slip away inside the Club.

"Mrs Taylor... Miss Raina, you can't come behind here. This area is only for official staff. Now as much as I admire your father, you cannot make such a demand..."

Ben doesn't hear the rest; he catches a glimpse of Raina pestering Lamont by trying to get around his desk to see the register and then ducks through the paneled oak doors. On the other side there is another world.

It's silent. And grand. Removed.

Empty.

Ben looks around frantically for stairs, an elevator, some-thing... There's a staircase on the right, sweeping into the function room under deep red carpet. He scoots up it as fast as a man who has lost count of how many times he's made love to his wife in the last eighteen hours can scoot.

At the top is another reception area, similarly furnished. He catches his breath while he looks left and right. There are numerous doors along both sides of a wide, carpeted hall. At the other end of the hall is another staircase to the third floor. How is he ever to find his father in this?

Cliff

Cliff hurries along the first floor hall until he comes to the service staircase. He mounts it two steps at a time and reaches a door with the Second Floor sign on it. With a complete set of the service keys in his pocket, he yanks open the door and sticks his head out. Here's a sight he half expected: Ben wandering from door to door, trying each doorknob.

"Ben... Ben..."

Ben looks in his direction, sees him and hurries towards him.

"He's not here according to Lamont," Ben greets him.

"Well, he *is* here," Cliff says. "I have the guest list from the service manager's office to prove it. And I have the keys."

"How?"

"I'll tell you later. Where's Raina?"

"She distracted Lamont so I could get inside."

Cliff nods. "Good work. As soon as you are inside your father's room, I'll go get her."

"So where is he?"

"Next floor. Room 3C. And according to the service register he had breakfast in his room this morning. Let's go."

They continue up the service staircase and cautiously open the door onto the third floor, peering out while keeping their cover; in yet another reception area, a small band of men are gathered, sipping champagne, slurping whiskey and eating finger food.

"Not a bad way to spend the afternoon, is it?" Ryan remarks. "Good food, pleasant surroundings, cigars and all the influential friends you could want. You don't look impressed, Ben."

"How many daughters have become the seal on some business partnership at one of these?"

"One less now I gather."

"We'll have to wait till they leave."

"That could take a while."

"Raina…"

"I'll go look for her. You continue here."

"Just don't come back without her."

"She's a lively girl, Ben."

Ben inspects the progress of the reception. "That's Raina."

Cliff steals his way around the back corridors until he finds himself at a door leading into the main lobby. He cracks an opening and peers through. Raina is seated on the lounge, drumming her fingers on her knee. Lamont is fidgeting behind his desk.

Cliff waits; a businessman enters the Club and heads straight to Lamont's desk. Lamont is distracted. Cliff lets himself into the lobby and takes a seat next to Raina.

"Oh, for heaven's sake, Mr Ryan," she gasps.

"Sorry," he whispers. "See that door over there…"

She nods.

"We're going through it in three seconds. Follow me and don't look back. Lamont is distracted but we don't have much time."

Cliff slinks away; she follows him. On the other side of the door she clasps her chest and takes several deep breaths.

"Where are we going now?"

"Third floor. Ben's already up there."

They climb the stairs, Cliff on the lookout for staff and other personnel. Because of the time of day, the lazy part, the place is deserted.

Except for that reception going on upstairs.

Energetic Raina manages the flights as well as he does. When they reach the third floor exit, Ben is still peering through the slit in the door. He looks around and sees Raina; she steps into his arms and he holds her close.

"We need a plan," he says over her shiny head.

"Now that we have Raina, I have one."

Raina looks up expectantly.

"We're a lively bunch, a party, intended for your father's room. I have the key, but we should knock first, pretend we've been admitted – I'll unlock the door while you two cover me."

"The door might be unlocked," Raina says. "Why would Ben's father feel threatened in this fortress?"

"Good question, Mrs Taylor," Cliff says. "As long as the threat doesn't come from within the fortress itself."

The pair stands goggle-eyed. Cliff hears movement and low voices in the stairwell. "We've got to move. Party time, remember?"

"Yes, Mr Ryan," Raina says. "I know what to do."

And she does. As soon as they move into the hall, she starts laughing and making small talk in a big voice. Ben holds her hand, kisses the side of her face and she laughs some more.

"Your father will love this idea," she says.

The men look up from their whiskey and finger food with idle curiosity. Cliff moves his gaze swiftly over the group; he doesn't recognize a single face, so he concentrates on their diversion.

"I've heard so much about your father," Raina prattles.

"From whom?" Ben banters.

"*My* father, of course!"

While Raina is making breezy small talk, with Ben doing a pretty good job of following along, Cliff moves into the gap between the two of them and the door. Standing there in front of the door, his back to it, he looks like the odd man out, but in those seconds he casually reaches behind him and tries the doorknob.

"Hey there! You! What are you doing there?"

The door is locked.

Poker face in place, he waits for Raina and Ben to make their move.

"Mr Polkingham?" Raina declares. She moves towards the man she's identified as Polkingham, drawing Ben forward with her. "Is that you, Mr Polkingham?"

"Miss Raina?"

"Mr Polkingham! Yes, it's me. How lovely to see you."

Cliff turns and bends over; he inserts the key to Room 3C into the lock.

194

"And you, my dear. My, how charming you look! What are you doing here?" Polkingham converses.

He has to jiggle it before it will turn.

"Meeting my brand new father-in-law, of course. I married Ben this morning. Ben, this is Mr Polkingham."

He lets himself into the room where it's dark and the air stale.

"Sir. Pleased to meet you."

"Didn't quite catch your last name, son."

"Did I not mention it? Oh, listen, Ben, your father's calling for you..."

He resists the temptation to lower his voice and call Ben's name, and clears his throat loudly instead.

"Oh, yes, we definitely must go. Lovely to see you again, Mr Polkingham. My kindest regards to Mrs Polkingham. Good day."

"But there's no one..." Polkingham is saying when suddenly the pair almost falls through the door.

Cliff hastily closes it behind them, inserts the key and quietly turns it.

"Phew!" Raina sighs.

"Good work, Raina," he says.

"Thank you," she breathes. "It was fun."

"Always. Who's Polkingham?" he asks.

"Friend of my father's. He's a bit of a lamb, believe it or not. He won't make any trouble."

"Well, he seemed to think that no one occupies this room."

"Are we in the right one?" Ben asks.

Room 3C is gloomy; every shade is down and it's difficult to see anything but vague outlines of furniture.

"Yes, definitely. Let's get some light and fresh air in here." He crosses the room to one of the windows; he throws back the drapes, puts up the shade and opens the window.

Ben does the same for the second window. Light floods the room and crisp, fresh air streams in.

And then a deep, stern voice says, "Who are you people..."

Raina lets out a short squeal.

"...and what is the meaning of this intrusion?"

Ben

Ben swings around at the sound of his father's voice.

The old man is sitting on a bed, shielding his eyes from the afternoon light now inundating every corner of the room.

"Ben," says Raina in a shaky voice.

Suddenly, his father is on his feet. They stare at one another across the room.

"What are you doing here?" his father grinds out.

"I could say I want to introduce you to my bride, but that would only be half the story," Ben says coldly.

His father rubs his chin and looks utterly confused. "Your bride?"

"Raina Montgomery-Taylor."

"Raina Montgomery?"

"Raina, you remember my father, Richard Taylor…" She comes to his side and slides her hand into his; she's trembling.

"How… nice to see you again, Mr Taylor," she says valiantly.

His father's gaze bores into her. "But… were you two… I was at your father's several nights ago…"

"We were married this morning."

"No, no… it can't be right… Have you any idea what you're doing, Ben?"

Ben frowns. "What do you mean?"

"No one just marries Montgomery's daughter. How did you convince him?"

His father appears to be deeply disoriented.

"Doesn't matter how I convinced him, I just did."

"I don't believe you; this is a ruse."

Ben shrugs. "Suit yourself…"

His father edges a glance at Ryan. "Who is he?"

"Deputy US Marshal Cliff Ryan. He's the other half of the story and the real reason I'm here. Ryan, meet my father…"

Ryan seems to have been waiting for the introduction. He walks across the room and shows his badge. "Mr Taylor, I'm glad we were able to find you."

"Why?" says his father, peering at the badge.

"To tell you that your wife is safe."

His father flinches and looks Ryan straight in the eye. "Caroline… Are you sure?"

"Very sure. She is with your daughter and your nephew in Cheyenne under the protection of Laramie County law enforcement."

"My God… you people are real…"

"Mr Taylor?"

His father's knees buckle and the bed catches him; he sits hunched and confused. "Caroline…"

Then Raina is on the move; she pours water from a glass pitcher into a tumbler and hands it to his father. "Here, Mr Taylor, drink this."

He takes it, staring blankly at her. "Raina?"

She nods with a tentative smile. "Yes. You're not yourself, Mr Taylor."

"You married my son?"

"Yes."

"Good God…"

"Drink, Mr Taylor. It will help clear your head."

Raina returns to Ben's side. He holds her there for a moment, a surge of deep and unexpected tenderness towards her pulsing through him.

Ryan, meantime, has found a chair and places it in front of his father. "Mr Taylor, when you've had that water, we have to talk."

His father downs half the glass in one go. Ryan takes the tumbler and puts it on the nightstand.

"Go on, Mr Ryan…" he croaks, and clears his throat.

"What are you doing here?"

"For God's sake, I'm being held here against my will, Marshal, you have to believe me. Threats, terror... even blackmail. Ben, you must believe I would never do anything to hurt your mother..."

"Slow down, Mr Taylor."

"I had to do whatever he said, or he said he would kill Caroline. He said he had already dealt with Ben..."

"Dealt?"

"Had him killed. That Donnelly. He was going to do it."

"Ben is fine. Caroline is fine. Tressa is fine and the baby. Your family, Mr Taylor, is alive and well. His plan for Caroline did not succeed. She was rescued before he could..."

"Who?"

"Luke rescued her."

His father's expression glazes over. "My brother's son?"

"That's right. One of Luke's more interesting traits is his impeccable timing. He was on his way through Omaha and decided to pay you a visit. He found your wife terrified after she'd been threatened by Donnelly and worried out of her mind about you. He convinced her to return to Cheyenne and to safety with him."

"He would do that?"

Ryan nods. "It nearly cost him his life."

"I...I am forever grateful to him."

"Mm. Now – who said he would hurt Caroline?"

His father's eyes fill with tears that start to drip onto his face. "I trusted him. I thought it would mean great things for all of us. I was greedy. He knew it. He used it against me."

Ryan gives a deep sigh. "Who?"

"Loren Bodecker... the cur. He's been keeping me here for weeks. I have to do what he says, go where he says. He contacts my business back in Omaha every two days and issues them my instructions. I've been stuck here in town for weeks. I make deals on Bodecker's behalf so that he isn't seen. I must do it or Caroline... She's all right?"

Ryan grips his father's arm. "Yes, Mr Taylor."

His father puts his face in his hands; his shoulders begin to tremble.

"So this is the one other possibility, Ryan," Ben says. "How did you know?"

Ryan answers with an enigmatic smile.

"Hummer was right about you."

His father suddenly lets out a great groan; he thrusts out his hands, grips the air and shakes them. "Why? What did we do to him?"

Ryan encases those trembling, enraged fists in his hands. "Be calm, Mr Taylor, please."

Ben feels a lump in his throat. Ryan's capacity for dealing with people on every plane is teaching him a lesson in compassion he won't easily forget.

"But why?" his father pleads.

"Simply this. Bodecker has great plans for himself. Wicked plans. Luke stands in his way, and Luke for all the terrible things that have happened to him, remains resolute. Bodecker has used you and Ben to try and break him. But he won't be broken and now he has become even stronger than Bodecker can imagine. Mr Taylor, we have Loren Bodecker in the Union Station lockup under guard. Donnelly was arrested several weeks ago and he is in my lockup in Cheyenne awaiting trial. You are not the only person Bodecker has ensnared, Mr Taylor, with false promises."

His father frowns deeply. "My nephew has taken on the likes of Loren Bodecker?"

"He's very determined. And so are many others, including your son."

"Ben has joined with him?" his father mutters.

"Oh yes. You don't turn the other way when the Alliance comes to town."

"I want to speak to him. I need to speak with Ben."

Ryan vacates his seat and nods it over to Ben. His father twists his neck in search of him. Ben takes the chair. His father stares at him through slotted eyes.

"This marriage, to Raina Montgomery... why'd you do it?"

Ben clears his throat. "Because I love her."

"You don't understand. Don't understand what Bodecker is capable of. Montgomery is a close associate..."

"Father, I married Raina because I'm in love with her and she is in love with me, no other reason…"

"But can you trust her? How can you be sure?"

"I am very sure."

"How do you know?"

"About Raina? – Father, I *know*."

His father's expression darkens as this registers. "But you took his daughter, didn't you? He only has to tell Bodecker and we're doomed…"

"Montgomery won't be doing that."

"How do you know?"

"I… I dealt with it. He won't be doing anything. I assure you."

"You sound very confident," his father accuses him. "Why are you so confident you've dealt with him?"

"Because I learnt from the best, didn't I? – how to deal with men like Montgomery, men like you. There will be no repercussions from Montgomery, and as for Bodecker… he'll be going up for trial in Cheyenne before long. And he'll be finished. You were weak, Father. You wouldn't listen."

His father reaches out and grabs his arm, pinching it. "Don't you see, Ben, Raina is your weakness now."

Ben's heart takes what seems like a giant leap into his throat. He restrains it from worse with many years of hard practice.

Raina comes to his side. "No, no. Ben and I are strong."

Ben takes her hand, brings it to his mouth and kisses her ring. "It's all right, Raina," he murmurs, "cut from the same cloth, remember?"

She catches her breath; her bright blue eyes flicker with comprehension.

His father lets go of Ben's arm and sits back. "Why did you desert me, go off to your cousin's? It was unforgivable."

"I went to look for Tressa; certainly not Luke. She knew the things I needed to know. About my heritage. I found the truth with her. You kept the truth from both of us all our lives."

His father grunts. "The truth is always subjective."

Ben exchanges glances with Raina; she shrugs, her humor restored.

"This Alliance of your cousin's – you are now part of it?"

"Yes. It is the right thing to do. Tressa loves and trusts him; she and her baby son are an important part of his life. And I will not disappoint her again. When I left you, Father, I'd already made my bid for independence. So, I understand what Luke is about, how he thinks, what he fights for. And I agree with it. It can't surprise you more than it does me, but that is how it is. We're not best friends, I can't say we even like each other, but we understand one another. You don't have to love your allies, only despise your common enemy. That is Bodecker. Not you. Not Raina's father."

"You speak like a traitor."

"Well, we're not in the North and South war now, are we? A different kind of war, perhaps. And one more thing. Mother and Luke are close. He rescued her; he put his trust in her; she carried out an act of bravery that saved him in return. There is a deep and abiding connection between them. Father, you cannot go on acting like a tyrant towards us. We expect more of you. A lot more. It's funny, but all our lives you've been keeping the truth about Luke from us and where do we end up? – with Luke, on his side. It doesn't look Yankee and it doesn't look Confederate. It just looks like the truth."

His father looks stubborn and confused. "You...you'd better go..." he says in a jaded voice. "They'll be back..."

"Who will be back, Mr Taylor?" Ryan asks.

"Bodecker's men. I haven't seen them since yesterday evening, but they'll be back."

"No, they won't," Ryan says decisively. "Bodecker is behind bars and his men have not had access to him."

"No, no," he rants. "You don't know what he's capable of..."

"Collect your possessions, Mr Taylor. It's time we were leaving."

THREE

So from the bosom of darkness
our days come roaring and
gleaming...

Henry Wadsworth Longfellow
Fragments

Jennifer

Jennifer steps down from the train onto the platform, watching for ice. Despite the bright sunny afternoon, the wind is tearing through the depot, intense with chill. She holds her hat to her head with one hand, her luggage ticket in the other. A young porter takes it. He tips his low-slung cap and disappears. Anxious, she looks around her, keeping her emotions in check. Bitter-sweet Cheyenne...

"Just the two, Doc Sullivan?"

Her eyes come into focus on the boy with her luggage. He grins.

"Budd..."

"Aw, you remember me."

"And you me."

"You made my Ma better last winter, and my little sister. Wouldn't forget that, or you. Me and Jeff tossed to see who would get your luggage. It's good to see you back again." He carries her one suitcase and one carpetbag to the end of the station and sets them down; then he grabs her hand and shakes it enthusiastically. She rummages in her purse for his tip. "No tip from you, Doc Sullivan." And then he is gone, back to his work.

Before she knows what's happening, someone is bending over her cases, saying, "Where to, Doc Sullivan? I know! The Faradays'. No problem."

"Who...?"

He stands up, holding her bags, grinning from ear to ear. He's the father of her young porter, and a taxicab driver.

205

"Mr Aiken, I just saw your son."

He chuckles. "My vehicle is over there. The Faradays' place?"

She looks about. "I...I hadn't... yes, please."

Mr Aiken nods and expects her to follow him. "I'll wager young Mrs Faraday'll be happy to see you. Great friends, you two."

"They don't know I'm here," she says.

Mr Aiken loads her luggage in the back of his buggy and then holds out his arm to help her step up into it. As they get underway, Mr Aiken starts to talk.

"Lots been goin' on here in town since you left, Doc Sullivan."

"Oh? Do tell."

"Sheriff Ryan caught the man who shot poor Miss Keaton. Bad business. Got shot himself."

"Is he all right?"

"'Course. Take more than a stray bullet to put him down. Then a few days ago, the Alliance all comes into town, a-swaggerin' like they own the place. A joy to watch."

"The Alliance?"

"Sure, you remember the Taylors and the Keatons."

"Of course. Why are they here?"

"The man responsible for Miss Keaton's murder, a man named Donnelly, his trial is comin' up. They came into town for the trial. All of them. Even the cousin and her infant. And Mrs Keaton. Ethan Benchley and his son. And some other young feller. Reckon I heard he's another cousin, you know, the girl's brother. Anyhow, the talk is Luke Taylor is a key witness for the prosecution..."

"Luke..." she breathes.

"There's rumors flyin' every place, but I don't how many of them is true. Latest though – Sheriff Ryan got deputized to US marshal by that Hummer and they've gone off on some secret mission. You know, I don't like to speculate myself, I hear a lot drivin' my vehicle every place, but I wait to read it in the Tribune before I settle for the real thing. They got this new reporter. Emmaline Roberts. She ain't scared of nothin', that one. Charlie Quaid prints whatever she writes and she's got a lot to say. Everyone reads her articles. You kinda get the sense she knows a lot about what's goin' on."

Jennifer stares at the buildings passing by without seeing them.

"You all right, Doc Sullivan?"

She nods. "I'm a little out of touch."

Mr Aiken chuckles gently.

"Ain't hard to do these days."

Mr Aiken deposits her bags on Meg's porch and even though he insists that her ride is 'on the house', she is equally insistent on paying him.

"Mr Aiken, you have a family to feed, now take my fare."

He takes it shyly and tips his cap. "Good seein' you again, Doc."

"Likewise, Mr Aiken, and give my best to your wife."

"I surely will. You take care now."

She waves him off the porch and then turns her attention to the house. *So, Meg Faraday, let me see you explain your letter in person.* The letter that is burned onto her brain...

My dearest Jen, I hope this letter finds you well. We all miss you terribly. Please do not be anxious. I have never lost faith in my belief everything will turn out in the end. I know Luke loves you. I am entirely certain of it. I know whatever he chooses to do in his life he is always thinking of you. You must believe this, Jen, and hold onto it no matter what. I cannot tell you anything else, but Cam assures me that you and Luke will find your own path together. I think it comes down to this; you must do what you feel you must and Luke the same. If you are torn between the need to go to Provincetown or wait for Luke you must put that anxiety to rest in whatever way you see fit. I can hardly believe Dermot has asked to see you after all this time. Indeed you must be curious. It might be important, significant, or even affect the rest of your life. Be strong, Jen, like I know you can be...

A great many words, Meg Faraday, but what is behind them? We shall see what you have to say face to face!

Jennifer lets herself in. It still looks the same and smells the same. Like home.

"Meg..." she calls, pulling at the fingers of her gloves. "Meg..."

It's not until she's actually removed both gloves that someone appears – a tall, thin woman with an angular face and an excessively suspicious expression. She's brandishing a broom like a sword – *en garde!*

"You're not going to attack me with that?"

"That depends. Who are ya?"

"Jennifer Sullivan. Who are you?"

"Constance McConnell. What're ya doin' here?"

"I…" Jennifer raises her chin. "What are *you* doing here?"

"I work here," says the woman with a brusque nod.

"Why haven't I met you before and where is Meg?"

"I started workin' here the day before that purdy blonde reporter Miss Roberts got shot out in the front yard and Mr Ryan pulled her out the snow and jacked her up in front of the hearth like he wanted to roast the answers out of her, and why should I tell ya a single thing about Mrs Faraday?"

Jennifer can't make sense of a thing she's saying. "Why are you so suspicious? I'm Meg's best friend. She's never mentioned me?"

"I ain't good with names. And Mr Faraday gave me strict instructions."

"Cam…" Jennifer breathes in confusion. "What…instructions?"

"Ya just blew in, didn't ya? Don't ya know what's been goin' on in this town the last two months?"

"I will if you tell me."

She lowers the broom. "Nah. I'll get Mrs Faraday to do that. If ya are who ya say ya are. She's asleep – her afternoon nap. My job is to make sure she has it and…"

Jennifer slowly backs into the parlor, saying, "I'll just sit in here, in that chair there and I won't move until Meg comes down."

Constance McConnell grunts. "I should make ya wait out on the porch, but, well, it's cold out and ya look like ya could be who ya say ya are. But if ya ain't and any harm comes to that young woman, Mr Faraday will have me…"

"Yes, Miss McConnell, I understand…"

"It's Mrs. My man died in a mine cave in down in Colorado. He was a prospector. Got in way over his head." She gives an abrasive laugh. "Well and truly, if ya get my meanin'."

"Yes, I get it," Jennifer says, taking the winged armchair. "Ah, do you think Meg might be ready to wake up. You know she shouldn't overdo the afternoon nap and not be able to sleep tonight."

"Huh! So yer a doctor now? Ev'rybody's got an opinion."

Then Jennifer hears a familiar voice. "Constance, what is all this noise! Who are you...?"

"There's a young woman in the parlor. Says she's yer best friend. Huh! If I had a dollar for ev'ry person who said they were my best friend, partic'ly when Mr McConnell's mine was producin' an ounce of gold dust ev'ry day..."

Jennifer, grinning with relief, says, "What happened to Mr McConnell's gold, Constance?"

"JEN!"

"By the time I got back from the funeral, someone had jumped his claim..."

"JEN!"

Meg appears in the parlor doorway, heavily pregnant, her eyes as round and brilliant as full moons.

"I got some of what was comin' to me because I fought for it, but I was just a woman and the mine was Mr McConnell's. Gold's all but gone now; put the young'uns through school. Kept some for my old age. It's what Mr McConnell woulda wanted."

Meg's puts her hand over her mouth, her eyes now brimming with merriment.

"So, Mrs Faraday, ya reckon ya know this here young woman?"

Meg removes her hand and tries to be serious. "Yes, Constance. You may stand down. Please make some strong coffee for our guest."

"Certainly, Mrs Faraday. Ah, sorry, Miss... I'll make certain ya get an extra helpin' for supper."

All goes quiet in the hall.

Not long after that Meg breaks into a fit of giggles and Jennifer quickly gets up and closes the parlor doors.

"Stop that, she'll hear you."

Meg shakes her dark curls from side to side. "No, she'll be too busy singing her old Texas cowboy songs." Between giggles, Meg sings in a deep gravelly voice, "*I ride an old paint... and we're alone Doney Gal, in the rain and the hail...*"

Giggling herself, Jennifer tries to hush her. "Who *is* she?"

"Our cook and my jailer," says Meg. "Cam's idea, of course. Never suspected he had an evil bone in his body until he hired Constance."

"She's perfect."

Meg's eyes flash. "I knew you'd side with Cam over this..."

"No, silly. Not about that, ever. I mean she's a perfect character. I bet she has more stories than the city library."

"Well, I wouldn't know. I don't encourage her. I know Cam wants a healthy, well-rested wife, but if he wants a sane one I refuse to encourage that woman!"

"Is she a good cook?"

Meg throws up her hands. "Yes. After every supper Cam is so pleased with himself." She imitates Cam: "See what an excellent idea this is."

"A better cook than you? I find that hard to believe."

"Your sister-in-law is a better cook than me..."

"Well, Jeanne I guess is..."

"Better than everyone we know. After all, when it comes to the culinary arts she taught me everything I know. But apart from her there's me, right? It's my only talent and I worked hard for it."

Jennifer shrugs. "Men."

Meg's eyes go fierce. "Men with wives who are expecting their first child."

Jennifer smiles. "I bet Cam can't keep his eyes off you. Look at you. You're glowing. And in the midst of winter. He walks through that door every evening and there's you. No wonder he thinks Constance is an excellent idea."

"Mm. I thought you'd come around to his way of thinking."

Meg comes to her and hugs her, her round belly coming between them. Jennifer kisses her cheek and laughs. They part, holding hands. But as they look at one another the laughter disappears. Meg swallows.

"You received my letter?"

"You are going to tell me what it means."

"I can tell you some things, Jen, but the things you really want to know it's not my place to tell. Oh, I was hoping you'd come back, but I wasn't allowed to write that."

"Not allowed? Why?"

"It was... *is* a very difficult situation. I'm sorry, Jen, really sorry." Meg releases her hands, walks to the sofa and sits down. She pats the place next to her. "Make yourself comfortable, Jen."

Cliff

Union Station Police Precinct
Denver

As Cliff leads his unusual band through the door, Hummer gets off his seat with the greeting, "Ah, Ryan, so this is your latest catch!"

Cliff puts confused, disoriented Richard Taylor into a chair beside Cornwall's desk. He makes the introductions.

"So, Mr Taylor," says Hummer, "we meet at last."

Ben stands by with his customary inscrutable expression arrowed on his father's blank face. Raina, on the other hand, is wide-eyed and as lively as ever.

"Well, bust my britches if that ain't Raina Montgomery," Hummer says to Cliff under his breath. "What's she doin' here?"

"Let me introduce you," Cliff says. "Raina, this important looking gentleman is US Marshal Dan Hummer; he is in charge of our mission. Hummer, I'd like you to meet Mrs Raina Montgomery-Taylor."

Hummer removes his cigar and puts on the charm until the Mrs Taylor part sinks into his brain. "Taylor?"

Raina gives him a lovely, vivacious smile. "That's right, Marshal. Ben and I were married this morning."

Hummer takes the hand she's offered him and gives it a genteel squeeze. He looks at Ben and says, "Busy day."

"You should congratulate the groom," Cliff says, grinning.

Hummer grabs Ben by the shoulder. "You wanna tell me how this came about, Ben?"

"No. None of your business, Hummer. But thanks for asking."

"Sure, don't mention it," Hummer replies and turns away, raising his eyebrows and rolling his eyes.

Ben's surliness has nothing to do with Hummer and everything to do with his father.

Cliff draws Hummer away from the others.

"So, how are things progressing with Clarke?" Cliff asks.

Hummer's chomping his unlit cigar once more. "All happened while you were away. The Big Parade. Clarke came in; Police Chief Lomery came in; Mayor Routt came in; the Governor, Ben Eaton, came in. All secret, mind. They looked at the warrant. Had a powwow and threatened to contact the Justice Department. I just told 'em plain: if they make a big song and dance about it, a whole lotta people would get a whole lotta publicity they don't want. Better if they let me and you handle the whole thing quietly. They thought about it some more. Agreed. And then left one at a time."

Cliff digests all this and asks, "When do we leave?"

Hummer rips out his cigar and a second later jams it back in. "Heck, Ryan, you're one cool customer."

"I'm dancing on the inside."

Hummer chuckles. "Yeah, we got what we came for. Reckon we should pull out in the morning."

Cliff rubs his brow. "The longer we stay the more likely the press will get wind of it."

"Cornwall has been givin' the pesky varmints a few diversions. Clarke and the others are too scared about their own necks to say a word now. I reckon we could pull it off. Say, Ryan, Richard Taylor don't look so good."

"Yeah, he's had a rough time."

"How's that?"

"Bodecker held him prisoner, threatened to kill his wife, convinced him Ben was already dead..."

"Ah, your other hunch. You're a freak, Ryan."

Cliff shrugs. "The indictment list just keeps on growing."

Hummer throws a glance over his shoulder. "And those two?"

"Without Raina we wouldn't have found Richard Taylor the way we did and as fast. There are some things you can't explain."

"Mm, they look like they could use a honeymoon."

"Yep."

Raina is exactly what Ben needs, being lively, adventurous and compassionate. They understand one another and where they've come from. A meeting of minds and hearts. And it happened it an instant. Some people are brave enough, perhaps desperate enough, to act in that instant.

"Where did he meet her?" Hummer asks.

"I have a hunch," Cliff grins.

"Care to share?"

"Nope," Cliff says and shoulders out of his coat while Hummer splutters his disappointment. "There are a lot of people for you to take back to Cheyenne tomorrow, Hummer. Think you can handle it, with Ben's help?"

Hummer frowns. "Cornwall offered Allan to help with the Severini family. Ben can look after his Pa. That leaves me and... What about you?"

Cliff lowers himself wearily into Cornwall's seat. Richard Taylor is still staring at the floor. "He needs a doctor."

Hummer looks; nods. "Sure. Now what about *you*?

"Porterfield."

Hummer sighs. "Porterfield... Shoulda guessed."

"By the time you get all these folks squared away in Cheyenne and you've briefed Cam, I'll be in North Platte."

"How do ya know Porterfield's even there?"

"He's there. He thinks the heat is off. His laboratory alone must be worth a great deal, not to mention his stash of drugs. 'Ironpants' wouldn't have bothered searching Porterfield's house either. He's not about to help Luke or me after what happened. Trust me, Hummer, we need Porterfield."

"Somethin' you're not tellin' me, Ryan?"

Cliff comes clean about Marvin Tucker's drug habit, and Porterfield being his supplier and 'a scientific colleague' of Bodecker's. Hummer grunts his displeasure with Tucker.

"When we get back to Cheyenne, Hummer, this whole story is going to break – explode more like – and while I'm stuck in Cheyenne, Porterfield will escape – again. I need to be in North Platte when it happens, not a hundred miles away."

Hummer studies him without letting up for several harrowing minutes. Finally, he remarks, "This is the messy part for ya, ain't it, Ryan. Ya need Porterfield to clear your name and Luke's. And the Roberts girl. Make that ornery Judge understand that when ya get a hunch ya can't ignore it."

"Porterfield, according to Tucker, is a colleague of Bodecker's. It's another connection to the conspiracy between Donnelly and Bodecker. The more we have the better. While Walker looks the other way in North Platte, Porterfield goes on with his activities, his own and Bodecker's. We have to shut him down – now – before it's too late. At least give it a try. You have his arrest warrant."

Hummer frowns, thinking hard.

"Listen, Hummer, I'm past caring about Judge Callaghan. If he wants to have me resign as sheriff, or have me impeached, so be it; that was Luke's life at stake and that's all I have to say on the subject. But Porterfield nearly killed him, and if Walker won't arrest him, I sure as hell want to try."

Hummer opens his mouth to speak when he's interrupted. They hadn't noticed Ben step forward.

"What's next? My father needs to rest and I don't want Raina sitting about here any longer. Not to mention Montgomery's carriage outside drawing attention."

Hummer unplugs his cigar momentarily. "Good thinking, son."

Cliff gets to his feet. "I'll help you find a hotel and organize a doctor."

Raina says, "I know of a hotel, not too far from here. It's discreet and if Ben and I don't register as a couple then it won't draw attention. Ben can register with his father."

"And won't Miss Raina Montgomery checking into a hotel draw attention?" Hummer asks.

"No. They know me. I stay there off and on since my father remarried."

Hummer looks as though he would like to fully understand that remark, but Cliff diverts him. "Looks like we have a plan. Raina, you take the carriage. Ben and his father and I will arrive after you."

"Okay," Hummer says, mauling his cigar, "but get straight back here, Ryan. We haven't finished our little talk."

While Ben and Raina help Richard Taylor towards the door, Cliff says, "What's really bothering you, Hummer?"

"Honestly, Ryan? I'm to be the one to tell the Roberts girl I let ya go off on your own to North Platte again?"

Cliff feels the blood drain from his face and then rush back again. "That's it? *That's* your objection? Telling Roberts? She knows what I have to do, Hummer, if that's any of your business."

Hummer chomps down hard. "Roberts ain't the girl for ya, Ryan, if your intention is to keep on chasin' after hunches."

Cliff glares at him. "You want me to do my job or not? What's got into you? Now dig up Porterfield's arrest warrant, if it's not too much trouble."

"Aw, don't take it so hard," Hummer says, shifting his feet.

Cliff grabs his coat and hat and strides away. "I'll write her a letter if that'll make it easy for you."

"Easy for *me*," Hummer yells after him.

Those words ring in Cliff's ears for hours.

Jennifer

"I'd better start at the beginning. The day after you came through here from San Francisco, Luke followed. Jen, are you listening to me?"

"Is he here in town now?"

"Yes, but..."

"How long?"

"Jen, you are going to have to let me tell this properly."

She begins to pace. "Where is he?"

"I... I don't know exactly. Cliff organized it all. The Keatons have rented a house in town. Ethan Benchley and his son are staying in a boarding house. They are protecting a witness; supposed to be protecting Luke as well, but you know how he is..."

"You don't know?"

"There are many things I don't know. And others I am not allowed to talk about. Even to you. Unless Cam says I may. But if you sit down, Jen, I will tell you what I can. Please."

"I can't sit, Meg. Just..." She takes a deep, steady breath, "...talk to me."

"You won't interrupt?"

She shakes her head.

"Well, as I said, Luke followed you. He came straight to us to find out where you were. Cam quickly asked him to help in the investigation of... of who killed Miss Keaton. Luke said he would but he had to find you first. Cam pressured him, but he resisted. Then something... a thing happened..."

"A thing?"

"Cam and Luke had a huge falling out."

"A falling out?"

"Yes. Luke was furious with him. They are not reconciled, Jen."

"What happened?"

"Well, all I can tell you is Cam did something that Luke can't forgive him for, to do with Miss Keaton's murder."

"Oh," she mutters and sits down at last.

"Cam was devastated; he still is. You know how it is when you say something and you can't take it back, or you want to and the other person won't let you. I think that's what happened as well. Anyway, Luke left for St Louis that same night. He left to go to you. But something happened on the way…"

"Something always happens on the way," she exclaims, getting to her feet again.

"Something dreadful."

She looks at Meg; there is moisture welling in her eyes.

"He got hurt?"

"To cut a long story very, very short – yes. Badly hurt. If it weren't for Cliff, he'd be dead."

Her heart is racing now.

"Sit down, Jen. You look so pale…"

She sits for Meg's sake.

"I can't go into detail. It's not my place and of course I can't speak about anything to do with the trial unless Cam says it's all right. Jen, I wanted to write and tell you everything, but Cam wouldn't let me."

"Apart from the fact that there had better be a very good reason for Cam to dictate what you can and cannot write, why couldn't Luke write and tell me what happened himself?"

"I want you to ask him that, not me. *You* have to ask him."

"He excluded me," she murmurs.

"He's a man!"

"And that explains everything?"

"Pretty much." Meg adds soulfully, "A brave one, though."

But Jennifer can't help feeling baffled and frustrated by the whole thing.

"Jen, I think you should remember that what happened to him wasn't his fault; he was on his way to you…"

"I understand that, Meg, but how can he get into trouble on a train?"

"He… he got off in Omaha."

"Now I don't understand. Omaha? Who goes via Omaha? You go to Denver and change trains. Take the Kansas Pacific and continue via Kansas City…"

"From what Mac told me, he got on the first train that morning. The UP to Omaha. I…I think he was still upset. Apparently, he decided, since he was there, to see his uncle, Tressa's father, you know…"

He detoured. She was his first thought, but he…

"That's when all the trouble started. It's very long and complicated and it's not my story to tell."

"Fine. He can tell me. Where does he live?"

Meg shakes her head. "I don't know. I haven't seen him, except once across the street in town and he tipped his hat. Cam would know…"

"You and Cam have secrets from each other?"

"Luke isn't a friend anymore, Jen, you have to understand that. He's a witness, Cam's key witness. I miss him and I've missed you. All I want is for you to be happy. I don't understand why something always happens to come between the two of you. You still love him, don't you, Jen? That's why you are here?"

"Yes," she sighs.

Meg manages a smile.

The coffee arrives. Constance is humming. While she pours, she says far too brightly, "Ya sure are purdy, Miss Sullivan. My boy Arthur is lookin' fer a wife. He's got good livin' down in Colorado Springs. Ya could do a whole lot worse."

"Thank you, Constance," Meg says. "I'll finish pouring…"

"Sure thing, Mrs Faraday." She exits, singing this time.

"I can just picture you living in Colorado Springs," Meg remarks gloomily.

"I could do a whole lot worse."

They stare at one another.

Jennifer jumps up. "I'm going to look for him."

"Wait for Cam," Meg suggests, sounding a little desperate.

"Oh, I intend to see Cam," she says from the hall, stretching on her gloves. "I'm heading there right now."

"It's getting late. Jen…"

"You stay there…"

"Oh, this darn stomach… I can't move…"

"Constance!"

The woman pokes her head into the hall from the kitchen. "Yes, Miss Sullivan?"

"Don't let Mrs Faraday out of this house!"

"Yes, Ma'am!"

"Not you too. Jen, come back."

Josh Bridger gets to his feet the moment he sees her. "Dr Sullivan, this is a surprise. How nice to…"

"Yes, Josh, and you. You're looking well. Is Cam in there?"

Josh adjusts his glasses. "Ah…"

She tries to catch his eye. "Well?"

"Yes, well… he's having a meeting. I really don't think I should interrupt him since he asked…"

Her heart sinks. "Oh, of course…"

"But since it's you I'll tell him you're here."

Moments later, Cam emerges with Josh on his heels hastily closing the door behind him.

"George!"

Seeing Cam after a long stretch is almost like seeing Frank after one, and when he warmly hugs her, she almost succumbs to his affection.

"Don't George me! This is your fault, Cam Faraday."

Cam looks confused.

"Meg told me you upset him – don't worry, she didn't tell what *it* was, but that he took off on the first train and ended up in Omaha! How could you?"

"You make him sound like a little boy."

"He is a boy, a lost little boy, but he was my lost little boy and…and…"

Cam draws her away to chairs and puts her in one. "Take a deep breath."

She glares at him.

A twinkle emerges in his eye. "What happened with Dermot?"

"Nothing happened with Dermot," she whispers loudly.

"You haven't seen him?"

She groans a sigh. "What's got into you, Cam? Did you predict that I would sacrifice Luke for Dermot – blood is thicker than water?"

"I'm sorry, George."

"No, you're not. You tried to influence my decision."

"Yes," he confesses. "It's a mess here..."

"Mess?" A tremble begins in her knees.

"...and I thought you would see Dermot and then the mess might get sorted out in the meantime."

"What mess?"

"With Luke. And between Luke and myself. He's co-operating – as my key witness, but he's unhappy and he's been through a great deal."

"I need to see him. Urgently."

Cam frowns; a wobbly, unsure grimace.

"What is that look for?"

The look continues.

"He doesn't want me?"

"I wouldn't say that."

"Where can I find him?" she mutters, determined.

Cam's look of uncertainty drifts across to his office door.

"Cam!"

His eyes flicker between the door and her and back again.

She snatches a soft breath, understanding, but Cam hears it.

"Josh didn't announce you. He doesn't know you're here."

"You think you are sparing me?"

"George, he's not the same, at least I don't think so. It's not like him to..."

"And you know the whole book on Luke, do you? – every chapter, every last word, every second a page is turned?"

"No, I would never presume..."

"You let him down," she accuses.

"In *his* mind," Cam rasps. "You know how he is with anything to do with Miss Keaton..."

To her own deep and regrettable pain, she knows. Clearly, Cam has suffered, and it is probably unfair to heap any further blame on him, but her loyalty regarding Luke is defined and rigid, and nothing, not even a lifelong friendship with Cam, will shake it.

"Oh, Cam, how could you?"

He pales, opens his mouth to speak, closes it, and then looks down at his hands. He shakes his head and shrugs his hands. "What do you want me to say? – that I put my job ahead of Luke?"

"How could you?"

"All right. But will you stop saying that? At the time it was the right thing to do, but he can't see it that way, and in light of the way Miss Keaton died, I guess I can't blame him, but..."

"Cam, you are scaring me..."

All at once, he takes her hand and holds it tight between both of his. "You might not believe me, George, but I'm proud of you for coming back, for his sake and yours."

It is her turn to look down. No one knows the deep and true reason for her return, and no one will ever know if she can't make this right... if it can ever be made right...

She takes back her hand. "May I go in?"

Luke

He expects Cam, but what he gets is a strange mirage. He feels the blood completely drain from the top half of his body, his heart pounding frantically to restore him before he faints. The hallucinations, the persecutions, were gone he thought. No one told him that they could revisit weeks later. That in the moment when he needed her the most, craved her presence till it hurt like a thousand pins being jabbed into his skin, till his chest felt like a train lay on top of it, that she could appear and torment him. It hurts. Doesn't anyone understand how much?

His eyes start to water. Her figure flickers and blurs, wavers like the mirage that it is. And he looks away.

Self-pity feeds the torment, Ethan is counseling him, and he has to think beyond himself to the next thing, whatever it happens to be. So now when he looks back, ready to move on to the next thing, the mirage should be Cam and he will conquer these bedeviling tricks his mind wants to play because every particle in his body wants and needs Jennifer.

But before he can complete this move in his mind, a voice soft and full of pain says, "Are you so disappointed you can't bear to look at me?"

She speaks? He looks back and stares at the figure of Jennifer across the room. He's lost his mind. It's happened; he'd been waiting for it to happen, didn't know how it would manifest itself, but this speaking apparition of Jennifer…

"Say something… anything…" the Jennifer apparition urges.

A man who can't tell the difference between what's real and

what's not is a man who has lost his mind. She seems real, but she seemed real to him in Porterfield's basement and for a long time after that. He's not normal – yes, some days are better than others, but why do they keep treating him like he is normal?

He hears himself say, "Just leave me alone."

Her shocked expression seems odd.

And instead of disappearing she comes towards him with the whispering rustle of skirts and soft measured steps on the polished boards beneath his feet.

He instinctively pulls back.

"Luke," she says with her doctoring face and tone this time.

He feels utterly bewildered and confused, detached from his body and yet aware of its physical discomfort.

"Look at me…"

He *is* looking at her. Jennifer. Everything about her is the same. Her porcelain skin with the sprinkle of pale freckles across her nose; her soft-red lips; the sweep of her chestnut hair and the loose lock by her cheek; and those eyes, emeralds of fire, a sea of green grass… everything he loves gazing up at him.

"Look. At. Me."

He stares. A peculiar feeling is spreading through him. His befuddled brain produces a vague thought that she could be real. It's not impossible that she could actually be standing there…

Wishful thinking. These painful bouts of melancholy are nourished by it. When melancholy devours hope, it becomes stronger, increasing in strength until hope turns into despair and it feels like there's no turning back. She's given up on him, he knows that. Known it for weeks. It's what he wanted, wasn't it? Desperate for her, but desperate for her not to know him this way. Very likely crazy. Unclean. Not worthy of her…

That peculiar feeling is growing so determined, though, his skin feels like it is vibrating.

"But you can't be real, because if you are, then I *am* mad because I can't tell the difference. When I look away and then look back, you will be gone and Cam will be standing there…"

She reaches up; he strikes out, trapping her wrist in his hand. That feeling streaks across the surface of his skin. His heart pounds and thunders. Beneath his hand he feels her trembling, detects her pulse as it races through the heel of her glove to his fingertips.

"Don't look away," she whispers. "Please, Luke, don't look away."

"Where did you come from?"

"I got off the train several minutes ago."

"If you were real you would be afraid."

"Of you?"

"Of what you've just walked into."

"I'm… shaking, I don't know what to say, I've lost you… I have never been more afraid than this."

He releases her. "Stop tormenting me!"

She starts to back away. Further and further…

Soon the bout will be over. Please be over soon. He squeezes his eyes shut while it happens.

When he opens them again, Cam is standing there, just as he expected.

"You're back."

"What happened?" Cam demands. "Why did she leave?"

"What?"

"George… what did you say to her?"

"What do you mean?"

"Luke, I don't know what just happened between the two of you…"

"She was real?"

"What are you saying – of course she is real."

All at once a huge invisible wave swamps his mind, drags it under, then tumbles it around and tosses it out to reveal calm sea and clear sight to the horizon. The last time he knew something like this feeling, in North Platte, the blindness had gone from his eyes and he could see: the room, Cliff and Doc Kincaid. Then and only then did he realize Cliff's rescue was truly real. Then, like now, he was shaken to the core, but he knew he was going to be all right. His prayer was answered. Hope was real. Despair had lost.

His Jennifer is real.

"It's all right, Cam, you'd be right to ask if I've taken leave of my senses."

"I would never suggest such a thing," Cam says, "but... are you all right?"

"I will be. I think I will be. Now."

"Then go. With my blessing."

Luke finds his feet. He grabs his coat and hat and runs.

He catches sight of her walking past the courthouse steps and tears after her.

When he catches up, he throws himself in front of her. She pulls up with a gasp.

"I'm sorry," he pants, drinking her in and turning weak at the knees.

She looks away. "There's no need to be. You've changed your mind..."

"Changed my mind," he echoes desperately. "You don't understand... Jennifer, can we..." He takes a steadying breath. "May we please stop running away from each other?"

"It's all right. You don't have to do this. I understand..."

"You couldn't possibly understand. I don't understand it myself. Please..."

He doesn't wait for her reply; cupping her elbow in the palm of his hand, he leads her away.

"Where are we going?"

"Some place private."

Cliff

Cliff draws Ben aside. "I've talked it over with Hummer and I won't be going back with you to Cheyenne tomorrow. There's a train for Ogallala at six this evening."

"You're going after Porterfield."

"That's right. I don't intend to let him off the hook just because we've netted the big fish."

"He's back in North Platte?"

"I believe so."

Ben looks around at Raina, who is adjusting the drapes on the windows. Nearby Richard Taylor sits hunched and disoriented on the end of his hotel bed.

"She's a strong woman," Cliff says. "She'll help you with your father, which in turn should help you keep an eye on Hummer and his charges."

Ben's gaze returns. "What else?"

"Police officer Allan March is escorting a family who is under witness protection. A woman and her two sons. They'll be on the train but not with you. You don't have to do anything, just be aware of them in case something happens and Allan approaches you."

"What could happen?" Ben asks, his eyes narrowing.

"I'm not going to pretend this will be a happy ride, Ben. It's tough keeping your eyes peeled for trouble."

"You know you're doing it again."

"What?"

"Taking a risk. The same kind you took in Watt's Landing with Emmaline."

"Thanks for the critique. One more thing. Don't believe a word Marvin Tucker says. He can't be trusted. Understand?"

"Yes. What about Bodecker?"

"What about him?"

"Like I said, Ryan, this is risky. Why don't you come back with us and then go to North Platte?"

"Hummer's at the top of his game; he knows how to expedite a couple of prisoners. Just stand back and let him do his job, which he'll do even better knowing our witnesses are well taken care of. I'm asking you to keep an eye out."

"Bodecker's a famous man. You really should come back with us, Ryan. We can't afford to mess this up."

"That's why you are going to reassure Hummer he has nothing to worry about."

"He hasn't, he won't..."

"Good. Understand, Ben, the Judge is going to have me stripped of my position as sheriff at the end of all this. So the next time I set foot in Cheyenne it'll be because I have Porterfield. All the loose ends are going to be tied and when I step down there'll be nothing left to hurt Luke or the Alliance ever again. And justice for the deaths of a lot of good people will have been served."

Ben looks a little startled. "Sure, Ryan, I understand."

"I'll talk to Cornwall and arrange for a second police officer, to help Hummer and his prisoners. Denver owes us that much after harboring the man all this time."

"I guess they do at that."

Cliff holds out his hand. "Good luck, Ben."

Ben grabs it and they shake, firm and sharp. "Same. See you in Cheyenne. Just one thing – what should I tell Emmaline?"

Cliff sighs and wonders how Charlie Quaid would be clueless as to what's going on when it seems everyone else knows.

"You'll think of something."

Luke

Cheyenne

"You shouldn't be staying here," Jennifer murmurs when they reach the shabby front door of the old rooming house.

"A few blocks from the courthouse is good for me."

"No human being should stay here. It's unfit. A fire-trap."

"Then where would we all live?"

He lets her inside, fishing in his coat pocket for his room key as he leads her up the narrow, well-swept old staircase which creaks and groans under their weight.

The two small children, Jody and Delia, who along with their mother occupy the large room next to his smaller one, are playing marbles in the upstairs hall. The brother and sister are aged eight and six, and are slowing getting to know him; their mother works two jobs and long hours and when not in school the children are often alone or in the not so attentive care of their landlady. They're good kids and he would like to help them, but folks have got their pride and he hasn't worked out how to go about it yet.

He steers Jennifer around them and they smile shyly as he and Jennifer pass.

Delia, who likes to sing and has a sweet voice, says, "She's pretty, ain't she, Jody?"

Her older brother whines, "She's a girl."

"*I'm* a girl."

"Hush up and have your turn."

"He ain't allowed to have a girl in his room. I heard Mama say so when that other girl came."

"Who cares? Now if you don't have your turn I ain't playin' with you. And if you run and tell I ain't ever playin' with you again."

"Other girl?" Jennifer asks as he unlocks his door.

"Tressa," Luke tells her, holding it open for her.

Her glance is wary as she passes him.

His confidence shudders. He closes the door and as he turns around, suddenly feeling weird and unsure, he notices her surveying his room with a critical eye.

"I know. It could be cleaner..."

"It could be clean."

"You've been in this part of town before."

"Yes, of course, many times, and to this building, but I never expected to see you living in it. I've not seen those children before. Do they go to school?"

"Jody is good at arithmetic."

"And the little girl?"

"I think she wants to be a doctor when she grows up."

Her glance is droll before it chews him up and spits him out.

He removes a stack of newspapers from the best chair.

"I don't think I'll be staying that long," she says.

He stands there holding the papers.

Then he seizes the moment. "I'm sorry."

"For?"

"I came after you."

"You went to Omaha!" And her green eyes flash. He stands mute in their brilliance. She scoffs in frustration and folds her arms, glaring at him.

He dumps the newspapers. "Okay. I went to Omaha and I got sidetracked..."

"Would you care to explain that?"

"In a moment. Let's go back a few steps. Maybe you could explain how, when you said you would give me time to think, I get back to your hotel the following morning and you're gone!"

Her face falls, but she soon rallies, holding her chin high.

"Well?"

"Well, what?"

"You know what."

"All right!" she rasps. "All right! I got scared and I ran. I'm a coward. A… a chicken."

"You, Jennifer, a chicken?"

"I was upset. You were upset. I thought distance, patience, time, thinking time for you, would all help. And then in St Louis I had a revelation. I… wasn't being wise or considerate; in truth, I ran away."

"From me? Knowing how much I loved you? You wait four months after I leave Cheyenne to follow me and be with me. We spend twenty-four heavenly hours together blissfully happy, the happiest either of us has ever been in our lives, you then tell me what I need to know, I don't react the way you expect, so you run away."

"I… I don't know why I do the things I do. I'm beginning to because of you."

"Oh yes, we're a great revelation to each other."

"Well, you didn't exactly take the direct route in following me, did you? You found something to do along the way, from what Meg tells me."

"Cam…" he begins hotly and quickly controls his temper. "I found out something about K…"

"Oh?" she says, but her eyes flash a warning.

"I did attempt to follow you," he says and has to sit down.

"Most people go via Denver," she points out.

He regards her with a sigh. "You know, we're so alike sometimes it scares me."

"How?"

"I didn't really follow you, did I? I ran away as well. From Cam and what he did, from Cheyenne and all its ghosts, from that moment when K was dead in my arms knowing it could have been prevented, from the pain I get being separated from you…"

"You know what I think? I think the pain of Kelley's death is greater than any pain you get from being away from me. Whatever it was that Cam did, it was to do with Kelley, wasn't it? And it was *that* pain which drove you to Omaha."

He goes cold.

"If you won't admit it to me, at least admit it to yourself," she says, and although her words are painfully direct, her tone of voice tells him it is difficult for her to say them. Meanwhile, he's trying to deal with intense recall of the moment Cam told him about Loren Bodecker's face in his file and what it could mean.

"How could I ever be sure anything you did would not be motivated by or instigated in *her* memory? Right now, I am pretty certain almost everything is."

"No, you're wrong."

"You need to deal with this, Luke. You loved her and if she hadn't rejected you, you wouldn't have given me a second glance."

Sweat breaking out over his body, he says, "I don't know how you can even say that after San Francisco."

Now it is her turn to stop and turn pale. Yet she holds his gaze with typical courage.

"All right," he says quietly, "I loved K. But you know me, and you know if I had been in love with her the way I'm in love with you I would have pursued her until she changed her mind about me. The thing is she did change her mind. She did fall in love with me, but by then it was too late. I'd seen you. Then I met you. I knew I wanted you, but you had to be beyond my reach, so I stored you away. Even when Ethan and my mother coerced me into making an agreement with K for the sake of the Alliance, I rejected it at first; then as things got more desperate for us, I told Ethan I would do my best – but it was you I wanted and loved deep in my heart. My relationship with K was difficult and complicated. Pure and simple feeling was needed between us to fix the past, and that was never going to happen while I loved you. I tried, but I wasn't strong enough. You were the one and nothing I could do was ever going to change that. I'm sorry I couldn't make you feel that in San Francisco."

San Francisco is a powerful memory. He's not sure how she can throw it back in his face. There's a rosy blush creeping into her cheeks as he holds her gaze. Maybe she's remembering it, too; at last she takes a seat.

"Jennifer, I think about you every second of the day and night. And if I wasn't stuck here in town…"

"Stuck? What do you mean?"

"I'm under a court order to stay in town. I can't leave or I'll be jailed. I thought Meg or Cam would have told you."

She shakes her head. "I haven't had time to be told anything except Cam did something to upset you and now you won't be friends."

He leans forward. "It *was* about K. And I admit I wasn't thinking clearly when I left town that morning. That I still didn't have a clue what to say or do to make you realize that I didn't care about Dermot, only about you and how to convince you that we could be happy together. You ran, Jennifer. I didn't know what to do. I admit I diverted to my uncle's place to give me more time to think."

"Can't you see, Luke, it's all about her?"

He sits back, frustrated with her. "No. It's all about you."

"Well, if it was all about me, why didn't you make contact with me? You shut me out, how am I supposed to take that? I waited and I waited. I gave you the time you asked for. I thought I'd lost you! After telling you about my life, about Dermot, I thought you no longer wanted me; and then Meg's letter came, telling me you did still love me and that I should believe if we are meant to be together we will be. It made me realize running away was wrong, that I should come and find you. My mistake – you are still here doing what you were doing when we first met!"

He starts to shake. It happens every so often, when he gets weary or overwrought. It will pass soon enough, but he needs to lie down for a spell. How long the symptom will stick around the doctors in town can't tell him. They said he was suffering from melancholia and mental trauma because of what happened to him, particularly as his memory of his time in Porterfield's basement still haunts him so vividly, and that the shaking and anxiety is part of the strain of it. In other words, it is all in his head. But how can he tell Jennifer? He won't stomach her pity or her doctor's compassion.

"You're unwell, aren't you?" she says quietly.

"What makes you say that?" he replies, tucking his hands in his armpits.

"You are pale, you have dark circles under your eyes, you are

233

perspiring and now you are shaking. When I came upon you in Cam's office you weren't yourself. You were disoriented. You didn't think I was real."

"So?" he counters. "That can happen to anyone."

"Meg told me you were badly hurt, and if it weren't for Cliff you would have died... is that true?"

He gives a shrug.

"Is it true?"

He doesn't answer.

She gets up and comes to him. She looks down at him and he looks up at her. She can't help being a doctor, and he does love that about her, but...

"Give me your hands."

"They are my hands and you can't make me."

"What?"

"I think you should go."

"Go?"

Her closeness brings on the feelings of adoring love he has for her and he has to muster all his strength to resist them. Her eyes tell him of her confusion, but he looks away, saying, "I think we've said enough for one day."

"But..."

"You should..."

"I'm not leaving," she butts in. "The reason – the only reason – I returned to Cheyenne was to find you, and now I've done that I'm not leaving until I know what has happened to you."

He wrestles with his tie. "I don't need you here."

"So you turn into some kind of monster when the shaking starts?"

His gaze flies up to meet hers. Delicate lines of confusion wrinkle her forehead. In her eyes, a green prairie grass sea...

"I don't need a doctor," he mutters, tossing his tie away.

She moves across to his washstand and he watches her pour water from the pitcher into the bowl. Her gracefulness was one of the first things he loved about her; watching her soothed him like nothing else could. She takes a towel and squeezes water through it, her dainty white fingers reminding him of a painting.

"I *don't* need a doctor," he repeats.

"Do you forget those times you came to me last year? – with Tressa, because she fainted in the street, then Wilson Cutter shot you in the leg..."

"What has that got to do with anything?" he mumbles, as water trickles through her fingers into the basin.

"Take off your coat and vest and whatever and lie down." She carries the basin and towel to the nightstand beside the big old rusty bed. "You trusted me."

"I just wanted to see you again."

She actually laughs; he hasn't heard her laugh in so long – not in real life anyway...

"Luke, you trusted me. Come over here and lie down. You need to rest."

"I knew this would happen," he mutters.

She returns to his side. "That I would want to look after you? Luke, any red-blooded woman who wouldn't want to look after *you* has something wrong with her."

He thinks about this as he looks into her eyes. Sees the gentle humor playing about her lips.

"Now come and lie down on this old bed. If you don't want to tell me I won't push you. I will just wait until you fall asleep and then go ask Ethan."

Other people may be able to resist Jennifer, but not Ethan.

"That ain't fair," he says, getting to his feet to remove his clothing.

"And neither is keeping me in the dark. Was that in your plan for convincing me we could be happy together?"

Down to his shirtsleeves in his cold room his shakes intensify.

She frowns and looks away towards the bed. "Lie down."

There's nothing for it but to do as he's told. She covers him and then sits on the edge of the bed and wipes the sweat from his face and neck with the wet cloth. It is amazing the effect she has on him; within minutes he feels better.

When the toweling is done and his skin feels refreshed, she holds his trembling hand in both of hers.

"You should sleep," she says.

Sleep scares him.

"What are you afraid of?"

"No questions," he murmurs.

"Then why did you bring me here?"

He watches curiosity play over her face. "This much you can do. Nothing more. I don't want you to know…"

"Then… then we are through, you and I…"

"Through?"

"We have a problem, a serious one."

His temper flares. "I don't want your pity."

"Like I didn't want yours for Dermot?"

His breath gets caught in his chest. She's winded him without a single punch. "That was different."

"Mm. So different. I couldn't trust you with my unhappy story and now you can't trust me with yours. You trust me with your life, with the life and health of your family, but not with whatever it is you're not telling me? I told you my story and then – like a coward – I didn't wait around for your considered response." She looks down at their joined hands. "And still I don't know what that is."

"Well," he says and swallows. "Well… I never pitied you, not the way you mean. I admire you. Your courage and tenacity. And if I were you I would be proud of what I'd achieved in spite of Dermot. I'd be flaunting it. I wouldn't be hiding it. Every time you do, he wins. He's succeeded in what he set out to do – but don't ask me what that is exactly because I can't understand a man who wouldn't welcome a child into his life no matter how she came about."

She looks up with twinkling eyes. "Thank you."

"That night on the pier I had a whole heap of stuff I wanted to say to you, but everything seemed trite and shallow."

"Trite and shallow? Not possible. I think when I am with you all the bad things, the painful things, seem different. As though there is a purpose to them. We have spent so much time apart from one another. Do you think we will ever be able to trust that the love between us is strong enough to prevail?"

Her question, asked with such innocent longing, is beyond him to answer.

She smiles at him sadly, her lovely doe eyes shiny with moisture. "Looking around this room, I think I understand."

"What you do understand?"

"What you are feeling. But you can't go on like this. This is not who you are."

"I've changed."

"No, you haven't."

"Yes, I have."

"How?"

"You saw how I was when you came upon me in Cam's office."

"You thought I was a figment of your imagination, didn't you?"

"Not my imagination, something else…"

She frowns sweetly; he's said too much.

"Luke, you are not mad, if that's what you're thinking."

"How do you know?"

"I don't know a person more grounded in reality than you."

"Things change."

"What things?" When he doesn't answer, she says, "You were disoriented and confused, and there are many circumstances where…"

"Name one," he tests her.

"Starvation, dehydration, fever and delirium, ill-treatment, trauma to the head, abuse of alcohol…"

"I said one…"

"Then there are drugs. You're a little sensitive to opiates. Remember with your leg I adjusted your morphine dosage twice before I got it right? Well, probably not since you were mostly in and out of unconsciousness at the time. I wasn't happy with your response to it. And you could manage pain. Just not the sight of blood…" A smile creeps about her mouth.

"I said just one…"

She leans closer to him. Reaches into his soul with her gaze. "Tell me what happened? Tell me now, quickly, don't think about it, just say it."

"I was drugged."

"With?"

"Morphine. And some weird mushroom."

Her expression darkens. "What happened to you?"

"The drugs poisoned me, blinded me, and nearly killed me. Cliff saved me in time. He got a doctor and they…"

"Nursed you through the withdrawal."

"The first and worst part, yes. Cliff endured the rest on the way home. Then Ethan."

Sweat pours out of him now; he pulls his arm from her grasp and covers his face.

"Just go, will you? Now you know."

His arm is yanked back. She twists it and he knows all too well what she's looking for. She finds them. The red marks where Porterfield stuck his filthy needles.

"Are you dependent?" she asks abruptly.

"No. I don't know! I'm going crazy not knowing. I haven't had anything since. All I know is I'm not right in any part of me."

"You went blind?"

"I was taken against my will, drugged and held in a pitch dark basement for days. When Cliff found me I couldn't see. I didn't know he was real for hours."

"In Cam's office, you thought I was a hallucination."

He snatches back his arm and once again covers his face. "If I have a craving in me, Jennifer, it's for you. I know how to get you back in my dreams, but I have to fight that every moment. You're the only one I've told that to. With the drugs I dreamed about you all the time. It got to the point when I couldn't tell if I was high or dreaming or awake. You would come and go constantly."

"What did I do?" she asks, her voice trembling.

"You loved me."

"I loved you?"

"After a while I could make you come to me. I held you. Made love to you."

He hears the sharp intake of her breath.

"I lay in my own filth for days. I had no control over anything."

"Anything?"

"Nothing."

She goes quiet.

Good. Now maybe she'll go and he can feel unworthy of her in peace.

"You missed me, wanted me that much?" she asks. "You never dreamed about anyone else?"

"In my lucid moments that Ethan would come get me. But it was Cliff who came. He dragged me out of that disgusting place and stripped me and put me in a bath. I was filthy. He said he was going into town to fetch a doctor. The next thing I remember is waking up in a bed. I was still blind. There was a doctor, Kincaid, a kind man, trustworthy. They cared for me. It's a long and complicated story how Cliff came to be there and what we had to do. He risked his job. We're both in trouble. And Emmaline..."

"Who is Emmaline?"

"A reporter."

"Oh... my taxi driver mentioned her."

"By the end of the trial I have to be found innocent of murdering a young prostitute and assaulting a deputy trying to escape, and Cliff has to prove he didn't desert his position as sheriff. Emmaline helped him. The Judge said she was protected by the first amendment, but she can't leave town either. We're both stuck here."

"You didn't do those things!" she gasps.

"No!" he snaps, shaking hard; his muscles are beginning to hurt. "Everyone seems to know that except Judge Callaghan and Walker."

"Walker..." she murmurs. "But the trial isn't about you and Cliff, is it?"

"No. It's about Loren Bodecker and his crony, Donnelly."

This time his arm is pulled away gently.

"I understand you can't tell me things because of this trial." Then she holds his hand, puts it up to her face. Beneath her cheek she rests it. "Why didn't you send for me? Luke, you needed me. You didn't need to fight this on your own."

He can see the hurt in her eyes and has to shut his own.

"Luke?"

"Because this is ugly," he grinds out. "I wasn't fit to be seen. I'm not fit to be anywhere near you."

She sobs against his hand. He feels her lips on his skin, and then his hand pressed hard against her soft forehead. He opens his eyes. She weeps quietly in the shadow of his arm.

He struggles and sits up. "No, don't do that... don't, Jennifer... I'm not worth it..."

More tears keep coming. Yet these are tears he understands – he shed a million just like them on the pier the night she told him about Dermot. Pity's not the cause of them, but hard sorrow and a desperate sense of helplessness.

He reaches for her and holds her against him, staring down at her face with its glazing wash of tears. Gently, he uses the unbuttoned cuff of his shirt to wipe them away.

"I love you," he whispers over and over, kissing those hot, wet cheeks and drenched eyes. "I swear to you I haven't stopped since the moment we met..." It all seems to work because her distress eases.

"You'll be all right," she tells him between sobs. "It just takes time. I promise you."

"Are you sure?"

"Yes, yes, I'm sure."

"These symptoms – they're not because I'm dependent or mad or..."

"No," she chokes on a sob. "You had a dreadful experience. The body and the mind take time to heal and they don't do it at the same rate. Oh, Luke, I'm so sorry."

He looks into her face as he cradles it in his hand. "I know what you're feeling."

She gives another gentle sob, her eyes deep green and coming to the fullness of comprehension. "You do?"

"It hurts, you feel angry and frustrated. You know it ain't your fault, but it sure as hell feels like it should be, because you weren't there to stop it."

"Yes," she says.

"I want to be honest with you about something."

From behind her sparkling wet lashes her eyes widen and sweep beautifully over his face. His heart takes flight. A feeling begins to grow inside him that he hasn't felt for a very long time.

The one feeling that can expose the darkness of Porterfield's basement, shatter it and blow it away forever.

"I know I should have gone to Denver, and you were right about how I let my distress over what Cam told me about K become more important than finding you, but my ending up in Omaha saved the Alliance in the end, Tressa and Adam and the Keatons, and Tip, but mostly saved Ethan because Cliff and I got there without a moment to lose..."

She gulps. "Saved Ethan?"

Oh boy. Those two.

Smitten with each other.

But he understands her since San Francisco and her revelation about Dermot. He ain't the only one Ethan is father to.

"And I would do it all again."

"Luke, I..." she says quickly and then thinks better of it.

"It's all right. I feel the same about Ethan. My whole life."

"And you would go through this whole ordeal again to save him? Oh, Luke. Does he know that?"

"I think so. I told him so."

"What did he say?"

"He told me he had work to do."

Her eyes sparkle and a small grin forms on her lips. That feeling inside him is strengthening, maybe even gaining the higher ground.

"So, you were being the hero again, were you?"

"No, I think that honor definitely goes to Cliff."

"Mm. I'm not so sure."

"C'mon, lie here with me, it's cold. I promise the sheets are clean."

"In a moment. What you just told me, what you said about saving everyone, that you would do it again – don't you think that it makes something very beautiful out of what you consider ugly? That in those moments when you felt unfit to be seen, you were most beloved by those who love you?"

He takes her in his arms and settles her beside him on the bed. Holding her close, clinging to every word, he lets her warmth and beauty and spirit run through him.

"Love and honor are so much a part of who you are, Luke – why do you think people care so much for you? I understand the drugs made you feel unclean, particularly because of how you were treated, but they are only drugs. I look into your eyes and I still see you. Not a monster."

He wants to close his eyes and sleep with her, safe with her, let her chase away his demons like he knows she can, but he can't afford to wake up and find he was only dreaming again. Surely madness would take him then.

"My blue-eyed boy," she whispers. "Go to sleep."

"Not yet."

"I'll be here when you wake up."

"Not yet. Keep talking to me."

"I will, just close your eyes."

"Not yet."

He doesn't know when it happens; one minute her gorgeous green eyes are gazing into his and she's convincing him there isn't a time or circumstance in his whole life when he will ever be unworthy of her, and then sleep.

Ethan

Ethan hasn't seen the boy for hours; maybe that ain't so strange, but they agreed Luke would check in at Ethan's boarding house every afternoon at five o'clock. Gone five thirty and the boy never showed. These days Ethan leaves nothing to chance.

He clomps along the upstairs hall, his ears collecting a myriad of domestic sounds from behind the drab walls along the way. One day soon he's gonna finally convince Luke to move out of this joint and move in with Tip and him. He knocks lightly on the door of Luke's room and what happens next nearly knocks his socks off.

Jennifer opens the door to him. Her face lights up, which makes his insides turn to mush, and she declares his name in a loud whisper... "Ethan!"

"Jennifer!" he practically chokes. "Jumpin' Jehosaphat!" He steps inside, closes the door and she hugs him. Stunned, he puts his arms around her, patting her shoulder. "Ain't you a sight for sore eyes! Where'd you come from?"

"Shhh," she says, stepping back. She indicates the bed.

Ethan spots the boy flat on his back, deeply asleep. His arms outstretched, his face smooth, his body fluid. He looks young again, the way he used to before Porterfield. Maybe young ain't right; innocent – yeah, he looks innocent again, the way he use to before Porterfield. Ethan gives an approving nod.

"He's all right?"

"Yes."

He looks at her, smiling. Her eyes are shining at him. He pats her cheek.

"Where'd you come from?" he asks again.

"I arrived this afternoon."

"He's been needing you."

"I know. I'm sorry I didn't come sooner."

"Well, the boy didn't want you around while he wasn't too good. As a man I can understand it. But now... well, Jennifer, I'd say your timing is perfect."

She gulps. "It is?"

"Sure," Ethan says. "You get that potbelly firing?"

"Yes, it was like an icebox in here."

"That's the way he wanted it. Look at him. Finally sleeping like he ain't got a care in the world." Ethan goes to the end of the bed, folds his arms and stares at him. An image pops into his head of a carefree seven-year-old boy on the back of a cowpony in the dusty corrals of Diamond Bend, chasing a steer with a lasso in hand, the thing swirling wide above his head...

"How much has he told you?"

"Just enough. What do you see when you look at him that way, Ethan?" she whispers, moving to his side.

She's uncanny this woman, but he already knew that.

"A boy," he says. "What do you see?"

Their eyes meet.

"I am not leaving him again, Ethan," she says with a tremble in her voice.

He gives her a sloping smile. "I told you I see a boy. When he's smart enough to stop you slipping through his fingers I'll see a man."

She gives him a soft, confused flash of those green eyes. "That's a little harsh."

"I guess. But that's the way of it." He glances at Luke again. The boy stirs a fraction, his head moving to the side. "So," he says, looking around the room. Back copies of the Tribune are open and scattered over the small table. Well, they have that in common. "Been doing some reading I see."

"I thought I should at least know what every other citizen knows."

"Mm. It ain't good."

"When he wakes…"

"You'll be here," he says.

"Yes."

"I'll let the others know he's in good hands."

"Do the others know about me?"

"Tressa'll know. He tells her most things. But you're worried about John and Amy."

"Yes. I know what they… what they wanted."

He blames *that* for the whole crazy business. If Luke had been free to court Jennifer last summer, he'd have her by now. A lot of things would be different. But no, John and Amy and Sara had to insist on yet another alliance, one that was never gonna turn out happy. One that made the boy believe he had no right to this incredible woman beside him. The guilt he suffered when Kelley died weren't fair; he didn't deserve it. Ethan should have been stronger. Should have resisted the others and told the boy to go with his instincts. He should've taken better care of him.

He turns to her and takes her firmly by the shoulders. "Jennifer, you promise me something here and now…"

Her wide green eyes bore into his. "Yes, Ethan…"

"You stand shoulder to shoulder with him and you stake your ground. I don't imply you have to be mean about it…"

"Of course not, Ethan…"

"Can you do it? Can you look John and Amy in the eye and do it?"

"I want to."

"But you're scared?"

She nods.

"Yeah, well, imagine how Luke feels. He loves these people like his own flesh and blood."

"Don't they love him as if he's their flesh and blood?"

"Yes, honey, they do. Jennifer, you gotta make a decision here. Every one of us, right now with this trial coming up, thinking and recalling all we can about what's happened, we're stuck in the past and can't move on just yet. But we need hope. Something to jump up and shout that beyond this hard time the future still exists. Luke more than any of us, I reckon, but John and Amy, too. They're not the kind of folks who look back for long. Not in their nature, I guess. Tressa'll tell you that. But the past don't seem to want to go away for them."

"But..."

"Hush now. You gotta be strong against the memories. You can't let 'em hold you back, pin you down. There's no right or wrong here. There's only courage. Now, I reckon you got a lot of that, so don't be selling yourself short, don't be telling me you don't want to walk into John and Amy's house with Luke by your side and let them see what I see, what I saw all along and should've done something about."

Her eyes tell him she's thinking hard. "I appreciate everything you just said, Ethan."

"Well, now, you two take care of each other and we'll see you when we see you." He plants a kiss on her forehead. "When he wakes up, tell him I was looking for him. I'll be at the Keatons if you need me, 18th and Evans. Guess you know where that is."

She nods that shiny chestnut head of hers.

"The one with the fancy white woodwork around the porch. Got a porch swing, too."

"Thank you, Ethan."

Ethan gives her chin a shake. "Keep it up."

"I will."

Out in the hall, he stops and takes a deep steadying breath. Then sighs it away. Long time since he uttered a prayer, but he says one. He's just so darn grateful.

Luke

Luke opens his eyes to that all too familiar feeling of confusion.

"Jennifer," he breathes, always the first and last and everything in between... And she is right there beside him, sitting on her side of the bed reading the Tribune.

"Hello," she says coolly.

But the room feels warm. Lamplight from the nightstand casts a glow about her face.

"I didn't make any of the past few hours up, did I?"

"No." She puts the paper together, saying, "You did not. I've just been catching up. Reading Emmaline Roberts actually. She writes about you with great authority. Quote..."

She rustles the newspaper open again and holds it up.

"His enemies tried to keep him down and they failed. His return to Cheyenne is the story of one of the great journeys, from the very pit of darkness to the resurrection of determination and endurance. Unquote. She knows the whole story, although from what I can gather, the rest of Wyoming is still in the dark. I think readers are supposed to assume that your pit of darkness is Kelley's murder and no one really knows what happened to you yet – not until the trial will it be exposed."

He regards her closely. Oh, he's not dreaming. Jennifer is back and she is not happy for Emmaline to be an authority on him.

Excellent.

He grins up at her. "She's a reporter, Jennifer."

"Well, that article at the very least reads like she's part of the Alliance, or something."

247

"She was for a while. She kinda got involved with us. That's how she knows so much, as you rightly pointed out. Jennifer, there's something you should know about Emmaline…"

"And what would that be?" she says tartly, folding the Tribune into quarters and then eighths.

"Emmaline is Cliff's girl."

The newspaper is suddenly still. "Cliff's girl?"

"Mm."

"*Our* Cliff? *Our* Cliff Ryan is in love with a reporter?"

He chuckles. "He's got it bad."

"And what of Emmaline Roberts? Is she in love with him?"

"Crazy about him, I'd say."

She grunts and gives a thoughtful frown. She slaps the newspaper against her knee. "You leave town for a few weeks and look what happens!"

He laughs some more; she's funny and it feels good to laugh again. He sits up, rubbing sleep from his face, pushing his fingers through his hair. Her shoulder touches his arm, her face glows up at him. He reaches out and fondles her cheek and it sends tingles up his arm.

"I like waking up to you reading the paper next to me."

"I meant what I said before you went to sleep," she says softly. "You did hear me, didn't you?"

"I heard. I want to believe you meant it and it wasn't part of my treatment and recovery."

"I guess if you were easy to convince there would be no challenge. Remember you liked to say: Jennifer, put your cool steady hand on my forehead and tell me everything will be all right?"

He smiles. "I remember."

"I loved you so. My heart used to beat so fast when you came near me…"

"Used to?" he murmurs, holding her face in his hand.

"You know, Luke, you'll never know if it was part of your treatment and recovery or not if you don't kiss me."

So it begins, tenderly, like a first kiss. With the rush in his head dissolving like sugar into his blood and sweetening his whole body, he begins to float. He can feel her breathlessness and her rapid pulse beneath his fingers as he holds the side of her throat and her face. He wants her, but not like he had her in Porterfield's black hole, with dark urgency and pitiful gratification.

"I love you, Jennifer," he says. "Please don't do this because you hate to lose a patient."

Suddenly, his face is between her cool, steady hands and she's gazing fixedly into his eyes. "Have you forgotten San Francisco?"

"I was hoping you hadn't."

"I will never forget San Francisco."

"I think about it every waking moment."

"Do you believe, really believe, what I said before you went to sleep?"

"I have scars up and down my arm…"

"To remind you of – what does Emmaline Roberts call it: your great journey from the very pit of darkness to the resurrection of determination and endurance."

"Jennifer…"

She gives his head the gentlest shake. "If I remember rightly, you have a scar on your leg, and at the time we dubbed it a memento of your heroic attempt to capture Wilson Cutter. Emmaline's correct. You have been on a great journey, longer than she knows, and great journeys leave scars. Signs. A map. A journal. In the mind and on the body. You give your whole self to every-thing you do. Luke, you could have surrendered to the drug that made you dream about me, but you didn't. You were making tough decisions every day. To do that you must have felt deep in your heart that there was a chance for us."

His eyes begin to sting. She completely understands him. Frankly, it's scary, but her intelligence and intensity enthrall him.

"I want you in my life more than anything in the world," he declares.

"And I feel the same about you. Why do you think I came back? I had to see for *myself* that you didn't want me anymore."

"Since the moment I set eyes on you I've never not wanted you."

"And I the same," she says. "You sell me short if you think I would stop because you have acquired a few needles scars on your arms, because you've suffered and you still are suffering. Luke, I cannot stop loving you. It's never going to happen to me. Not if your arms fell off, or even if you did indeed go mad. Do you understand?"

"Yes..."

"So you must see that what you've been through these last weeks and the way you see yourself because of it makes no difference to my feelings for you. If it did then I would be the shallow one."

"That's impossible for you..."

"And for you," she counters sweetly. "You still love me, don't you, despite what Dermot did? You got angry and wanted to shoot him..."

"I scared you."

Her eyes tell him so.

He lifts one hand from his face and kisses her palm. She's trembling a little; he takes her firmly in his arms, cradled across his chest, her face close to his.

"I'm so sorry."

"You couldn't help it."

"No," he admits, "I couldn't help it."

"So what hope is there?"

"Didn't you just say that I felt deep in my heart there was always a chance for us?"

"Then if you trust my love for you and yours for me, what chance are you prepared to take?"

A light switches on in his brain.

"There's one..."

"One?"

He has to swallow. "The one I was prepared to take in San Francisco, but it got interrupted."

"By my running away..."

"Partly. But mostly by my reaction, how I felt... Suddenly, what I wanted for us seemed totally out of place. It wasn't enough. Like I said before, trite and shallow. The future I saw in my plans didn't seem right."

They stare at one another, she with an intense, expectant look about her, and he swallowing hard. The darn thing is on his lips but he can't bring himself to say it. He's gone numb.

Suddenly, she's unraveling herself from his arms; she's off the bed, standing by the table and chairs, threading her arms into her coat.

"What are you doing?"

"I...I just remembered Meg will be worried about me. Worry is not good in her condition."

He scrambles off the bed. "You're not leaving?"

"This is not so much leaving as slipping through your fingers," she says, pulling on her gloves.

"What are you talking about?" He stubs his toe on the leg of a chair. Excruciating pain shoots through his foot. "Dang!"

"Now what?"

"Have a heart, Jennifer," he says as he hobbles in agony towards her, "I'm only just getting used to the fact I probably ain't gonna go insane anytime soon."

"I guess that should be a mitigating circumstance," she says. "How's your toe?"

"I think it's broken," he says, catching her around the waist and holding her still. "What do you mean *should be*?"

"I can't leave your side for a moment," she exclaims, looking down at his feet.

"Answer me," he says and draws her close.

"How many will there be before... before..." She stops and clams up completely.

How many *what*? Before *what*?

"Tell me straight," he says seriously.

She shakes her head.

"Why can't you just tell me?"

"Why can't you?"

He pushes fingers through his hair. There's a tremor starting somewhere in his body. Porterfield didn't make him a coward, but he did make him doubtful.

"I can't make you," she says. Tears appear to be collecting along the bottom rim of her eyes.

Make him what? He slides his arms around her and holds her. Her hands rest flat against his chest, a neutral position for her.

"If you hold so much doubt about us, now would be a good time to say so," she says.

"Doubt about myself equates to doubt about us?"

"You have to trust, Luke."

"I do!"

"No, you can't commit yourself to me. You know there'll always be something, don't you? Something you will place between us – like Omaha and Kelley."

He blows a huge sigh, releasing her at once, turning away. "Don't start that again."

"You can't bring yourself to even say it!"

He turns on her. "You make me tongue-tied, all right?" He groans his frustration. "I look into your eyes and you overwhelm me."

"But… but we're past all that…"

"No, we're not," he punches out. "If it was so easy, Jennifer, so darn easy to… Look at me. I'm shaking. And don't you dare ask me if I need to lie down."

"I…"

"I know we love each other, I know we think the same, and I know it counts for a lot, but deep down who am I compared to you? I hold you in my arms, I make love to you, I want every minute to be with you. When you told me about Dermot in San Francisco, nothing drove it home to me so clear."

"Dermot does make a difference," she murmurs, looking bleak.

"I only know how to love you. I don't have the solution to every problem. And I can't compete with your brother."

"Frank? – what has he got to do with anything?"

"I'll never be as good as he is. He's the one you measure by, ain't he?"

She looks down at her hands and fiddles with the cuff of her gloves. "Who do you measure by then?"

"You know the voice in my head is Ethan's, but it's a guiding voice. A father's voice…"

"Frank has been my father."

"Yes, but you told me, Jennifer, that without him and Jeanne you wouldn't know true love. If you see us as some version of Frank and Jeanne, then how do I live up to that?"

She doesn't answer. He watches her fiddle endlessly with her gloves, her coat buttons, her gloves again.

Very gently, he says, "I only know how to love you, Jennifer."

"And...and you believe after the life I've had I don't think that you loving me is some kind of miracle? The voices in my head are Frank's and Uncle Michael's and Jeanne's and Meg's and Cam's telling me I deserve to be happy. I dismissed them for twenty-five years until you walked into my life, and then I began to have hope that if you could love me the way you do then perhaps they were right after all. And you say I make you tongue-tied. Your love *overwhelms* me, Luke. So much so that I can't bear to lose it. But if nothing else it has taught me that I deserve to be happy, that I can be if I want..." Suddenly, she looks up; her eyes are flooded with tears. "Are we through? Is this the true impasse?"

It's a while before he can bring himself to say, "You told me you can't stop loving me, that it would never happen. How could you find happiness with someone else if you still love me?"

"What do you mean by that?" she asks, wiping tears from her cheeks.

"It means we're through over my dead body."

"Huh! Your dead body is not beyond the realms of possibility if you continue the way you're going!" She starts pacing furiously, her eyes flashing at him every couple of steps. "You're arrogant disregard for your own welfare seriously diminishes the length of your future!"

Why doesn't she just slap him in the face?

"And yours, is that it?"

"Mine and our..." She stops dead in her tracks.

"Our what?"

"Never mind," she grinds out and turns away again.

"No, there's no never mind. You just called me arrogant. You think I'm arrogant?"

"Oh, what does it matter? There's no future for us, is there? It was a mistake. We were a mistake."

"You think I'm irresponsible."

"That's not precisely what I said."

"You see? Loving you ain't enough. I gotta be responsible and trustworthy and humble and all things to all people. The way your brother is!"

She clenches her fists and glares at him. She stamps her foot and utters a sharp, angry groan. "Stop saying that! It isn't true!"

"Well, what's true then, Jennifer. Tell me what's true."

"You are not prepared to make a commitment to me. Admit it."

"I am not prepared to be Frank!"

"Fine. Fine! Don't be responsible or trustworthy. Be immature and non-committal."

He catches his breath. "Immature?"

"That's what I said."

"You may have noticed I'm not standing here hurling insults at you!"

"Oh no? You are accusing me of not being able to differentiate between the relationship I want with you and the one my brother has with Jeanne. I'd say that was a pretty hefty insult!"

"You wanna put that in words I can understand?"

"Oh, you understand. Go on, I can take it. Throw another at me. This is the first real fight we've ever had and I'm beginning to enjoy it immensely!"

"No, I'm bigger than that at least."

"Is that what you think, Mr Honorable? Too gallant to insult a woman? Don't let Emmaline Roberts' stories about you go to your head, will you?"

"We're getting off track," he points out.

"You'd like to think so, wouldn't you? Well, maybe I don't want to be committed to a big-headed, immature, irresponsible, untrustworthy ne'er do well."

"Ne'er do well?" he squawks. "Ne'er do well? A quaint turn of phrase. I'm glad I could stick around so you could use it. Okay, so I'm only a ranch hand. It didn't seem to bother you before."

She sucks in a sharp breath. "Now you're accusing me of being a snob?"

He is?

"No," he says. "I'm not."

"Then what?"

"Nothing. I thought you loved me because of who I am, including the ranch part. Is that wrong?"

She throws up her hands in frustration. "No!"

"So that's not the ne'er do well part?"

She sits down at his small table. The chair is rickety and he hopes to God it doesn't break from under her.

Even from where he's standing he can see her trembling. Is she conceding? Then she starts pulling something from around her neck, a chain... He goes cold. His Liberty and Property ring emerges on its long golden chain. She pulls and it snaps free.

"Jennifer..."

She slams it on the table, takes her hand away and looks up at him. *We will not be slaves...* an engraved message from long ago.

"Jennifer, what are you doing?"

The ring winks in the lamplight, taunting him. *Sons of Liberty.*

"I gave you that to keep," he murmurs.

"The truth is out," she says, "and I'm free."

"So what you are telling me is that no matter what I do from now on it won't ever be good enough. I take that back and I got nowhere else to go."

"You don't want me, Luke. You only think you do."

Only a mother cow mourning for her dead calf could look or sound sadder.

He lets out a huge sigh. "Now I know I'm not crazy, because compared to you I'm utterly sane. We have one fight – the only one we've ever had – and suddenly I don't want you? I've never wanted anything so much in my whole life, but that don't mean it's any easier to get. Particularly now I know what you really think of me!"

But all the fight has gone out of her. She gives a heart-wrenching sob and buries her head on her arms beside his ring. He swallows about ten times before he gains some measure of understanding. A good fight might clear the air, but she's had a lifetime of fighting Dermot's cruelty. What she needs is love and only love. If only he could be sure his love was enough.

"What if I fail, Jennifer?"

"Then I have very poor instincts," comes her muffled reply.

"I can't promise not to be irresponsible and untrustworthy and arrogant, at least at first, because I'll fail. I'll disappoint you if you think I can be better."

She turns her head and looks up at him with smudged cheeks. "I said those things in the heat of battle. It got to me that... what you said about Frank."

"Well, you're not the first person to call me all those things."

"I never want to be the first, second or any placed person to call you those things because I never... I don't believe... You don't disappoint me." She buries her head again.

In the wake of her concession, he swallows his fear and pride, and cuts to the heart of the matter at last.

"Maybe I should give you a list of the things I wanted from you before you decide what to do with my ring."

Her fingers creep a little across table until she has the chain in her grasp. "I'm listening."

"I wanted us to decide where we would live so that you could be the best doctor you could be and I could still keep my ties to the Diamond-T. I could never permanently leave Ethan and Tip, or be too far from them. And I wanted you to accept there are some things I wanted to explore about myself, namely my drawing and a peculiar desire for storytelling, that what I am now I might not be in two years, or five, ten."

"Go on..."

"And... and I wanted us to have a family together... though your own experience of family life, and what happened to your mother when she had you, might make it difficult for you. Even so, I believe together we could manage it. Jennifer, I wanted you to be my home and my life. I feel safe with you, I always have. I wanted you to accept that I love you more than anything else in the world and that I put your happiness above my own, so I wanted you to accept sacrifices from me, whatever I'm prepared to do so that you'll be happy." He feels strange. Calm. "I wanted to marry you, Jennifer."

Again she turns her head to look at him, her cheek flushed and eyes bright with tears. "And you don't any longer?"

"Did I say that?"

"You said you were tongue-tied."

"I got over it," he says. He goes to her and crouches beside her. "A good fight will do that." He gazes at her tear-stained face, his heart set to burst while that strange calm feeling drifts through his blood. "I want this, Jennifer, more than anything."

Her fingers clutch at the golden chain; her eyes follow it and then rest on his ring, mellow in the lamplight.

"My ring," he murmurs, recalling the terrible day he left it for her, with a pain-filled letter, in despair over K's death, but desperate for her not to forget him.

"Put it on my finger."

He looks back at her; her green eyes are glowing at him. His heart skips a beat. "It's too big for you. Which one?"

"You know which one."

"You didn't take much time to think about my demands."

"I know you and I believe your intentions to be true."

"Thank you. Did we just get engaged?"

"I believe so."

"Shouldn't you tell me first what you want?"

"You already know. The same as yours for me. Since we want the same for each other and the same from each other, why are we fighting?"

He smoothes his hand over her hair and down her cheek. "I don't know but I think we needed it. We never said the things we should have said in San Francisco maybe. And I keep behaving like an arrogant, irresponsible, immature, untrustworthy ne'er do well."

"I'm sorry about Frank," she says, sitting up. Her cheeks are deep pink in that porcelain face. "You are not incorrect in what you say. And I understand I wasn't being fair to you. Despite your reservations, in honor and honesty you are like him, but other than that..." She shrugs ever so sweetly. "He thinks twice before taking a walk after lunch on Sundays; you don't think twice about chasing after an outlaw. You're exciting and unpredictable and I can't help being attracted to that. From the very beginning it made me feel that life held so many possibilities."

"I'll try not to be quite so unpredictable," he says. He takes each of her hands in turn and removes her gloves. "Reckon by the time we're old and gray I'll be boringly predictable."

She smiles, takes his hand and fills his palm with the ring and its golden chain. She closes his fingers over it. "There is something I have to tell you. I know you love me, that you want to marry me. I had to know before I tell you because I can't let what I'm about to say influence you."

"Okay, now you're scaring me." He takes her hand and slides his over-sized ring onto her finger. Whatever she has to tell him can wait a few more moments. "Marry me, Jennifer?"

She leans forward and kisses him. He draws them both upright, unbuttons her coat and pushes it off her shoulders to the floor; then folds her arms around his neck, wraps his arms around her and kisses her back. It seems an age since he embraced her this way. The tender passion, the warmth of her love and desire, what he feels and knows deep inside him when they are together, return in abundance, rich and exuberant and overflowing, to renew him.

"So that's yes?"

Luke

She said remember San Francisco. After he found her on the pier, not long after the *Pacific Treader* had sailed, they walked into town and spent the rest of the afternoon together. They didn't say much at first because the fact they were together seemed to be enough. They ate in a fine restaurant and looked at stores and sat on park benches and didn't even notice the cold wind blowing. He found San Francisco fascinating before she arrived; now he knew he would remember every detail.

And he does. As his mind wanders back, her full green eyes regard him intensely.

Evening fell, cold and damp outside maybe, but not inside, where they were.

What happened between them had shades of Cheyenne, but it was different. It had the future in it, it had hope; no fear, no reservations. By that next evening, he wasn't sure how much more he could be in love with her. At that point, he still didn't know about Dermot; that was to come. And when it did, he thought the pain and anger of not having been able to protect her when she needed him the most would kill him. The revelation of her secret fractured them at their most vulnerable spot. And his reaction split them asunder.

"Don't think about Dermot," she urges him.

He caresses her face and gazes into her eyes. "When you say think about San Francisco I think about making love to you."

"I knew what was to come, telling you about Dermot. But I thought I'd lose you. It was reckless of me. I should have been the

259

one to say: making love the way we did is for people who marry and want children and a whole long life together, not for the two desperate characters we were. I should have said: if you still want me after I tell you about my life under Dermot then I will love you always and forever. I should have trusted. Oh, I've learnt a lot about myself since then. I should have been stronger and…"

"Will you stop?" he says and smiles, a little confounded. "Your vulnerability is very attractive to me, Jennifer. So you wished you were stronger in San Francisco. I didn't make it easy for you, did I? We were crazy about each other and we'd been lonely and sad and apart for months."

"But something happened."

He frowns. "What?"

"Luke, I…"

"You what?"

"We…"

"We what?"

She looks away; he follows her gaze and catches her eye. "We what?" he prompts again.

"You and I…"

"The two of us…"

"Mm, are…"

Her gaze penetrates like a shining sword.

What could the two of them…

Making love is for people who marry and want children…

"You're…?" he mumbles, stunned.

"I am…?"

"You… We… Are you sure?"

"I'm a doctor, aren't I?"

"Jennifer…" he gasps.

Is the old floor that uneven or is it just his knees giving way?

"A doctor who should know better."

"I reckon you're a woman first. The woman I'm going to marry and have a family with."

"What… what do you think?"

"No wonder you gave me the third degree on maturity and responsibility."

"You're not angry or upset or disappointed or..."

"No. Are you?"

"I love you and I want this more than anything."

"I'm sure I'm supposed to say that."

"You can, if you want..."

Her fingers play at the back of his neck; her eyes are shining with more beauty than he has right to lay claim to; he kisses her, passionately. The surprise starts to sink in.

At last it appears as though he will have what he so fervently wanted: Jennifer, a life shared with her, and a life that is part of them both. Now he really remembers San Francisco. He loved her until he knew every part of her, or thought he did. Loved her and held nothing back from her, so she would know he intended nothing would ever come between them. In that intent, it came to pass.

"Are you all right?" he murmurs in her ear, kissing it softly as he does so.

"Yes. It's very early days. Only six weeks."

"And you're sure."

"I'm sure."

"So when...?"

"October."

He lifts his face from the fragrant place in the hollow of her neck to look at her. "We'd better set a date to be married. How soon can Frank get here?"

"Here?"

"I can't leave town remember."

"You want to be married in the middle of all this Bodecker and Donnelly business?"

"Reckon we'll find the time. And the trial's not for another ten days."

"We haven't even told your family we're together, let alone about to be married."

"Tressa, Ethan and Tip already know about us. And Tressa's pretty good at this kind of stuff."

"At what exactly?"

"Letting John and Amy know stuff. She's gentle, and subtle."

"That she is. And your mother?"

"I haven't seen my mother for a very long time."

"She won't approve of me," she says with alarming authority.

"How do you know?"

"Because she wanted you to marry Kelley."

Tired of speaking about his mother already, he puts his face back in his favorite spot on her neck and kisses it. "I want you, Jennifer. Let's get married tomorrow."

"Let's give Frank and Jeanne and their tribe a week to get here."

He sighs. "A week then."

"And perhaps you should write your mother and tell her? A letter explaining everything, so when we finally meet the poor woman won't collapse from shock and disappointment."

"I'll deal with it."

"One more thing… Were you thinking about disclosing to anyone about… you know…"

"My only plan is to marry you and love you forever. Besides that, I will do what you want."

"You must have an opinion."

"I have."

"And?"

"They'll find out soon enough."

"You don't think it a lie by omission."

"Nope. It's our business, no one else's. I kinda like it that way. Between us for a while. When will it become obvious? Three, four months…?"

"Yes," she says. "You remember Tressa."

He lifts his head and grins. "Not likely to forget that… details."

And she laughs gently.

"Are you happy, Jennifer? Cause you look it."

"You make me happy."

"Then I don't want you worrying who knows what. We can fib about it forever if you want. And as for weddin's, I wonder why anyone would want to have one with all the fuss it causes."

"Even so, I think it will be a very special occasion."

"We'll invite all the necessary people…"

"That will include Cam."

"I know," he says earnestly. "And big brother Frank."

"He's a lamb, you know."

His heart melts. "I'd wish I'd been there, Jennifer. To help him take care of you all those years."

"I know you do," she says, caressing his face with the back of her fingers. "And I love you for it. But those years are gone. The present and the future are before us, and that's all that counts. Oh, I just remembered…"

"What?"

"Ethan stopped by while you were sleeping."

It's late when he walks her home. Although he thought the walk was too long and too cold for her, she insisted it wasn't and he should tell her how he came to be in North Platte and how Cliff came to save him. So he rugged her up well and they set off.

She listens attentively as his voice becomes more and more hoarse from talking in the cold evening air. Her interest in Porterfield and the laboratory is intense, and she becomes a little frustrated when he can't give her details.

"Cliff could give you more."

"I can see why you believe Cliff a hero. And I'd like to meet his Emmaline."

"Well, she's already told me she'd like to meet you," he says, chuckling.

"She knows about me?"

"She's the snoopiest reporter that ever lived. She knows about *us*. Apparently, there's been a rumor about us since last fall. Typical Emmaline, she dove right in and found out if it were true."

"Cliff told her."

He gives an impressed laugh. "Yes. How…"

"I suspected last fall he knew. He's too canny by half. Are they good together?"

"I wouldn't say they are exactly *together*. They have some challenges. But if I know Cliff, he's working at sorting them out. Strange, in a way… the girl he loves came into town to investigate his job, and his job is the very thing that could keep them apart."

"That's sounds intriguing."

"Well, I think you should meet Emmaline before I say anything more. There's the house…"

They stroll to the gate and stop. And look at one another.

"I have a feeling you have more to say," she teases him.

"Jennifer…"

"Go on."

"If I set one foot out of Cheyenne, I'll be in contempt of Judge Callaghan's order. If I were to walk into Lincoln County Nebraska, I'd be arrested for murder…"

"But you are innocent."

"But if I'm not cleared by the trial…"

"Do you really think for one second that Cam would let that happen?"

"He let…"

She stills his lips with a gentle finger. "I don't say this very often, but you're wrong. Cam will fight tooth and nail for you."

He removes her finger. "I wish I had your confidence."

"I know your trust in him has been shaken…"

"Jennifer, if I end up in jail, what will you do?"

"You *won't*."

"But I could."

"Then I would spend every moment of the day and night working to prove your innocence and have you released. I wouldn't rest until it was done, no matter how long it took."

He swallows hard. "Honestly?"

She sighs, a little frustrated. "Granted getting married next week is very risky, but you and I are no strangers to risk. We like that about each other. Think of it this way. You and I being married before the trial sends a clear message to all the doubters. You are innocent, so innocent in fact that I am prepared to marry you, and all our friends and family will stand up for us."

He gazes at her in awe for having uttered the exact words he needed to hear.

"I'll walk you to the door," he says, grinning.

"What will we do tomorrow?"

"You need your rest. I'll call by late in the morning."

"Not too late. Maybe I should meet you…"

"No, I'll call."

He leads her through the gate and draws her close to his side as they stroll to the Faraday's front door.

She leans into him and kisses him. "Not easy to say goodnight, is it?"

"My mother used to say the sooner you go to sleep the sooner tomorrow will come."

"Then I will go."

But neither of them moves. He holds her fast, kisses her neck, her cheek, her brow. "I'll be back in the morning, I promise."

"I take comfort from the fact that you can't leave town."

"You do that. I'll go when you open that door, walk through and close it behind you, and only then."

If nothing else, he wants to leave her with an image of him not leaving her.

Ben

The Mile High City

Raina is seated in front of the mirror at the dressing table, brushing her glossy dark locks, when he exits his father's adjoining hotel room. After leaving the door slightly ajar, he goes to her and sits next to her on the wooden seat, his back to the mirror, their hips touching. It becomes a love seat. Her closeness makes his head swim and the rest of him like a magnet for her soft curves; her scent reminds him of white damask roses glorifying the last days of summer, cozy, triumphant and heady.

"He's still fast asleep then?" she asks and tables her brush.

He slides his hand down the shiny, tumbling cascade that is her hair. "The sleeping draught the doctor gave him is working. Should be feeling a whole lot better in the morning."

"I think so, too. It's amazing how a good night's sleep can make you feel."

He grins at her and changes his position on the seat, straddling it so that she fills the space between his thighs. Her eyes are dancing, sprinkling Raina light wherever her glance falls on his face. He feels illuminated from the inside out when she does this. He slips his arms around her waist and holds on because it makes him light-headed and silly. When he's had his fill of Raina light, he nestles his head on her rose-scented shoulder and breathes her in, and wonders how this much delight and beauty could possibly be all his.

"Raina," he sighs.

"It has been a long day," she murmurs. "The best day…"

266

"The best."

"Mr Ryan would be well on his way by now."

"I guess."

"I hope we'll be all right without him."

"Can't see why not. Hummer's been at this marshal's game a lot longer than Ryan."

"Well, you wouldn't know it. Still, there's something strange about Mr Ryan..."

"Strange?"

"Something poignant. He's terribly efficient and wonderfully clever. But something troubles him. You can see it in his eyes."

"I don't look at Ryan's eyes."

"I pray he'll be all right, out there on his own with no one to help him, or look out for him."

"Raina," he says, highly amused, lifting his head to look at her, "you just said he is efficient and clever."

"But you told me he was taking a great risk going to North Platte. Taking risks puts an edge on everything. You know that."

"I know that," he says softly.

"I wouldn't like to be the woman waiting back home for him," she remarks. "Is there such a woman?"

"Emmaline," he tells her.

"Put yourself in their shoes for a moment, knowing how *we* feel about each other..."

And because his Raina suggests it, he does. And is promptly glad that he can step right back out of Ryan's shoes into his own again. Separation from Raina is unthinkable...

"Cliff and Emmaline – please, God, look down on them and reunite them soon."

"Prayers at bedtime," he grins.

"We really don't know very much about one another, do we, Ben?"

His grin broadens. "Every minute's a revelation."

"I like it."

"Oh, Raina, so do I."

Emmaline

The next morning
Cheyenne

Emmaline sets off for work early, her hands pushed deep into her muff. As she passes *his* house, she keeps her head down and her eyes averted. Looking at it only increases the deep pangs of separation that have been unmistakably etching themselves onto her insides. She really should take a different route.

Why couldn't she be like Celina and fall for a man like Harrison – normal job, steady hours, a home relatively close to their mother? Warm climate...

She pokes her head in the county sheriff's office and says good morning to Mac. He's always comfortingly pleased to see her, even when she asks – as she does now – for an overnight report on Cheyenne.

"Nothin' you'd be interested in."

She takes him at his word.

"Send that cub reporter down here; I'll toss a few neighborhood squabbles his way."

She grins and says, "You haven't seen Dillon Kerr this morning by any chance."

Mac's eyes narrow. "Should I have?"

"He's gone quiet, hasn't he?"

Mac gives a decisive nod. "I'm hopin' that's a good thing."

"I guess."

His eyebrows move from side to side. "You all right, Emmaline?"

"Certainly."

He pushes his mouth around pensively. "Okay. Off you go now."

"Bye, Mac." She stops at the door and regards him over her shoulder. "Mac..."

"Don't worry. I told you, as soon as I hear somethin' you'll be the first to know."

At the Tribune, she's so early the cub hasn't even arrived to make the coffee yet. She takes her notebooks from her satchel and sets about her work. While there is her everyday work, developments she must soon venture out to find, there is also her major story, the one she originally came to Cheyenne to get and turned out to be nothing like it was supposed to, and is to be published in installments after the trial.

Mr Quaid likes to tell her it's worth a lot of money to him in syndication; it's worth a lot more to her in reputation and status. But deep down she knows that is not why she writes it. She has a profound regard for her subjects and something close to awe for their story. She writes with a smidgeon of subjective affection for them even though she shouldn't, a word here and there, a phrase... Mr Quaid critiqued some of her early drafts and told her to start steering an even course or he'd rewrite it himself, although she detected a smile on his face as he said it.

Not complete, or in order, she writes some bits on some days, other bits on other days. Sometimes she can't bear to write about Cliff, sometimes she can't write about anyone else. For his part in the story, she has great difficulty in remaining objective, particularly when she reads his recount – penned just for her in *that* notebook – about his time in North Platte. Since he's been gone, she hasn't been game to read it at all. Even now she thrusts that particular notebook back into her satchel and out of sight.

Somehow it all has to come together.

For an hour she pours over her account of her time with Sheriff Ransford and Deputy Chase Deloight, that incredible journey from Laramie to the Diamond-T. She wants every detail to be clear and precise and it takes time. She wants to leave room in her narrative to weave in Donnelly's simultaneous movements. Perhaps Cliff's time in North Platte and Luke's experience at Porterfield's could also receive this treatment, but she doesn't want one to detract from the other, so amazing are their exploits.

Sensing a lot of movement around her, Emmaline looks up. The whole Tribune staff is at work; she hadn't noticed.

Mr Quaid saunters up to her.

"What time did you get in?"

"A little early."

"I like that about you, Roberts."

"Thank you, Mr Quaid. But I know that look…"

"Jennifer Sullivan arrived in town yesterday afternoon…"

"Jennifer Sullivan!"

His eyes light up. "I can see that it means as much to you as it does to me. There's a story here, Roberts."

"I'm sure there is, Mr Quaid, but can it have anything to do with…"

"If it's got to do with Taylor, it's a story the Tribune wants. Now go find out why she's here."

"But…"

"She's a lovely woman, Roberts. I'm sure she'll give you a fair hearing."

"Yes, Mr Quaid."

Yes, Mr Quaid. No, Mr Quaid. If she wasn't the principal depository for the entire Alliance versus Donnelly and Bodecker story, there would be nothing to stop Charlie Quaid from running her life. In some ways he treats her like his prized Hereford, but she has a feeling he's determined to turn her into a full-blooded news reporter by ordering her here, there and everywhere, and having her do his bidding.

"It's a scoop, Roberts. Don't let it get away from you."

"I won't," she says. She stops his departure with a raised eyebrow.

"Yes, Roberts?"

"How widespread was that rumor about Taylor and Sullivan?"

"The two were seen together a lot last summer and fall. Nothing compromising, but they did seem to develop a solid friendship. A beautiful, intelligent woman and a handsome determined hero seemed like a perfect match to me. It's well known that Sullivan supposedly *helped* Miss Keaton in an eleventh hour appeal to the governor against the extradition of Wilson Cutter which saved Taylor's as...bacon, but by my observation I'd say it was the other way around."

"Oh?"

"Sullivan was tight with the governor because she pulled his kids unscathed through scarlet fever. Miss Keaton had no such claim on the governor. I liked that about Sullivan; she had no qualms about calling in a marker when it was needed and, boy, did Taylor need it."

"Seen by whom?" she asks, backtracking.

"Roberts..." he steams. "By me! Okay. I didn't spread the rumor. I kept it for the right time. Now's the right time and it's in the hands of my best investigative reporter. So go investigate and come back with the story. I'll write the background. You get the rest. Turn it into whatever you like. But I want the story, Roberts."

"I'm on it," she says jauntily, but in her stomach is a very cold and nasty feeling.

Luke

A cold wind whistles under the awning of the telegraph office. Luke blows on his hands to warm them up.

"Come on, Ethan, I need your help on this."

"She's *your* mother."

"You've known her longer than me."

Ethan doesn't even seem to hear that; he's drifted off again, his arms folded, hat down low and a faraway expression on his face.

"Ethan!"

"Sorry. I'm just so dang…"

"Don't say it," Luke mutters quickly. "Not again."

Ethan grunts and gives him an indignant look. "I'll be excited and there ain't nothing you can do to stop me. Write your own telegram."

"I'm trying, Ethan," he says in placating tone. Actually, he can't help grinning. Ethan rolls his eyes.

"It's kinda rushed," Ethan says, "for your mother, I mean."

"Well, I ain't waiting around for something else to wreck it up. With the trial coming up, she said a week and a week it is."

"Something I have to tell you," Ethan says in a low voice.

"What?"

"I, er… I told Amy and John. Not about the weddin' – didn't know that last night. Just about the two of you. Hope you don't mind."

"Why?" he asks, outwardly calm.

"Because I owed it to you."

He stares at Ethan, wondering what to say.

"Just write the damn telegram," Ethan grunts and looks away.

He swallows hard and looks down. "I don't know what you think you did, Ethan, but you don't owe me a thing."

"Hurry up. It's cold."

"How'd they take it?"

"Well... hard, at first. Then we talked some more. They came around to thinking they'd expected too much of you. And that's the truth. They said they liked Jennifer very much, respected her. Were grateful to her for what she did for you. And for Tressa. John said after all she did, he shoulda guessed. I told him he had blinders on. We see what we wanna see, ain't *that* the truth. Anyway, I reckon it's gonna be all right. Awkward at first maybe, but... well, you got Tressa working on them."

"Thanks, Ethan."

"Hurry up with that thing, will you?"

"Yes, Ethan," he grins. "How's this? Dear Sara, hope you are well. Getting married in one week in Cheyenne. Can you come..."

"Not can you come."

"What then?"

Ethan frowns. He goes to speak and then closes his mouth. He repeats this a couple more times. Then shrugs. "Can you come."

Luke grins. "What about – hope you can arrange to come?"

"Better."

"Hope you can arrange to come. Missing you. Luke."

"Your loving son, Luke."

"Ah...Your loving son, Luke."

"Hurry up and write it down before we forget it."

"Hold on, what about Edith?"

"Hope you and Edith can arrange to come."

He scribbles it quickly and hands it to the waiting telegrapher.

The telegrapher comments, "New York to Cheyenne in under a week at this time of year. Yep..." he winks, "it ain't for everyone."

"Better to ask though, ain't it?" he says.

The telegrapher nods. "Can't argue with that."

It ain't a cheap telegram.

"Weddin's don't come cheap," Ethan remarks as they move away. "I gotta keep pinching myself. Are you sure she said yes?"

"I'm sure. Sending that telegram though... that had a kinda weird feeling about it."

"Yep. Ain't a man alive who don't feel weird about getting hitched. Just you wait for the ceremony."

He thinks of what binds him and Jennifer together for life; he's grateful for it. That tiny prospect has grounded him more in twelve hours than anything over the last twenty-seven years. And he wants it with a surprising fierceness that is growing minute by minute.

They stroll quietly up 16th Street, looking this way and that, until Ethan says, "Ain't that Emmaline coming our way?"

Cliff

North Platte, Nebraska

Cliff makes his way along Front Street. North Platte appears to have thawed somewhat since he last paid his respects. Although bitterly cold, the town less resembles the snow globe world he described for Emma in her notebook, recounting the time he last spent here searching for Luke. Life is stirring... a welcome distraction after the long and uncomfortable train journey; he feels stiff and kind of creaky, having slept sitting up half the night until a porter noticed his badge and found him a vacant bunk.

He arrives at Doc Kincaid's Dewey Street home, which stands rock solid like the Doc himself. It's a fine house, full of light and comfort. A substantial two stories, white-washed timber with shutters and fancy trim painted dark green, part of the bottom comprises his doctor's rooms. There is a side entrance for these, complete with its own stoop and small porch with a couple of bench seats. An outdoor waiting room, when the seasons allow.

He makes an entrance.

Kincaid is alone and standing at the reception desk, reading a schedule book.

"Morning, Doc," Cliff says, with a grin.

Kincaid looks up. Recognition and surprise follow. "Cliff, my boy!" He puts the book down at once and crosses over with his hand outstretched. They shake heartily. "How are you?"

"Still at it," he says and Kincaid's eyes widen.

"Came back for what you left behind?"

"You could say that."

"Come in. Let's talk. Belle will make us some coffee. Have you eaten breakfast?"

Belle remembers him and they chat like old friends. Angel of mercy that she is, she feeds him pancakes with a side of heaped bacon rashes and then leaves them to drink their coffee and talk, telling her husband she'll keep an eye on things.

"So, how is the young man?" Kincaid asks as soon as she's left.

"It was rough."

"Melancholy?"

Cliff nods. "Very, but physically he seems okay."

"Oh, it takes time for mind and body to get back on the same track, after what he went through."

"That's a neat way of putting it."

"Indeed. And you?"

"My arm has healed *and* I have a temporary posting."

"Deputy US marshal, I see. The work you did here, retrieving the young man, you achieved your goal?"

"We did, but we lost a couple of good men."

"Ah… I'm very sorry to hear that."

"It happens in this business. As you know, Luke and I had to leave in a hurry and I left something behind that I wish I hadn't."

"Doctor Porterfield."

"You haven't seen him around have you?"

"You thought he would return?"

"You saw his laboratory. It must be worth a tidy sum."

"Yes, you're right."

"Another question. Sheriff Walker – did you happen to hear if he searched Porterfield's house?"

Kincaid looks serious. "Firstly," he says, lowering his voice, "I took a walk along Porterfield's street only yesterday, in fact, and if I'm not mistaken there are signs of life. And secondly, I'm going to tell you this because neither Belle nor I approve of Sheriff Walker's methods. Walker spoke to us day before yesterday about what had gone on with you and Luke and Porterfield. He said that he knew a doctor in this town had helped you and if he found out which one it was, he'd have that person arrested and charged. I think he knew it was me. I think he was threatening me... warning me at the very least."

"How does he know a doctor helped us?" Cliff asks. "Even when Walker brought Luke and I before the Judge in Cheyenne, hoping to have us extradited, we never mentioned that anyone helped us."

"I don't know," Kincaid replies, one eyebrow raised.

"He's in on it," Cliff murmurs.

"I don't know," Kincaid reiterates.

"No wonder he was so desperate."

"You're going to have to be extra careful, young man."

"It makes sense."

"Did you hear me?"

"Yes," Cliff smiles, "I heard you. I did the right thing coming here first. I knew it would be."

"You have good instincts. I recognized that in you straight off, but I might add you're inclined to take a few risks. You're all alone here, aren't you?"

"It's a long story, Doc."

"I have no doubt it is. Well, you have to do what it is you have to do. Personally, I'd be very happy to see Porterfield gone from this town and you should know that Belle and I will do whatever we can to help."

Cliff gives another grin. "Then I'm not all alone here, am I?"

Emmaline

"Good morning, gentlemen," she says.

Luke's dark blue eyes are twinkling; his face is smooth and expression serene. If she's not mistaken, he looks well.

Extremely well. Mm...

"Emmaline, honey, you look kinda cold," Ethan says.

"And I live in hope of Judge Callaghan rescinding the order to prevent me leaving town before I freeze to death. Ethan, I hope you don't mind, but I need to speak with Luke."

Ethan looks amused, gives Luke a sidelong glance, tips his hat and says, "Guess I'll mosey along."

Emmaline thanks him. As Ethan is leaving, she observes Luke from the corner of her eye. The two of them have got the poker face down to a fine art.

"So, Emmaline, should we go someplace warm?" Luke asks.

She doesn't know where to start.

"Emmaline?"

"This isn't going to be easy because I respect you as a friend," she blurts out.

He regards her casually, but she can see him thinking. "The Cheyenne Hotel's in the next block."

A walk will make it easier to begin, so they set off. "Mr Quaid knows that Jennifer arrived in town yesterday."

"Yeah," he says, "she did."

"He wants me to investigate why she is here."

"Why don't you ask her?"

"Because it's an invasion of her privacy and yours, I imagine."

"That's strange coming from the snoopiest reporter in town."

"Aspects of this job are not pleasant. Investigating your friends is one of them."

"Why did Quaid ask you then?"

"Because Mr Quaid expects me to remain impartial and objective no matter what. In his world I have no friends in Cheyenne. I haven't the courage to tell him he couldn't be more wrong. Besides, at least this way I can control the situation."

"Thank you. I think."

"You're welcome."

"C'mon, here's the Cheyenne. Let's have it, Emmaline. Spill your guts."

"You got it all wrong, Luke. You are supposed to spill yours."

Inside the Cheyenne Hotel they find a deserted corner of the dining room and sit down.

"You look much better this morning, better than I've ever seen you since I've known you," she says. "You look very, very well."

"I am well, thank you," he replies. "You know, Emmaline, if you weren't a friend, I would have told you to get lost back in the street."

"Yes. And I appreciate it. But you have to help me here. I don't want to write a load of gossip."

"You know it's not fair. She didn't do anything."

"Mr Quaid reasons that when she called in a marker with the Governor over Wilson Cutter's extradition she planted herself squarely on the side of the Alliance. That means you. And that means a story."

"She's always been a friend of the Alliance. But she's a doctor first. Emmaline, I ain't gonna talk about her behind her back."

"I understand completely. Perhaps we could arrange for the three of us to meet and talk."

He looks suspicious and she can't blame him.

"I want to get this right, Luke."

"As good as your intentions are, Emmaline..."

"Doctor Sullivan doesn't strike me as the kind of woman who would let a man speak for her without her knowledge."

He looks taken aback.

She bites her lip. "Sorry..."

He gives a lopsided grin. "I thought I was being very off-handed."

"That's sweet, Luke, but..."

"Look, Emmaline," he says, sitting up straight, "we both got a lot to do today. If we got time, I'll..."

"It doesn't matter how late it is."

"Does anyone else know about this?"

"If you mean reporters, no. Mr Quaid seemed sure about that, but even he doesn't know much. He's surmising most of it. But Mrs Landers does. Talking to her is how I found out about you and Jennifer in the first place."

"I don't know any Mrs Landers."

"She's that strange little old lady who wanders around town saying she should be here and there... you know her... you gave her your scarf, I believe."

"Oh, her... How would she know?"

"She told me much," she says carefully. "She's different is Mrs Landers. Like she has second sight or something..."

"What's second sight?"

"You know – she can see things other folks can't. See things in one place when she's actually in another. That's why she tears off – you turn around and she's gone. One thing though: she keeps secrets. If you don't think to ask, she doesn't tell. She's sweet and kind and loves hot chocolate."

"I'm happy for her."

"There's one thing she told me and I think I'm going to tell you."

"I'm all ears, Emmaline."

"I don't think it will be easy for you to hear."

His eyes narrow. "Maybe I don't want to hear it then."

"Maybe you should."

"Not the ranting of old woman, Emmaline. C'mon..."

"She was the one who told me Loren Bodecker stayed with Donnelly during Ed Parsons' trial. Don't forget when that was investigated, Mr Faraday found witnesses. Anyway, I asked her:

did you see who shot Miss Keaton? She replied, and I quote: I should've. I was supposed to. Supposed to be there. But I went for hot chocolate and I didn't see...unquote."

His face has gone blank. She waits for his reaction.

"Like I said, the ranting of an old woman. The only one who should have seen it coming was Cam."

She stares into those blue eyes, now burning with indignation.

"Apparently not."

He shifts his position, grunting madly. "What are you saying, Emmaline? That this Mrs Landers is some kinda... I don't know... angel who failed to do her job properly? That's just plain..."

"I guess what I'm saying is that nothing is as it seems, ever. We get so busy being fixated on one thing that we fail to consider another."

"It was Cam's fault."

"Didn't you blame yourself at first?"

"Yes," he mutters.

"Then you found out Mr Faraday knew about the sketch of Bodecker in your file and you blamed him."

"Why are you taking Cam's side?"

"To get you to see that there is more to see – just like Mrs Landers. She blames herself and what has she got to do with it? But she sees everything, all at the same time. She never said Mr Faraday should have seen it, and I believe if he should have seen it Mrs Landers would have said so."

"Emmaline, you're crazy. You want folks to think you're half-baked?"

"Mrs Landers was right about you and Jennifer. She could very well be right about this."

"Does Cliff know you take Mrs Landers seriously?"

"You mean does Cliff know I'm half-baked?"

He bursts out laughing. When he's finished, he sits there, his eyes dancing, wrestling a grin off his face.

"I'm not half-baked," she retaliates. "I have an open mind, something you could do well to cultivate yourself."

"Well, Emmaline," he says, "I'll think about it."

"Good. Now don't forget what we talked about before."

"Jennifer," he murmurs.

She gets to her feet. "Any time of the day or evening."

"Emmaline, how do I know you're not going off to snoop around on your own?"

She sits down again. "I'll show you and Jennifer everything I write, I swear on the great name of Pendleton…"

"Great name of *who*?"

"Whom. And I won't snoop around. This is a Tribune story and I value my neck too highly to compromise Mr Quaid's scoop. Have a nice day."

She picks up her satchel and scampers out of there. Yes, he's a tough nut to crack but she thinks she might have done it.

Luke

The tall woman with the scratchy voice opens the Faraday's door. It's been a while but she's not someone you forget in hurry.

"Mornin'," she says. "Welcome back."

"Good to see you again."

"Constance McConnell."

"Luke Taylor."

"Yep, I remember yer name."

"I'm calling for Jennifer."

"Ah, the pretty one with the fancy voice, gorgeous green eyes and hair the shade of a dark chestnut filly."

"That's the one."

"Ya know, young feller, I'm under strict instructions from Mrs Faraday that when ya call I'm to see to it ya come in and sit in the parlor."

"If it's all the same to you, I'll wait right here."

"Where I come from, when a gentleman comes a-callin' on a young lady, he comes in and sits a spell, polite an' all."

"I got my reasons."

"Have ya now."

"Is Jennifer up and about yet, Ma'am?"

She grunts. "I'll check. Stubborn, ain't ya? Mrs Faraday warned me."

He turns away and Constance McConnell leaves him in peace while mumbling something about how manners seem to have gone the way of the dinosaurs.

Meg appears several moments later and with her a memory of

a happier time: the first occasion he saw her, on Jennifer's backdoor step, with her bright cherry brown eyes and perky dark curls.

"Howdy, Meg," he says and clears his throat.

"Do have any idea how happy Jen is this morning?" she says gently. "I so want to give you a hug."

He twirls his hat in his hands. "It's good to see you again."

"You look fine. Very fine. Not at all sick like Cam said."

Her stomach, swollen with Faraday junior, reminds him of what he has to look forward to.

"You look very fine yourself, Mrs Faraday."

Her smile sparkles as she takes his hand and leads him inside, and when she closes the door, all sorts of ghosts fly about him.

"It's not so bad, is it?" she says.

"If it's all the same to you, I'll wait right here."

"Whatever you might think, we still love you, you know," she says as she walks into the parlor. Constance's pointed lecture on manners seems to be getting to him and he follows her.

"I've told Jen that I am here to help. Anything you need doing, I will see to it. Well, actually, Constance will probably see to it because I'm allowed to do nothing."

"Is that dissent I hear from you, Mrs Faraday?"

"In bucket loads. But enough about that. I want to shower you with my congratulations."

"Thanks."

"And Cam will, too, when you see him next."

"Oh?" He tugs on his tie. "What did he say?"

"Well, he hugged Jen. That was all. He was smiling, then he left for work, quickly. Jen thought he might be on the verge of tears. Personally, I think he was smug about knowing before Frank. Are you going to sit down?"

"No, I..."

But Constance interrupts, abruptly marching in with a tray. "Coffee and cake, as ordered." She puts the tray on the table, saying, "Ya can't have cake 'til after supper, Mrs Faraday."

"Why?" Meg gasps.

"Still want a figure after the baby's born, don't ya?"

"I'll see about Mrs Faraday," he cuts in.

Constance gives him a steely look. "Ya look like the type who'd spoil a woman with child. Mr Faraday knows what's best for his wife. I carry out his wishes. Cake after supper. Small piece."

"Aye, aye, Captain," he says.

Constance is rolling her eyes as she leaves and runs into Jennifer at the door.

"Ah, Miss Chestnut, yer boy is here. Watch him with that cake. He's a soft touch with Mrs Faraday."

He can hear Meg expelling indignant grunts as Jennifer comes towards him, her face so radiant it almost stops his heart.

"You came back," she teases him.

He catches her in his arms and looks into her eyes. "I promised I would."

"Jen, may I please eat a piece of cake?"

Her eyes sparkle back at him. "Eat whatever you want, Meg. By the time you've nursed that babe for six months you'll be skinny as a rake."

"Oh, Jen, you are an angel. Do you two want any? No? Don't mind me then... Oh, this is so good... I don't know why Constance makes cakes at all if all she intends to do is torture me."

Kissing Jennifer is his only goal. There wouldn't be a cake in the world capable of distracting him. Meg goes a long way away.

Later, they notice Meg is not in the room. Neither is the cake.

"Think we scared her off?" he suggests.

"No, Meg is preoccupied. I need to have a quiet word with Cam about her."

"Is he doing something wrong?"

"Very soon she'll have an infant on her hands and her life will no longer be her own. He should be spoiling her, not marshaling her."

"I thought having a baby is supposed to make you happy."

"Don't worry," she murmurs, kissing his lips softly. "It will..."

"I'm happy now," he tells her.

"You're a softy. I heard Constance say you're the type to spoil a woman with child."

"Will you let me?"

"Gracious, yes, after all you've put me through."

Constance appears. "Where's the cake?"

"I have no idea," Jennifer says. "Constance?"

"Something on yer mind, Miss Chestnut?"

"Will you tell Mr Faraday whenever you next see him that I want a word with him this evening?"

"Sure thing, Doc Sullivan."

When Constance is gone, his bride-to-be says, "I've been thinking. We need a place to live. And, well, I have a place."

"Ah, I know that place...."

"It's private and still furnished – everything's under dust covers, all my medical things are in crates back in St Louis, but the residence is perfect for us, except it's my house and your memories... of course, if it takes you back to a time that... I understand." Her voice dies away as she dismisses her own idea.

"I want to live there. With you," he says.

"You do? And you don't mind it being *my* house?"

"Ah. You being a woman an' all. I thought you accepted my point that we would live where we needed to so you could be the best doctor you can be."

"I...yes, I accepted it."

"There you have it."

"Our Cheyenne home?"

"My heart never really left it."

"I miss it," she murmurs. "And you in it."

"You did good there," he says. "Tell me something... about Duffy. Where is she?"

"Didn't you know? Duffy is still here."

"No. Why didn't she come see me?"

"She doesn't read the papers very often and she went to live with her Irish friend, Kathleen Quinn, who moved into a homestead out of town. You remember Kathleen."

"You don't forget a woman who sews your long johns into short johns..."

She starts giggling. "Fond memories?"

"Why not?" he grins.

"Well, anyway," she says, clearing the giggles from her throat, "we should definitely pay Duffy a visit."

"She waited for you to come back, didn't she?"

"She believed in us."

"I've missed her. Shame she didn't come and look after Meg."

"Oh, yes! So, what have you been up to this morning?"

"Sent my mother a telegram first thing."

"I need to send one to Frank and Jeanne."

"Sure. But I don't want you traipsing all over town…"

"Don't worry, I won't."

"There's something else…"

"A whole twelve hours have passed since I've seen you; I'd be surprised if there wasn't."

He explains his meeting with Emmaline.

She stares at him, speechless.

"Say something."

"This Emmaline must consider you a true friend."

"She's a friend to us both. And she knows what could happen to your reputation, as do I, if rumors start and get out of hand. I believe she can stop that from happening. Jennifer, I know this is going to make things tricky and if this ain't how you want our weddin' to be, if you want to call it off until after the trial and get married someplace else, like St Louis…"

"I said to you once that I'd rather be accountable for my behavior than constantly looking for excuses for everything I did or for what happened to me."

"I remember." She was suturing his hand… a lifetime ago.

"This is not being accountable. Our love affair in Cheyenne last year and again in San Francisco has had far reaching repercussions. And I would take the consequences…"

He swallows hard, finding it difficult to remain calm.

"Here me out," she says softly. "I would take what's coming to me, except that there is more at stake than just you and me. There's the distress a scandal would cause for our family and friends. And there's…there's…"

The tiny prospect. The expression in her eyes melts his heart.

"What kind of parents bring a child into a world of deceit?"

"I don't know what kind of father I'll be," he says. "I only know I love you both so much and want to protect you."

"Luke," she whispers, "he's so tiny, so new and unexpected, and you love him?"

He shrugs, hoping to diffuse some of the emotion.

Neither of them speaks for a long while.

A rim of unshed tears appears in her eyes. "I've just learnt something about you," she whispers. "I… what I really mean is that I'd forgotten for a moment why you do things and you just reminded me… When I stop trusting that, that's when I get into trouble."

He's not sure what she's talking about, but it sounds like she's coming around to his way of thinking.

"Think of a reason for being back in town," he murmurs.

Just then, Meg re-enters the room. They turn their heads to follow her progress to the sofa. "Oh, you two are so sweet together. Jen, now I feel terrible eating the cake behind Cam's back."

With one eyebrow raised, Jennifer lifts her bright green gaze and meets his. "Don't fret, Meg. We'll fess up when he comes home and beg his eternal pardon for the sin of eating cake against his express wishes."

"What? Oh, Jen, it's *good* to have you back. I've missed you."

Cliff

Now there is less snow piled up on the roof, Wilma Young's dilapidated house on the edge of town looks sturdier than when he saw it last. Smoke drifts pleasantly from the chimney, which heartens him. He steps up to her door and is about to apply his knuckles to it when it's pulled wide; Wilma and her bright blue eyes greet him.

"Enemy of my cousin, well, ain't you a sight for sore eyes. Look at ya! Never thought I'd be seein' you again."

"Wilma," he says, with a wide grin, "good to see you."

She's beaming at him. "Now there's a smile to warm an old woman's heart. Well, come in, what're you standing there for…"

"I have a favor to ask you."

"Course you have. What are enemies for? Say, how's the young feller. The cute lookin' one…"

He chuckles. "He's doing okay, partly thanks to you."

"Aw, I did nothin'. Just give him some milk is all. Come in, I said. Don't stand there yappin' on my doorstep."

She stands back and waves him in.

"I hate imposing on you, Wilma," he says as he enters.

"You come here 'cause you can trust old Wilma."

She closes the door behind them. The interior hasn't improved, but the fire is burning strong.

He removes his hat. "You're right."

"Course I am. Though I got some sad news."

"Eliza Bensen?"

She nods. "Came down with pneumonia 'bout a week after you and the lad left. Doc Kincaid did what he could but she passed on, God rest her soul."

An acute twinge of sadness pinches him. "Wilma, I'm sorry…"

"I miss her, but, well, I reckon she's gone to a better place."

He agrees with a nod. But he should've done more.

A moment passes before either of them speaks.

"Folks got their pride, Cliff," she says.

Still…

"We gave Eliza a mighty fine send off. Mariah and Nell from the Nebraskee Bite paid for everythin'. Lotsa folks came. Buried her in the town cemetery; she's even got a genuine headstone with an angel. You should see it!"

He swallows and says, "I'm glad, Wilma."

"Yep. They're fine gals… So, can I get you somethin'?"

"No, thanks." Time to move on from Eliza's passing and his regrets to what's got to be done. "Wilma, did Sheriff Walker bother you at all since Luke and I've been gone?"

"Nope. Never see hide no' hair of that character. Stays clear of folks like me, unless I was disturbin' the peace or botherin' folks for handouts or somethin'. Don't do neither, so he don't have no call to come down on me."

"Mind if I leave my stuff here? I got work to do and I need a…"

"A place to hide out. Why didn't you just say so in the first place? You on the run again…? Hey, wait a minute, what's that on your coat? Deputy US marshal. You're a lawman?"

"I thought you knew that, Wilma."

"Nope. Never did. Thought you were helping a friend. You *were* helping a friend, weren't you?"

"Yes. Luke's a good friend."

"He was in such a state…" she murmurs, shaking her head from side to side. "How is he? Did I ask that already…?"

"What he is, Wilma, is an important witness, a key witness. I believe the man that harmed him is still in town. I need to find him and arrest him and take him back to Cheyenne with me."

She whistles softly. "Won't that cranky sheriff have somethin' to say about it?"

"I think he just might."

She waves her wrinkled hand around. "Heck, stay here as long as you like, Cliff. Ain't no skin off my nose. Be glad of the company. You look like a neat houseguest. I'm afraid the house ain't so neat though."

"The house is great." He digs into his pocket. "Let me know my board. Here's some in advance. Buy some food. And whatever else you need. Not too much though."

"I get it," she says and taps the side of her nose.

Jennifer

Cheyenne

Jennifer closes the door on noisy Eddy Street and lifts her glance to the Tribune's front desk. She recognizes the gentleman behind it, although he would never stoop so low as to be one of her patients.

"Doc Sullivan," he says, his eyes widening. "What a pleasant surprise."

"Good morning, Mr Simons." His sister was a different matter; Jennifer delivered her baby girl, a difficult labor that lasted most of one summer night. "I trust your sister and her family are in good health."

"They are indeed," he grins knowingly. "How can I help?"

"May I speak with Miss Emmaline Roberts?"

"Sure," he says off-handedly. He looks around. "She came back from an assignment a short time ago. Around the corner, near the window."

A pretty, well-groomed young woman, with dark blonde hair looks up from writing at her desk as Jennifer approaches.

So, this is the girl who stole Cliff's heart. Interesting…

"Miss Roberts?"

"Yes. Can I help you?"

"Jennifer Sullivan."

Miss Roberts' face becomes a parade of lively expressions. "Oh…oh, won't you please sit down."

Jennifer takes the chair by the desk. "I heard you were looking for me."

"I was… I mean I am."

"Good. Well, here I am."

"Then let me start by saying how very pleased I am to meet you at last."

A Southern accent? Very charming.

"I have heard a great deal about you, Miss Roberts. And I have managed to read some of your work since I got back into town. It's very good."

Miss Roberts thrusts a pencil behind her ear and relaxes in her chair. "Then you know what my job is here at the Tribune."

Jennifer holds the light brown gleam in the young woman's eyes. "I know."

Miss Roberts looks intense suddenly and leans forward. "I want you to know that you are not obliged to tell me the truth," she says in a hushed voice. "And that anything you don't want me to print you tell me is off the record."

"I understand."

"Good." The pencil is extracted from her ear and she reaches for a notebook. "So, why have you returned to Cheyenne, Dr Sullivan?"

"As you know, Meg Faraday is expecting a baby. I believe she needs my help and my company. This is her first baby and it can be a little daunting. Meg has no family here. She's from Boston, and although her mother is very likely planning to travel here nearer to the birth, I thought Meg could use a close friend."

Jennifer watches Miss Roberts jotting calmly as she speaks.

"And where have you been since you left?"

"In St Louis. With my brother and his family."

"Why did you leave Cheyenne? You had a flourishing practice here and that's no mean feat for a female in a man's profession."

"I hadn't seen my brother for some time. And I needed a vacation. Doctoring is a demanding occupation."

"You had a very long break, though. Several months in fact."

"I wasn't wasting my time, Miss Roberts. I undertook further study at a teaching hospital in St Louis. There is always some new surgical technique that needs to be learnt."

"That's interesting," Miss Roberts says. "So will you re-open while you are in town?"

"I haven't decided yet. Looking after Meg Faraday for a while is currently my intention. But I will be returning to my residence while I'm here."

Miss Roberts opens her mouth to ask yet another question when she stops, looks beyond Jennifer and then says, "Dr Sullivan, you remember Mr Quaid..."

Jennifer swivels in her chair to see Charlie Quaid making an entrance.

His jaw drops a fraction. "Dr Sullivan, how lovely..."

"Mr Quaid, always a pleasure..."

"Where's Taylor?" he says, looking around madly.

"I beg your pardon?"

"Luke Taylor. Where is he?"

Jennifer frowns. "I have no idea. He walked me here and then continued on with Meg Faraday. I think he was walking her to her husband's office."

Charlie Quaid looks utterly perplexed; he charges across the floor towards the door of the building, opens it, sticks his head out, evidently scouring the street for signs of Luke.

Miss Roberts shrugs as Jennifer exchanges glances with her.

The editor charges back. "What's going on?"

"Mr Quaid, perhaps you should explain yourself," Jennifer suggests.

"No...no," he says, flustered, "carry on, Roberts. No, wait. Why was Taylor walking you and Mrs Faraday?"

"Well, he found out I was in town, called by the Faraday's this morning where someone told him I was staying, and told me Miss Roberts was looking for me to do an interview on why I'd returned to Cheyenne. I must say I thought it very strange that my return was newsworthy, but I'm happy to talk to Miss Roberts. He advised me that she is a very scrupulous journalist."

"And why *have* you returned, Doctor?"

"To attend to Meg Faraday, in her confinement. Her house-keeper is a very efficient woman. I thought Meg could use some spoiling before she has an infant to care for."

Charlie Quaid grunts. "And Taylor walked you into town for what reason?"

"Meg wanted to see her husband and he offered to escort us. We did some catching up along the way."

"Everyone knows that Taylor is not on speaking terms with Cam Faraday."

"I always found Luke to be very courteous, so I suppose he thought it a necessary courtesy to pay a call on me as I did do a lot for him and the Alliance when they were in town last year. I appreciated his gesture. And he could hardly avoid Meg. I didn't perceive a problem between them."

Charlie Quaid is clearly not happy.

Meanwhile, Miss Roberts is shuffling papers. "May I get on with *my* interview, Mr Quaid?"

"In a minute, Roberts. So how did you find Taylor after all this time? Some say he's been through more than hard times since Miss Keaton was shot."

"I can imagine it must have been very difficult for him. They were very close, weren't they?"

"Heard they might have been engaged."

"Miss Keaton was a fine young woman and her death was a terrible shock," Jennifer says earnestly while thinking how easy it is for Charlie Quaid to walk the fine line between the requirements of his profession and common decency.

"Excuse me, Mr Quaid," says Miss Roberts, "I believe you gave *me* this assignment."

"So, how did you find him?" he persists rudely. "Apart from courteous."

"Off the record, sad but determined," Jennifer says, lifting the words directly from one of Miss Robert's articles. "You know, Mr Quaid, I won't be answering any more of your questions if you keep ignoring Miss Roberts this way. I know how demanding it is to work as a woman in a man's profession and I really don't approve of how you are treating her."

He blinks in surprise. "Oh. Yes. Very well. Good day, Doctor. Go ahead, Roberts." He leaves, mumbling under his breath.

"Sad but determined," Miss Roberts murmurs. "You *have* been reading my work."

"Interview over, Miss Roberts?" Jennifer asks.

"I think so."

"It's been interesting."

Miss Roberts smiles. "A great pleasure to have met you."

"Will you write anything?"

She shrugs as if she thinks the whole business extremely mundane. "Perhaps we'll meet again."

"Perhaps. I should be settled in my house within the next day or two. Please feel free to call by."

Miss Roberts grins. "I'd like to chat with you. Off the record."

Out in the street, Jennifer breathes a sigh. Miss Roberts is a peach, and Charlie Quaid a piece of old jerky. In spite of his hound-like tendencies, she feels confident that Miss Roberts has the situation within her control. So, with that hurdle behind her, she lifts, only to realize that a new hurdle looms up ahead...

By the time she reaches the door of the Keaton's rented house, she is exhausted. The tiny prospect is beginning to make his presence felt. For a long time she has counseled and attended to women in the same condition. Inside her head she can hear her own voice speaking to herself like she is one of her patients. *You must take time to rest.* Luke was right; she can't traipse all over town.

The door opens and thankfully Luke is on the other side of it. She goes straight into his strong arms; he boots the door shut and holds her tight. She melts into his warm embrace, while he whispers in her ear, "I got you..." And then, "How was Emmaline?"

"She's a good person. Loyal and true. And how did *you* fare?"

"The church is booked for next Thursday, that's a week from tomorrow. And I sent your telegram to Frank."

She acknowledges a distinctly peculiar reality in telling her family that she is to be married. Emotions swirl around inside her; thoughts and fears come and go. He smiles at her and gives her a tender kiss on the lips.

"So," he whispers. "The Keatons..."

"Jennifer?"

They turn their heads to find Tressa standing in the hall, smiling at them.

Cliff

There is still plenty of snow on the ground in Porterfield's street and the sun's reflection is bright and harsh. It's getting near lunchtime and there's still no sign of anyone in or around Porterfield's house.

A faint and familiar aroma drifts into his nostrils every so often. It could have seeped out of the walls over time and permeated the surroundings, or it could be a recently conjured odor being carried on the cool, wispy breeze.

So, either he eats lunch and gets warm, or he presses his instincts into action...

He ventures to the door of Porterfield's nearest neighbor and knocks on it. A middle-aged woman opens up to him.

"Afternoon, Ma'am. Cliff Ryan, Deputy US marshal."

"Good afternoon, Deputy Marshal." She looks put out as she views his badge. "What do you want?"

"Ma'am, I'm hoping you can tell me if the gentleman who lives in the house at the end of the street is at home."

"The scientist fellow?" she asks and frowns disapprovingly. "Are you here to remove him, because if you are the whole street would be ever so pleased."

"How so, Ma'am?"

"It's the smell, you see. And of course, he's ever so *strange*. It used to be such a pleasant house and a fine family used to live there before he moved in."

"Do you remember the name of the family who used to live there?"

"Ever so nice neighbors, they were. The Barretts. It's a while ago now since they moved out."

"Did the Barretts say why they were leaving?"

"From what I recall I think someone wanted to buy the house and offered them ever so much money. But Mr Barrett didn't want to sell up. He had a steady job and the children were doing well in school. Then he lost his job in town, although I was never quite sure why. Don't think they said. Not long after that, they moved out and the scientist moved in. Such a sad day. A real fine family that one. And now we're stuck with that weirdie."

"Have you seen him recently?"

"How recent?"

"Yesterday, today…?"

"There was some trouble about a month ago. Some strange goings on in the house. My husband reported it to the sheriff, but by the time that sheriff got around to paying a call everything went quiet down there. The smell stopped, too. Then a few days ago, I noticed the smell back again. He's a sneaky fellow. You have to be lucky to see him. Be looking out your window at the right time. Be shoveling snow at the right time. Know what I mean? I told my husband I figure he waits till there's no one around so he can sneak about. What's he do in there anyway?"

"So, he's home then?"

"I believe he is," she says, studying him with a frown. "The children two doors up like to play knock and run on his door. What are you going to do, Deputy Marshal?"

"Well, I'm going to knock on his door."

She gives a nod of approval. "Anything I can do?"

"No, you've been very helpful. Just close your door. Stay inside. Thank you, Ma'am."

With the woman secured back in her home, he marches on Porterfield's house. But he doesn't knock. He knows from experience that Porterfield has the place locked up like a fort. All the drapes and blinds are closed. All the windows and doors locked. Including the front door; Porterfield clearly isn't making that mistake twice.

He makes his way around to the side entrance, to the door that opens directly into the laboratory. He puts his ear to it, can't hear anything, but notices the smell is stronger. He takes a deep breath and with all his strength kicks at the door. The first kick dislodges the lock; the second thrust breaks it; the third busts the door open.

And there it is, Porterfield's lab, laid bare; at the sight of it a familiar disgust washes over him. It's operational, but there are small packing boxes everywhere, hovering in the gloom, being revealed one by one as the stream of daylight penetrates.

He steps inside and looks around.

Behold Porterfield, cowering in a corner, pistol in hand, his aim shaky but otherwise accurate.

"You!" he exclaims. "What do you want?"

"You, of course. I came back for you, Porterfield."

Porterfield looks set to fire his weapon; Cliff slams the door shut and ducks behind a table just as the pistol explodes.

Cliff steadies his breathing. "Are you sure you should be firing that thing with all these chemicals around?"

"Get out!" Porterfield screeches. "I'm going to kill you."

In the renewed gloom, Cliff skulks around the furniture. "This place must be worth a lot of money to you that you'd risk coming back for it."

"I read in the papers what you did to Donnelly," Porterfield says.

Cliff doesn't respond. He begins his approach.

Porterfield moves out of his corner. Cliff follows him. As soon as Porterfield's back is to him, Cliff jumps him. They struggle while Cliff slams Porterfield's hand repeatedly on the floor until he cries out in pain and releases the pistol. Cliff sweeps the weapon out of reach. He pulls Porterfield's arms behind his back and manacles his wrists. Then he drags Porterfield to his feet. He whips out his Colt and holds Porterfield at the point of it while he catches his breath and Porterfield stops his moaning.

"You're under arrest, Porterfield, for attempted murder."

"What! Are you crazy, Ryan?"

"No. But a lot of people think *you* are. Maybe it could be your defense." Cliff gives him a shove. "Now, let's go. Move."

Porterfield refuses. "My laboratory…"

"I'm supposed to feel sorry for you? What you do here – did here – disgusts me in every way imaginable. Now get moving."

Porterfield finally does as he's told. "Where are we going?"

"To see the sheriff." Cliff picks up Porterfield's pistol and pockets it.

"Walker?" Porterfield squawks.

"This town elected a new sheriff since I've been gone? Of course, Walker. Got a problem with that?"

Porterfield goes quiet, walking almost politely through the door and out into the startling sunshine. "No."

Sonofabitch.

Luke

Secrets suit Jennifer. They make her self-contained disposition intriguing and her bursts of spiritedness dazzling. This particular secret she carries does all this and more. Those first awkward moments with John and Amy, when everyone is going out of their way to appear warm and friendly, are carried by the graceful way she has with people; he's seen her handle patients with the same thoughtful and kind objectivity that is peculiar to doctors. He knows how nervous she was about facing them; this is how she decided to handle it. The success of this approach gives her confidence; everyone relaxes.

If nothing else, the Alliance loves a good strategy. Over lunch they tackle the latest: to hold a weddin' without the newspapers getting wind of it and destroying their privacy.

Hopefully, someday soon they won't need strategies. But for now this particular caper gives people who are accustomed to being active something to do.

He reflects on the strategies he and Mart once concocted for dealing with Ed Parsons – how naïve they were. When Mart's predicament worsened, that naivety was swept away by the fight for survival, a fight with a relentless nature. And nothing will change until the day Donnelly and Bodecker are convicted and imprisoned, and these dark and difficult days are a memory.

Jennifer begins to tire. She's strong, but this intense afternoon is the culmination of a long journey from St Louis, an emotional evening sorting out a melancholy ne'er do well, and a busy stretch foiling Charlie Quaid. He reminds her that she is expected at the

Faradays' and fetches her coat. He holds it for her and she threads her arms into it; she says her goodbyes.

"When will I see you?" she asks as he's walking her home to Meg's.

"Well, you never know when we could run into each other…"

Her soft-red lips curve into a knowing smile.

"…but other than that, definitely tomorrow morning at your house. You can help me get it shipshape."

"I can help *you*?"

"Mm," he says. "And then we'll take a trip to Kathleen Quinn's place and tell Duffy what's going on."

"They live way out of town – I don't think you can go."

"Oh. I forgot about that. Then *you* can take a trip to Kathleen's place and tell Duffy what's going on."

"Soon. There's plenty of time."

A buggy appears alongside them. "Take you someplace, Doc Sullivan?"

"Oh, Mr Aiken…"

"Call me Clive, Doc."

"Oh. Certainly. Clive, I was hoping to run into you. I may need you for some errands over the coming week. Luke, you remember Clive Aiken. His wife, Rebecca, and little daughter, Maisie, were my patients last year."

"I recall. Good to see you again, Clive. How's the family?"

"All doin' as well as can be. Fine seein' you again, Luke. Good to have the Alliance back in town."

"Much obliged, Clive. Good to be back."

"See you and the Doc have been doin' some catchin' up. And I'd be happy to help with those errands, Doc." He gives a wink. "Nothin' is too much trouble for Doc Sullivan."

Nothing.

Cliff

"You got some nerve, Ryan."

Cliff turns the key in the lock of Porterfield's cell and removes it, the whole set on the saucer-sized key ring clinking as he does so. After giving the door a good shake, he glares into Porterfield's stricken face and holds it until the scientist gulps and looks away.

"You hear me, Ryan?"

"I hear you, Walker," Cliff says as he watches Porterfield sink down onto his cot. Then he turns to Walker and glares at him instead. "I have a pretty clear idea of what you've been up to, Walker, and if you get any ideas about trying to thwart my plans to take Porterfield back, if you get in my way, I swear I will hound your butt until it's sitting on a cot just like that one in the state pen. Got it?"

Walker scowls back until his eyes begin to water. "Where do you get off, Ryan...?"

"How much do you get paid for running interference on Porterfield's operation? Because it's not just *his* operation, is it? It belongs to Loren Bodecker..."

Walker's face goes white. "You better not try sweeping me into that pile of shit, Ryan."

"Oh, I'll do more than try if you interfere. Just how deep you're into this muck, Walker, I can't even hazard a guess."

"I'm warning you, Ryan..."

"It's simple, Walker. I have a warrant for the scientist and you are going to co-operate."

"You can't prove a thing."

"Maybe. Maybe not. I've spoken to the people you've sworn to serve and protect. They don't like the job you're doing. And they don't like the scientist. You interfere and in actual fact I won't have to do much of anything. Democracy will have the last word. And I have a feeling you have an aversion to losing."

Walker's face sags and he suddenly looks old.

"Now, I have some business to conduct out at Porterfield's house. I need a deputy to help out. In the meantime, Porterfield stays locked up – and healthy."

Walker grits his teeth. "I'm gonna haunt you to the ends of the earth for this, Ryan. You're gonna be looking over your shoulder till kingdom come."

"And one more thing, Walker. The family that used to live in Porterfield's house – the Barretts. Start locating them. Tell them their house will be vacant in a couple of weeks."

"The Barretts? They got..." Walker stops.

"They got what? Blackmailed? Extorted? Threatened to within an inch of their lives? The Barretts are probably lucky to be alive, considering they were unlucky enough to own the house most suitable for Porterfield's operations. The perfect place. North Platte. Central to Omaha, Denver and Cheyenne. Find the Barretts, understand? And have the house cleaned before they move back in."

Walker nods, his face downcast and ashen.

Cliff gives him a scathing look. "Where's my deputy?"

"You can have Nelson," Walker says. "He's cleaning rifles out front."

"He's not the one who got bashed is he?"

"No," Walker says as they make their way out of the lockup. "He resigned and left town."

"I wonder why."

Emmaline

"Roberts!"

Emmaline jumps and looks up. "Yes, Mr Quaid?"

"What are you working on?"

Having her boss bark at her when she least expects it has become a part of her daily routine. Even so, Mr Quaid looks more peeved than usual.

"My story."

"Did you go down to Dillon Kerr's office today?"

"Yes. After lunch. His assistant said he'd left town for a day or two."

"And?"

"And he wouldn't tell me where and neither would the ticket clerk at the depot..."

Mr Quaid thrusts out his hand. "Show me your copy."

Emmaline shuffles through some papers. "As you can imagine, it's not very..."

"No excuses, Roberts."

She finds the piece, such as it is, and hands it to him. He reads it and grunts, then hands it back.

"Abysmal. Someone knows where he went. Find out. *Whatever it takes!*"

"Whatever it takes?" she gulps.

"That's what I said. So, where's the copy on Jennifer Sullivan?"

"I haven't written anything on her. I..."

"What?" he explodes. "What did I tell you?"

"Mr Quaid, with all due respect, the woman came to town to

see her friend. I hardly think that is newsworthy. Simons' mother-in-law came into town last week and we never printed that."

"Roberts!" he yells. "You write up your interview with Jennifer Sullivan and have it on my desk before you go home. Is that clear?"

"Actually, I'm deaf," she says through gritted teeth. "Could you say it louder? I didn't quite hear you."

She puts her head down and pretends to write something. From the corner of her eye she can see him blustering and dithering. Finally, he storms off.

"You'll get it at the end of the week if you're lucky," she mumbles under her breath.

Barely three minutes later he's back. He dumps several sheets of paper in front of her; they are filled with his uneven handwriting.

"This is the background information as we discussed earlier."

She runs her gaze over the words and gets the gist of it.

Although somewhat vague, relatively speaking, here is the beginning of a good old-fashioned scandal and she wants nothing to do with it. She measures her anger and looks up.

"Somehow I think my interview with Dr Sullivan would look very stupid and insipid as the denouement to this! In fact, I think the whole thing is stupid."

"I know you like these people, Roberts. Taylor and his Alliance buddies. You wouldn't be trying to cover for them, would you?"

She reaches for her satchel, gets to her feet and starts tossing in her papers and pencils.

"What are you doing?" he asks.

"If you are insisting that I write such complete and utter garbage, I'll have to leave. I don't write nonsense, Mr Quaid. I thought we understood that. I'm a serious journalist, not a gossip columnist, and frankly I'm shocked and disappointed in you. You always impressed me as a man for whom news is…"

"Oh, lighten up, Roberts," he declares. "And stop packing. You know very well you can't leave in the middle of the biggest story of the year!"

"I could change newspapers."

"Huh! You're loyal to a fault, Roberts. You'd never sell out the Alliance to the Bugle, which is what you'd be doing."

"Who said anything about the Bugle? There are other publications in town that would be glad of a decisive boost in circulation."

"Roberts, sit down!"

She ignores him. "If you want to turn the Tribune into a scandal sheet that is your business, but I will not make it mine."

Mr Quaid blows a huge sigh and strings his fingers through his hair so many times it hangs limp around his ears.

"What is it with you and these people?" he mutters.

"I don't write gossip. I write factual accounts that mean something."

"I repeat," he says in a low voice, "what is it with you and these people?"

"You've been reading my stories all this time and it has never crossed your mind even for one minute how fighting alongside them has affected me? You put me in the middle of their war, Mr Quaid, and I'm lucky to be alive. Am I supposed to remain cold and untouched by what's happened to them? What happened to me? This is reality. Real life. What you want me to do is to trivialize and hurt people who not only don't deserve it but who are busy with the reality of surviving. You want to degrade that by publishing silly stories about matters of which you have no real knowledge, you only think *might* have an element of truth in them."

He walks towards her, his eyes slotted and glittering. "Let me tell you something, young lady, I've been in this business as long as you are old. You can't tell me anything I don't know."

She finishes her packing while he's talking and then leaves her day's copy on the desk. "Bully for you."

"I'm warning you, Roberts."

She loops the long handle of her satchel around her neck and settles the fat weight of it on her hip.

"We have a contract," he says.

"Perhaps you don't know, Mr Quaid, but I am very familiar with contract law. My contract with the Tribune states that I am to investigate and report on the official investigation into Miss Keaton's murder. I've done that. I will be able to prove in any court of law that since I have fulfilled the conditions of my contract

307

anything else you ask me to do which is not relevant to said contract is not part of it. I believe our contract has expired."

His face falls. "That's my story you have in that bag, Roberts."

"Fine, have it," she says and starts unloading harmless pieces of copy from her satchel.

"Roberts, you have got to learn to be objective and impartial!"

"I told you. I nearly died – twice! And that was just the beginning."

"Roberts…"

"You might have noticed that my inability to meet your objective and impartial requirements has given the story a certain highly desirable quality which would regrettably be amiss from the work of a writer who had not experienced what I have experienced! You put me on this beat, so you either like it or lump it!"

Mr Quaid glares at her for some time. She holds on, barely breathing. Then he throws up his hands and every nerve in her body jumps.

"You're right," he announces. "Damn you, you're absolutely right."

"Thank you," she mutters, "but I'm not writing the…"

"I heard you."

"May I return to my work?"

"Yes. I'll…er.. I'll spike the Sullivan story – for now."

"Very well."

Mr Quaid gives her one last stare before he retreats down the hall and into his office. His door closes with a decided thud.

She clamps her hand on her chest and tells herself to breathe. Then, more collected, she sheepishly looks around her. The staff is standing about grinning at her. All at once they break into applause. The cub puts a steaming cup of coffee on her desk and winks cheekily. The applause dies away as one by one they go back to their work, grinning from ear to ear.

Then she exhales a deep breath and sinks into her chair.

Cliff

"I ain't so much a deputy as Sheriff Walker's gofer," Nelson tells him as they stride down Front Street. At barely nineteen, the kid is eagerly learning from Walker what he ought not to be learning.

"Did you take an oath to uphold the law?" Cliff asks him, spying their destination up ahead.

"Sure I did."

"I expect you to conduct yourself like a lawman."

"Yes, sir. I can shoot real good."

"We're serving the Court on this assignment, Deputy."

"What does serving the Court mean, Mr Ryan?"

"It means you won't be required to shoot."

Cliff halts.

Nelson pulls up a second later. "I can read and write as well."

"Good…" Cliff examines the sign writing on the store window.

Bernard W. Brown,
Photographer
No occasion too big or too small!

"This kind of shooting excepted," Cliff says, smiling at the kid.

Nelson frowns. "Yes, sir."

Cliff arranges for Bernard Brown and his assistant to meet at Porterfield's house in one hour. Then Cliff marches Nelson across town to the house itself. Nelson starts whining as soon as they enter.

"Pee – yew!"

"Don't touch anything. Get out that notebook and pencil I gave you and write what I tell you."

"Yes, Deputy Marshal." Nelson fumbles for his equipment and stands poised to begin. "I might need help with my spelling…"

Cliff dictates that, under warrant, he kicked in the door of the laboratory and found Porterfield, equipment and boxes; Porterfield pulled a pistol and threatened to shoot him; he apprehended Porterfield and put him in the lockup; Sheriff Walker is co-operating and has loaned him Nelson; they hired a photographer; they intend to search the house and the laboratory and document everything they find. Spelling challenges are surmounted.

"Hard to see in here, Deputy Marshal."

"I know. The lamps are almost burnt out. Brown will probably bring his own magnesium flashlamps for his photographs. So, now we go room to room until Brown arrives."

Nothing much has changed since the day he found Luke. Even the room Luke slept in smells the same. The bedclothes are roughly piled up on the mattress, but the odor is unmistakable.

"Pee – yew! What died and went to hell in here?"

"No one. By the grace of God."

Cliff has a plan for this sad old house, as soon as Brown has finished photographing it. A simple one, but one long overdue.

Brown arrives on time. He's a professional gentleman in his middle thirties. His younger assistant, John Frasier, is loaded up with lamps and plates, camera and tripod.

Cliff takes him to the laboratory.

"Can you shoot in this light, Mr Brown?"

"As I understand it, you want to keep things exactly as you found them. I brought flashlamps, but if you want plenty of detail, I can try a longer exposure and it would help if we could open the shutters on those windows."

"I'm on it," says Nelson.

Cliff helps him with the stiff shutter hinges.

Light pours in, flowing over the benches and the equipment and across the floor. Cliff looks around, mesmerized, squinting against the glare.

Even Nelson seems flabbergasted. "Look at all this stuff..."

"Don't touch it."

"I know. There you go, Mr Brown."

"Let's hope there's nothing too flammable in here..." Brown says.

"It'll be fine," Cliff tells him.

Brown and Frasier spend several minutes setting up each time Cliff requests a different aspect of the laboratory photographed.

"This is probably the last," Brown says. "You know, Deputy Marshal, I always wondered what went on in this house." Brown disappears under his black veil to line up his picture. He reappears and says, "This is it."

Sensitive now to the explosive flash, they shield their eyes.

"Where to next?"

The kitchen.

The downstairs bathroom.

The storeroom.

Then the bedroom where Luke slept.

"I only have three plates left," Brown announces. "John can run back into town if you want more..."

"There's only one other place. It is pitch black without the doors open, but if you could try..."

Brown nods. "This is a real eye-opener, Deputy Marshal."

"Yep." Cliff leads the way downstairs.

"And it won't come cheap."

"I am not after souvenirs, Mr Brown."

"I don't recall this ever being done before, Deputy Marshal. I don't get why you need it."

"To convince a judge."

Into the cellar...

"Oh, my God..." Brown stands and gapes.

Frasier covers his nose with a hastily procured handkerchief.

"Pee – yew!"

"Thank you, Nelson. Let's not stand around. I've already seen enough of this place to last a lifetime." Cliff lights a fourth lamp. "Well, Mr Brown? What do you think?"

"I'll take two in this light with the flashlamps and then I want those basement doors opened for the last."

"Good. I'll work on the doors in the meantime."

"Exactly what do you want me to picture here, Deputy Marshal?"

"The area around the cot ideally. One from up here looking down on it. Another one closer."

"You want me to get close to that thing?"

Cliff looks him in the eye. "I knew a photographer in Chicago, my hometown. He took photographs of the battlefields during and after the War. There are some things that shouldn't be forgot."

Brown's hairline shifts backwards about an inch. "I've seen such photographs."

Frasier says, "You'll get your picture, Deputy Marshal."

Cliff heads out into the afternoon cold to work on the basement doors. He digs out residual snow from the hinges, and yells a warning to the others inside to stand back. They call out that they're ready; he takes aim and shoots the rusted padlock. And again. The busted padlock flies, while the reports throb across the neighborhood in chilling waves.

He waits for Brown to tell him that he's finished taking the first two photographs. As he's tugging the solid basement doors into submission, Nelson joins him and lends his wiry strength to the effort. Soon the basement is open to the outside world for the first time in a very long time. The putrid miasma pours out of that black abyss like a fume.

"Feels like we're lettin' loose a new sickness out into the world," Nelson says. "Or maybe settin' the old house free of it."

"Write that down, Nelson," Cliff tells him, panting, impressed with the kid's insight.

Nelson retrieves his notebook and starts scribbling.

Cliff grins. "And credit your name."

Nelson nods.

The photograph is taken.

Brown and Frasier pack up and leave, telling Cliff to check in tomorrow afternoon on the progress of the photographs.

As Nelson helps close up the basement, he says, "Now what?"

"Light's starting to fade. You can go. That was a good afternoon's work, Deputy."

"You want my help tomorrow?"

"There's a lot of stuff in the laboratory and the house we need to box up and put on a train back to Cheyenne. You up for it?"

"Sure. I'll be here."

They shake hands, much to Nelson's surprise and delight.

"I'll have the notebook, Nelson."

The kid hands it over.

"And Nelson?"

"Yes, Deputy Marshal?"

"You are under no obligation to tell Sheriff Walker what we did here today. None. If he pushes it, you tell him I told you he's to ask me. Clear?"

"Yes, Deputy Marshal."

In the soft fading light of what was a bright day, Cliff goes from room to room and opens every drape and every shutter he can find. The Barretts' house fills itself up with the pearly light of dusk and the promise of starlight.

He secures the house as best he can and heads back to Wilma's. He stops along the way to reassure a gathering of concerned neighbors that everything is fine, but it's not safe yet to enter the property, and that he will return tomorrow.

Luke

Luke returns to the Keatons' house around suppertime. Although Jennifer wanted him at the Faradays' for supper, this is where he needs to be tonight. Through the back door windowpane and beneath the folds of its filmy drape he spies Amy preparing supper, her familiar enthusiasm for the task comforting, and John seated at the table reading the Bugle, an indignant look on his face.

He knocks politely and enters. Their faces light up. He can't ever remember a day when those faces didn't light up when they saw him. As a boy it took him a long time to understand why they liked him; he always thought he had Mart to thank for it, until it became apparent that it didn't matter if he was with Mart or by himself they always had time for him.

John folds the newspaper, saying, "Pull up a chair."

Amy asks, "More potatoes then?"

"You don't mind?"

"As if you need to ask," she says and starts peeling.

"So," John says, "what brings you back?"

"I wanted to thank you."

John folds his arms. "For what?"

"You know what."

It might be easier if John's Keaton-blue eyes didn't remind him so much of K's. But he doesn't want it easy; he wants them to make it as hard as they feel necessary. He holds John's gaze for a long minute, wishing K would walk through the door.

Amy stops peeling and sits down next to John. "We just want to know what happened."

"With K and me?"

She nods; she and John swap glances as if they're preparing for some more terrible news.

Luke swallows hard. "I'll start at the very beginning."

"Good idea, son."

"I noticed her, soon as she got home that first time from New York. She was real pretty. Had loads of spirit. I knew I had feelings for her but I needed to know if she felt the same. She told me in no uncertain terms to back off. She didn't want me. And considering our past, it wasn't unexpected. Before I could think of or do anything else, she took off back to New York. And then we went looking for Mart. We spent some long, hard, cold hours in the saddle, John. Long thinking hours. I began to understand what had taken place. She always hated me, but I never hated her. My feelings came from that place, but hers came from the other direction. It was harder for her. I realized I loved her but I wasn't in love with her. I was just getting past our childhood and moving along.

"By the time we brought Mart's body back to Cheyenne, I think K had begun to work out her feelings. But there was still some bitterness between us. Possibly we could have resolved it and at least try being friends, but we were grief-stricken over Mart. And then I met Jennifer. At that very time. I looked at her and the pain over Mart seemed to go someplace far away. I fell so hard for *her* that K, for all her beauty and spirit, never had a chance. I tried to make it go away. Tried until I thought I had successfully convinced myself that I dreamed Jennifer up in some grief-stricken stupor, but knowing how I *should* have felt about K only made it harder for her to be the woman she needed to be.

"Tressa returned from Omaha; I met her here in Cheyenne and with Adam on the way she needed a doctor. I trusted Jennifer so she became Tressa's doctor. And I knew I hadn't convinced myself of anything regarding Jennifer. I never told Jennifer how I felt about her because how could anything ever happen between us; I mean, look at who she is and look at who I am, so there was no use harboring a false hope. Tressa and I came home. Again, I tried to put Jennifer out of my mind.

"Then Sara and you both wanted an arrangement between K and me. I rejected the idea at first because I didn't trust K. She knew that. She knew I thought she wanted me to take her to Cheyenne to get justice for Mart. It *is* what she wanted, but she did have feelings for me. She wanted us to be partners for Mart's cause and she wanted more with me, but she didn't know how to get it. When I finally saw that she was sincere we made a pact between ourselves, an alliance of own. *Our* Alliance, John, the one between you and Mart, Ethan and me, she despised, and the hatred for it went deep. She resented me for it. But we made our personal alliance, on the strength of her feelings for me and what you and Sara wanted. I told her I would never break it – no matter what, I would always be true to it. I swore I would protect her with my life.

His voice cracks; he clears his throat and sits up a little straighter in his chair.

"So, then... when I explained to her that I was going back to Cheyenne to get Wilson Cutter, she got angry. She wanted me to take her and I refused. It wasn't what the Alliance wanted, I told her. She didn't care about the Alliance, and she threw the alliance, the understanding, between us back in my face. She broke it there and then. I begged her to wait, be patient until I got back and she told me she would never *ever* wait. That was the end. I was angry with her because at our very first test, she didn't live up to our agreement. I know it's my fault, too; I would never blame her entirely. Our past still haunted her. We never trusted one another the way two people should.

"In Cheyenne, Jennifer saved my leg after Wilson Cutter almost shot it to pieces. A strange thing happened to me with her. I felt safe with her. I didn't know if it was right or not, but it deepened how I felt about her. She cared for me in a very professional manner, but nothing could stop how I felt about her. I was drawn to her more than ever. We became good friends. And we helped one another. She became involved with Alliance business – she captured Wilson Cutter – and I needed to protect her from Ed Parsons' murderous intentions. Still, it seemed to me that she looked after me more.

"I kept my alliance with K. I kept Jennifer as a friend. K came to Cheyenne with Edith. I began to feel the weight of Ed Parsons' trial and balancing my feelings for two women. K still hotly rejected the Alliance and our heart's alliance, but started to prove herself to me. She began to realize that I wasn't as worthless as she thought. I was torn between them. I knew what you and Sara wanted. But I deeply loved Jennifer. But by the time K and I had sorted our feelings and come to some understanding, which was on that very day Dan Hummer tried to extradite Wilson Cutter to Denver, I was already involved with Jennifer.

"She'd been hiding her feelings for me as well. I was with her one day, helping her with a patient, and it slipped out how I felt about her. She wanted to know where I stood with K and I told her that I knew for sure that K didn't want me. As soon as I surrendered to my feelings for Jennifer, life seemed a lot easier to handle. I guess that's what love should do. Lift you up.

"When we found Mart's journal that was a hard time. K was so upset I thought I'd have to give up Jennifer to make it right for K, but I couldn't turn my back on Jennifer. She has harsh things in her past, within her family, and she needed me. As hard as it is to say it and for you to hear it, K and I never loved each other the way you wanted us to. I loved Jennifer. K loved her independence. She rejected me more times than I can count and it got to the point where I was always going to choose Jennifer, even if Jennifer and I weren't going to last. You see, I'd learned how it should be. K thanked me for making such a gallant effort and then told me only the very deepest love can survive the kind of life we lead. She had her own wisdom about the outcome which I appreciated. She planned to return to New York with Edith. I never told her about Jennifer. I would have, especially as she was coming to know and admire her. Honestly, I don't know how she would have taken it.

"In spite of everything, we still managed to become friends, the kind we should have always been. That was the only thing I could be glad about at the end, although for a very long time it wasn't nearly enough. I broke our alliance in a far worse way than she ever did. It took me a long time to understand that the way she valued her independence over her feelings for me exonerated me from blame. I couldn't protect her every minute and she wouldn't have wanted that. She never did, even at the very beginning when I offered it to her. She was a free spirit. And that's how I'll always remember her."

He comes to a halt; words have suddenly deserted him. It's all out on the table now. He realizes, as his eyes come back into present focus, that all this time he's been speaking to a knot in the table. He looks up.

Their stunned, pale faces alarm him. He considers making for the back door and bolting into the night.

Uncannily, John says quickly, "Don't you move."

Luke swallows and tries to remain glued to his seat.

"That was the God's honest truth, weren't it?" John says. "And you kept all that inside you all this time?"

He manages a sharp nod.

"You were going to give up Jennifer because me and Amy and Sara wanted you to marry Kelley?"

"I couldn't give up Jennifer," he replies, feeling two inches tall.

"But you were going to."

He shrugs.

"Even after Kelley died you were going to," John persists.

"I couldn't do it," he says, recalling that day on the pier in San Francisco. "Jennifer came after me on the same day I planned to leave for the Hawaiian Islands; I didn't go because I couldn't leave her. We realized we should be together. Jennifer's past got between us temporarily, and what happened in North Platte, but we've fixed that now."

"Well, I'm sure that is her business and we got no call to be knowing it, so there it stays, between the two of you."

Again, words dry up in Luke's mouth.

"No wonder Ethan was steamed up like a train yesterday," John mutters.

Still, he is unable to comment.

"Well," John sighs. "In desperate times, people tend to do desperate and foolish things. You and Kelley seemed like a good idea at the time. Sara was convinced she loved you. To be honest, we liked the idea but your mother sold it to us. But, Luke, we like Jennifer very much. She's a brave young woman, kind and sincere, and she's got a smile that'd melt ice. Luke, you must have felt a lot of loyalty to us to put yourself through what you did. I know how much you loved Mart. That there's nothing you wouldn't do for him ever. I just wish you hadn't tried so hard to ditch your own happiness in the process."

His eyes wander back to the knot.

"Thank you for what you said about Kelley," Amy says. "And for being so honest. You know we love you, Luke. We want you to be happy. It's plain as the nose on your face that Jennifer makes you happier than either John or I have ever seen you. You deserve it."

Her words float around in his head for a bit. "Thank you," he murmurs. "And thanks for hearing me out." He shifts in his chair, saying, "Maybe I should be go..."

But the door opens and Ethan and Tip come barging through.

"Good. You're here. We were just talking about you," Ethan says noisily. "C'mon. Let's have a drink. What do you say, John?"

"Ethan, you got the best timing of anybody I know," John chuckles.

Luke catches his Keaton-blue glance and gives a lopsided smile.

Ethan grabs him firmly by the shoulder and says, "Luke's got the best timing of anybody we know. I went by the telegraph office before it closed, sniffing around for a reply from Sara. And what do ya know? Here it is!"

Luke's heart lurches. Ethan takes one look at his face and bursts out laughing.

"What does it say?" John asks.

Amy's gone back to her peeling, very fast peeling.

Tip has raided the pantry for whiskey and starts setting up glasses.

Ethan reaches into his pocket and brings out the telegraph paper.

"Well, go on, Ethan," Amy urges him, "what does it say?"

Emmaline

Emmaline excuses herself from Nan Morris' supper table and, with a throbbing headache, heads upstairs to her room. She rummages through her satchel for Emma by Jane Austen and then curls up on her bed, clutching the book.

What am I going to do with you, Emmie? You can't even bring yourself to look at the inscription...

I can't ask him to give it all up, Celie, not when he's so dedicated and so clever. It is his life, not mine. I have no right.

But, Emmie, I think he wants you to ask him. He wants you to be so secure in your feelings for each other that you think you have the right.

Even if you are correct about this, Celie, no one has the right to ask another human being to give up who they are.

Emmie, that's not what you would be doing. Think. Think about what that Mrs Landers told you. Think about why he gave you the book. What it means to him. He's been waiting for you. Waiting for you to change his life. Direction and meaning beyond the here and now. Think, Emmie, think...

Cliff

"This is a fine stew, Wilma," he says, tucking in.

Wilma laughs. "You must be one hungry critter."

He looks up and smiles at her. "Yes, but it's still good."

She gives a gracious nod of acceptance. "I was a fine cook in my day, long time ago now, but some things a woman never forgets."

"Will you tell me about 'your day' one day, Wilma?"

"I'll think about it, but often it don't do a body good to dwell on the past."

"The past led you here. I have a... friend who thinks Luke and I should build you a home of your own for all the help you gave us."

"I appreciate the thought but I wouldn't accept it. I got my independence and my pride. And my help is mine to give. Reward don't come into it." She slices more bread for him and pushes it his way. "This *friend* wouldn't happen to be a woman..."

He swallows and takes a slice. "She would."

"She's the one, is she?"

"One? Oh, I see. I said a *friend*, Wilma."

She chuckles, shoveling stew onto her spoon. "You should learn to say *friend* in a different tone o'voice."

"You are too clever by half," he complains with good humor.

"Been known for it. So, are you gonna give up your wand'rin' ways for this one?"

He considers her lusty chewing as she waits for his answer. "I'm thinking about it."

"What makes her different from all the others?"

"How many do you think there've been, Wilma?" he asks, both amused and bothered.

"Lookin' at you…"

"I don't know how I look to you, but…"

"Like a man who takes things serious."

"Oh," he says and resumes eating.

She gives a nod and asks, "So what makes her different?"

"I fell in love with this one."

Wilma beams at him across the old rickety table. "The one," she chuckles. "What does she think of your job?"

He swallows his mouthful. "She hates it, but she understands how important it is. Her father is a sheriff and she lived with what it did to her mother. Honestly, things could be better."

Wilma chews thoughtfully, studying him. "Couldn't fall in love with a simple woman?"

He shakes his head. "Guess not."

"That's the attraction?"

"Guess so."

"She's got a lot to say for herself, I'll wager."

"You got that right."

"Good for her," she laughs.

"Have a heart, Wilma," he says, reaching for the bread again.

"Not me. You're too good-lookin' and sure of yourself to suck any pity outa me!"

"Wilma…"

"No, no. I feel sorry for the One…"

"Emma."

She grins. "For Emma. Now that's pretty."

"You really want to talk about this, Wilma?"

She looks surprised. "Don't *you*?"

"I guess it helps," he concedes.

"Sure it does. You got some job ahead of you, and part of you just wants to be with Emma…"

"Some pity at last," he grins.

"A smidgeon. Just what kinda woman is she?"

"She's a reporter. A good one."

"A reporter! Didn't see that comin'."

"Me neither."

She laughs and says, "I'd sure like to meet her someday."

"I could probably arrange that."

"Are you safe in the hands of a reporter, Mr Lawman?"

"This one I am. You'd like her – she's independent."

Wilma grins. "Course she is. What would you be doin' with a needy woman?"

"Didn't say she doesn't need me."

"Oh," Wilma sings, "likes humility in a man, does she?"

He lets that pass and says, "I think Emma's like me. She hadn't been looking for anything and suddenly it appeared before her eyes, and surprised her."

When Wilma doesn't reply, he looks up from his meal. Her blue eyes are studying him without the usual candor.

"Something wrong?"

She shakes her head. "Not that I can see. Finish your supper."

Luke

They've taken to reading and re-reading Sara's telegram and toasting to it, much of it at his expense. Even Amy is smiling, although they're rowdy and she tries to hush them every few minutes. Then they get him to hold the baby while Tressa joins in.

"From Aunt Sara? Let me see. Let me read it."

It gets passed over Luke's head until it reaches Tressa, who reads it out loud.

"Luke. Is this some kind of joke to get me home? I forbid you to marry anyone. Don't do anything till I get there. Love Sara. P.S. you should have told me you were back. Oh, dear. Aunt Sara doesn't sound very pleased, does she?"

Another loud cheer goes up. All he can do is roll his eyes.

Caroline joins them, looking perplexed by all the noise.

"Oh, Mama, you must read this from Luke's mother," Tressa says, grinning.

If it makes Tressa smile, it's not all bad.

Caroline reads. "I'm afraid I don't understand."

More cheering and the glasses clink.

"Oh, how I long for the day of Sara's return!" Ethan revels.

Adam grizzles about all the noise, so Luke takes him to another part of the house where it's quiet and the ticking of the mantle clock exceeds the distant sound of the bizarre party in the kitchen.

Before long, Caroline joins him.

"Here... let me take him for a while."

He's happy to pass Adam into her arms; her grandmother name seems to be Gram, which he kinda likes.

"I'm very happy for you, Luke," she says, rocking Adam, whose hands, shaped like chubby starfish, reach out for her jeweled broach.

"Thanks, Caroline."

"Jennifer is lovely. Somewhat *interesting* profession for a woman, but it hasn't seemed to have affected her."

"No. But you can't be conventional and be Jennifer."

"There's not a great deal conventional about you either."

"You think so?" he smiles.

"I think you can appreciate that in one another. From what I could see today you seem very happy together. Who could ask for more? Even so, you're not concerned about your mother?"

"I think it's a waste of time worrying what Sara will think."

Caroline switches Adam to her hip and rocks back and forth. He grizzles a bit more. "He wants his toy horse. I can't believe Tressa picked him up without it."

"Jennifer came with me when I bought it for him," he reminisces. "She said, this looks like the perfect gift from a man who wants his baby cousin to love horses as much as he does."

"Which goes to prove she is also a good judge of character."

"I want to thank you, Caroline."

"Good heavens, what for?"

"For being so brave..."

"You already did that..."

"If you hadn't done what you did, I'd be dead and Jennifer would be alone."

Caroline studies his face with all the shrewdness of years spent fathoming a man like Richard Taylor. "So you're thanking me on Jennifer's behalf."

He gives a lopsided grin.

She appears to want to further the conversation when loud knocking on the front door interrupts her. "Heavens, that sounds desperate!"

"I'll see who it is."

Luke opens the door to Mac and a host of people standing behind him obscured by the shadows.

"Evenin', Luke," Mac says.

"Mac. What's all this?"

"You're not goin' to believe it," Mac says with a shake of his head. "Still, d'you mind if we all come on in…"

"If my wife is here, I demand to see her at once," a deep voice booms from the darkness behind Mac.

"All in good time," Mac says over his shoulder.

Caroline comes to Luke's side. "What is going on? Oh my… who are all these…"

"Caroline, is that you?"

"Richard!" she gasps. "Richard…"

"Get out of my way…" A tall gruff man pushes his way through and stands on the doorstep, his gaze boring into Caroline's face like he doesn't believe it's her. "Caroline…"

Voluminous feeling surges from Luke's chest to his brain, routing all thought except for a strange sense of recognition… he should know this man… doesn't he?

Caroline rushes past him, still holding Adam, and thrusts her free arm around the man's neck. His arms clasp her so tight that Adam begins to cry.

This man… this is his uncle…

Caroline is sobbing. "Richard, this is Adam, this is your grandson…"

Mac shifts his feet. "Folks, I'm real happy for you, but can we please get off this porch and into the house?"

Luke watches in a daze as Caroline leads her husband towards the parlor.

"A right pain in the you know where," Mac says in a voice so low only Luke can hear. "Well, that's not all I brought for you."

"What's happened?" Luke asks.

"When we're inside," Mac persists.

Luke steps back, paying closer attention to the folks standing behind Mac, a woman and two boys around Tip's age. If he's not mistaken they are Italian. "Come on in…"

"Thanks," says Mac. "Where are Ethan and John?"

"In the kitchen. I'll show you."

The woman and the boys file past him.

"Lock that door," Mac orders him.

Luke complies and leads the group down the hall to the kitchen. Everyone crowds into Amy's sacred cooking space.

Mac explains, "These folks are the Severini family. This is Rosa – Signora – and her sons, Alfredo and Gianni. They are now under the protection of Laramie County law enforcement. Witnesses for the prosecution of Loren Bodecker, no less. They need a safe place to stay until the trial is over."

Signora wears a sad, almost shameful expression. Her sons stand sullen and quiet, looking on.

Mac continues, "I want you all to know that Dan Hummer brought Loren Bodecker in this evenin', about half an hour ago. He's in the lockup and so is that lawyer Marvin Tucker. Cam is there now."

"Wait a minute, Mac," Ethan says, "I've had a few whiskies. D'you say that Bodecker is in your lockup?"

"Yep."

"Oh, my," says Amy. "This is unbelievable…"

"Well, you can believe it."

"Where's Cliff?" Luke asks, feeling like Amy.

Mac doesn't look too happy. "He went to North Platte."

Luke goes cold. "Porterfield…"

"Hummer said Cliff brought all this about. I mean, Hummer don't give away glory lightly, so I'm thinkin'… Well, anyway, apart from Richard Taylor in your parlor there, there's another sur…"

"My father!" Tressa gasps. "My father is here?"

"Sure. Your brother found him. Had a hard time and ain't real sure what's what…"

Tressa catches Luke's eye before she hurries from the room.

"So, where is Ben?" Ethan asks.

"He's comin'. I left him talkin' with Cam and Hummer, makin' his report. And now these folks here need a place to stay, can I count on you?"

"We've plenty of room," says Amy.

In actual fact, the walls are bulging.

"They're more'n welcome. Leave 'em with us," John says emphatically.

"Ethan," Luke says, "we need to get down to the jail."

"You and John go. I need to speak with your uncle. All right with you, John?"

"I reckon so."

Luke swallows a lump of confusing emotion.

Ethan grips his forearm tight. "You think about what you're doing. You think about Jennifer, y'hear?"

"I hear you, Ethan."

"Tip, go to Emmaline's and see if she's still there. If she doesn't know, she'll want to. Go with her to the jail and stick with her."

"Sure, Pa." Tip slips out the back door.

"Thanks for that, Ethan," Mac says, "I promised the girl and I haven't had a chance…"

"That's what we're here for, Mac," Ethan says.

Then Luke hears that gruff, obnoxious voice coming down the hall towards them. Once more that disconcerting feeling rises in his chest…

Richard Taylor stands in the doorway of the kitchen, his face and body heavy-set with aggravation, at each shoulder Caroline and Tressa. Luke studies him in a kind of shock. Sharp bursts of recognition slash into him like a carving knife, chiseling a memory back to life. Blue eyes. Brown hair. Strong shoulders. His father, returned in likeness. The man's savage eyes come to rest on him. Luke can't breathe… face to face with a reflection of his father after sixteen years… Pa!

"You! Morgan's brat!"

"Richard!"

This man is not his father.

This man is not.

His Pa had kind eyes. Not those of a savage…

He wants to fly away but whichever way he turns he runs into ghosts, mostly of his mother suffering the torment of Morgan's loss, and that childhood feeling of despair. He feels sick and cold. Wishes he were Tip, fetching Emmaline. Instead, he must face this… this demon uncle.

"You," his uncle says, "you are the cause of all this!"

"Richard! Richard, no…" Caroline rebukes him.

But the distress in her voice brings Luke to his senses. He'd felt a protective inclination towards Caroline since the moment he met her and an even stronger one when he found out this despicable man ditched her for Bodecker. And what he did to his own daughter… words fail at every turn.

"My son has betrayed me because of YOU!"

That does it. The feeling in his chest explodes. He rushes to take a swing at him.

"Luke, no!" cries Tressa.

Ethan grabs him and holds him back. "Leave him to me."

His blood is coursing; inside he's steaming. He grapples with Ethan to get to the demon. "No, let me… just once…" But Ethan's strength has him flailing.

"Luke… I know what you're feeling and I'm glad you're finally taking account of it, but not this time, not right now."

"Let me go… Ethan… let me go."

"Leave him, Luke." How is it that Ethan – puffing, red-faced, full of whiskey – is stronger than him? "Leave him to me, son." Ethan pinches his face between strong fingers and demands his focus. "Leave him to me."

"Luke, please," Tressa says. "I… I'll never ask of you another thing, just…"

Her voice, the sound of her sad pleading, causes the waves of aggression inside him to falter. He finds himself easing off.

"Good man," Ethan puffs, slapping one of his cheeks. "Good. Now, go down to the jail with John. Remember what I said about Jennifer. And then go back to your room. Or the Faradays'. Don't come back here tonight. Understood?"

He nods and straightens himself up. Ethan gives his chest an affirming thump.

"I'll meet you outside," John says, making a move.

"I got the buggy we came in out front, you can ride with me," Mac says. "Give me a minute more to instruct the witnesses."

"Are you sure my uncle is a witness?" Luke mutters.

"Accordin' to Cliff he is and that's good enough for me."

Luke snatches his hat from its peg and gets himself out into the cold night air.

Ethan

"So, Richard Taylor, you ain't changed," Ethan says. "Sit down."

"Who are these people?" Morgan's brother says, his voice bitter and his face red with strain. They are all staring at him. Amy in particular, he notices, stares hard at the traces of Morgan's likeness. She opens her mouth to say something and thinks better of it.

"This fine woman," Ethan says in her stead, "is Amy Keaton. Everyone who stays here does so through her hospitality. She and her husband John, who just left with Luke, are Tressa's in-laws. Mart's parents. You say one word against them and I'll kick you out, no matter what Caroline has to say about it, y'hear?"

Richard's eye bulge. "I don't take orders from you, Benchley!"

"So you remember me, then?"

"You and my brother should've stayed in Texas!"

Caroline grips his arm. "Richard, please. Let's all sit down and be calm. *Please*, Richard."

This seems to work on him favorably. He grabs a kitchen chair and sits on it.

Amy finds her voice. "I'll show Signora and her sons where they can rest and clean up…"

"I will help you," Tressa says.

They lead the Severini family away, leaving him and Caroline with Richard.

"The boy was going to attack me," Richard says. He runs his trembling fingers through his already rumpled hair.

"The boy is a man who took one look at you and remembered his father for one instant and then recalled your meanness in the

330

next. He saw in your face what we all see – Morgan's likeness, which gladdens us – and then we remember that you are nothing like him."

"Ethan, that doesn't help," Caroline says, taking the chair next to her husband's.

"It's the truth. All you had to do, Richard, was reach out to the boy and Sara."

"Morgan reaped what he sowed," Richard grinds out. "And so did you, Ethan."

Ethan feels the blood drain away from his face and then boil up inside him. "And you haven't?"

"My son has betrayed me because of Morgan's son. Morgan and his unconventional and undisciplined ways. He passed them down, didn't he?"

"I raised Luke since he was knee-high. Me, Red Sky and Sara. We gave him cause to be proud of who he is and what his father was. A brave man..."

"A brave man..." Richard turns up his lip.

"And his son is a brave man," Ethan punches out. "Courage always was a Taylor trait if I remember; your own son has it, and your daughter."

"Tressa!" he exclaims. "My daughter behaved like a..."

"Richard..." Caroline cuts in.

Ethan knows what Caroline stopped the bastard from saying. How come she don't smack him in the mouth he can't figure.

"Don't get me started on how you treated Tressa," Ethan grinds out, getting madder by the minute. "That gentle girl? And you call yourself her pa?"

Richard glares and snarls.

"Listen to me, Richard," Ethan says, spreading his hands on the table, "since the moment Luke and Ben met they've been coming to an understanding. Ben knows where he comes from; he knows his heritage, the truth you tried to keep from him. And he's proud of it. The two of them are gonna bring this family together and there ain't nothing you can do about it."

"Bravo, Ethan. Feel like a big man, do you? Have you been rehearsing that heap of rubbish? Listen up, you Texan waste of space, I don't *want* my son coming to any understanding with that brat you raised…"

Ethan stands up, his hands and feet tingling with the urge to flatten him and then kick his miserable behind all the way to China.

"Well, John and Amy had a hand in raising the boy, too. They were a family to him when his own family – that's you, Richard – couldn't be bothered…"

Caroline looks up with deep hurt in her eyes.

"Sorry, Caroline," Ethan adds, even though it's too late. He plunges onward. "So, if Luke and Ben are finally reaching an understanding in spite of you, Richard, then that should be telling you something."

Richard sighs loudly. He looks haggard and sick. And like he can no longer put thoughts together. Sure enough, he goes quiet.

Ethan folds his arms. "Luke is going to confront you, Richard. I stopped him from laying you out cold tonight, for his sake, and Tressa's, not yours, but I won't interfere again. You're gonna have to take whatever he dishes out and that's a fact."

"You can't let Luke hit Richard, Ethan," Caroline pleads. "He's weak; he's been through a hard time…"

"It's up to Luke now."

Richard mumbles, "Just let him try …"

Luke

For most of the ride John and Mac talk non-stop, which doesn't bother Luke since his mind is still in Amy's kitchen, careening about like a sloop in a gale... occasionally a name or place seems to pop out of the air and reach his ears, as if normality is trying to bring him back to life as it was thirty minutes ago, but that hell-born image of his uncle refuses to leave him alone.

Ethan's right. He is finally taking account and while he doesn't like where his mind is right now, there is a feeling inside him telling him that not only can't he run from this but that he doesn't want to.

As the county sheriff's building comes into view, his mind begins to clear, as if another instinct is taking over. If his uncle is a demon then surely Bodecker is the father of lies. Everyone's mind should be clear for that prospect.

They pull up and get out; an icy wind whistles clean through his ears, slices through his clothes and hits his hot skin, effectively restoring his whole being to its normal state.

Inside, the scene is tense but surprisingly calmer than he'd expected. In fact, no one would suspect that Loren Bodecker had been arrested and jailed pending trial for a whole range of crimes.

There's no throng, no controversy and no excitement. Just Ben, looking pale and tired, pacing outside Cliff's office; an elegant-looking young woman sitting in a chair nearby, watching Ben pace and as if she knows him; and Tip, who comes forward to greet them, his sloping smile and black-eyed glance both a greeting and a summation of the situation.

Tip tosses his head slightly and Luke follows the direction of it

333

to see a bemused Emmaline sitting amid the wait-chairs. If ever he needed to fulfill his promise to Cliff, now would be the time, but Ben comes towards them. He and John shake hands. Mac tells them to sit and be patient until Cam returns from the lockup.

Luke sighs and removes his hat.

"You've seen my father?" Ben asks him.

"Yeah."

"And?"

"Ethan's dealing with it."

Ben says nothing; merely nods. Ethan commands indisputable respect.

"It couldn't have been easy, finding him," Luke imagines out loud.

"More pleasant than you think... I want you to meet someone." Ben looks around to the young woman on the chair; she gives a small smile and stands up. "Raina, this is my cousin Luke Taylor; and this is my good friend and my sister's father-in-law, John Keaton. Gentlemen, this is Raina."

"A pleasure to finally meet you both," says she.

Ben clears his throat. "We were married yesterday."

If the bottom fell out of the room Luke couldn't be more shocked.

John starts chuckling. "Now that's a fine thing. Congratulations to you both," he says. "Ma'am, Ben is a fine young man." They start to chat, Raina's face becoming animated and twice as pretty.

"Well?" Ben says, staring straight into Luke's face.

Luke sticks out his hand. "Congratulations."

Ben grips it and there's an unexpected moment of connection between them that has nothing to do with their physical contact.

"Another story destined for Liberty and Property," Luke murmurs with a grin.

"You think?"

"I'd say so. Hope I get to hear it someday."

Ben smiles and says nothing. And Luke gets the impression that the telling might be some time in coming.

John and Raina are still conversing. Raina grows prettier and more charming by the minute. Tip joins them.

"And Cliff..?" Luke asks.

"They carried a warrant for Porterfield's arrest and Cliff had a hunch Porterfield had returned to his laboratory. Hummer could have ordered him not to go, but he didn't."

"Hummer knew better." He looks around at Emmaline and thinks about what to do next; he excuses himself and joins her. "Emmaline..."

She doesn't hear him.

"Emmaline," he says louder.

She looks up and breathes a sigh. "Oh, it's you."

"Are you worried about Cliff?"

"No, er... it's just... Walker."

"He has the right badge this time round. He'll be fine, trust me. So, this is some scoop you got here. You're the only reporter in the place. Where is everyone?"

"Enjoying their supper, if they had any sense."

"Where's your notebook? I expected to hear you were down in the lockup annoying the heck out of Cam and Mac."

"No, they won't let me."

"But it's still a scoop. First on the scene. It'll make sensational reading: Bodecker arrested! Now that don't happen every day..."

"I guess not."

"You guess..? Emmaline, I think you should head on down to the Tribune and tell them to hold the presses while you get this story. Better yet, you stay here and wait for further developments – Cam will be out soon – and we'll send Tip to the Tribune. You can write him a note to give Quaid."

"Very well," she sighs and reaches for her notebook on the chair beside her.

"Emmaline," he urges, "snap out of it."

"I'm sorry," she says, hurrying now.

"Don't apologize to me. You *will* be apologizing to Quaid if you let this slip through your fingers. I don't imagine that's a pleasant experience."

She looks up, grinning and more like the Emmaline he knows. "No, it's not. Don't worry, I'm on it. Thanks."

"Don't mention it." He leaves her as she calls Tip over.

A minute later, with Tip having left for the Tribune, Cam emerges from the lockup. For the first time in a long time Luke is glad to see him; with Cliff still away, at least someone has control over the whole business. Emmaline pounces. As calm as ever, Cam gives a long statement that she madly scribbles down in her notebook, and while she writes, the rest of them listen.

Cam tells them how, where and when Loren Bodecker was apprehended. That at this stage he has been charged with several counts of conspiracy to murder and the list of charges is growing. That he will be arraigned before Judge Callaghan tomorrow afternoon and it is hoped he will be held without bail until trial. That he is refusing to answer any questions put to him and has asked for his lawyer Dillon Kerr.

Also arrested was the attorney, Marvin Tucker, on the charge of taking a bribe as an accessory to conspiring to murder. He will also be arraigned tomorrow.

Cam gives a concluding statement, particularly for Emmaline's benefit, although he is clearly affected, about the grave and serious nature of these crimes, that the territory of Wyoming cannot permit Loren Bodecker to get away with terrorizing innocent people for his own gain, and that citizens should not allow the man's standing in the community to influence their zeal for prosecution and discharge of justice.

Emmaline asks a series of questions, the first of which refers to Dillon Kerr being out of town, but while Cam makes his answers, Luke finds a seat and lets the whole business sink in. Truth be known, with one thing coming on top of another, it's a bit much.

He feels a hand on his shoulder and hears John say…

"Son, I'm taking this news back to the others now. Got lots more detail and Amy'll be worried."

He looks up.

"Will you be all right?" John asks.

"Yeah. I'll come by tomorrow."

"Take your time. You know we're always there if you need us for anything. Oh, Tip got back. Said Quaid was holding up the press for Emmaline's story. She's got that look in her eye." He smiles some encouragement. "Ben and Raina are coming home with me for now. They're keen for her to meet the rest of the family. I expect they'll find their own accommodation before the evening's out. It's gonna be all right, Luke. We're nearly there now."

"Sure, John, thanks."

"Tip said to tell you he's sticking by Emmaline for a while longer. Well, take it easy, son," John says and walks away.

Luke's gaze becomes fixed on one particular spot on the floor. All goes strangely silent, except for the buzz of his thoughts and the occasional distant and eerie noises coming from the jail cells at the back of the building.

Someone says, "Want to know what's going to happen next?"

The question resounds in his head like a taunt. He becomes aware of someone sitting beside him.

And Cam's voice… "My prediction is that shares in Bodecker's empire are going to plummet and a lot of people are going to lose a lot of money. The exact extent of ruin across the territory and beyond no one can accurately predict, but it will happen. It will be painful and confusing. It may even be deadly."

"Folks made their choice."

"Yes, but I still feel sorry for them. Like sheep without a shepherd."

"Mart would have said that."

"I know. That's why I said it. Nothing's changed, Luke. We are still putting on the mind of Mart to do this. At least I am."

Luke glances sideward. Cam's earnest brown eyes are staring at him with concern way beyond what Luke deserves.

Cam clears his throat. "I will prosecute Loren Bodecker with every last breath in my body if I have to, and it may come to that. Or it may not. The enormity of the evidence against him will be countered by public opinion and the weight of big business. It may not end happily for anyone. Either way, I will never forget that Mart gave his life for this, and that you made a promise to him to see justice done and you have never given up on it."

Luke sits forward, his elbows on his knees, needing to avoid Cam's gaze since he can't escape it.

"I know I disappointed you," Cam continues. "And you know how sorry I am. When you marry Jennifer, I'm afraid by custom you adopt the Faradays. That wouldn't have been such a bad thing for you at one time. We haven't changed, Luke. Not in how we feel about you, or how much we want you and Jennifer to be happy. And I am convinced you will be happy together. She has already thoroughly shamed me over causing you to detour to Omaha. One more 'how could you, Cam?' and I was ready to leave town. But not at any time in all the years I've known her have I seen her as happy as she was this morning. I think what I'm trying to say is that whichever way this ends, you have the greatest treasure of your life already in your hands."

Deep down Luke recognizes the truth of this, and the right person to whom he should admit it...

"I've never put her first, have I?"

"Not until yesterday, I don't think so. Not because you didn't want to. With all of life's pressures, sometimes it's not always easy to know how. It takes time and effort to work it out, which, if I remember, was something you were endeavoring to do. Women are complicated creatures – and I don't know a woman more so than Jennifer – so the process can be complex, for us anyway. They seem to know exactly how it should be done."

Luke smiles reluctantly at the floor.

Cam sighs and says, "One thing I've learned. They'll make you a better man if you learn how to make them happy."

Luke looks at him. "Have you been home this evening, Cam?"

Cam frowns. "No, not yet."

"Are you headed that way now?"

His frown deepens. "Should I be?"

Luke gives a laugh. "C'mon. I'll ride shotgun."

Emmaline

Mr Quaid is beaming, a welcome change from the barking of earlier.

"I don't know how you did this, Roberts."

He resumes his reshuffle of the front page, his fingers covered with ink smudges and switching letters from the upper case and the lower with deadline speed.

Their sub-editor and prepress manager, Will Dobson, goes along behind fixing all Mr Quaid's errors.

"I have friends in the right places," she tells him, watching Dobson keenly.

"All right, Roberts, no need to rub it in."

"I think she does, Charlie. I still can't believe it." Will Dobson is an Englishman – a 'Londoner' he describes himself – and she adores listening to his strange and lilting accent. "Lucky there's just a handfuluvus here really. And the press boys. And we're not abou' to tell a soul. Wha' abou' 'im over there?"

Dobson indicates Tip, who's got bored and is standing by the window looking out into the dark.

"Tip?" she says. "He's an angel. He won't tell anyone."

"Roberts, your affiliation with these people is beginning to irk me," Mr Quaid says.

Irk? Huh!

"Not my problem," she retorts.

He looks up. "What's that supposed to mean?"

Dobson gives him a hurry up. "Don't wanna be 'ere all night, now do we?"

Mr Quaid dithers about. "No, no, of course not."

"I fancy Mr Faraday's statement at the end, Roberts," says Dobson. "A nice touch, that."

Tip wanders back. "How much longer?" he asks. There isn't a trace of impatience in his voice, only curiosity, but Mr Quaid bites as always.

"What are you here for again?"

Tip folds his strong, capable arms and says, "If I employed someone as valuable as Emmaline I'd see to it that she was well-taken care of."

"She's a reporter, Benchley."

"Your *ace* reporter."

Mr Quaid grunts. "Go back and look out the window some more, will you?"

"That's the copy then. Now for the 'eadline. We only got so much space," says Dobson, maneuvering Mr Quaid out of his way. "I know. Why don't we move this piece 'ere to the stop press on the back page where we woulda put Roberts' piece 'cept that it's all too excitin' for the back an' all."

"Well, it *was* front page stuff," Mr Quaid points out.

"Oh, that's daft, that's wha' it is. Look 'ere, we can make a decent 'eadline if we do that. Wha'd'ya say? Who cares for the new price of wool anyhow? Bodecker don't own sheep anyways. You can go now, Roberts, if you want, if you trust me to give you a none too shabby 'eadline."

She nods. "I trust you, Dobson. And thank you."

Already he's searching around in his upper case for his largest, tallest, fattest letters. "Don't mention it."

"Good night, Mr. Quaid."

"Night, Roberts. Benchley."

According to Ben, Cliff wanted to have Porterfield firmly in his grasp before the news of Bodecker's arrest spread to North Platte. Mr Quaid, guarded and jealous to a fault, had already assured her this scoop belonged to the Cheyenne Tribune. He didn't intend to wire anyone until the whole story broke tomorrow. The Tribune would be out on the streets tomorrow morning. As long as the darkness lasted, Cliff's window of opportunity remained open.

Donnelly

Donnelly stares through the row of cells to the very last one on the end, where Loren paces the floor of it, side to side, back to front, corner to corner. How could he let this happen?

"What are you looking at?" Tucker asks him.

"Not you, you weasel," Donnelly retorts. "Didn't ask to bunk with you, so keep your trap shut."

Tucker rolls his eyes. "You know why I'm in this hellhole with you?"

"Don't give a crap."

"Because Loren sent for me. He gave me a fist full of notes to ask the Severini boy to maverick you, Donnelly."

"Shut the fuck up."

"He's not your savior."

"You're lying."

"Ryan walked in on the deal. I had the money in my hand."

Donnelly scowls. "You ain't that kind of lawyer."

"It was more money than I've ever seen in one place. You know where Ryan is now? He's gone after Porterfield."

Donnelly feels ill. Porterfield wouldn't know about Loren; he'll resume his operation. He'll be right there in North Platte ready for Ryan to pluck.

He tugs at his collar with his sore hand and winces then swears at the pain. Freakin' bullet wound – since that bastard Ransford shot him at the Keatons' ranch house the damn thing won't heal up. Good thing Ransford got what was coming to him…

In the next two cells are his mavericks – Jacobs, the miserable

SOB who failed to get the shot on the Roberts girl, and Carter, the other Cheyenne shooter, the first half of his job done right, but the clean-up of Jacobs' mistake foiled by Ryan, who shot and wounded him. Then there's Cole and Tyner, the remaining two snipers from the team he sent to Bright River to deal with the Alliance.

He wants to kill the lot of them. Quiet, downcast, and almost confused, the mavericks form a buffer between him and Loren. If Tucker is telling the truth, then Loren thought Donnelly couldn't keep his head, thought him a liability. If it were true...

When Hummer and the deputy sheriff brought Loren in earlier, Loren never gave him a second glance. Maybe it *is* true. Loren ain't treating him like a brother or a partner, that's for sure. Suddenly, the lockup outer door opens and the attorney, Sturrock, strides in. An armed deputy stands by the door and keeps guard while Sturrock marches down the block to Loren's cell. He pushes himself against his bars and strains to hear their conversation, but it's conducted in a whisper, their mouths barely moving.

Sturrock strides back.

"Hey, Sturrock," he says.

Sturrock stops. Looks down his nose. "Yes, Mr Donnelly?"

"What's going on? Where's Dillon? Why ain't he here?"

"I am not Dillon Kerr's keeper," Sturrock says.

"What's Faraday up to?"

"Donnelly, your trial is proceeding as planned. We discussed your defense."

"Sturrock, I've been locked up for weeks..."

"It's called incarceration, sir. On Mr Faraday's recommendation the Judge removed the option for bail, if you remember. You get out on the day of your trial and sit in the courtroom while I present your defense. Unfortunately for you, this latest development has given Mr Faraday even more ammunition. I will return in the morning to discuss this with you. Let me just say that Faraday has several important witnesses under protection. Although I will have access to their statements, even I do not know who they are. If a jury of your peers is not satisfied with our case, sir, you will go to prison, or you will be hanged. Considering the charges, hanging is likely. Prepare yourself. Goodnight, sir."

Sturrock gives Tucker an arrogant glance. He checks his exit and says, "Who represents you, sir?"

"I'm an attorney," Tucker says, "I'll represent myself."

"I see. What are the charges against you?"

"There is one. Accepting a bribe, accessory to conspiracy to murder."

"You were apprehended with Mr Bodecker?"

Tucker gives a sharp nod.

Sturrock stares at Tucker for a moment, then his gaze shifts to Donnelly. The way Sturrock stares at him gives him the creeps, but in that moment he knows what Tucker said is true.

He can feel himself begin to perspire. And he tugs on his collar.

"It ain't true," he bursts out.

Sturrock steps away and begins to walk.

"It ain't true," he shouts again.

Sturrock disappears through the lockup door with the deputy.

"But it didn't happen, thanks to Ryan's timely intervention," Tucker says, a bit too smug for his liking. "Not yet anyway."

He turns on Tucker, who steps back in his cell. "I could snap your neck with my bare hands, so shut up!"

"Just like you did to the girl on the train?"

His brain feels ready to explode.

"Why?" he bellows down the cellblock towards Loren.

Loren looks up. "Look at you," he yells back. "Tucker's holding it together better than you."

"All the time I've been locked up I ain't said a thing and you know it."

"Faraday is going to screw you."

He grinds his teeth. "And you."

Loren laughs. "He can try."

"You should've listened to me a long time ago, Loren…"

"Keep your mouth shut," Loren snaps.

Donnelly retreats to his cot and slinks down under his blanket. There used to be only one man he hated in this world. Now there are two. Funny, neither of them is Loren. If he were Loren, he'd probably do the same thing. But if he were Loren he would've got rid of Taylor and Ryan a long, long time ago.

It's all too complicated now. That's Loren's weakness. He likes things complicated. He likes the means. He likes the game. Something Donnelly could never understand, especially when the end could be so clean, so short and simple.

"You don't have a little something, do you?" he asks Tucker.

"What do you think?" Tucker says and shakes his head. "You idiot."

Jennifer

She finds Luke sitting at the kitchen table, dishtowel in hand, his blue eyes shining, conversing with Constance. It appears as though he's supposed to be wiping up, but the clean, wet dishes are piling up around Constance's elbows.

"What's going on in here?" she asks.

"It's refreshin' to meet someone in this town who ain't afraid to talk about what really matters," Constance announces, adding a dish to the pile.

"Oh?"

Jennifer goes to him; he reaches for her, drawing her close, looking up at her like she's the center of his world; her knees almost collapse.

"What really matters?" she says, enjoying the feeling.

"A person's roots," Constance says. "That's what. Where ya come from. Take Mr Blue Eyes here. He likes my stories of Mr McConnell. He reckons they're important to this country. Now why do ya reckon he'd think a thing like that?"

Jennifer grins at him as he starts to look endearingly sheepish.

Constance grunts, quite fiercely. "Folks could take a lesson or two from him."

"Don't worry, Constance. I know how important stories are to Mr Blue Eyes *and* to you."

"There's a million of 'em..."

"I know. Constance, Luke and I can finish up here."

Constance narrows her eyes. "Tryin' to get rid of me?"

"Take an early night and do something for yourself," she suggests. Luke's hands tighten playfully on her waist.

Constance drops the dishcloth and starts drying her hands on her apron. "Can't refuse an offer like that, although ya don't look like the type who can wash dishes…"

"I'll wash," Luke pipes up.

"That's more like," Constance says with a satisfied nod. She unties her apron, hangs it on the back of the door where her coat and hat are waiting. She puts them on, saying, "Tell Mrs Faraday I'll see her in the mornin'. Night, folks."

She's gone.

Jennifer shakes her head. "Why would she assume I couldn't wash dishes? I'm a doctor, for heaven's sake. I wash people and the bits of them they'd rather not know they had."

"She's your regular old-fashioned character. She means no harm; better still, she takes your mind off things. Sit."

"How's your leg?"

"The day it can't hold you will be a sorry day."

She sits on his knee; he pulls her close. Once she has looped her arms around his neck she studies his face for a long while, not only because she loves it but because so many things have happened in twenty four hours she wants to know how he's holding up.

"Stop looking at me like that," he murmurs. "I'm fine."

"I believe you."

On top of everything else that's happened she still needs to tell him about Dermot.

"How goes it with Ma and Pa to be?" he asks.

"Much better. You know, I never thought that Cam and Meg would ever have a problem communicating. They always seem so open to one another."

"Well, they're hardly an old married couple, are they?"

The delicate rebuke brings stinging warmth to her cheeks.

"No," she admits.

"And it's easy to get on different tracks, even if you think you're on the same train."

"You are very insightful."

"My middle name, didn't you know," he grins.

"Be patient with me?"

"I seem to recall I got a lot of patience when it comes to you. Besides, there's something else you need to tell me…"

"I… How did you…?"

"I gotta do something when you look at me that way. Sometimes I just look right back into those eyes of yours for the pure enjoyment of it, and sometimes I work on what you're trying to say to me."

"Oh?" she says, averting her eyes now.

He laughs softly. "I reckon I might know what it is."

"You couldn't…"

"I could. Try this. Frank and Jeanne are the best part of your family, the only part you want to own. But there is Dermot, and two other brothers. I forget their names…"

"Joseph and Miles."

"As for Dermot, well, would he want to know you're getting married? Would Joseph and Miles want to know?"

"Am I getting heavy?" she says, shifting a little, "because I can sit on…"

His arms firm. "Jennifer…"

"Yes?" she murmurs, fiddling with his collar.

"Talk to me about Dermot. I promise – I swear – I won't do anything rash. Say something stupid. Run out of the house. Or do anything to cause you to run away and never want to come back."

"You can do that?" she says, giving his ear a tug.

"Ouch. Yes."

So she tells him about the summons Dermot issued her by telegram to return to Provincetown, and he listens thoughtfully.

"And when I asked Frank what he thought Dermot wanted, he only said that Dermot's old."

"How old?"

"I don't know."

"Old as Ethan?"

"Ethan's not old…"

"'Course not, what was I thinking… Older than Methuselah?"

"Who?"

"Not heard of him? I'm kinda surprised. Nine hundred year old character in the Bible."

"Nine hundred! That's not possible."

"Always the science with you…"

"Luke, Dermot always seemed old to me. I haven't seen him in years. I've no idea."

Jokes aside, he is cleverly scrutinizing her face. She might want to hide, but she knows she can't from him.

"Well, there are two things you could do maybe," he says. "You could go now and put off the weddin' until you return. Or, you could wait until after I've cleared my name and we could go together. I prefer the second…"

"Or I could not go at all."

He frowns. "Are you sure you'd want to do that?"

"The thought of facing him makes me want to run away."

"Is that why you came here to me instead?"

She walked straight into that one. A tough question, but fair. And she must take it like a grown woman, not like the unwanted child that every thought or conversation about Dermot makes her feel.

"You asked me the hard question; I'm going give you the hard answer. I was going to Provincetown and then I discovered that I was… that we were…"

"Becoming a family."

She bites her lip. "Let me explain… I didn't know what to do. I was torn. You didn't communicate with me. As I said, I wasn't sure you still wanted me. I tried to work out what to do. Meg wrote me a letter saying she believed you did love me, that if we were meant to be together it would happen. So I began to think that this separation between us could be a test. The very last thing I wanted to do was see Dermot, but… well, coming back to you seemed almost as hard if you had rejected me. Then… then everything changed. The… er, the test changed."

He closes his eyes, lines of anguish creasing his forehead.

"What?" she whispers.

"I'm just thanking God for this child. And for you."

"Luke…" She caresses his face.

"You saw how sick I was without you."

She rests her forehead on top of his. "Yes. I'm sorry. I'm so sorry."

"You're brave, Jennifer. You never shrink from facing the hard things of life. It's one of the first things I loved about you. But I don't want you and our baby to go anywhere without me," he says. "If that's selfish I'm sorry, but I just got you back."

It's been such a little time since he's been well...

Now, at the sound of fear in his voice, she folds her arms around him and holds him close. "I'm not sure I could face Dermot without you anyway." She releases him and takes the face she adores so much between her hands, marveling afresh at the love he has for the new life inside her. In his ocean blue eyes she sees the vulnerability of a lately healed man and it almost breaks her heart. "I just want us to be married. To be in this world together. It's all I want. I won't ever regret it. Even if I regret never seeing Dermot again, it won't ever be a bigger regret than if I left you now. So don't let me go."

"I won't let you go," he says. He puts his face on her shoulder; she can feel his breath hot against her neck. "I won't ever let you go."

Ben

They lay side by side in the dark, holding hands, in yet another hotel room. He'd be lying to himself if he didn't admit that he's fed up with hotels… and he'd thought about 'home' a lot since Raina.

"Your mother was so lovely to me," she says softly into the darkness above her. "So kind and so polite – and after the shock we delivered. She… she welcomed me with open arms, like family."

Considering that's at least the tenth time she has uttered similar remarks, he decides he should counter it or she might keep on saying it all night and he had other plans. Except she beats him to it…

"Ben, until I met her it didn't occur to me that I was gaining a mother. What a wonderful thought! I think after the shock wears off she might think of me as a daughter, too – what do you think?"

"Yes, I…"

"And your sister… I was so honored to meet her. Such a sweet soul. I feel like her sister already. I'm going to love having a sister. And darling little Adam! One thing, though… I confess, Ben, it will take me some time to warm up to your father."

"Take all the time you need. I don't expect miracles, Rain."

He knows she needs stability, a home of her own, but she'd decided for herself she didn't want that until she'd found her mother. For now, being together was home, in some ways more complex than buying a house, finding furniture and hiring a cook.

"You were pretty wonderful with them yourself," he says. "And, Rain, I swear we will find your mother, if she is out there we will find her and bring her home to you."

Emmaline

Exhaustion pushes her into bed, with her fingers still cramping and black with ink. She usually applies great diligence to her efforts to keep Nan Morris' sheets free of ink, but the ability escapes her for now.

Dawn is a couple of hours away.

After spending all night at her desk, the story is up-to-date. All the parts she couldn't bring herself to write or polish – done; and the challenges she had encountered streaming everything together – all surmounted.

She gave it an ironic title, *Empire for Liberty*, borrowing from President Jefferson – and Mr Faraday, who, in response to one of Miss Keaton's letters in the Bugle, wrote: *do we not live in the heart of President Jefferson's 'empire for liberty'?*

Her final task was scratching the title at the top of the first page. She didn't intend to explain it or defend it; she intended for people to contemplate it, in relation to the story beneath it and what was happening all around them. And she had a strong feeling that Miss Keaton would have liked it, too.

Only one thing remains. A few hours' sleep. Her head comes to rest on the pillow, sinking blissfully into the downy cloud; her body surrenders its satisfied weariness to the warmth and coziness of her bed, and she sighs herself into slumber.

FOUR

But who shall dare
To measure loss and gain in this wise?
Defeat may be victory in disguise;
The lowest ebb is the turn of the tide.

❦

Henry Wadsworth Longfellow
The Light of Stars

Preston Roberts

The following morning

Never in his life has he been west of the Missouri River before this trip. That his daughter has done it makes him proud. So she didn't have to do it in a covered wagon, but still she went where no other Roberts or Pendleton ever went before. No member of the family had ever been daring enough to venture into the Western frontier.

No one except Emmaline.

She'd had trepidations; her Mama said she did.

She has problems now; Celina insists she has.

All right; he'll be the one to go.

Emmaline knows trepidation and problems. She knows how to deal with them. She's a scrapper; an inventor. She thinks on her feet and her impulses don't scare her.

He misses her; has missed her… she's still his little girl.

And if this ain't the train journey to beat all train journeys.

The sun's climbing. Slowly. He was warned – winter in these parts retreats very slowly.

Emmaline hates the cold.

He's about to find out exactly how cold in approximately five minutes. The train is reducing speed again. They are approaching Cheyenne.

After scooting across vast plains and stopping in fascinating frontier towns, Preston can't help but feel he has left the old South and the insistent North a long way behind.

His anticipation at seeing his daughter and discovering how

she likes the West really takes hold of him. His blood is pumping. Is it as wild as they say? As the legend purports?

The train slows into the depot. Clouds of steam are expelled into slanting rays of morning sun, making strange shapes out of a platform full of people. He reaches for his luggage on the rack above and alights from the train.

The chill hits him hard. Crisp and invigorating. He shoulders his way to a vacant space and surveys the scene of people scurrying every which way with a newspaper in their hand, often calling out to one another, their faces pale, or flushed, their eyes bright, or dim.

A young porter comes by…

Preston inquires as to what is going on.

"You haven't heard?"

"Heard what? Just got off the train, son."

"Loren Bodecker's been arrested."

The boy takes off.

Who is Loren Bodecker?

A paperboy stationed at the exit has several copies of Emmaline's newspaper… The Tribune. Hastily, he buys a copy.

LOREN BODECKER ARRESTED!

An exclusive report by Emmaline Roberts

Emmaline!

As he's marveling at her name right there in the newspaper, someone canons into him, knocking him sideways. He straightens up while the rattled gentleman apologizes and then takes off again.

After folding the newspaper under his arm, he picks up his bag and heads out into the street. He promised to send a telegram as soon as he arrived, but the queue at the telegraph office winds down the sidewalk for half a block.

He asks someone for the location of the Tribune.

The young man informs him politely, but adds, "You sure you want to go there this morning? You'll be lucky to get near the door."

Preston tips his hat. "I'm sure."

It is safe to say that Cheyenne is in uproar.

The news of this man Bodecker's arrest occupies every

overheard conversation and passing remark he encounters. The town reminds him of a woman who having looked down at her feet and discovered she's in the center in an ants' nest, picks up her skirts not knowing where to step or which direction to go.

Outside a handsome brick building, in what appears to be the center of town, a large and noisy throng of people is gathered. He stands at the back and surveys the goings-on.

A sandy-haired man, dressed warmly, addresses the crowd.

"You all need to go home," he shouts. "It won't do you no good to stand here all day."

"We want to know what's going on with Bodecker, Mac..." someone yells from nearby.

The crowd erupts with strident solidarity. The man Mac quiets them again.

"Dillon Kerr ain't in town. You'll have to wait 'til..."

"You can tell us, Mac," a gentleman calls out from the side. "Is it true what it says in the Tribune?"

"Bodecker has been arrested for conspiracy to murder," Mac says, like it's the hundredth time that morning.

"Are we going to lose everything?" asks another.

"I can't answer that question. I'm sure that someone from Bodecker's company will let everyone know as soon as possible what is goin' to happen. For now I suggest you go about your business as usual. The whole town can't shut down or we'll *all* go out of business. I'll make sure a representative of Bodecker is out here at two o'clock this afternoon to talk to all of you. Deal?"

The crowd grumbles and starts to disperse.

The man Mac watches them intently, his hands on his hips.

He asks someone, "The sheriff?"

"Acting sheriff," the disgruntled gentleman replies. "Sheriff Ryan is out of town for a few days."

Preston finds a sunny place to sit and read Emmaline's story. Now all the pieces begin to fit together.

A group of three men stride past him, full of haste and purpose.

"How did the Tribune scoop this?" says one.

"How should I know?"

"You know, Roberts," says another, "she is always…"

He doesn't hear the rest. He follows them down the street since they are going in the direction he wants to go. They even stop outside the Tribune building, whine a little more and shake their heads, then keep on going. He watches them until they disappear into another building in the next block, which unless he is mistaken appears to be another newspaper called The Bugle.

He smiles to himself as he enters the Tribune building.

Inside, the disheveled lobby is so crowded with people he has to push his way in and then struggles to close the door.

A tall man dressed in a baggy suit, his tie hanging loose around his neck, looking like he hasn't been to bed all night, stands on a wooden chair trying to calm them all.

"This is all we know for now. Go bother Bodecker's company secretary and his attorney. And leave us alone."

The doors suddenly open behind him, and the noisy crowd, who is being coerced by Tribune staff to leave, sucks him out into the street again.

The haggard-looking feller follows them outside.

"Go on. Go home."

"We need information, Quaid," someone shouts.

"Told you. I don't have any more right now."

"What about Roberts?" shouts another.

"She's working on it," the man Quaid replies.

"She out-scooped the Bugle, didn't she, Quaid?" declares someone else. "They didn't see this comin'."

"That's right. Now if there are any Bugle spies among you, I won't be saying anything else, so go home or back to work."

The man Quaid retreats back inside his building. The door snaps shut behind him. Preston is still out in the cold.

Finally, the crowd gets the message and disperses. Preston tries the door again. It's locked. He knocks politely.

Someone from inside shouts, 'Go away'.

"My name is Preston Roberts. Emmaline Roberts is my daughter and I want to see her immediately."

He knocks again, more forcefully. A man's face appears at the window, the shade having been pulled aside, and peers out at him.

Preston lifts his eyebrows expectantly and peels back his coat lapel. The man at the glass sees what Preston intends for him to see, then turns away.

A muffled voice declares, "Did you know that Roberts' old pappy is a sheriff? He's got a badge to prove it."

Preston smiles. The door is unlocked and he is admitted.

The man Quaid appears to be waiting for him.

"So you're Roberts' father."

"Indeed."

"You're very welcome, sir. I'm Charlie Quaid, editor-in-chief of the Tribune."

"Pleased to make your acquaintance, Quaid. Come at a bad time, did I?"

"Big story," Quaid says apologetically.

"My daughter?"

"I'll show you."

"Thank you."

"Hope you're as proud of her as we are," Quaid says as they walk. They reach another open area where several desks are arranged. His daughter is seated at one, her head at an angle, writing, seemingly oblivious to all the fuss. His chest swells.

Emmaline! He always knew she was destined for a life very different to her sister's. Both girls had emerged from childhood with intelligence, beauty and grace, yet with totally different goals. Celina, determined to marry and move in society, chose Harrison. Emmaline, typically, decided on the most difficult thing she could find. Rejected by law school, she turned to journalism. At least that fraternity didn't ban her, merely tried to ignore her.

Not any longer it seems. At least one corner of the Wild West has taken to his daughter.

"Emmaline," he says.

Emmaline

At the sound of her name she looks up and can't believe her eyes.

"Sheriff..." she murmurs.

He makes that face where the top half frowns and the bottom half smiles. He hates her calling him sheriff.

"What are you *doing* here?"

The emphasis on 'doing' irritates him as well.

She shouldn't bait him. She shouldn't.

He comes towards her, twirling his hat in his hands. She rests her writing implements and gets to her feet.

"It seems I have come on a busy day," he says.

She lets him kiss her cheek and then stands back. In his eyes lurks the usual disappointment. In hers, undoubtedly, he sees the same.

"And I'm hearing your name all over town."

"Sit down, Sheriff. You've come a long way." She arranges her visitor's chair closer to hers. "Come. Sit."

"I wanted to talk to you, but..."

"Are you checking up on me?"

"Couldn't we go somewhere more private?"

She takes a good look at him while he makes himself comfortable. He looks well, if anything younger and more handsome than when she last saw him.

"That would be three months," she says aloud.

"Pardon me?"

"Since I last saw you."

His eyes hold her gaze steadily. "I went home a month ago to find you had left. Your mother informed me where you had got to. She says to give you her love by the way."

She feels herself stiffen. "So, you went home..."

Her father's gaze becomes difficult to hold. "And I stayed."

"Stayed? What do you mean?" she asks, wishing he wouldn't talk in provocations when he wanted her attention.

His steely sheriff's stare is impossible. "That's what I came to talk to you about. That, and to check on you. Your mother is concerned."

"Why did she feel the need to send you?"

"She didn't *send* me, Emmaline."

"And Celie, how is she?"

"*She* sent me," he says, with a dry smile. "She insisted I come. Meanwhile, your mother thought the frontier had borrowed you long enough. She said I was to plead with you to come home."

"Well, as you can see, that is impossible right now. I'm in the middle of..."

"Yes," he interrupts soberly, "I've witnessed what's going on."

She has to swallow. "What's the matter with Celie?"

"You would know that better than I."

She feels the weight of his comment and holds her tongue.

The Sheriff gets to his feet. "Any further conversation between us, Emmaline, will be conducted in private arrangements."

She looks up at him. A shiver traverses her spine.

"You look tired, Emmaline," he remarks.

"I spent a long night writing."

"And this looks to be a long day ahead."

"Quite possibly."

"And how do find the cold?"

"A challenge I am managing."

Just then, Mr Quaid appears at her desk. "Ah, Roberts, pleased to see a familiar face from home, I bet."

She gets to her feet, feeling weary and off-center. "Yes, Mr Quaid. You've met my father then?"

"Certainly. Didn't expect him to be a lawman. Well, I guess that would explain why you have no problem dealing with the lawmen in this town, eh, Roberts."

The remark is too true to be comfortable. She glances at the Sheriff to find the comment has caused a cavernous frown to appear on his stern face.

"Like I said, you are very welcome," Mr Quaid adds, turning to her father. "But I'm afraid I can't spare her just yet."

"I can see that," the sheriff says. "Do you let her out for lunch?"

Mr Quaid squirms. "Usually, but I can't vouch for today."

After the long night, the early morning and all the upheaval she will collapse if she doesn't eat lunch. Quickly, she says, "I'll eat lunch today."

Mr Quaid meets her gaze; they squabble silently for a moment and then he gives in.

"I'll have copy ready for you by deadline, Mr Quaid."

He knows she means what she says, so he politely retreats, leaving her alone again with the sheriff.

"Where shall we meet?" her father asks with a gleam in his eye she can't fathom.

"The Cheyenne Hotel at noon. If it is busy we can go someplace else, it's just easy to find."

"Accommodation?"

"Yes, not grand, pleasant."

"Good enough."

He likes his creature comforts, the Sheriff, but he would hardly have been the respected lawman he turned out to be if extravagance was at the top of his list when traveling.

"Your mother was right. You're working too hard, Emmaline."

Then he departs, with a flash of his dark brown eyes which leaves her in no doubt that if she doesn't turn up for lunch at the Cheyenne he won't be pleased.

She could spend the morning pumping herself full of coffee, racing around town, talking to anyone who will give her any information about Bodecker's business interests and what's to become of them. However, she decides to let Simons get the details on these, which he seems very pleased to do, and turn her focus instead onto something of a mystery, something that is beginning to bother her almost as much as it does Mr Quaid... what has become of Dillon Kerr?

Ben

Ben spies his cousin at a table near the window, he's eyes riveted to everything and nothing as he stares out into the street. Ben's approach, however, doesn't escape him; nothing really escapes him. Such vigilance must be wearying, and yet it seems second nature, leaving Ben to wonder if he will ever understand this cousin.

"Mornin'," Luke greets him.

Ben takes a seat. "Got your message."

Will you and Raina meet with me for coffee at ten in the dining room of the Inter Ocean Hotel? Luke.

Considering he and Raina are staying in the hotel, the request is practical and easy.

"Where's Raina?"

"She'll be along in a few minutes."

"She settling in okay?"

Ben nods. "So – what's up?"

"Your father and I almost came to blows last night."

"Oh?"

"I thought you should know. But I promise it won't come to that again."

Ben fiddles with the silverware. "Spoken to Ethan then?"

"Briefly. All he said was it was a long night; he didn't want to talk details."

Ben sighs and prods at the white linen tablecloth with the fork.

"I'm sorry," Luke says.

Ben looks up. "What for?"

"We didn't get to be the cousins we should have been."

"Shouldn't I be saying that?"

"This ain't about fault or blame, it's about regret. And, I was angry with you for not being like Tressa. She had it tough, but maybe you had it tougher."

"Right or wrong, what brought you to that conclusion?"

"I remembered my own father when I looked at yours. For a moment there was Morgan Taylor returned to my life. And then I looked closer into your father's eyes. It wasn't real. Morgan was truly gone. Instead, your father's hatred for him burned across the room at me. And I reacted. I've never seen a look like that in your eyes. It had to be tough to live with that all your life and be expected to carry it on like a family tradition."

"Fine," Ben says. "Can we move along now?"

Luke's gaze bores into his. "No, we can't. We're family."

"Did Tressa put you up to this?"

Luke's intensity lasts about two seconds longer and then he dissolves into laughter. He has an infectious laugh in that it's warm and kind. Ben knows how tough his cousin is, the depth of his resolve and the steeliness of his determination, but when he laughs it's easy to forget.

"Ethan then?" Ben says, feeling the ice melting.

His cousin shakes his head, chuckling, reaching for his glass of water.

Ben looks away to find his beautiful Raina is walking towards them.

They all have coffee together. Luke behaves like a gentleman in that he doesn't ask for details of how and where they met, although Ben detects a flicker of curiosity behind those astute eyes.

He and Raina realized after a while that the whirlwind and secretive nature of their marriage gave folks the impression they shouldn't pry. And they get caught up in the obvious and deep attraction between them and forget the rest. Even his own mother and Tressa accepted a trite explanation, for now anyway.

Raina shares with Luke her impressions of Ryan, which are insightful, amusing and seem to feed the part of Luke that needs reassurance of his friend's welfare.

Luke talks about the Diamond-T, which captivates Raina's imagination.

"Did you like it there, Ben?" she asks, her irresistible blue eyes shining with expectation.

He nods, smiling at her. "Although I don't think I experienced it the way you're meant to. Luke was sick, Ethan injured and Tip worried. Emmaline was wandering all over the place talking to people and scribbling in her notebook. Ryan couldn't keep still. He and Emmaline had a couple of arguments."

"Did they?" Luke says, amused.

"And that was *after* the trouble subsided."

Raina laughs.

"How is the Diamond-T normally?" she asks Luke.

"Very peaceful and quiet. Just how I like it."

This strikes Ben as odd. "Quiet? You?"

"Think you know me, do you?" Luke says with a grin, shifting about for his coat and hat. "C'mon. There's someone special I want you both to meet."

Emmaline

Emmaline locates Dillon Kerr's residence, a two-story house near the center of town. The man is unmarried and lives alone. Even so, she approaches carefully and waits for the street to clear before she slips into the passage beside the house and around to the back.

The yard is boring in its simplicity, crying out for release from its dull existence. Buds of Spring long to thicken the branches of one tall tree in the center; several branches have been broken off and lay scattered about the yard and around the small porch. The porch itself is bare of garden implements or furniture. Snow remains piled around the base of the stoop and she has to pull herself up and over it with the help of the railing. Her footprints, either in mud, slush or snow, are visible from the porch when she looks back over the way she came, but she can't be worried about that.

She steps up to the back door and peers through an uneven division in the window drapes. Inside it appears dark and quiet. Ever so carefully, she tries to turn the door handle. The door is locked. Well, that would've been ridiculously easy... She gleans the back porch for a suitable hiding place for a key. There is only one.

After taking a small, slender branch discarded by the tree, she uses it to poke the lintel over the back door. A black key falls onto the porch, clattering on the boards. She retrieves it quickly. It's covered with dust and dirt, and hasn't been used in a long time.

She frowns hard at the key; she should resist this, but she's not sure how. This is wrong, isn't it? But it needs to be done and she's the only one who can do it. She once chastised Cliff for breaking into Ed Parsons' place. Then they found the maps of Bodecker's

366

Empire on the wall and stood there discussing what it could mean. She desperately wishes Cliff were here now, to fight with her about the ethics of breaking and entering for a good cause. If he were here would she be doing this at all?

Her mind is made up. She peers around her for witnesses and seeing none she shoves the key in the lock and turns it. The click causes a rush of blood. It's all or nothing now.

She opens the door and enters into a small mudroom with two pairs of old boots scattered directly across her path. Gingerly, she closes the door behind her, and after taking a steadying breath she locks herself in. A risk perhaps, but she doesn't want anything to seem unusual or anyone barging in on her without warning.

And now... Dillon Kerr's home. Dark, perfectly still. She has a view, however, straight through the mudroom to the kitchen into a parlor and even beyond to a large open space which is probably the entrance hall. With the boots negotiated, she creeps through to the parlor. There is no sound but for one clock ticking somewhere nearby.

Off one side of the parlor there is a door, which she peers around to find his study; she pushes the door wide and enters. His chair looks like he just got out of it and she catches her breath. But everything is somber, gloomy and eerily still. If she is to be as good at this as Cliff, she needs to stop worrying about someone catching her and focus on what she came for.

She goes to Kerr's desk and begins a methodical investigation of it. Everything on top amounts to nothing more than personal possessions and correspondence. The drawers are next. First, the shallow one beneath the desktop. Inside, resting on green felt is a small pistol, its handle inlaid with mother of pearl or ivory or something similarly exotic. Bullets float around in its vicinity. The only other objects are a letter opener, in decoration a twin for the pistol, and a small brass key. She furthers her inspection to include the back of the drawer. It's not unusual for men like Kerr to have secret compartments. But this drawer has none.

Carefully, she lifts the key and then slides the drawer shut.

The key is a match for the stack of drawers on the right hand side. She unlocks the top drawer and pulls it toward her.

The drawer is packed with file folders and papers, all of which need sifting. She pulls each one out and eventually has to sit down and tell herself to breathe. Each is a dossier on some very familiar people. Luke. Ethan. Cliff. Mr Faraday. The Keatons. Mac. Marvin Tucker. Mr Quaid. The Governor. The Mayor. And compilation folios such as The Mavericks and The Association Members. At the bottom, however, is hers – and beneath hers is Miss Keaton's.

Her inclinations fluctuate between acting on the chill running down her spine, on the one hand, and her stinging curiosity on the other, but both are tempered by time and situation. At this point she must keep moving. Returning the dossiers to the drawer precisely as she found them, she vows to come back to them if she has no luck finding a clue to Kerr's whereabouts.

The second drawer contains stationery equipment, ink and pencils and the like.

The third has personal correspondence, which after a short dispute with her integrity, she examines for clues. Nothing.

The fourth and final drawer slides out at her bidding. There is but a single white envelope inside. She turns it over to find it is not stuck down. Inside there is a tatty scrap of paper with a name and address written on one side and on the other the words: *When all else fails.*

She takes out her notebook, copies down the words and then the name and address, which are not familiar to her.

As she puts everything back the way she found it, she reflects that Dillon Kerr went missing some time before Loren Bodecker arrived in chains. He couldn't know that Bodecker was arrested at that point. Could he? How? Did someone tip him off? Who?

She moves on, sleuthing around the parlor and all the downstairs rooms. Cold, dull and uninviting. This is no home; this is a house where a solitary man lives, and a not very nice man at that.

Time to make a start on upstairs.

The staircase is wide and has dark red carpet running down the middle of it. Every few treads it creaks, so she takes each step with great caution and has to tell herself to breathe.

She peeks into a couple of small rooms which have no furniture in them. One room, however, holds an ornate desk. An upstairs study is more likely to contain secrets perhaps? Her hands begin to tremble. She has a feeling that causes her scalp to prickle. But she needs to do this no matter what the cost.

She tiptoes to the desk.

On the green leather inlay of the desktop there is a telegram. She doesn't need to pick it up and touch it; she can read it perfectly: *Loren compromised. You know what you have to do. Lamont.*

She quickly starts jotting and has barely finished when she hears it – someone murmuring. She almost drops her notebook and juggles it firmly into her grasp. After expelling a deep breath and taking a fresh one, she creeps out of the room and into the hall. More murmuring. Like someone turning restlessly in their sleep. She follows the sounds down the hall until she finds the source; the door is slightly ajar. She teases it wider and puts one eye around it to see a comfortable, well-furnished bedroom.

Expecting to see Dillon Kerr talking in his sleep, the reality is infinitely stranger.

There is a woman, not much older than herself, with her long brown hair flagged out over the pillows, and a lurid pink eye mask over her eyes to shut out the light. She wears not a stitch of clothing, although a rumpled sheet covers her to her waist. All about the room articles of a woman's clothing are scattered; but some articles belong to a man.

The woman stirs again. "Dill... Dill, where you'd go?"

A familiar voice growls, "Still not satisfied, Eva?"

Emmaline pulls herself out of sight, staying her erratic breathing.

Dillon Kerr. Sounds place him in the room. He must have come from an adjoining chamber.

"You know I'm not," the woman purrs. "Come here."

Emmaline hears the bed creak and groan. She hears the beginning of what she should not be hearing. But they are also talking and every investigator knows that pillow talk can be invaluable.

"Why must you leave town, Dill? I want you here with me."

"You saw the telegram."

"Why do you act so secret?" she purrs again.

Emmaline imagines a lot of pouting.

"To get out of this, pet..."

"Out of what?"

"You know what, Eva. As I was saying, I must put people off the scent."

"You went and came back..."

"Well, Lamont and I have ways of communicating which you really shouldn't worry your pretty head about. Now, where were we..."

Neither says anything for a time. Emmaline thinks Kerr has put an end to the woman's protestations and she can sense and as well as hear their passion heating up. She's feeling uncomfortable and is about to leave when the woman says in a restless, breathy voice, "I much prefer you to Loren, Dill. Loren has no finesse."

"I've always wanted you," he says in a husky voice. "It was worth the wait."

So that's it. He's been having an affair with Bodecker's woman; he found out from this Lamont person that Bodecker had been caught – probably communicated from a telegraph in a secret location – so he went into hiding with this woman to carry on the affair.

"How much do you want me, Dill?" she asks. "How much do I mean to you?"

Emmaline considers this. They seem like perfectly reasonable questions in light of the situation.

"I'll take you with me," Dillon Kerr mutters passionately.

"What if Loren catches up to us?"

"He's going to prison."

"You came back for me, Dill."

A minute follows where only kissing sounds can be heard, as well as Eva's vocal appreciation of Kerr's amorous attentions.

"I want you, Eva," he says. "And I want you with me."

Soon it becomes obvious there is to be no more talking. The woman's groans become more insistent and fervent. Time for Emmaline to leave. She creeps and scampers. Pretends she's a mouse. She can hear them from the bottom of the stairs, however, their passion inhibited by nothing it seems. Strange to discover Dillon Kerr a passionate man. Appallingly disloyal though.

She hurries to the back door, stopping to debate whether she should use the time to return to the files in the downstairs study.

Have you lost your mind entirely, Emmie?

Celie is right. Knowing they are there is enough for now.

She lets herself out the back door. Once she has relocked the door she must find a way to replace the key. With the lovers so engaged, now would be the time to make a noise if it came to that. She notices a fat log stump lying at the bottom of the stoop. It's heavy but she manages to lift it and drop it by the door. It wobbles as she steps up onto it and she uses the door frame to steady herself. Reaching up, she slides the key back into place on the lintel. Again she struggles with the log until it is back precisely in the position she found it.

Pretending she's invisible, she ducks across the yard, along the side passage and stops. She waits for several passers-by and then darts through the front garden and out into the street. With her satchel clutched to her stomach, she inserts herself into the ebb and flow of townsfolk, all the way deep into town, until Cheyenne swallows her up and she at last feels safe. She makes for the Cheyenne Hotel. The clock in the lobby tells her it's almost eleven.

The desk clerk says, "May I help you with something, Miss Roberts?"

She shakes her head and goes back out into the street. Who does she tell? Mac? Mr Faraday? Mr Quaid? Anyone? No one? What disturbs her above all else is the perverse way she wants Kerr and Eva to get away and live happily ever after... They love one another and aren't scared to show it or to live it.

Looking this way and that, desperate to steady her bumping heart, she leans back against the outside wall of the Cheyenne.

She wants Cliff. No one else. Only him. Have him gaze at her with those Love's Philosophy eyes. Have him hold her. Have him be to her what Dillon Kerr is to that Eva woman.

"Oh, my," she breathes. "This is not good..."

She never expected to feel this way. She loved him. It stood to reason that she would want him. Yes, they had shared certain moments and those particular encounters had produced powerful feelings. But this was overwhelming. So much time and effort had been expended in squashing her enormous feelings into a tiny box, roping it up with a thousand impossible knots so she didn't feel the frustration of having to deny herself. She didn't expect overhearing Dillon Kerr and his woman declare their passionate intentions and acting on them would shake the whole arrangement loose.

"Emmaline…"

She looks up. "Sheriff."

"Are you all right, child?"

She doesn't know how to answer.

"You're early," he says, taking her arm and leading her inside again.

"I'm all right…"

"No, you're not. I think your sister may have been right. Let's sit down."

She puts herself into the Sheriff's hands for the first time in a long time. She hasn't allowed him to be her father for years. She knows it hurts and frustrates him, but he knows his relationship with her mother hurts and frustrates her, a standoff in which neither is prepared to surrender.

A glass of water is thrust into her hand.

"Drink."

She sips. If water could cure what currently ails her, she'd drink the town water supply dry. She allows the rhythm of the hotel to penetrate, the sounds of its occupants at work and play, the excitement in their voices over Bodecker, the smells from the kitchen, the perfume of a woman nearby, the pungent odor of a gentleman's cigar as he puffs madly over diverting conversation…

Slowly, slowly, she feels herself return to normality. It is a mark of the Sheriff's patience that he's still there.

"I'm sorry," she says.

"Something happen?"

"Yes… no… yes…"

He frowns. "Emmaline, I'm your father…"

"I know," she says lightly.

The frown deepens.

"Go on," she prompts him.

"I can see how involved you are here... Listen, Emmaline, I came here not only because Celina begged me to. Although her pleading alerted me to something you and I need to sort out right here and now..."

"Sheriff..."

"Emmaline, I don't appreciate being called that by my daughter and you know it," he declares, not so patient now.

She takes another sip of her water and then jams the glass down on the table.

"Then don't talk to me," she snaps.

They glare at one another; she makes a move to leave.

"I don't have to be here talking to you for another an hour, so until then I have work to do."

He lets her go.

And that hurts.

You are such a contrary creature, Emmie. Poor Papa...

Don't start that, Celie.

Then a hand comes out and grabs her wrist. She starts and looks down.

"There is something I have to tell you, Emmaline. And for once in your life you need to listen."

Luke

With a final wave of her hand, Jennifer steps back through the door into the kitchen. Luke closes the door behind them and observes her for some kind of reaction to his cousin and the sparkly-eyed Raina, but she is silent, her mind closed to him.

"Well?" he says, moving away from the door to where she has stopped by the stove, her arms folded, deep in thought.

"I think you are both trying very hard," she says.

"To?"

"Get used to one another for a start." She looks up, her green gaze penetrating.

He gives a quick nod.

"Raina is charming," she says and smiles. "Her eyes dance, did you notice? I can imagine for someone as serious as Ben that would be a delight. They clearly adore one another. And as for making a commitment they put the rest of us to shame."

"That they do," he says, linking his arms around her.

"Not the depth of their commitment, you understand…"

"I understand…"

"The swiftness of their action…"

"I know…"

"Do you know how he secured her away from her father – he sounds like a tyrant…"

"I don't know Ben well enough to ask the personal questions."

"Mm, I noticed. Luke, if you don't ask the personal questions, as you call them, how do expect to grow closer to him?"

He shrugs. "I guess it'll happen naturally."

"Oh, I see," she humors him.

"Ben and I've said enough for now," he concludes, happy with their progress and not about to succumb to any female pressure to do more.

"And what about his father, your uncle?"

"Hope he's had a good night's sleep because I'm heading over there now."

Truth is, the thought of confronting the man makes him sick to his stomach, but he has to do it.

"And what kind of questions will you be asking *him*?" she says archly.

"I don't expect it to begin or end well. He hates me and I hate him."

"*Do* you hate him?" she asks intensely.

"Shouldn't I?

"I think you should think about it carefully. What part of you hates, Luke? The child, or the man? I know from experience that a child is defenseless against such terrible emotion. On the other hand the adult can wield many weapons."

He bows to her expertise. "Go on."

"Do you really want to hate him? Will that help Ben and Tressa, and Caroline? You said yourself he brought your father back to life for a few moments. He is your father's brother. Surely that is something to celebrate. Your father did not hate him…"

"No, but he hated my father. Because my father's dead, he's transferred it all to me."

"You should be flattered," she mutters, startling him. "You should prove to him that hate holds no place in your family. He may think *he* holds the high ground but the way things are going he'll soon realize, if he hasn't already, that life as he knew it has been blown away and a new order is about to begin. Yours and Ben's. He's going to resent it but he'll have to accept it. *You* hold the high ground, Luke. You and Ben."

Staggered, he mutters, "I should pity him?"

"If you want to control the situation, hate will be a useless tool, but pity might come in handy," she says. "You need to stay on top, control the *high* ground…"

"Jennifer the Ruthless," he jokes.

She shakes her head, gently admonishing him. "I know you. You can't hate the way your uncle hates, Luke. It's not in you. You are your father's son. You have better things to do and more important emotions to express. If you could hate even for one second the way your uncle does, you would have killed Wilson Cutter in cold blood for what he did to Mart, but you didn't. You did what Mart wanted, your version of it at any rate. You are a loving man, Luke, not a hateful one. Your strength and determination come from goodness and compassion. And I don't believe for a moment, after all that you have been through, and all the enemies that surround you, that Richard Taylor is the one who would weaken you."

Her words never leave his mind as he makes his way to John and Amy's place. He recalls the moment atop the cliff in San Francisco Bay when he dealt with the pain and the darkness of his father's death. Somehow he has to connect that achievement with confronting his uncle.

Emmaline

"It can't wait one hour?"

"Now, later... It won't make any difference," he says.

Reluctantly, she accompanies her father; his hotel room typically overlooks the street. She has a perfect view of busy 17th Street in both directions as she stands surveying it by parting the muslin drape with the back of her hand. Perhaps she shouldn't be too harsh about his choice of room – which he would have asked for specifically – she would have requested the same. Cliff would have requested the same...

Cliff. *Ashcliff... Where are you? I need you here.*

Even though her father has this mysterious 'something' to tell her, she wishes he would leave and let her think.

Pull yourself together, Emmie. It's not the end of the world. Everyone who ever loved someone feels the way you do at some point...Love grows. Escapes. Gets out of control...It's something to celebrate...

Celebrate? Are you crazy, Celie?

"Emmaline, come away from the window," the Sheriff says.

She flinches and glances at him over her shoulder. Hands on hips, he looks troubled. She releases the drape and grudgingly gives him her attention, which mollifies him somewhat.

"I'm listening," she tells him.

"You're not yourself, Emmaline. Anyone can see that, especially someone who knows you well."

"Well," she says, choosing her words carefully, "be that as it may, Sheriff, you came to Cheyenne to tell me something. I did not ask you to come."

He looks skyward and blows a sigh.

"Fine," he says. "Obviously, there is no way of addressing this in a manner that will make it easy for you. You don't want me to make it so."

She takes fright at this. "I didn't say that," she says hastily. "I do have things weighing on my mind…"

"Then, for God's sake, sit down and make this easier on both of us."

She drops into the chair by the window. Though why she should make anything easy for him she doesn't know.

He draws and exhales a steadying breath. "Your mother and sister *did* want me to come here and check on your welfare, that is true. But there is something else and I had to tell you face to face, not in a letter. Emmaline, your mother and I have reconciled."

Her mind goes blank – what he said makes no sense to her…

"What did you say?"

"I moved back into the house. With your mother and your brother."

"She… Mama took you back?"

If she's not mistaken, he looks like he feels sorry for her.

"But… but she…she…"

"We never stopped loving one another, I think you know that."

"Don't speak to me," she says, turning away, knowing no such thing. "Just don't speak to me…"

"No, you are going to listen."

"No. You made her miserable. You can't… She can't want you back…"

"Emmaline, most children *want* their parents to reconcile."

"I…"

"*You* don't want me back, and that's the truth."

"Every time you had to leave town she was anxious. You didn't see it, but I did. It made her miserable. She would cry and…"

"And she would pick herself up and get on with her life. She had guts, your mother. She knew what she was getting into. Knew what she had to do and she did it."

"That's just your way of looking at it."

"No, it is hers. Ask her yourself. She'll tell you."

"I saw what it did to her with my own eyes. I saw her kick you out and tell you not to come back…"

He swallows hard. "When your baby brother was seven…"

"She had had enough."

"Your mother knew how to be a sheriff's wife better than any woman alive. True, she worried about me, worried I'd be hurt, and sometimes I was. But we made the most of our time together and we bore the times we were apart. We were strong for ourselves and for each other. That is, until I made a mistake…"

"You're darn right you made a mistake…"

"Emmaline, you have three brothers and a sister. None of you are a mistake. You are the result of how much I loved your mother."

She catches her breath.

"Now I've shocked you."

Tears sting her eyes. She grits her teeth. "I'm not a baby. *What* mistake?"

The Sheriff takes another deep breath. "I know all this time you've been thinking your mother got sick and tired of the way we lived, and that's why she told me to leave. Emmaline, I hurt her. After everything she'd done, all that we meant to each other…"

"Just tell me…"

"I was unfaithful to her."

"Un…unfaithful…"

"I had an…"

"An affair?"

He nods. "A very brief one."

"Why?"

"Does that matter?" he asks, his voice pained.

"Yes, it matters," she says. "And don't you blame my mother…"

"Emmaline," he says, "I blame *myself*, every day."

"Why?" she repeats. "Explain this to me."

"In a marriage there are dark patches, times where if things aren't working well between you, things come unstuck. It happened to your mother and me when your brother was seven. You may not think the two of us have ever been young, but we have been, and still don't consider ourselves old. Ten years ago, Emmaline, I was fit and strong as I ever was, and your mother as beautiful as the day I married her. But we had five young children and a lot of responsibility. It all took precedence over our relationship and we drifted into a workaday pattern; we forgot that the passion we started out with needed nurturing. And then one day I went off to work on the other side of the county for a few days. I was lonely. I was tempted. I succumbed. By the time I returned home to you all, I realized what I'd done. Your Mama knew something was wrong, I couldn't hide it from her, and I confessed…"

Feeling nauseous, she chokes out, "Was that… the only time?"

"I realized I'd broken the vows I made to your Mama on our weddin' day…"

"And since then?"

He doesn't answer right away; her insides sink to a new low.

Then, "I tried to make it right, but she was too hurt. She never wanted to see me again. And when I spent time with you children she refused to see or speak with me. In time, she healed enough to get back on speaking terms. We had to, for your sakes."

"I remember the day you left."

"Do you? I'm not surprised. I remember the look on your face. You thought me the worst person in the world, I'm sure of it. But not because of what really happened, Emmaline, but incorrectly because of my job and what you thought it did to your Mama."

"Your job was to blame. It took you away."

"No."

"Then we were to blame. The five of us. We were too many for her and you were away a lot. She worked too hard and you betrayed her."

The Sheriff lets out a loud, exasperated sigh. "Emmaline, you and your brothers and Celina are not to blame. This is between your mother and me. I'm telling you because I know how our history has shaped you, and I don't want you to take out my shortcomings as a father on any prospective relationship of your own. You are at that interesting age, Emmaline. Look at you. You're lovely. And so full of spirit. Some extraordinary young man is going to come along and want to sweep you off your feet and you are going to tell him that all men are dogs because of me! I know you, Emmaline."

Tears burst from her eyes, burning and stinging. Misery is not far behind.

"I don't want that to happen to you," he says gently. "Your mother knew me; she knew being a sheriff was important to me; she never resented it, not the way you always thought. She said you and I have that problem, not her and me. She thinks you perceived her struggles so sensitively that you mistook them. She said you were different to your brothers and Celina. She wishes she'd been stronger, for your sake. She blames herself. She said if I wanted to come back to her I had to make it right with you. That's why I'm here, Emmaline. I want your Mama."

She cries into her hand.

"Why do you think I've never stopped trying to get her back?"

"Is that what you've been doing?"

"If you think about it, Emmaline, you know it's true."

"So you've never betrayed her since?"

"I can see that question is important to you, but I'm not going to answer it. It's not relevant and not your place."

She takes her hand away and glares at him.

"Emmaline, you are by far the most challenging obstacle I have faced in my goal to get your mother back into my life. It's like telling trees and rocks to switch places. Emmaline, I want my beloved daughter back too."

"How touching! And just how am I your beloved daughter, Sheriff?"

He looks deeply hurt. "I taught you to ride and shoot. To be yourself. To be confident. I was proud of you. Of how clever you were, even as a child. I went to the university and argued – to no avail – that they let you into law school. Then I argued for you when your mother didn't want you to go to that college. She won't be a lady when she comes out of there, she said. But you were. Then I convinced her to let you become a journalist. I convinced her to let you come to Cheyenne. In only the short time I've been here already I've seen how much you have accomplished. You are amazing."

"Thank you," she mutters, quite astonished at him.

"It's not enough, is it?"

"I don't know what to say. I didn't know most of that."

"I will always fight for you, Emmaline. Protect you. That is unconditional. And my right as your Papa. But your Mama has put a condition on *me*... Please, answer me this: will you give me your blessing to return to your Mama?"

"*My* blessing...? *Mine*...?"

"Yours."

"You love Mama that much?"

"I have always loved her that much. And you. We are a family, Emmaline. That's why I worked so hard. Why I never stopped working. Why I lived in another house but never truly left our home. Why I saw you all so often. I love my family. All of you are worth whatever I need to do, even facing my toughest critic – you – and saying how sorry I am."

"The others... what do they think?"

"I didn't tell them about the affair, although I think Celina has worked it out. Anyway, she and Johnny and Nick are very pleased your mother and I are back together again."

It feels like forever since she's seen them...

"And your baby brother... well, Sam is fine. I think he may even go to college now, at least apply himself to something. I never realized how deeply he felt the need to take care of his Mama."

"Man of the house," she murmurs.

"They don't see me the way you do, Emmaline," he declares softly.

"That's why you told me and not them."

"I'm sorry."

She looks straight into his eyes and sees for herself that he is genuine.

"I don't know what else to say to you..."

"I...I wish..." she stammers, "I wish it had been different."

"I know," he says, clearly grief-stricken.

She shrugs and wipes her tears away. There is a strange calmness to her devastation which leaves her lost for words and feeling just plain lost.

"I... I should go."

"Go? You can't go. Look at you."

"I have work to do. Copy to prepare." She gets to her feet.

"But…"

"Don't you understand, Sheriff – I *have* to work. Please, go back to Mama. She loves you. And you can't help who you love…"

She gives his tall figure a wide berth as she leaves, but when she gets to the door he delays her, again his hand on her wrist. She looks up at him, despising the painful vulnerability she feels.

"Is there someone, a young man?" he asks, frowning.

"I have to go or I won't make deadline."

He takes his hand away. He isn't sure of her; doesn't know her as well as he thinks…

But then, "Emmaline… I'm your Papa…"

Whether he holds out his arms or whether she puts herself into them, she doesn't know. All she can be sure of is that he comforts her with fatherly tenderness while the heart-broken thirteen-year-old girl inside of her weeps.

Luke

As he walks along 17th Street, crosses and weaves and shoulders a path, he works on his memory, so hard in fact that once he's turned into Evans Street, not far from John and Amy's on the corner with 18th, he has to rest on the sidewalk. Nearby is a bench seat made out of a split log and he sits, takes off his hat and wipes his brow. Searching through memories of his boyhood, searching for something that could help him with his uncle, he's left scratching his head. But it's cold without his hat on. He's about to fix it to his head again when a vision of Red Sky comes to him, filling his mind with her presence, filling his eyes so that he sees nothing but her.

"Red Sky…" he murmurs aloud.

Her form becomes so vivid he has to suppress the urge to reach for her. She is wearing her princess dress, which is what he always called her buckskin dress and shawl, adorned with beads, fur and feathers, and trimmed with a deep buckskin fringe; she holds her feather fan; from her ears, shells and other ornaments dangle; in her jet black hair another sloping spray of feathers. Her wide-set eyes glisten like black amber as she gazes at him, her full mouth curved into a gentle smile. She is so young and beautiful and proud she takes his breath away.

"My little one, Luke."

He closes his eyes.

She promised him she would never truly leave him. In the few times this has happened since her passing he has never ignored her; he would never ever turn away from Red Sky.

And suddenly he's nine years old; he and Red Sky sit together on the shady porch steps of the house on their Red River ranch in Texas. They look out across the sun-drenched yard to the corrals where his Pa leans on the corral fence looking off into the distance at something. Above him sparkles a blue summer sky.

"What's Pa lookin' at, Red Sky?"

"I do not know. Your father likes to think, little one."

"Why is that?"

"You are young. One day, you will like to think also."

"No, I think at this age, Red Sky. I been thinkin' about somethin' I overheard yesterday..."

"Your father and mother talking."

"How'd you know that, Red Sky?"

"You are everywhere you should not be, little one!"

"Yeah, it was them that were talkin' about how my uncle hates us. Pa wrote him a letter, see, and I think he got one back and I don't know what it said but Ma was upset so I guessed it weren't good."

"Your poor mother, she who is so kind."

"My uncle hates us all so much and I reckon I'm supposed to hate him back. That bothers me a lot. Is that what Pa's thinkin' about now, d'you think?"

"Little one, hate is not for you. That is why you are not happy to hold it in your heart. You believe in freedom, Luke. And this makes your heart strong, very strong."

"I guess."

"The bad feeling between your father and his brother is like war with long truce. The fighting is stale; there is no struggle. But there is no surrender; they do not forgive and they do not sue for peace. It troubles me, because they are kin."

"But I think I do hate my uncle. I never even seen him."

"One day you will deal with it."

"I don't know. Aw, just look at how Pa likes to think. Maybe he's thinkin' about us leavin' Diamond Bend."

"I believe he is thinking this, little one."

"He sure does love this country, why does he want to leave it?"

"This land is tired, and wounded..."

"I don't ever want to leave. I wanna stay here, right where I was born. I'm Texan. This is my country. Not someplace up north on the frontier with homesteaders and sojourners."

"Your kin, Luke, this is your country. You are born to them, not to a land, for lands can be left. There are many paths to take you forth, many gates to open and shut, before you understand this and be content. To be truly free you must unlock your heart, then you will discover the things you seek."

The memory begins to fade; he wants to cling to it and never leave, but as it dissolves a sense of being wrapped in love's embrace replaces it. He feels warm inside and out.

He breathes deep... Red Sky's familiar scent of buckskin, eagle feathers and the white lilac perfume Ethan always gave her fills him up before it floats away, and the wintry Cheyenne street returns.

Richard

One minute Caroline was seated on the sofa talking to him and the next she's mumbling a few words and walking out. He's missed something; it's been happening constantly... blanks in his thinking, missing things...

How does he rid himself of everything that's happened and clear his mind?

There are voices out in the hall, Caroline's and a man's. Young and low. His son! Returning to show remorse this time perhaps... instead of showing off the new wife. How could he ever forgive Ben for what he did, keeps on doing – joining up with the traitors.

He stands up and paces the hearth rug. He can't keep still for long either. Befuddled, nothing he does or says makes sense. How to right it... how to right it...

Caroline reappears. "You have a visitor, Richard."

He looks up from the patterns on the rug.

Standing in the doorway is his young and virile brother. He bristles.

Morgan! No... that's not right.

Confused, he frowns. Stupid, stupid brain. Not Morgan. The son. The troublemaker. With a stony blue stare, like he is superior.

He glares back at the upstart to put him in his place.

Sonofabitch...

Ah, what's this now?

The son's expression now seems uncertain.

He pounces. "What do you want?"

"Would you be willing to speak with me, Uncle?"

"Asking permission? How polite! Had a change of heart from wanting to pound my head into the dust?"

"Richard," Caroline gasps.

He has a distinct need to dismiss Caroline; she gets in his way.

The son says, "Don't look at her that way."

"What are talking about?"

"When a woman is bothering you that's the time you should be paying attention to her."

"Who taught you *that*?"

"Women," the son fires back, but smoothly, like he thinks it's funny.

Caroline's cheeks dimple and blush. The son grins at her.

Got the ladies wrapped up then. Same as Morgan.

"Will you speak with me, Uncle? I think we need to get this situation between us figured out. At least reach an understanding of some kind. Do you agree?"

Caroline has been looking up at the son with clear admiration and abruptly transfers it across the room to him. There is such hope in her glance; such conviction. How can he disappoint her again? When he thought he had lost her, his whole life veered out of control. He never dreamed it was she who held his world together. Learning to include her, acknowledge her position, would be a promising start.

"I might," he concedes to score some points with her.

Her eyes sparkle at him. Why does she still love him? The strength of her loyalty now could be a result of her guilt over having deserted him earlier, but he's not inclined to hold to this view. Besides, he'd liked to believe she loves him. Someone has to.

"Ah," he stammers, lost momentarily under Caroline's influence. "Sit then."

"I'm sorry I tried to fight you last night," the son begins as he sits. "I reacted. Memory is a powerful thing."

Puzzling is this change of attitude.

"I was in a dark place," the son continues. "And it was strange looking at you. Seemed like my father had come back to life after all these years. It never occurred to me that you would look alike, well, resemble one another the way brothers do."

He'd been thinking the same thing. "You look more like him than I. Very like him. He closely resembled your grandfather, while I am more like our mother."

"If you say so, but I saw my father. And now I am ashamed that you, his closest living relative apart from me, are the very person I tried to attack."

"Ashamed, are you?" he barks in callous amusement. "Don't be. Your father wouldn't be ashamed of you for that. He'd have wanted you to!"

"I don't believe that."

"Then you might look like him, but you are not like him."

The son looks uncomfortable.

"If you intend to carry on in this conciliatory manner..."

"I do," the son says firmly. "And there is a very good reason why."

"Oh?"

"You are no longer in control of your family, Uncle. Your son is."

He feels acute pain in his chest. "It's not right."

"Ben and I want to make this work. And what's more, we are going to."

"So you and Ben see eye to eye, do you? Think I'm getting my just deserts, do you? I tried to keep Ben from this, spare him from knowing the traitors..."

"Traitors?"

"Your father betrayed his family heritage of liberty and freedom and yet it is he who is held up as the model of our heritage. I will never understand that."

"Neither do I," the son says.

He can't believe his ears. "I tried to spare my children the shame of knowing relatives who disgraced the heritage of Taylors' from the time our forefather Matthew got to this country..."

"But you kept them from knowing their heritage. To be strong you need to have all the facts. I told Tressa about Matthew and Elizabeth, about Daniel and Roberta, about James and Lara. She barely knew anything. As much as my father shamed our heritage of liberty and property in your eyes, he kept safe our heritage by passing the stories on to me. Can you be so proud of them if you refused to share them?"

"I... It may look that way. Yes..." he thinks, rubbing his forehead, "it looks that way, but you should understand the complications. Our parents favored your father. I was different in their eyes and because Morgan was like them, they thought more of him than me, even when your father went off into the world and left them. *That* I didn't do, despite my unhappiness. Eventually, I rejected my heritage because of them. Even in my successes I could not compete with your father. I resented it, yes, with all my being, but when Morgan turned his back on everything we had been taught, I could not forgive or condone."

The son looks thoughtful and then says, "I agree, he did fight for the wrong cause, and yes, he should have fought on the side of the abolition of slavery, but he did exercise his right to choose, his right to take up arms..."

"Don't you think I haven't thought of that? Of course, he did. And Ethan. But it doesn't excuse them, not in my book. Morgan turned his back on our heritage, your heritage, he lived one but passed on another... well, in that sense, maybe the war taught him a lesson. Did he not speak of it with you?"

The son shakes his head. "I learnt more from Ethan over the years. Ethan..." The son clears his throat and continues, "Ethan is Texan-born."

He scrutinizes him carefully. "You defend Ethan, but not your father."

The son looks rattled. "Yes. All right. Don't ask me why..."

"I know why," he says with a grunt. "Your father knew better. He wasn't a Texan by birth or by upbringing. He was a son of liberty, just like you."

The son is quiet, wearing a pained expression on his Morgan-like face.

He wishes the son *were* Morgan so he could tell him just what he thought of him.

What the heck, close enough; may as well get some of it off his chest... "I wanted nothing to do with any of you. Wanted to forget you existed. I didn't want my children growing up with the son of a confederate. I didn't abandon you and your mother to fate when your father died. I had already refused to acknowledge your existence. I'd wiped you out of my world and my family's world a long time ago."

The son grows pale and looks sick. "You speak of being a son of liberty. Do you think you acted like one?"

"I gave up seeing myself as one of those brave and noble boys long, long time ago, when it became clear that in being different I didn't fit the mold. I'm not brave or noble, and I don't believe in causes. I tried – once. Didn't turn out right. Didn't fit the mold."

The son stares at him for a long time. He wonders if the boy will ever speak.

Then, "Ben... fits the mold."

He grunts, affronted. He recalls Ben's restlessness over the last few years and unhappiness over the past twelve months, and ponders on it now.

"Whether you taught him unthinkingly or whether it comes natural..."

"You think that saves me in your eyes, don't you?"

The son looks taken aback. "I don't know what saves you. Tressa... Ben... Caroline... they are truly good people, in spite of you or because of you, I don't know. And I don't care."

He has to laugh at this. "You care. It's your weakness. Do you think if Morgan cared he would have left you and your mother and sister to go fight for a cause that went against everything he'd been taught?"

Heat grows in the son's expression, with cheeks gaining color and eyes sparking.

Again, he is stared at for a long while, and he can see the son exercising restraint.

"I care nothing for your morals and your values," he tells the son. "I truly don't care. Your fight against Bodecker has divided my family. That and when Tressa got herself messed up by marrying your friend."

"Really?" the son counters through his teeth. "I think Tressa saw in Mart who she really is."

"You're an idealist, your other weakness. So, have we finished?

Because I really have nothing further to say. You understand my position and I understand yours…"

"You're half right. Your position is clear. You might be interested to know mine in more detail. What I think about *your* weaknesses."

"You come here to insult me? Nothing short of what I expected."

"Not insults. The truth."

"According to you."

Suddenly, Caroline says, "Listen to him, Richard. Let him say what he's kept inside him all these years. He's just a boy…"

He considers his wife and her words. Then he looks at the son, who looks like Morgan did the day he left home in search of his own life… there's something about the son. It's in his eyes.

"You have suffered," he says, thinking out loud.

"Excuse me?" the son gulps, puzzled.

"Did I really cause that suffering, or should you really be blaming your father?"

The son doesn't say a word; he's thinking again, something he does a lot of it seems.

"It was your father who caused your suffering, not me. Granted I didn't ease it and whether I should've or not depends entirely on your point of view. What you suffer now, under this sway of Bodecker and his cronies, you can thank your father for. He left Diamond-Bend and Texas for Wyoming. No one made him. He thought he was some great frontier man, but all he did was set you upon a path of suffering. So don't blame me for what he did."

"I don't blame you for that… and I think dwelling on the past is unhealthy. I've righted the past in my own mind, all except you and where you fit. I understand things in your family weren't good for you and caused you to cut yourself off, but I don't have to agree with it. I believe you were jealous of my father and your mean streak was the true point of difference…"

"How dare you…"

"It's my turn, Uncle, so keep quiet and listen. I never said my father was perfect. And in spite of his obvious faults, he was kind and cared about people. He treated people well and he respected them for who they were. You demand that your family be the people you want them to be. You're some kinda tyrant. And the twist in all this, Uncle, is that *you*, who rails against the South, are a hypocrite. No one was free under your roof, and then Mart Keaton walked into your office and rang the liberty bell loud and clear, so clear that Tressa responded to it with all her heart. It set off a chain of events you couldn't control, because in spite of what you tried to do, freedom is a spirit that can't be contained. It's a part of who we are, as people. I can't explain it any better than that, but if a whole civilization couldn't manage to hang on to slavery, then who d'you think you are to think you can enslave your family's will to yours. There's a cold, silent war been going on and the tide's turned. You're losing, Uncle."

He recoils inwardly and sits back. Where did the son learn to talk like that? How dare he talk like that…

"Richard," Caroline whispers.

He looks at her, feeling old, his head aching. She nods gently and looks with pity into his eyes.

Pity. Is that all he can expect for the rest of his life?

"Now, here's the thing," the son continues, "I don't know if you and me will ever get along, but Ben and I are making progress. This family will grow strong, we are both determined. We've lost time, but with the family expanding, we'll make up for it. We're moving on, Uncle. You can come with us, or stay behind, or maybe Caroline will pull you along with her. No matter what, the old days are gone and you better get used to it. Now that's all I got to say."

All he can do is stare at the son, who before long gets to his feet.

"I think we understand one another, Uncle. I'll see myself out, Caroline."

Caroline nods; she looks miserable.

Before the son walks out, he says, "You might try making the people who love you happy once in a while."

He has to take that on the chin; funny, but as he looks at downcast Caroline sitting beside him he wonders if she's ever been happy with him, except perhaps at the very beginning of their marriage, when they were starting out and life was ahead of them.

They were at that age now when most of life was behind them. But they'd been successful, hadn't they? Why shouldn't she be happy then? Success leads to happiness in the truest sense. He thought she felt the same. Has he been wrong all these years?

"He's smart, don't you think?" Caroline murmurs.

He concedes with a weary nod. Her eyes sparkle a little.

"I remember Sara said once that she was determined to educate their children well, no matter where Morgan took them. What a grand job she has done. I think that young man is destined for something."

He grunts, annoyed.

"Don't be downhearted, Richard. I believe this family, all of us together, will make you proud someday. Surely that is something to look forward to."

He reaches across and takes up her hand. Surprise darts into her eyes.

"We need to talk," he says.

She steadies herself, much to his amusement, and says, "Very well, Richard."

Faraday

On the steps of Loren Bodecker's building
Downtown Cheyenne

Faraday checks his watch. Two o'clock precisely. Thomas Dyer holds his hands up to the crowd, pleading for their silence.

Political life in Cheyenne had got a little complicated of late and it wasn't helpful in the midst of all the upheaval. Tom Dyer had been elected ex-officio mayor since Francis Warren resigned in February to take up the post of Governor of Wyoming, relieving Elliot Morgan who'd been acting governor since Governor Hale passed away in January. A special mayoral election had been called for March 17th, but Tom, meanwhile, has a lot on his plate.

From his vantage on the sidewalk, Faraday looks out across the throng. Members of the press, overly keen, take up all the places near the front. He can't spot Miss Roberts among them though. He lets his eyes wander to look for her, but Tom Dyer clears his throat, alerting Faraday to his duty. Eyebrow raised, their stand-in mayor expects Faraday's full and unfailing support.

Someone yells out, "Where is Dillon Kerr? We want to know what's going on."

Tom launches into a speech, not telling them exactly what they want to hear, but more of what he wants them to know, which isn't much.

Faraday scans the crowd once more looking for familiar faces. Luke, Ethan, Ben Taylor and John Keaton stand as a group near to the back. He's surprised, however, to espy Miss Roberts with them. Beside her is a distinguished older man he doesn't know. She has her notebook out and writes as Tom emotes his rallying of the business community. In the face of its imminent collapse, what else could he do?

As for Miss Roberts, she should be at the front. If he didn't know better, he'd say she is standing in the protective shadow of the Alliance.

He spies George at the back but on the opposite side.

Tom makes his final point and then hands the gathering over. "Faraday..."

Exposure to Cheyenne's disgruntled citizens suddenly becomes an unsettling reality.

When he casts another glance at the Alliance, only Miss Roberts and the older gentleman remain. He skims the scene to find they have all changed positions. Ethan is near the front on his left. Ben Taylor on his right. John Keaton stands in the middle of the crowd. Luke walks past George and hovers in that vicinity.

Good God, they are protecting *him* now.

Another glance at Miss Roberts; the older gentleman has also moved. And Miss Roberts is working her way to the front.

Faraday begins.

"Everything our Mayor has just said is true. Loren Bodecker is to stand trial for conspiracy and murder. Information and confirmation from Denver and Omaha have been pouring in all morning and it is true that, for the moment, Mr Bodecker's business concerns are in disarray; the price of shares in his public companies has plummeted. We are facing a challenging prospect, there is no doubt about it. I understand that this is a difficult time..."

"Where is Dillon Kerr?" that same journalist yells out again.

"His whereabouts is unknown. He left town before anyone knew Mr Bodecker had been arrested. So whether he knew or didn't know is not something I can tell you. Now, Mr Bodecker's trial will commence on Monday week."

"Mr Faraday, that is the same day as the Maverick mastermind Donnelly's, is it not?" This from Miss Roberts.

"Yes, Miss Roberts," he says. "It is."

"So they are being tried together?"

"Yes."

A huge ripple of sound escapes from the stunned crowd. Faraday holds up his hands.

"Would you care to update and confirm for us the list of charges, Mr Faraday?" Miss Roberts asks, her pencil at the ready.

"Yeah, get on with it, Faraday," another reporter calls out.

It never ceases to amaze him that the others take their cue from her.

"Mr Bodecker and Mr Donnelly are charged with conspiring to murder Miss Kelley Keaton..."

The crowd reels.

"...Sheriff Dave Ransford, Deputy Jim Crogan..."

They gasp as one.

"Also, the sheep farmer John Adams from Dickson and several other poor souls. Mr Donnelly's indictment includes an additional count of murder for that of the young woman, Cadie McClements."

"The prostitute on the train?" a reporter calls out.

"That's right. And then there are the attempted murders of Miss Emmaline Roberts and Luke Taylor."

This time the crowd is very vocal.

Boldly, Miss Roberts asks, "Have the accused maintained their innocence?"

"Yes. But the prosecution has many witnesses and will work tirelessly to bring the perpetrators of these crimes to justice."

"But what is their motivation for such crimes?" he is asked by another young reporter.

"The motivation for these crimes and other acts will become clear as the trial progresses. I will not be a party to any efforts to sensationalize and speculate on what has happened. Suffice to say, it is in everyone's best interest to see this thing done properly and securely."

Miss Roberts asks, "How long do you expect the trial to last, Mr Faraday?"

"It will not be rushed because investors think it should be. All the evidence will be thoroughly presented and examined."

Someone from the middle of the crowd yells, "And what if you're wrong, Faraday? What if they are innocent? Or what if they are acquitted?"

"I am confident that the people of Cheyenne can put aside their own interests to form a jury which will be able to intelligently and faithfully consider the facts in evidence and deliver the correct outcome."

A Bugle reporter asks, "Why didn't Sheriff – sorry, Deputy Marshal – Ryan return with Dan Hummer and the others?"

"I believe he had another lead to follow in the case."

"When will he be back?"

"Marshal Hummer tells me a few days."

"What is the lead?"

"I can't discuss that."

"Will there be another arrest?"

The questions begin to flow. He answers them one by one. The crowd stays to listen. A glance at Tom Dyer. He shrugs. No attorney or representative from Bodecker's company has shown up, despite Tom's repeated request.

Then, striding down the sidewalk towards them, flanked by two men on his right and one on his left, is the attorney Sturrock. They are immaculately dressed in dark town suits and carry black leather attaché cases. With grim expressions on their faces, they come to Faraday's side and overwhelm his place on the sidewalk.

"We wish to address this crowd," Sturrock announces.

Faraday steps aside for them.

"My name is Sturrock. This is Buchanan, Watson and Ellicott. We will be defending Mr Bodecker and Mr Donnelly. We have visited with our clients and Mr Bodecker has asked Mr Buchanan to read a statement."

Buchanan steps forward, solemn to the point of contemptuous, oozing experience and self-confidence. "Mr Bodecker says, 'Dear citizens and friends, I am entirely innocent of the charges brought against me. I will fight this injustice with every bone in my body. I will fight to have your confidence restored. While I am undertaking this important work, please do not neglect the work of our empire, the prosperity of this great territory. Work and work hard to keep the wolves at bay and to silence the howls of our district prosecutor for my blood. I will see you all in court. Sincerely, Loren Bodecker.' That is all."

Silence.

Buchanan moves back into line.

Suddenly, a huge cheer explodes from the crowd, followed by clapping and more cheers. Meanwhile, there are handfuls of people standing quietly, looking unmoved or confused.

Luke now has positioned himself at George's shoulder. The older gentleman from before has reappeared at Miss Roberts' side, and while she puts finishing touches to Buchanan's statement, he stands guard over her.

Tom Dyer restores some order.

"Thank you, gentlemen," he says to the attorneys. They nod and disappear into Bodecker's building, locking the door behind them.

Tom dismisses the crowd and then, with a dip of his hat brim in Faraday's direction, takes himself off as well. Townsfolk disperse in dribs and drabs, a great many speaking excitedly as they go, some shaking their heads, some still utterly perplexed. Most of Faraday's thought is consumed with the knowledge that the jury will come from these unhappy, confused people. *That* and it seems he has four of the wiliest looking attorneys he has ever set eyes upon with which to do battle.

He gradually becomes aware of Miss Roberts and the older gentleman bickering. As the Alliance has since gathered around Luke and George, there is no one left to hear them but him.

The gentleman approaches him.

He sweeps off his hat and says, "Sir, my name is Preston Roberts. Emmaline is my daughter."

Which would explain a great deal.

"Cam Faraday. A great pleasure indeed to meet you, Mr Roberts."

Faraday offers his hand and Preston Roberts shakes it firmly.

"Likewise. I apologize that my daughter and I cannot hold a civil conversation in a public street, but I just found out, listening to you, that she was nearly murdered, twice. This is true then?"

Faraday understands his incredulity. Looking at Miss Roberts it is difficult to believe how anyone could want to harm a hair on her head, let alone shoot her.

"I'm afraid so, Mr Roberts."

Miss Roberts steps up, looking uncharacteristically fragile and out of sorts. "Hello, Mr Faraday."

"Miss Roberts. Neglected to tell your family about your narrow escapes, I see."

"Yes, wouldn't you?"

Faraday presses his lips together and steals a look at Preston Roberts' face. The man is pale, although his eyes are glowing.

"I'm sorry to be rude," she says, "but I really need to get back to work. I have a deadline. Goodbye, Mr Faraday. I thought you were very brave."

"Thank you, Miss Roberts."

"You'll need to be, don't you think? Those attorneys look like something from a prosecutor's worst nightmare." She smiles wanly, gives her father a hesitant look and hurries off down the street.

Faraday has a smile ready for her father when he finally stops watching his daughter and looks around.

"She's an extraordinary girl," Faraday says.

"A proud father thanks you. So, how lucky is she to be alive?"

"Do you really want to know?"

"That bad?"

"Mm."

"But how... what...?" The man jams his hat back on his head.

"She had a very good man keeping an eye on her. Our sheriff, Cliff Ryan."

"The gentleman that's out of town temporarily?"

"The same."

"I must remember to thank him."

Faraday smiles. "What do you do for a living, Mr Roberts?"

Preston Roberts pulls back his coat. A familiar silver object winks in the afternoon sunshine.

"Oh. Sheriff Roberts..."

"Orange County, Florida. I'll be retiring in two months. Emmaline's mother has had enough. I think it's time to take stock."

"You know, you should stay in town until Cliff returns. Thank him in person."

"Oh, I plan to, Mr Faraday."

Luke wanders up and begs pardon for the interruption. "Cam, we all agree that you shouldn't be standing around in the street."

"Oh?" Faraday looks around. The Alliance, including Tip Benchley whom he hadn't spotted previously, has moved in and is guarding him at closer quarters.

He folds his arms, greatly amused. "Luke, you know Preston Roberts?"

"Sure; Emmaline introduced us."

"Yes, but you didn't tell me you have also recently escaped with your life," Roberts says.

Luke's dark eyes quiver. "Sorry about Emmaline, Mr Roberts," he says. "If it weren't for Cliff..."

"Ah, we've been over that," Faraday says. "Emmaline didn't mention her father is a sheriff?"

Luke frowns. "No, I..." A smile breaks out on his face.

"Is there something more I should know?" Preston Roberts asks.

"Emmaline is a good friend. And I'm pretty sure I'd be dead right now if it weren't for her," Luke says.

Preston Roberts gives Luke a hard look. "Why do I get the feeling I'm never going to know the whole story?"

"Er... you will," Luke says. "Excuse me, would you? Some things I gotta do..."

Preston Roberts tips his hat and Luke strides away.

"That one," says Roberts, "is trouble."

Faraday chuckles. "With a capital T."

Cliff

Brown looks up from his desk when he spies Cliff coming through his door.

Cliff shakes his hand. "Mr Brown. How goes it?"

"Very well, Deputy Marshal. I think you will be pleased."

"Progress?"

"John and I worked late. They're done."

"I'm much obliged, Mr Brown."

"You're welcome. It's not every day you get an assignment like this one. Here, let me show you. We've created the images in whole plate size, so you have pictures eight and a half inches by six and a half. You wanted details and we've captured plenty. Whoever looks at these will be clearly informed. There is no mistaking what you're looking at."

He spends ten minutes with Brown perusing the photographs, which are excellent in size and clarity, giving a precise and accurate picture of Porterfield's operation. The images taken in the basement, powerful in every respect, send a shiver down his spine.

Brown notices. "John and I did that, too, even though we saw it yesterday with our own eyes. You say your friend survived this?"

Cliff nods, his eyes watering as he stares at the cot in the photograph.

"Anything else I can do for you, Deputy Marshal?"

"No. Your work is excellent, Mr Brown, thank you."

"I will store the plates until you inform me otherwise."

"Much appreciated. How much do I owe you?"

402

He relieves his pocket of a small fortune.

Before he returns to Wilma's, keen to secure the precious photographs in his bag, he heads to the telegraph office, facing the prospect it might not be operational. Since the news came through about Bodecker's arrest, the business end of town has become restless and searching for news; top that off with the newspapers' incessant demand for updates. He'd heard the telegraph lines had jammed.

A sign on the wall of the telegraph office tells him that until the situation calms down the telegraph office is closed to anything but emergencies – and lawmen.

Open for him then.

"Write what you want, Deputy Marshal," the telegrapher says.

Mac. Expect me tomorrow afternoon with Porterfield and evidence. Cliff.

He hands it over. "How long till you send it?"

"Right away."

He reaches for another paper. "And there's one more."

"Always happy to help a deputy US marshal, but best keep it brief."

Dear Emma. Be home tomorrow afternoon. JAR.

Emmaline

Waiting for her hot chocolate to arrive at her table, wondering where Mrs Landers might be for some diverting conversation, Emmaline dabs at her eyes with the corner of her handkerchief…

Ashcliff. Her father. Dillon Kerr and Eva. Her father *and* mother. Ashcliff. Her woeful ineptitude at handling any of it, all of it. Back and forth, over and over. When will this introspective torture desist? Leave her be? Ever end? She came to Cheyenne to do a job she really wanted, that's all; not all this. How much more?

"So, Roberts…"

Mid-dab, she looks up. She had to ask the stupid question, didn't she? For here is the ready answer: Jacob Hunter, investigative reporter for The Bugle.

"Mr Hunter…"

"Got yourself a good old-fashioned head cold, Roberts?"

"No, I've been crying."

He invites himself to sit at her table. "Nice try, Roberts. So…"

"So what is it you want?"

"I've been watching you, Roberts."

She blows her nose.

"You might be interested in what I've seen."

She pockets her handkerchief. "Well?"

"Me and my buddies at the Bugle, we've been wondering how you know so much…"

"About what?"

"The Alliance. What else? Now, everyone knows you got in good with them, but like I say, I've been watching you. Saw you and Taylor sitting pretty snug in the Cheyenne Hotel. In fact, I've seen you two together more times than I can count..."

"Mr Hunter, don't come crying to me in clichés because when all the talent to be a top grade investigative journalist got divvied out you only got the scraps."

Jacob Hunter gives a laugh.

"Crumbs, more like..." she adds.

Hunter, impervious to her insult, continues on with even more insinuations which she doesn't entirely hear because she's too busy trying to decide if she's blushing or about to faint.

Her and Luke?

Well, if that don't beat all.

When Hunter stops to draw breath, she says, "No one's stopping you from buying Luke Taylor a cup of coffee and picking his brain, Mr Hunter."

Another laugh, a scowling one this time. "Taylor barks no comment and walks away. But for you, Roberts, he's got all the time in the world. And he... well, let's just say, he looks comfortable with blondes."

"You're an idiot," she says, neither blushing nor about to faint. "And that's the truth."

Her hot chocolate arrives.

"Something for your friend, miss?" the waitress asks.

"He's not my friend and he was just leaving."

The waitress's gaze travels suspiciously over Hunter before she departs.

Hunter rolls his eyes and gets to his feet. "There's something going on with you and Taylor," he says, "You're kinda good-looking and he's a hero. I'll be watching you like a hawk, Roberts."

"Mass on Sunday is at eight. I'll tell Father Nugent to expect you."

Jacob Hunter leaves with an irritating know-it-all smirk on his face.

She retrieves her handkerchief and dabs some more at her eyes as hot tears leak out of them. God must think she has a sense of humor.

Faraday

"How goes it in the cells, Mac?"

"I got those two prison guards watching them round the clock," Mac explains. "Hope it's enough, Cam."

"We are doing the best we can."

"Don't I know it," Mac sighs. "Still I don't like it."

Faraday nods. "So noted."

Just then, the delivery boy from the telegraph office runs in and stands at the door panting. What's his name? – Johnny, Jeff, Jeremy…. He spies them standing inside Cliff's office and makes a beeline for them.

"Urgent, for you, Mac," the boys says and hands Mac a telegram in an envelope with URGENT stamped on the top.

Mac jumps up from his chair. "North Platte?"

Jeremy shrugs. "Got another one."

"For?" Faraday asks.

"Emmaline Roberts at the Tribune."

"That's our boy!" Mac exclaims, ripping open the telegram.

Jeremy hangs back.

"There's no reply, Gerald," Mac tells him, tossing him a nickel. "Well, get going with that one. Miss Roberts can't wait all day."

Gerald takes off with a grin, pocketing his coin.

"I can never remember that boy's name," Faraday says as he waits patiently for Mac to digest the telegram.

"Three brothers. They all look alike." Mac looks up, his eyes bright, saying, "Here…" And he hands over the telegram.

Faraday reads.

He's not sure what he ever did to deserve this happy piece of news.

Mac starts shuffling about. "You know, he never said he was gonna bring evidence. Just Porterfield."

Faraday hands back the telegram. *Just Porterfield* will be quite something.

"What evidence but?" Mac asks.

"We shall just have to wait and see."

"Gees, Cam, where am I gonna put Porterfield? We're all booked up."

Faraday makes a move to leave. "You'll think of something, Mac. You always do."

Emmaline

"This has been some day," Mr Quaid says, receiving her copy.

Emmaline hopes he doesn't see her hand shaking.

"Simons said you got a telegram."

She nods, clutching both hands behind her back now.

Mr Quaid looks and waits in anticipation.

"It was private," she says. "Nothing to do with work."

"Oh," he says, disappointed. He cheers up. "Still we all worked hard today. There'll be plenty for Tribune readers to digest in the morning. So what's this copy about, Roberts? Took you long enough." He starts running his eye over it. "Ah, Mayor Dyer and Faraday's gathering this afternoon. Mm, Simons said you swapped stories with him, he thought you were looking into Dillon Kerr."

"Well, I was... I did, but I still need to check another source..."

"Oh? Have to say, Roberts, at times your sources worry me."

"Er... well... Since my father got into town things got a little disjointed, so I want to be sure of what I'm doing before..."

Mr Quaid holds up one hand. "Say no more, Roberts. Even I concede you've had a busy day, what with writing all night to finish *Empire for Liberty*. I like the title, Roberts."

"It *is* borrowed, Mr Quaid."

"I know," he says lightly, but his eyes are giving her the once over. "You look beat, Roberts. Really beat. Go home and get some rest." He turns to leave her in peace, then stops. "This Dillon Kerr story... you sure there's no problem with it...?"

She holds herself very steady, clenching her hands. "If there is, I'll let you know."

"Mm. You know where I live," he says. "So, if you need help."

So much for go home and get some rest.

Finally, he leaves for good. She slumps into her chair, pulls out her pocket watch and checks the time. She's expected for supper at the Keatons' at seven, with the Sheriff; John Keaton, it seems, has taken a shine to him. That gives her an hour and a half to find some solace and counsel in the only place left to her.

"Sit yourself down, Emmaline Elizabeth."

"But I'm interrupting your supper."

"That's true. But it'll keep for a bit. Of course you're welcome to join me..." Father Nugent stands at his sideboard, a quizzical expression on his face, poised to take a second plate.

"Thank you, Father, but I'm due at the Keatons' for supper."

"Ah. Fine people the Keatons. Called on them a day or two ago. Congregationalists. God-fearing to the last. Salt of the earth and with the strength of ages. Although how an Irishman like John Keaton got to be a Congregationalist I'll never know. Well, supper with the Keatons. That settles it then. Let's go and be comfortable." He leaves plates and supper behind and directs her into his small but cozy parlor. "That chair by the fire is the most comfortable one in the place. I keep it for people just like yourself."

"Like me?" she says and settles herself into it, appreciating the warm hearth.

"You look lost, Emmaline," he says kindly, taking another chair opposite hers.

She feels her chin wobbling.

"You miss him, don't you?"

She nods.

"And he's been missing you, I have no doubt about that. He loves you, Emmaline."

Tears prickle her eyes. "How... how do you know that?"

He gives a gentle laugh. "I've known since the day you and I met. He came to guard you in Mass, remember? I thought you as interesting a couple as I'd ever met – at that stage you were pretending you didn't have feelings for one another. I thought you were rather hoping they'd go away."

It was that obvious?

"He came to me that afternoon. He asked me how could he come to understand what happened at Mass. We talked about you. About your faith. It affected him a great deal, Emmaline. And then he asked me, Will you teach me to become a Catholic, Father?"

"Er... I'm sorry, Father. I don't think I heard you correctly."

"Oh, I'm sure you did. I questioned him about whether he could separate becoming a Catholic from his feelings for you. He said he didn't know but he was willing to find out, if I could help him. I gave him a long lesson that very afternoon. Then, his work took him away. But when he came back, he took up his lessons again. Just as I suspected, he knew all the rules and requirements in a very short time. And he is making good headway on his catechism. He's a curious fellow, did you know that?"

"I... yes."

"He asks the curliest questions. Well, I do my best to answer them. And sometimes I have no answer at all. He doesn't seem to mind. Anyhow, Emmaline, while I was happy with what he knew in his head, I didn't know what he felt in his heart. And then the other day he came into the church and sat there, plainly upset. He sat and he sat, and he let the peace of God into his heart. I saw it happen with my very own eyes. His choice to do this was an interesting one. And profound."

A mantle clock ticks with loud precision in the ensuing silence. Father Nugent reaches for his pipe and tobacco.

She suspects the day Father Nugent is referring to is the one when Cliff got upset and angry with Judge Callaghan, the day he gave her Emma by Jane Austen...

As Father Nugent prods tobacco into the bowl of his pipe, he says, "I don't think he'd mind me telling you this. You didn't know already it seems..?"

She shakes her head.

"Mm, I wonder when he planned on telling you."

She shrugs.

"Saving it, eh? For when he needed it."

There's a twinkle in his eye as he lights his pipe and puffs it into life.

"It's a grand story. And you probably don't realize just how instrumental you've been. His love for you got him into the church building, but it was your love of God that got him curious about God Himself. Ah," he says and starts puffing, "I love curious people. They don't want to die wondering." He gives a chesty chuckle. "Now, Emmaline Elizabeth, what is your story this fine evening?"

The smoke from his pipe drifts her way, fragrant in a relieving fashion, although how he expects her to speak after that revelation... as if today wasn't emotional enough.

Time ticks away.

Father Nugent patiently waits for her, puffing, watching the delicate smoke as it mingles with the soft orange glow of the fire.

She must put Ashcliff out of her mind. Not think about what his wanting to become a Catholic means. As happy as she is that he wants more meaning in his life, such as faith and hope, she can't ignore what Cliff's intentions towards her have been for some time.

"I can see I've taken the wind out of your sails," Father Nugent says with gentle humor.

"Yes," she says, forcing herself to speak.

"He is a good man, Emmaline Elizabeth, and he thinks the world of you, did you not know that?"

"I know that he...he loves me. He told me."

Her satchel with Emma by Jane Austen safely tucked inside sits on the floor beside her chair. She may as well have a ring on her finger... she feels very hot suddenly.

Father Nugent beams. "Good."

"I... I took your advice, Father. I examined my feelings and I confronted them. Now I know why you were so insistent I do so."

"You see, it wasn't so hard, was it?"

"Yes, it was hard. He didn't tell me he was seeing you for instruction."

"The man's a little on the ruthless side, I'll grant you that, but I think it goes with the job. A job you don't like."

She swallows hard and pushes herself to speak. "No, but he is so very good at it, and so many people depend upon him. I had a telegram from him today. He's coming home tomorrow."

Father Nugent stops puffing and murmurs, "Alleluia!"

"Yes. I have plenty to think about between now and then."

"Do you, Emmaline?" he asks with a kindly expression.

On that thought, she marshals her strength. "Father, something happened today. I did something wrong, illegal, and I will confess it outright in a moment, but in the process of what I did I found out some important information, and in the process of discovering the important information I stumbled into someone's, well two people's, privacy. What I heard wasn't my right to hear..."

Father Nugent's expression sharpens.

"I can't deal with this, Father. I need Cliff and he isn't here and I don't know what to do. I came to you and I'm glad because I can see now that's what Cliff would want me to do..."

"Calm yourself, Emmaline. Tell me what happened. Although I think we should make this parlor a confessional..." With that he extracts his purple confession stole from his coat pocket, shakes it out of its neat roll and puts it around his neck.

As he makes the sign of the cross, Emmaline does the same and proceeds as if she were in his confessional in the church. Then she confesses she broke into Dillon Kerr's house. That she snooped around until she came upon Kerr and Eva. That in their intimate state she heard Kerr's plan to take Eva and get away under the cover of darkness.

"Tonight?" Father Nugent asks.

"Well, yes. There were no signs of it, no luggage or anything."

"What made you do it, Emmaline?"

"I'm sorry, Father. I don't know what happened to me. I desperately needed a story on Dillon Kerr. I never suspected for a moment he was still at home. I took nothing; put everything back as I found it..."

"Took nothing? You wrote nothing down?"

"I..." She stops and thinks. "Yes, I wrote things in my notebook."

"You stole information."

"Yes."

"So you know all this and no one else does. Not Mac, or Mr Faraday?"

She shakes her head. "Who do I tell? I had no right to be there. They were being intimate and I listened to it!"

"You know, Emmaline, not many people would consider the feelings of Dillon Kerr worth the value you're placing on them right now. Only a truly noble person considers their enemy as valuable a human being as themselves."

"I heard the passion in his voice, Father, for her, for Eva. And hers for him."

"But that might be all it is. Passion. Are they married?"

"No. Eva is Loren Bodecker's woman and Kerr stole her away from him."

"Are you sure it wasn't lust, Emmaline? Carnal relationships outside of marriage are grave and require serious scrutiny. Lust is sinful, as you know."

Tip a bucket of cold reminder all over her! She feels a shiver.

"I'm surprised that you didn't consider this at the time."

All she heard and considered at the time was the longing they had for one another expressing the longing she feels for Cliff.

She has no answer for him.

"Sorry to be so blunt, child," he says. "Even so, you shouldn't have been there. And you did intrude upon their privacy. And what to do with the information."

She nods.

"You know, Emmaline, you just admitted to illegally breaking into another person's house for the purpose of stealing whatever information you saw fit to take. But I can't tell anyone. And even if you tell someone that you've told me I can't say one word about it. Anything you tell me is off-limits to Mac or Mr Faraday or even Cliff if he were to ask. So I understand your predicament."

"That's your job, Father. But mine is exactly the opposite."

"Is it?" he says, searching her face. "God gave you a conscience and the good sense to know how to use it. I've seen how much integrity you have, Emmaline. But you made a mistake, breaking into Dillon Kerr's home, invading the man's privacy, and now you must face the consequence of your actions. What does your conscience tell you to do – even though you're fighting it?"

She likes this question; she needs to speak her conscience, give it the freedom it deserves. "My conscience, which seems to have been non-existent at the time of my wrong-doing..."

"Ah, good..."

"...tells me that being a reporter tends to compromise who I am from time to time..."

"Mm..."

"And had I listened to my conscience this morning I would have never succumbed to Mr Quaid's insistent pressing to get a story on Dillon Kerr and I wouldn't have gone to his home."

"Mm. And why weren't you listening to your conscience?"

"Because something else happened, Father..."

He frowns and exclaims softly, "There's more?"

"My father came to town this morning. Things have not been so good between us since my mother told him to leave our home ten years ago. He's a sheriff, you see..."

"Oh. I'm beginning to see a great deal," he says.

"And all this time I thought that my mother got fed up with him being a sheriff because it made her miserable and that's why she made him leave. But he came all the way from Orlando, Florida, to tell me different. And that they are reconciling. And that my mother is taking him back. And that he being a sheriff wasn't why they separated. No, it was because he'd been unfaithful to her. Unfaithful to her! I don't know how to understand that, Father. Why would he do that? He tried to explain it, but to me it still said that his job caused loneliness and division between them... When two people love one another, they're not supposed to let that happen..."

Father Nugent says nothing for quite some time while she sobs into her handkerchief.

"Emmaline, children act out when their parents do something as hurtful as leave the family home. Seen it quite a bit over the years. It can be a terrible time. And, Emmaline, I believe it's happened to you twice. Once, ten years ago. And again, this morning when he came and reminded you of that terrible time. Seemed to throw all your pain back in your face because he and your mother are getting back together again... saying, forget about it now because all will be well again."

"Father?" she queries, wiping her face.

"What was the first thing you did when you found out your father had been kicked out of home by your mother?"

She recalls it, bites her lip and can't look at him.

"I can't tell you what I did, Father, but I did go to confession a month later."

"That's comforting," he says.

"I'm not a *child* anymore, Father."

"It takes a long time for some hurts to heal, Emmaline. Beyond childhood and deep into adulthood. And sometimes not at all. But I believe you will, in time, forgive your father because – correct me if I'm wrong – in your heart you recognize he is a good man."

"I guess."

"Although now I know your father is a sheriff, I understand your aversion to Cliff's chosen profession. You know all about sheriffing. The thought of living the same life as your mother is abhorrent to you."

"I'm confused," she admits. "About him…"

"I don't wonder. Only the pair of you can work that out. A little prayer would help."

"Yes, Father. Now may we return to my conscience?"

"Of course."

"I think what you are telling me is that my father coming to town is a mitigating circumstance when it came to my ability to know right from wrong this morning."

"Yes, I think it very likely indeed."

"Father, I can't let that happen again."

"I don't think you will."

"No," she says thoughtfully.

"So, Emmaline, what does your conscience tell you to do now?"

Faraday

Faraday gets up from his chair and stretches his tired muscles. "It has been a day longer than most, Mac. Are you heading home?"

"Soon. I want to check in with my guards. Two more arrived on loan from the Territorial Prison an hour ago. Need to make sure they hear from me what kind of devils they're guardin'."

"Good idea," Faraday says, recalling the first two already patrolling the lockup. They tend to stand with one hand on their side arm or clutching a rifle across their chest, their Prison Guard badge extremely visible to their charges.

"You get yourself on home to Mrs Faraday."

"Give my regards to Pat."

He's about to step out into the evening's cold air when he runs into Miss Roberts, who is not looking where she treads. Her head is down and he catches her by the shoulders before she collides with him. She looks up; her face is white and her eyes rimmed red.

Miss Roberts crying?

"Oh, I'm sorry, Mr Faraday. Are you going home?"

"That was my plan. Do you need me for something?"

A look of discomfort darkens her expression. "Yes… You and Mac. I won't keep you long."

"Well, let's go to his office."

Faraday observes her from the corner of his eye. This is not the Emmaline Roberts he knows and she hasn't been all day.

"Here, Emmaline…" Mac draws her a chair, which she politely declines.

"Go ahead, Miss Roberts," Faraday entreats her to begin.

416

She looks from him to Mac and back again. "I have some significant information regarding Dillon Kerr. I cannot reveal how I came about this information as it would incriminate me..."

"What have you done, Emmaline?" Mac asks.

"I... You must just listen, Mac."

He clamps his mouth shut.

"Go on, Miss Roberts," Faraday urges her.

"The words: *When all else fails* and an address..."

As she recites the address from memory, Faraday recognizes it.

Mac says, "That's the Severini family's address, ain't it?"

"I believe so. Go on," Faraday says.

"A telegram that says: *Loren compromised. You know what you have to do. Lamont.*"

Mac scratches quickly in his notebook.

"Finally, this remark by Dillon Kerr: *Lamont and I have ways of communicating.*"

"You heard Dillon say this?" Mac asks.

She ignores him completely; looks down at her hands. "Do not ask me who Lamont is. I do not know."

"Aw, Emmaline..." Mac whines.

"And you cannot reveal how you came by this information?" Faraday asks.

"If you subpoena me before a grand jury..."

He studies her down-turned face; perhaps she waits for the axe to fall, he doesn't know. "I don't think a grand jury will be necessary."

A look of agonized relief comes over her. "That is all I have for you, gentlemen."

"Does Dillon Kerr know you have this information?" Faraday asks.

"He does not."

Mac, meanwhile, who has been writing everything down, looks up from his notes. "Do you have any idea what it means, Emmaline?"

She shakes her head. The kind of gesture that could mean she has no idea whatsoever, or that she does have an idea but really isn't in a position to say.

"I was expected at the Keatons', but I'm not feeling up to it. I will be having a quiet supper with my father at the Cheyenne Hotel. Then home."

Faraday reads between the lines. The explanation, at least some of it, could be found at the Keatons, which is logical considering that the Severini family is staying there. If he wants to investigate, she will not be present. In fact, she will not be offering anything further.

She says goodnight and leaves them to observe her graceful departure with questions swaying in the air like colored lanterns at a summer dance.

"This line..." Mac consults his notes, "*You know what you have to do* from this feller Lamont..."

"Mm..."

"Glad I got those extra guards."

"Donnelly."

"Let's face it, Bodecker's chances increase without Donnelly. We know that."

"Mm, but if it's up to Dillon Kerr to see it done, then how much value does Kerr place on his friendship with Bodecker. There have been rumors..."

"Yeah, I heard. Kerr fancies Bodecker's woman. That Eva Tarrant."

"If he can have Tarrant, he might not want to increase Bodecker's chances."

They look at one another, astonished.

"Emmaline knows," Mac croaks.

"About Kerr and Tarrant."

"So, it's true. Kerr doesn't want to bump off Donnelly for Bodecker. He wants Tarrant."

"Mm. But we don't know who this Lamont is yet. So we can't assume Donnelly is safe. Think I'll pay a visit to the Keatons. With Hummer gone, Cliff not back yet, the only other member of the Bodecker search party in town is Ben Taylor. He might know this Lamont character."

"Good. I'll give my guards extra instructions."

They nod affirmation of each other's intentions.

Then Mac says, "How did Emmaline come by this, Cam?"

"I don't know. By the look of her, I'd say it cost her."

"Think I might try locatin' Eva Tarrant when I finish here."

"Yes. If she can't be found, we could assume that she and Kerr have run off together."

"A downright possibility."

"I'll have a search warrant for Dillon Kerr's place within the hour, Mac."

"That's good, Cam, because the Judge wouldn't give me one no matter how much probable cause I waved under his beak. Figured it was a reasonable request after Bodecker became a guest of Laramie County Jail and Kerr gone who knows where."

"Interesting."

"And one for Tarrant's place as well, I reckon."

"Good as done." Faraday buttons his coat. "What are we going to do with Miss Emmaline Roberts, Mac..."

Mac grins. "Leave her to Cliff, that's what."

The hour is late when Mac softly taps on Faraday's door with information and the result of the searches: there is no one home at Eva Tarrant's place, or at Dillon Kerr's house...

"Kerr's place is clean. Nothin' of what Emmaline told us, all the drawers, desks and closets, nothin' at all. He's pulled out for good this time. Nothin' at Tarrant's house neither. And none of Kerr's or Tarrant's neighbors and friends has seen either one of them for two days."

"So they have flown," Faraday says.

"Looks that way."

"Then Donnelly is safe for the present."

"Looks that way, too."

Faraday's thoughts drift to Miss Roberts before he offers some information in return.

"Lamont is a concierge at Bodecker's businessmen's club in Denver. According to Ben and Raina, he was there in the club when Cliff, Ben and Raina rescued Richard Taylor. Clearly, he was there somewhere when Cliff and Hummer arrested Bodecker."

"He alerted Kerr, who promptly ignored the warning."

"Preferring Eva Tarrant. An opportunity not to be missed."

"And that's that."

"Get yourself home, Mac. We will talk more in the morning."

Faraday cradles Meg in his arms as she sleeps; for him sleep is hard to come by. He searches for something else to feed his insomnia apart from Dillon Kerr and what Miss Roberts may have done to obtain the information.

"Cam…" Meg murmurs sleepily.

"Mm?"

"Kiss me?"

An easy request.

She needs reassurance and plenty of it – from you.

Her kiss in return is sweet with sleepy passion.

I know you want to protect her. Keep her and the baby safe. You do that anyway. Keep her safe in your heart, Cam.

Jennifer's the doctor.

He strokes Meg's sleep soft skin. She moves closer to him; they bump stomachs.

"Do you love me, Cam?"

"Silly question," he says.

"Then show me how much."

"One piece or two?"

She chuckles drowsily. "Had enough cake today. You don't want me to get fat."

"Heavens, no. What then?"

"There are some of Amy Keaton's cookies in the pantry."

"Coming right up."

Ben

The following morning

It's early. Ben's mind swings between the beauty of Raina's sleeping form and the things that need to be done. Her dark hair flows over one shoulder and fans out across her chest, almost concealing her breasts. She appears radiant, even in sleep. He gazes upon her with every kind of wonder and intention.

Yes. Intention. The things that need to be done.

He smiles at her veiled breasts.

She seems agreeable to go with him wherever necessary.

And these things must be done.

Her veiled delight beckons him... Forget the things that need to be done. Look at us.

He *is* looking. A three-headed horse could stroll in and he wouldn't drag his eyes away.

He's got to the point of no return. Well, no point that he wants to return from.

But Omaha also calls.

And he will answer.

Yet... first thing in the morning Raina's skin is incredibly soft.

At his touch she stirs lightly.

"Ben," she murmurs.

Excitement is unleashed with her waking. "Raina."

She stretches the sleep from her muscles and the veil slides away. He moves over her; she accommodates him.

"Raina, my sunshine. I don't want to rush this."

"We can try."

Her eyes are full of love; he smiles into them. He loves this joining with her. He inhabits her, he fills her, yet he is the one transformed. He rides among the stars. Raina's shining universe.

He was once so lost, without her.

Once, he scorned Tressa for falling in love with Mart Keaton – he didn't comprehend how it had transformed her. Now he cannot help but empathize with Tressa in her loss and loneliness without the man she loved.

He also understands Ryan's distraction on the train, leaving Emmaline, a job to do, and Hummer jabbering in his ear.

And Luke, wanting him and Raina to know Jennifer...

Love can't be contained; it escapes. And throws away the key.

Raina, who with loving patience waits out all his moments of deep thought, mostly because she is streaks ahead of him when it comes to thinking, asks perkily, "What are we doing today?"

"Let me see... would you want to come to Omaha with me?"

"Omaha? Really? For how long?"

"We need to allow a couple of days travel for the journey there and back... if we want to be on time for Luke's wedding, we could return by next Wednesday. I'm hoping four days will be long enough; we'll have to see how things are when we get there."

"Are you speaking of your father's business?"

"And my mother's home. The manner in which she left it... who knows what's become of the house. She never complains but it must be worrying her. And the business... I think it's still running okay but without my father at the helm..."

"Or you second in command..."

"...any number of things could have gone wrong since Bodecker got his hands on it."

"I think we should go at once if Mr Faraday will allow it."

"The trial doesn't start until a week from Monday. We will be back by then, hopefully with my parents' livelihood intact."

"Let's see Mr Faraday immediately."

"Mm, we will." He smiles at her bright shiny eyes reflecting her eagerness for life and adventure. "I adore you, Raina."

She adds a stunning smile to further distract him. "I never get tired of hearing you tell me."

"That's good. Because I'm going to be saying it for a long time."

"Over my grave when you're old and gray and need a walking cane and one of those ear trumpets so you can hear our grandchildren when they ask about me?"

"Now there's a picture," he laughs before he kisses her.

Cam Faraday listens with patience, then grants Ben's request.

"After all you and your mother have done, I think it's fair. It could be important to the trial to know more of what is happening to your father's business. And, if I'm not mistaken, the business is as much yours as your father's."

"It's supposed to be. Anyway, all our lives and our livelihood are tied up in it. I can't lose it. I have to do what I can."

He shakes Faraday's hand.

"Of course," Faraday says, his grip firm and sincere. "Good luck, Ben."

Ben buys two tickets for the sleeper UP to Omaha – a private compartment. If nothing else he wants his bride to be comfortable.

They find Luke next.

"We will do our best to be back in time for your wedding," Raina informs him.

"Thank you, Raina; it wouldn't be the same without you otherwise," his cousin says. "Are you all set, Ben?"

He takes Luke's meaning. "We'll visit the folks next. And say goodbye to Tressa."

"Good luck. What time does the train leave?"

They have just enough time to speak with his mother, who hugs them numerous times with relief and gratitude; farewell Tressa, Ethan and the Keatons; pack and get on the train.

As they pull away from the depot, Raina says, "You know, Ben, when I look back on the beginning of our married life I'll recall that, second to the bedroom, a lot of it happened on trains."

He locks the door of their compartment and draws down the shades. "Then let's make those train memories as pleasant as the bedroom ones."

FIVE

"O Eginhard, disclose
...the mystery of the rose."
And trembling he made answer
"...its mystery is love."

———— ❦ ————

Henry Wadsworth Longfellow
Emma & Eginhard

Cliff

A huge crowd is milling on the platform as he steps down from the train. Wooden barriers have been erected to keep a clear area for alighting passengers; others have to push through to board. What is going on?

He and Mac shake hands. "Good to see you, Mac."

Mac grunts. "Had a good gander at *yourself* recently."

He grins. "Looks like the town is expecting someone – that soprano is due this month, or is it next, what's her name ... strange, didn't know she was on the train..."

"Ya great lug, we're expectin' *you*. That's what they told me."

"Me?"

Reporters jostle among the noisy crowd of onlookers. As soon as he makes eye contact with them, they start shouting questions.

"Down, you mongrels," Mac snarls at them.

Cliff places Porterfield between them both for safekeeping.

"Don't ask me how they knew; they were all here when I arrived. Had to lay down some rules to keep them in line while I was waitin' for you. Hard to say these days who's friendly and who ain't. So this is Porterfield?"

"In the flesh. Meet Sheriff McNamara, Louis."

Porterfield inches a look around, trembling like a mouse inside his wrist manacles.

"Looks can be deceivin', I guess," Mac concludes. Then, "Who's this?"

"Nelson, Mac. Mac, Nelson. Walker's deputy."

Nelson nods shyly.

"Walker gave you a deputy?"

"I'm more of a go…"

"Deputy Nelson, stay close to the prisoner so Mac can focus on controlling this mob."

"Yes, Mr Ryan." Nelson crowds Porterfield a little more.

Mac clears this throat. "Much obliged, deputy."

They set off.

The reporters follow:

"Is it true, Sheriff – sorry, Deputy Marshal – that you are responsible for apprehending Loren Bodecker?"

"Can you tell us how you knew where to find him?"

"Who is the prisoner you've just brought in?"

"Where is he from?"

"What is his part in all this?"

He scans the group, searching for Emma.

"Expect a whole load of boxes at the office, Mac." With his grip tightening on Porterfield's arm, he asks, "Where is she, Mac?"

"Boxes of what? And I haven't seen her all day."

"Evidence from Porterfield's laboratory. Stick close, Nelson."

"Yes, Deputy Marshal."

Then, as they pass by the Welcome sign, he hears a voice…

"Deputy Marshal, according to Marshal Hummer you're something of a hero. What's your response to that?"

He pulls up; Porterfield winces. Standing on the plinth that raises the sign is the loveliest sight he's seen since he left. Emma. Wearing her dark red dress beneath her coat, and her red earrings. She wore this the day after the first bullet grazed her cheek, the same day he took the second bullet in his arm. She'd worn it other times since, but looking at her now it is the memory of that day which comes to him. He saved her that day. Saved her for this.

"Yeah, Ryan," someone shouts.

"Tell Roberts how it feels to be a hero," yells another.

"Come on, give us something."

He can't give anyone anything for the moment; he's too busy drinking her in.

"Easy, Deputy Marshal," Mac says. "Let's keep walkin'."

"She told them," he murmurs.

"More'n likely, come to think of it. I guess she figured you deserved a hero's welcome. I think you do, too..."

He turns his gaze from Emma to Mac. "Come off it, Mac."

Mac shrugs. "Go figure."

Cliff informs the pack he'll give them a statement at the county sheriff's office in half an hour. The reporters ease up.

As he decides to pick up the pace, he gives Emma one last glance. She's smiling at him. He puts his head down. Porterfield has to trot to keep up.

Cliff watches with satisfaction the despair on Donnelly's face as Mac tucks Porterfield neatly into one of the mavericks' cells.

"What have you done, Ryan?" Donnelly spits out, his hands wrenching the bars.

"Tied up some loose ends." He stands back between two rifle-toting prison guards and surveys the firmly locked cells and their occupants. Not a bad winter's work.

"Where's Dillon?" he murmurs to Mac.

"Flown the coop."

He frowns. "What does that mean?"

"Took off with Eva Tarrant we suspect."

"That rumor was true?"

"Appears that way. You should see the black suits Bodecker's got lined up to defend him and Donnelly."

Cliff catches Marvin Tucker's surly glance.

"He doesn't look too good," he whispers to Mac.

"He ain't."

Cliff wanders down to the end of the row to take a look at Bodecker.

"So, Ryan," Bodecker says. "Got all your pigeons, did you?"

Cliff folds his arms and scrutinizes the big man who's slumped on his cot and looking bored. "Heard you got yourself a fancy crew of black suits, Loren."

"Faraday won't make this stick. You should tell him that. Everyone in this town has got some part of their living tied to me. No jury will see fit to convict me."

"You got a point. Right now that's what it looks like. But wait till the trial starts."

Bodecker emits a muffled, grunting sound of disdain. "You're out of your depth, Ryan."

"No," Cliff says coldly. "You're out of luck."

Bodecker snarls at him and looks away.

When he gets back to his office, Luke is there with an unexpected hearty greeting.

"Look at you, Luke Taylor. You got your smile back." They shake hands. "What happened?"

"Jennifer."

"She's here?" he exclaims. "Well, good for her."

"Then you'll be pleased to know we got engaged – secretly. That lot out there..." and he thumbs at the group of reporters gathering in the outer office, "...don't know. Except Emmaline."

"Engaged?" he whispers loudly. "You finally had the sense to throw a lasso around the good doctor?"

"That'll be enough of that."

"You're right. I'm assuming it was a ring..."

Luke gives a laugh. "That's usually how it's done, in case you need to know."

He grins. "So when's the wedding?"

"Thursday next. You will be here, won't you?"

"Should be."

"So, tell me, how was Ironpants?"

"Doing his job for once. He sends his regards. Luke, I can't tell you anything about the job yet..."

"I know. Good to have you home. Jennifer's back in her house again. I know how happy she'd be to see you. Anyhow, I'll get out of your hair. Good work, Deputy Marshal."

Cam stands at his side while he speaks to the reporters. He can't see Emma, but that doesn't mean she isn't there, somewhere...

"I arrested Dr Louis Porterfield two days ago in North Platte and so far he's been charged with conspiracy and the attempted murder of Luke Taylor."

"With whom did he conspire?"

"Donnelly and Bodecker."

"This is yet another individual involved in this case. Just how many men have you and Mac got locked up back there, Ryan?"

"Eight. Bodecker, Donnelly, Tucker, Porterfield and the four mavericks, Jacobs, Carter, Tyner and Cole."

The questions continue for another ten minutes and focus on the trip to apprehend Bodecker as well as the detour he took for Porterfield. He feels weary of it all and he defers to Cam in the end. Thankfully, Cam has also had enough and he declares it over.

When they're gone, Cliff says, "I didn't see Roberts."

"No... probably at the back... So, what's next?" Cam asks.

"Come with me to see Judge Callaghan."

"The evidence?"

"The evidence."

Judge Callaghan finally sits back from his magnifying glass.

"Very impressive, Mr Ryan."

"I'm glad you think so, Judge."

"You didn't have these photographs taken merely to sway the jury, did you, Mr Ryan?"

"No, Judge."

"Mm," he grunts. He calls for his clerk, who dutifully appears. "Find Luke Taylor and have him here in my chambers within half an hour."

"Yes, Judge."

"If you can't locate him, Ethan Benchley will know where he is."

"Yes, Judge." The clerk scoots off obediently.

Cliff finds the Judge's eyes narrowed on him. "Do we need Miss Roberts as well?"

"Not presently, no," Cliff tells him.

"Mr Faraday," the Judge barks, "thank you for coming, but I won't be needing you. Mr Ryan and I have some things to discuss."

When Cam has left, the Judge tells Cliff to sit down.

"So, Mr Ryan. Clearly, you have been doing your job beyond the level expected of someone in your position and you've been doing that for some time. Now you bring me these pictures and I know what you expect of me. But your heroics and your dedication don't let you off the hook."

"I'll settle for letting Luke off the hook."

"Why?"

"Because you can see by the pictures the conditions in which he was being held against his will; Porterfield's laboratory, where the drugs that nearly killed him were made. We have all the evidence we need to restore his freedom. He didn't do anything wrong."

The Judge studies him thoughtfully for a long time.

"Why is his freedom so important to you?"

"He's innocent and restraining him isn't just."

"I repeat the question, Mr Ryan, I want the right answer. Listen, my boy, I know you've got a heart in there and I want to hear it speaking to me, understand? You wouldn't have got so angry with me last week if you didn't. Now, why is Taylor's freedom so important to you?"

Cliff expels a frustrated sigh. "What do you want me to tell you? That he's my friend, that I care about what happens to him?"

The Judge grunts. "That'll do for a start."

Cliff looks away, annoyed. "You didn't see what he went through like I did. He was tortured. And I don't like the innocent people of this world paying for the crimes of men like Porterfield."

"You didn't intend coming back without him, did you?"

"Porterfield? No."

"Again, you sent Marshal Hummer back to Cheyenne with a heavy burden."

"Dan Hummer can do this stuff with his eyes closed."

"You did the same thing you did with Miss Roberts."

"Fine!" Cliff exclaims. He gets to his feet. "When do you want my star, now or after the trial?"

"Sit down." The Judge mumbles heatedly, waiting for him to sit. "Why do you do it, Mr Ryan?"

"Because it has to be done."

The Judge takes to staring at him again. "You didn't have to bring me these pictures."

Cliff slumps forward, his elbows on his knees.

"Answer me this. And I want an honest answer this time."

He looks up, aghast. "Excuse me?"

"Well, a complete answer then."

"That's better."

"Did you and Miss Roberts strike a deal on the train to Laramie?"

"No, we did not."

"Then what prompted you, apart from your friendship with Mr Taylor, to give her the information she needed and then agree to let her take it to Laramie?"

Cliff looks at his hands. The time had come to let this cat out of the bag. Somehow, he has the feeling it is in safe hands. That he is in safe hands.

"I gave Miss Roberts the information because she was traveling to Laramie to do a story on Donnelly. She guessed much of what I didn't tell her outright. I believed if I gave her the knowledge it would help protect her, since her life had already been in danger on two previous occasions."

"You wanted to protect her?"

"Yes. Then, when she began to realize that in my heart of hearts I wanted to go after Luke, knowing the peril he was in, she offered to give the information to Dave Ransford in Laramie. I wouldn't allow it for several miles. But she insisted she could do it. I never doubted she could do it. And I trusted her. There came a long and difficult moment when I had to decide. I went with my instincts, not only regarding Luke's predicament, but about Roberts herself. Suddenly, I had my badge in my hand and I was pressing it into her palm, and I deputized her. It was a strange moment..."

"Good God, man, are you in love with this girl or not?"

He smiles at his hands. "Yes."

Silence.

Quietly, the Judge says, "Were you then?"

"Yes."

"Did she know this?"

"Not then. She does now."

"Was she in love with you at the time?"

"I believe so."

"This was an act of love?"

Cliff looks up quickly. "This was an act of justice, make no mistake."

"I got that part, Mr Ryan," the Judge says soberly.

"And a rescue. I knew what I had to do. And Roberts knew it, too."

"And she would willingly bear all the responsibility to see you do what you had to do."

"Yes. Without her, Luke would have died. He knows he is indebted to her. He has said so himself. Said as much to her."

"You took a risk that I find disturbing, Mr Ryan. But… I find it less disturbing knowing the bond between you and Miss Roberts is the anchor for it. It was an act of love and compassion, on both your parts. Some might think me sentimental, but I am as pragmatic as the next Judge. Love can be as firm and pure a foundation as justice. It didn't feel like a risk to you, did it, Mr Ryan?"

He shakes his head. "Odd, maybe, trusting her that much…"

"Mm. She is a courageous and honorable young woman."

"Yes."

"Now, Mr Ryan, doesn't that feel better?"

Like a clear July morning.

"I'm rescinding my bench warrant restricting Miss Roberts to town. She is free to come and go. As soon as my clerk returns I'll give him instructions on the matter."

"Thank you, Judge."

"As for you, I haven't yet decided. I'll make that decision after I have spoken with Mr Taylor. When Mr Taylor gets here, I want you standing at the back of the room and saying nothing while I ask him some questions regarding the content of these pictures."

"As you say, Judge."

Luke

"Have you seen these pictures before, Mr Taylor?"

He stares down at a whole bunch of photographs, unsure of what Judge Callaghan is asking.

"Sorry, Judge?"

"Do you recognize these photographs?"

"I don't know anything about…" The content of several of the pictures becomes clearer as he studies them. Memories begin to stir. "These are… these are…" He sinks down onto the chair behind him.

"Are what, Mr Taylor?"

"That is Porterfield's laboratory." The smell pours out of the photograph and straight into his nostrils. His stomach rolls. He senses the Judge's hard gaze on him. Why is he doing this?

"And this one, Mr Taylor?"

A photograph is pushed into his line of vision.

It's the basement: the cot; the filth; the blackness; the blindness; the foul stench; his flights of fantasy; his uselessness; his disgrace; his living nightmare.

Shaking, he thrusts the picture away. He feels faint; nausea swells inside him, all over, like every part of him wants to be sick.

"Mr Ryan had these taken when he went to North Platte to arrest Porterfield," the Judge tells him.

"Why… why would he do that?"

"I believe at the top of his list is to see you a free man."

"I'd rather wait for the trial than look at those again."

"Look at me, Mr Taylor."

He does as he's told. The Judge's gaze is relentless.

"Mr Taylor, some people believe it is beneficial to confront the thing you fear the most."

Determined not to give in to his weakness, he holds the Judge's stare for several more seconds; then he snatches up the pictures. "What do you want to know?"

"Tell me what each of those pictures means to you."

This is one of the most difficult tasks ever asked of him. To the best of his ability he does what the Judge wants, speaking about the contents of the pictures although he has no idea why he's doing it, while he fights building resentment towards the Judge for making him. The last picture is of the room he slept in, the room where Cliff and Doc Kincaid took care of him.

"I was saved in this room."

He's grateful the Judge doesn't question it or ask for details.

"The court made a ruling that if you were cleared of wrong-doing in the upcoming trial Sheriff Walker would have to give you up."

"I know that, Judge."

"I am going to rescind that ruling."

"Judge?"

"I do not believe you had anything to do with that young prostitute's death on the train, nor did you assault the deputy. I believe your story that you were kidnapped and held by Porterfield and drugged near to death. What Walker's intentions may be I have yet to discover, but I will discover them. I rather think that Mr Ryan knows."

"You believe me?"

"Yes, Mr Taylor. Watching you examine these pictures has made it perfectly plain to me you could not contrive such a reaction. That being the case, you are no longer restricted to town. You may come and go as you please from this moment onwards."

"Thank you, Judge."

"Don't thank me. Thank Mr Ryan. These pictures are intended for trial, Mr Taylor. Even though I regard them as a vivid and helpful representation of what transpired, it will still be up to Mr

Faraday to convince the jury. You are not permitted to speak to anyone about them, including Miss Roberts, is that clear?"

"Yes, Judge."

"Your restriction to town was not public knowledge; I expect the retraction of it to know the same courtesy."

"Yes, Judge."

"Miss Roberts has also had her ruling revoked."

"She'll be very pleased, Judge."

"As for Mr Ryan, I have examined his actions regarding Miss Roberts and I am exonerating him from any corrupt dealings, as I have her. Although it appears that a characteristic of the way Mr Ryan carries out his job is to take risks, I believe that he measures each one appropriately, in accordance with the people at his disposal. Miss Roberts a case in point; and Marshal Hummer yet another."

Luke stands up and reaches for the Judge's hand; he shakes it vigorously. "Thank you, Judge."

The Judge looks amused, if a little aggravated.

Suddenly, Cliff steps forward from somewhere behind him.

"Where'd you come from?"

"Out of the darkness and into the light," Cliff says, a smile spreading over his face. "Thank you, Judge."

Judge Callaghan nods. "You're welcome."

Luke looks from Cliff to the Judge and back again.

"You made these?" he asks.

"The photographer helped."

"Who's going to tell Walker the bad news?"

"Ah, that would be me," the Judge says. "Now, clear off, both of you, I have work to do."

Once outside, they wander off to nearest saloon so he can buy Cliff a well-deserved drink. He orders the good stuff. And finds himself in a mood for reflection.

"Ironical, ain't it... I finally get my freedom to leave town and all I want is right here. I don't have to go anywhere."

"Good to have the choice though."

"Damn straight. Here's to freedom!"

"To freedom. And good photographers everywhere."

"And Judge Callaghan." He refills their glasses. "To *the* best rescue and escape ever!"

"It wasn't half bad... To Arthur and Belle Kincaid."

"To the Doc and Belle! ...Wilma! If only she were forty years younger..."

Cliff almost chokes. "You or me?"

"She weren't making sparkly eyes at me, Sheriff."

"She called you cute, I'll have you know... or maybe it was cute-looking..."

"Now why would she go callin' me that for?"

"Beats me... I can't work out my *own* woman troubles."

"Did you really have a cousin who terrorized her at school...?"

"I doubt it... I'm the first of my kind to cross the Missouri."

"To the Big Muddy then... and the United States of America!"

"North, South, East and West!"

"Don't forget Texas..."

"Beg pardon..."

Their refilling and their toasting continue for some time; the basement disappears. The future comes into view again.

"To the future!"

"May it always be there!"

"And then some." He tables his shot glass for a spell. "So, Cliff, I got something I need to ask you."

Cliff

Once more he finds his kitchen table laden with culinary gifts. He'd had himself a shave, slept off most of the whiskey in a long, hot bath, and now he was ready to eat. One stew looks and smells especially good – Pat's; he recognizes the dish, and it's still warm. Well, that's where he should start, except that whenever his appetite gains the upper hand, thoughts of Emma smack it out of the way and demand his attention. Where did she get to after the depot?

He's about to spoon stew onto a plate when there's a knock on his front door. If people didn't keep bothering him at meal times, he might actually get Mac to stop calling him scrawny...

When he opens the door and beholds her, a slip of starlight in the cold evening gloom, his heart rate quadruples. "Emma."

"Am I interrupting your supper?" She's holding a parcel, and her satchel is securely attached to her shoulder as he remembers it.

He pulls the door wide. "Come in."

Once he has her in the building, he quickly closes the door.

She steps up and graces his cheek with a soft kiss; he feels her body linger and everything about this moment fills his head and charges his senses.

"Emma," he murmurs, almost shivering. Their eyes meet. His first and only instinct is to kiss her, properly, but for some reason she's got him double-thinking every move... what the heck... he's about to plant a kiss on her lips when she steps back and resumes her position on the rug.

She holds out the parcel. "For you – a welcome home gift."

Nonplussed, he takes it. "Thank you. What is it?"

"Something for your collection," she answers archly, taking off her gloves and stashing them in her coat pockets. Next she removes the satchel and drops it by her feet.

"That must be getting heavy by now," he says, his touch on her gift telling him there are books inside.

"Mm," she agrees. She starts on her coat buttons.

He helps her remove her coat and hangs it by his. With the winter woolens and the parcel and the satchel all shed, she is still wearing her dark red dress.

"Still Deputy Marshal I see," she quips, referring to his coat with the offending badge still attached; her eyes are now alight with something close to mischief. Talking loudly as she heads off into the parlor, she leaves him standing there. "Oh, all the lamps are lit. The room looks so inviting this way…"

He follows with the parcel in hand and he finds her in front of the hearth, her dainty hands held out for warmth, her ink-stained fingers wriggling as if to hurry up the process. Her satchel rests on the armchair by the hearth.

"Have you had supper?"

"Mm, thank you. But I fear I've interrupted yours…"

"It can wait a little longer. Sit down."

"If it's all the same to you, I'll get warm first…"

His backside finds the edge of the sofa.

"You must be tired after… everything."

"I grabbed some shuteye in the bath."

"How relaxing." She gestures at his parcel. "Open it."

"Come and sit by me."

"I will. Make a start…"

It's all too easy with women to miss the signs. But that was one.

"I got my freedom back this afternoon," she says. "I have a feeling you might have had something to do with that."

He unravels the string from the brown paper. "I had a chat with the Judge." He stops and looks her in the eye. "I told him about you and me."

"You and me? Oh."

"Emma…"

"You told the Judge," she breathes and looks away.

"It's all right."

She flicks a look at him. Her earrings dance and sparkle and distract… "You are the slowest parcel opener I've ever known."

He unwraps the brown paper; there are three books. He takes up the first and reads the spine. *The Manatee: Mermaid of the Tropics*. He lifts his gaze; she's smiling again, like she can't help it.

"What is a manatee?" he asks.

"A very strange marine mammal that lives in warm oceans."

"And the mermaid part?"

"Oh, that's fascinating, you're sure to love it."

He gives a laugh. And opens the cover. She has written:

Would tropical oceans and warm breezes be as foreign to you as the icy draughts of the Rocky Mountains are to me? Emma.

"I don't know," he says. "An invitation?"

"Just a thought," she says.

Amused, he puts that aside and takes up the next.

Tapirs: Mating and Habitat.

"Okay," he says, a little shocked, "what are Tappers?"

"*Tay-peers*. Any of several large, hoofed hog-like mammals of tropical America, related to the rhinoceros; they have flexible spouts, feed on plants, and are active at night."

"How active?"

"If I told you that would giving away too much of the plot."

"Really?"

"Oh, yes."

"Sounds like I won't be able to put it down. How is it not banned in thirty states?"

She laughs softly.

He grins and opens the cover to read her inscription.

You might not know me in the tropics. I am different there. In summer everyone is a tropical creature at heart. Late into the evening we sit and wait impatiently for a breeze to bring relief from the heat of the day. We laze on the front porch and sip sweet iced tea. And smell the honeysuckle and the orange trees. On the coast the sea air is thick with salt. When you finally lay down you can taste salt on your skin. You might not know me in the tropics.

He swallows hard. "You make me want to go there…"

"The tapirs don't wander the streets or anything…"

…and taste salt on her skin.

"…and I don't think anyone I know has ever seen one. Or even heard of them. Actually, they live down in South America…"

"Where did you get these?"

"The bookstore in town. I was spying on Dillon Kerr and… well, it's a long story. I…I miss being warm …"

"I know," he says. The longing for it is right there in her eyes.

"There's one more," she says, her glance directing him back to the parcel.

He places the Manatee and the Tapir by his feet, and takes up the third and last book. *The Holy Bible.*

"It's the Roman Catholic version," she explains hastily. Even more quickly, she says, "Father Nugent and I were chatting. He told me you have been receiving instruction from him. Although why you couldn't tell me… Perhaps that doesn't matter after all…"

"It matters," he jumps in. "I wanted to tell you, and I planned to, but I had to see if I could do it first."

"Can you?"

"I think I'm making progress. Did you inscribe this as well?"

"A little."

For James Ashcliff Ryan. Thank you for being my guard and my shield. God bless you. Always, Emma.

He looks up, an annoying lump in his throat.

"Catholics don't read the Bible very often," she says. "Priests don't like a whole bunch of folks drawing their own conclusions about God. We mainly look at the pictures, and the colored plates if there are some, and contemplate our sins. But you're different, so I thought it couldn't hurt to get you one to read. It doesn't mean that I'm trying to influence you or anything. It's just how I think of you."

"Your guard and your shield?"

"You have been looking out for me since I stepped off the train."

Okay, that sounded nervous.

"Thank you," he says, "for my books."

"You're welcome. I have things to tell you," she says when she notices him observing her closely. "A lot's happened since you left."

A very bad feeling comes over him. Maybe she didn't bring the satchel out of safekeeping for its contents. Maybe she is gifting him with books because she's giving Emma by Jane Austen back.

Books to replace her.

The signs are gradually coming into focus.

It would appear that *'awhile'* is coming to an end.

"Come sit with me while I eat," he says.

She never sat beside him on the sofa.

Emmaline

While Ashcliff nourishes himself with a helping of Pat McNamara's famous beef stew, she decides to tell him how Luke came by the telegram about Marvin Tucker and how they handled the find.

"Simple observation is a powerful tool," he reflects.

"You told Luke to watch over me."

This time he doesn't offer a response; instead, there's a glimmer in his eyes and a gentle, knowing smile on his lips.

"At times I couldn't discern between watching over me and trying to do my job."

He laughs; his affection for his friend is totally endearing. There is no competition between them, no envy, but great trust and an interesting helping of admiration of each for the other.

"He changed the moment Jennifer came to town," she says. "I've never seen such change in a person. He seemed completely well, overnight. He must have missed her terribly."

"So what do you think of her?"

"We've only spoken on one occasion." She tells him about the interview she conducted and how she put Mr Quaid off the scent. "She is astonishingly beautiful, with such a way about her – how did you not fall in love with her yourself?"

"Jennifer?" he frowns. "I guess she is pretty."

He never noticed? "Were you blind?"

He gives her the smile that causes her insides to flip over and makes her want to reach for a fan. "I guess I was…"

'Until you showed up' is fully implied.

She swallows and looks away, trying to right her insides.

After making inroads on his meal, he says, "This is good. Are you sure I can't tempt you?"

Tempt her?

He lifts his gaze, which is hardly innocent, looking for her answer.

Her mouth goes dry and she manages to shake her head. She convinces herself that the thought of telling him about her father is beginning to wear on her nerves. It's not *untrue*…

"Something the matter, Emma?"

"I'll make fresh coffee, shall I? I'm sure I can find everything."

"Sure," he says.

Relieved, she goes about her task. Coffee brewing, she asks, "Is there nothing you can tell me about your trip which doesn't involve divulging the secrets of the court and risk compromising the trial?"

"Emma, you are at present this town's most celebrated reporter."

"I know there has to be something. I can't wait until the trial starts; I'll go mad."

After a moment, he says, "Ben and Raina. Off the record…"

"Oh, yes! A very large surprise. I think his mother had to take pills."

"All I can say is they met in Denver and were married within twenty-four hours. And Raina was instrumental in retrieving Richard Taylor. Off the record…"

"Of course. You know, it's a very romantic tale. Something very kismet about it."

"If you say so. Just don't ask me where they met."

"That's precisely what I was about to ask."

He regards her with a soft smile as she stands by the stove waiting for the coffee. Its delicious aroma soon tells her it's ready.

Coffee pot (and pot holder) in hand, she pours the steaming liquid over the lip of his loaded silence and into his cup. And she asks, "Could you ever imagine yourself doing something like that?"

He looks up. "That's a provocative question."

"Well, you know I obviously intended it as rhetorical. How could they know so quickly? How did they not think about all the things that one has to think about?"

"What does one have to think about?"

"Still rhetorical," she says. "All relationships are different, I suppose. Raina is young. And Ben is such an unusual person. He can be kind-hearted one moment, and chillingly austere the next."

"Raina will be good for him."

"I think the chillingly austere might go."

While she takes her seat, he chuckles and says, "I think so, too."

She turns her coffee cup around on its saucer, suddenly uneasy. Talking about Ben and Raina might not have been the best idea because of...

"I missed you," he says.

... that.

Such a tender utterance forces the tumultuous emotions of the past twenty-fours to bear down on her. She finds herself saying, "Seems like an age since we stood upstairs, surrounded by your books..."

"Did you think about what we talked about that night?"

"Yes."

"You did?"

"I can't expect it of you," she says bluntly.

He frowns. "Ah. Care to define what 'it' is."

She shakes her head. "You define it."

"Seeing how I know what 'it' is?"

"Of course you know."

"Did you miss *me*, Emma?"

She throws up her hands. "What do you want me to say?"

"I want you to say 'yes'. Then we can move on to what would stop you from missing me in future and what would make you happy."

Whatever way this is meant, it is far too arrogant, too Sheriff Ruthless for her present state of mind. But the annoyance she feels, and the frustration she senses in him, drives her on. "I won't ask you to give up your work, you know that. I don't think that would be in anyone's best interest. Certainly not yours."

"How do you know?"

"Because anyone as good at their job as you, as dedicated and clever, should not be asked or convinced to stop doing it. It seems to me that you were born to do it. You possess the God-given ability and the talent to do this job for the good of people..."

"Emma, if I feel like the man I'm supposed to be because you are in my life, doesn't that tell you something?"

"Only that I could be a distraction from your true purpose."

He scratches his head.

She hopes he's fed up with the topic of conversation and goes to change it, but he beats her to it.

"Why did you come here tonight, Emma?

Oh, God.

A little prayer, Father Nugent said.

That's a little prayer.

Oh, God.

"Emma?"

Again, she can't answer him. Coward. Just tell him.

"Right now, Emma, I am very confused about what you want. You don't like my job, but you don't want me to change it."

She finds her backbone. "No."

"Me being a sheriff does not make you happy. Us being together makes us both happy. Can you deny that?"

"I won't let you."

"Are you going to deny it?"

"It's not going to happen. I won't let you do it. I won't be the one who's responsible. And you would regret it."

"No, I would not."

"I don't know a jot of what you did on your assignment, but I do know that you were extraordinary. Dan Hummer doesn't dish out praise lightly, but he praised you till his cigar fell out of his mouth."

"That's flattering, Emma, but all I did while I was away was miss you. I worked harder so I didn't feel it so much."

Her frustration at not being able to put him off and her inability to do what she came to do burns within her. "That's ridiculous. You're a grown man, not a boy."

"At least I have feelings that I'm not scared to..."

"You think I'm scared? Why does everyone think I scared! Why does this have to be about feelings, why can't it be what it is?"

They eye one another off for several very uncomfortable moments.

She can't bring herself to say it; he doesn't want to hear it. She backs down. He doesn't pursue it.

Instead, he clears his throat and says, "I haven't known you long, but long enough to know that something else is going on with you. Like your satchel, only invisible, it seems to be weighing you down."

Maybe if she could love a man who didn't pay her such close attention.

"There is something… else… I need to tell you. As I said, a lot has happened…"

"Then say what you came to say…"

That sounded cold and she jumps to challenge him on it.

"Emma," he cuts in, "take a deep breath and say it."

A deep breath? Good advice.

"Something happened while I was away…" he begins for her.

"Yes, while you were away… in fact, only yesterday, my father came to town…"

"Your father?"

"The same. The one who left home ten years ago. That my mother kicked out. He came to tell me that they are back together again. That he always loved her and she him. And all is forgiven."

"Well, that's…"

"You don't know the half of it. He tells me that my mother didn't care about him being a sheriff after all, that she knew it was something he had to do, that it was important to him, if he was happy so she was happy…"

"But…"

"There's no but. Only the truth. She didn't mind. Didn't mind! They could have told me, don't you think, before now."

"Yes…"

"No, my mother kicked my father out because…." She swallows the lump swelling her throat. She feels flushed and not in control, but what makes it worse is that she can trust Ashcliff with not only the private information but with her emotions. She loves him for it. Hot tears spring into her eyes.

"Because, Emma?"

"He...he was unfaithful to her. He took himself off and betrayed her. I'm supposed to forgive him for that. And understand my mother. He says it wasn't his job. But it was, it *was* his job. It took him away from her; he strayed..."

Her tears spill onto her cheeks.

"Trust," he begins and clears his throat, "trust is an important issue."

She can't speak, for as he's watching the tears leaking from her eyes, the beautiful compassion inside of him surfaces, softening his face, replacing the confusion and frustration that have been there since she arrived.

"Your parents are a family again," he says.

She groans at the thought. "You're taking their side."

"So you want them to be apart and miserable to fit your ideal of how things should be."

"How can you say that?"

"Because that's how you want us to be."

She swallows; more like a humiliating gulp. Maybe if she could love a man who wasn't so insightful.

"That's why you won't be with me, isn't it? You don't trust me. Why you're telling me this, about your father?"

"I do trust you," she says, wiping her face.

"Then at least trust me to know what's best for my life."

She pushes her head from side to side. "That's different."

"Emma, how can I make you understand? There are other jobs."

"One you love more? One that brings more satisfaction? That you do better?"

"I can think of two off the top of my head. It's time I grew up, Emma, and found out, don't you think?"

"You *are* grown up."

"It's easy to think so until someone comes along and makes you take a good look at yourself."

"It was not my intention."

"I know that. It's not something anyone can control. It just happens."

"Well, I won't be using you to negate my past."

"Emma, you don't have a past. Your father has a past; your mother has a past. You are caught up in the middle of it, perhaps, but it is not yours. Maybe your father came to tell you that."

She stares at him, stunned.

"Don't let them have your life, Emma. I can think of a much better use for it."

More stunned staring. This is a rout of mammoth proportions. She must counteract it at once, and raggedly pulls herself together.

"My…my career," she blurts out. "That is a much, much better use for it."

Surprise freezes his expression but jumps into his eyes; she holds her tongue and observes while those blue-green orbs flood with doubt and uncertainty. Relief almost betrays her. Almost.

He'll thank her for this one day.

"I'm sorry," he says, sounding hurt. "I was being selfish."

"Not at all."

"All this time, Emma, I thought it was my job that stood between us. Although, I have to say, I'm shocked you think I would stop you following your dreams."

She slips out of her chair and snatches another peak at him. Shock and confusion are etched into his face. She must be strong.

He'll thank her for this one day.

She takes a deep breath; tries to appear less ragged than she feels and smooth the rough edges of her contentious emotions.

"I asked you to define 'it'," he says. "Why didn't you tell me then?"

His counter-offensive.

She rallies again. "We weren't speaking about me."

He grunts. "Convenient."

"Well, I think I should say goodnight. I apologize for being emotional before."

"Oh, think nothing of it. They're only feelings and you didn't let them get in the way of succeeding at the job you came to do."

Ouch. Still succeeding by the sound of that remark.

"So what do we do now?" he asks.

"Do?"

"Yes, do, Emma. What do we do?"

"We...we have a solid professional relationship. That won't change..."

"Not to the detriment of your career," he says coldly, giving her a fair jolt.

But at least now it's done.

She manages to bid him goodnight before she darts out of his kitchen and into the parlor. With *Emma* whisked out of her satchel, she deposits the book on the chair and doesn't look back.

Outside, the night air is as cold as his last comment.

Emmie, Emmie darlin', what have you done?

Cliff

Jennifer Sullivan's residence
17ᵗʰ Street
Saturday morning

"There can be no doubt, Cliff. She has outsmarted you."

Jennifer forks more buttery fish into her mouth.

He watches, fascinated, as she relishes it.

"As improbable as that is, of course," she adds playfully when the mouthful has gone down.

"You seem to be enjoying that."

"I suppose you mean apart from the fact that it's delicious."

"Martha's breakfast steak is delicious, but I'm pretty sure I don't wear that delirious expression when I'm chewing it."

"Tease me if you must. But since you mention it, he rode out of town with Tip at God knows what hour of the morning to fish. They gutted I don't how many of the poor things. Then he returns, and while I'm sleeping, he cooks me some. Then leaves me a letter that begins with 'good morning, eat your breakfast' and proceeds to tell me what he's done and where he'll be this morning."

"And that's romantic?" he checks.

"You really should try some." Her eyes sparkle mischievously as she shovels another fork of succulent fish into her mouth.

"I'll pass, thanks. Like I said, I'm a steak man when it comes to breakfast. So where is Don Juan now?"

She swallows. "You know Mike and Grace Smith… He and Tip have gone to call on them."

He absorbs the significance of this. Grace Smith is a Shoshone

452

woman. Tip is the grandson of a Comanche chief. Luke's other love, after Jennifer, is horses. Mike Smith breeds Quarter Horses.

"He didn't waste any time getting out of town," he remarks.

"For which I thank you from the bottom of my heart."

He grins and says, "Getting under your feet, was he?"

"No. I think I was getting under his."

"I find that very hard to believe," he says, amused. Leaving town to look at horses with Tip and having Jennifer to return to and hang off every word he utters about horseflesh is exactly what Luke needs.

"You will be coming on Thursday, won't you?"

"I think the best man is supposed to attend the wedding, so, yes, I plan to come."

"He asked you?"

"Over some very smooth single malt whiskey."

She looks very pleased, which boosts his spirits considerably.

"I thought that honor would fall to Ethan, or Tip," he reflects.

"You don't think you would be his first choice?"

He shrugs. "Can we get back to my problem?"

"Certainly."

"Emma outsmarted me…"

"An inspired piece of bluffery, in my opinion. I know I'd be proud to have outwitted one of the cleverest men in Cheyenne."

"Is bluffery even a word?"

"This is the way I see it… she doesn't want you to sacrifice what you love and what you excel at for her. Actually, I don't blame her."

"Be that as it may," he says, "she pulled this 'what about my career' ruse out of the hat to put me off… it was very intense."

"I think so. If you believe she knows you well enough to know that you respect her plans and dreams…"

"Honestly? It wasn't stated, but it was definitely understood. I have shown nothing but respect for her work."

"Look, I know you've been saving the world as we know it in these parts, and in a man's mind that is what Cam would call a mitigating circumstance. But what it means to a woman like Emmaline is that for this to keep happening you need to stay committed to it. No, no... hear me out. You have declared your intention to give it away and do whatever it takes to please her, but what happens to the world as we know it in these parts, and what happens to you, the man she admires?"

His head is spinning. He shifts impatiently in his chair.

"Cliff, she wants you to be the person you are now. She likes that man. He's brave, smart and dedicated. He saved her life. Would she still admire that man if he lived another or lesser existence?"

"So... Huh?"

"You have to make her see that the two of you as a couple are not connected in any way to what you do for a career and what she does... That the two of you are a sublime entity on your own. Of your very own. That you exist beyond this world and bear no relation to it."

He gives a soft grunt. "So that's how Don Juan does it?"

She smiles. "With us it has taken a while to sort out our differences. I mean look at us, look at what we do. Anyone would say we have nothing in common. And who's to say we won't still be sorting it out in ten or twenty years."

She looks like she relishes the prospect more than the fish, which almost makes him envious.

"You and Emmaline, on the other hand, appear to be very well matched. She *does* realize you are a well-educated city boy who turned his back on his father's legacy out of a perverse yet typical desire to rebel against his father's politics?"

"Maybe she hasn't quite got it. Impressive summation, by the way."

"Thank you," she says jauntily.

"But in my defense, I can't get her to listen to me. Maybe if I'd failed to arrest Bodecker and Porterfield and I proved to be a lousy deputy marshal she'd have felt sorry for me... been a shoulder to cry on while I poured my heart out..."

"Now there's a thought, except that she probably wouldn't be attracted to you if you were the kind of man who needed a shoulder to cry on because you couldn't do your job."

"I meant..."

"I know what you meant, but then you are not being honest, even though some perceived weakness in you might be effective."

"I view the time Judge Callaghan chewed me up in Court as a lost opportunity. If I'd been sharper I would have played that for all it was worth."

"Well, don't start looking like a no-hoper now; she'll see right through it. Cliff, she may be a modern, independent woman, but you are going to have to court her the old fashioned way."

"Seems like every time I start I get interrupted."

"I sympathize. This isn't your typical situation. My advice: Let her know that you are still around. That you haven't changed your mind, that you are still planning to move on with your life, but you'd like her to be there when it happens. Stay strong, don't back down. That's, of course, you do still want her once you move on."

He begins to understand.

Sweetly, she adds, "Just don't move on too far away, will you?"

He smiles. "I'll try not to."

"You have to be true to yourself first, and ask yourself when you move on to do what you have to do in your life, and she still rejects you, will you be happy?"

He hears echoes of Nugent: Will you still want this if Emmaline Elizabeth rejects you?

"You really are a wise old owl, Dr Sullivan."

She smiles. "In this situation the only thing left is to calmly show her what she's missing out on. Be yourself."

Brilliant. Why couldn't he think of that?

Later that morning, he takes Emma by Jane Austen, a scented silk rose he bought from Pat, who makes them, and a note which reads: *Dear Emma, Are you absolutely sure, deep down in your heart and soul, that this is what you want? Nothing will change my mind about you. There never was and never will be another Emma in my life. You are she, just as my grandmother described you. Won't you reconsider? JAR*, and wraps the lot in the brown paper and string from the previous evening. Then he takes it to the Tribune and gets the cub reporter, who is hovering restlessly around the front desk, to deliver it to Emma's desk.

Around noon, when Cliff returns to his office after seeing Nelson on the train back to North Platte, he meets Emma's father, Preston Roberts, a vigorous yet distinguished gentleman, whose sincere and humble expression of gratitude for taking care of his daughter is peppered with his displeasure at 'Emmaline's recklessness'.

Despite Emma's disclosure of her father's past indiscretion, Cliff finds he likes him. In the course of their amicable conversation, Cliff observes the realization dawn in Preston Roberts' eyes that he is talking to a man who knows a lot more about his daughter than he probably should. Cliff knows he cannot keep his feelings for Emma cloaked during any discussion about her; Wilma taught him that. And a man like Preston Roberts is far too practiced at reading people not to notice. Still, he doesn't say anything; that time may yet come anyhow – or the way things are going, it may not.

Around twelve thirty, when Preston Roberts has left, he steps out of the office for a bite to eat and on his return Emma by Jane Austen is on his desk, recognizable by that same brown paper and string.

"Emmaline brought it by on her way home," Mac informs him with a curious look as he leaves Cliff to it.

Cliff opens the brown paper, which is starting to look weary. A note falls out. "If this gets lost I will bear no responsibility." The note he wrote her is tucked inside the cover of the book as if to reinforce how totally wrong he is. The rose, with its silken petals, looks unloved. He jams the sweet pathetic thing in an empty tumbler where it sits on his desk and mocks him.

That afternoon he returns home.

Circumspect, he places Emma by Jane Austen on his bookshelf where he decides it shall remain. It is, after all, his most cherished keepsake from his grandmother.

He gathers up his laundry and gives his house a cursory tidy.

At four, he heads back into town and drops off his wash to Wanda, his laundry woman, who tells him it will be ready on Monday afternoon.

He has supper with Luke and Jennifer at her house; then he and Luke go for drink and slowly take themselves off home.

On Sunday he oversleeps and has to rush to make Mass with the Roman Catholic Severinis in tow. He's still straightening his tie as he walks into the church. After the sermon, Nugent lets him sit in the back although strictly speaking he shouldn't, as non-Catholics aren't permitted to stay for the second half which contains Holy Communion. But Nugent is making some exceptions in his case – 'your job is so unpredictable, you need all the exposure you can get; we won't tell the Bishop, eh?' He suspects the Bishop is in the dark about a few things in Father Nugent's busy parish. Regardless, Cliff likes it, and he wants to see Emma. She sits about half way up the church, her father by her side.

Nugent makes a special effort to speak to him afterwards. The Severinis wait close by. He is due for another instruction session and they make the time. In the process of this, Emma and her father join them. Cliff's heart begins to behave like a train. Preston Roberts has a knowing look in his eye when they exchange pleasantries, which makes Cliff want to loosen his crooked tie. Emma politely introduces her father to Nugent. The gregarious Nugent delights in the introduction and they start talking.

Meanwhile, Emma says, "I need to speak with you, Mr Ryan."

Mr Ryan? That takes him back... He follows her to a spot several yards down the path. At this point she starts looking this way and that, craning her neck, giving the churchyard the benefit of her eagle-like glance. Alfredo and Gianni start looking around, too, answering Signora's panicky queries with shrugging arm gestures.

"Lose something?" he asks.

"What?" she says. Then, sheepishly, "No, nothing... Sorry, Signora, it's nothing, truly... oh, dear. Niente, Signora, scusi..."

Italian with a southern accent; he could listen to that all day.

"I didn't know you could speak Italian," he says. 'What else can you say?"

She frowns. "A few words. Um... I wanted to say how much I appreciate your efforts to change my mind but for the sake of the precious book, you really should learn to take no for an answer."

"Then Ashcliff Ryan would cease to exist."

"What is that? Exaggeration to my face?"

Hands on hips, he shifts from one foot to the other.

"Honestly. No, he wouldn't!" she declares.

"Yes, Miss Know-it-all, he would. And since I am he, and you're not, then I would know."

Her jaw drops. "Oh, Cliff, will you *stop* being so *contrary*."

He blinks. *Him?* "Something else we have in common, Emma. And you needn't worry yourself about the book. It keeps suitable company on my bookshelf."

She goes to say something and thinks the better of it. He knows her; she is curious about what company Emma by Jane Austen is now keeping...

He tips his hat. "Good day, Miss Roberts. Always a pleasure. Excuse me while I reassure the Severinis."

"Of course," she murmurs before she leaves him and joins her father.

As father and daughter depart via the churchyard gates, Nugent walks up to him and says, "Not going well, I see."

"She really doesn't have a clue," he derides gently, watching her, pondering how her rejection doesn't make him like her less and in fact want her more.

"Perhaps you should give her one."

"No," he says, resigned. "She has to come to this all on her own. Until she starts listening to me, it's the way it has to be."

"Well, forgive me for saying so, but watching the pair of you a minute ago, I'd say things are just starting to get interesting."

Ben

Taylor Mining Company,
Farnum Street, Omaha, Nebraska
Monday morning

Rob Gardener comes towards him with his hand outstretched.

"Ben… how very good to see you…"

Ben grabs that hand and grips it firmly. "And you, Rob."

He's back! Back in the building he swore he'd never return to unless his quest was fulfilled. Well, there's not only that but more. Much more. He knows who he is, where he comes from and, better still, where he's going.

"You could not have come at a better time," Rob says.

"Bodecker?"

"Precisely. What happened with him? One day we were getting regular instructions from your father and everything was going along like normal. Then comes the news of Bodecker's arrest. Since then everything's gone crazy."

"There's only so much I can say, Rob, but let's go and talk."

"How is your father? Where did he get to, Ben?"

"I'll explain."

Ben offers Rob the very best explanation of the situation without saying more than he should. Efficient, hard-working Rob seems to understand that all the explanation he's entitled to concerns the business and who will be in charge now that the boss has given himself time off in Cheyenne.

"You run the operation while I'm gone, Rob, just like you have been."

"If you're happy I'm happy."

"I'll make sure you get paid accordingly."

"Thanks."

"I'll be within reach if you need me."

"There's no chance that Bodecker will be acquitted is there?"

"Always a chance, but the trial doesn't concern us here. Only keeping our business strong. My father made a mistake bringing in Bodecker. And now we are working to fix that mistake."

"What do you think were Bodecker's true intentions?"

Explaining Bodecker's base intentions are not possible, but what he says for Rob's benefit is true enough. "We have always been a strong, healthy business. I believe that in the long run Bodecker didn't intend to ruin the company; he intended to take it over. Force us Taylors out. Fortunately for us, he was arrested before that could happen. You have done an excellent job here. Not a number out of place. Unfortunately, everyone has got the shakes. We need to formally kick Bodecker off the Board, take back what's ours and make sure everyone knows he's gone. We need to reassure our customers, ease the minds of our shareholders and allay the fears of our miners and workers. Taylor Mining is here to stay. We will spend the rest of the day timetabling the operation and get moving on this, Rob."

"Sure, Ben. I'll round up the others now. Contact our lawyers. How long are you staying?"

"I have to return to Cheyenne Tuesday evening. After that, the trial starts. It could be weeks before I'm back, but we'll be in touch regularly and you know how to reach me if you need me."

Rob nods. "And your father?"

"Bodecker's betrayal hasn't done him any good. He needs a long rest, be near family..."

"Sure, Ben. Tell him we're thinking of him, won't you?"

"I will, thanks. One other thing. I got married."

Rob beams at him. "Married? Congratulations. And the bride?"

"Raina Montgomery."

Rob's jaw drops. "You married Raina Montgomery?"

"You've heard of her?"

"You hadn't?"

"No."

"Guess you've got no call to be reading the society pages. My wife gives me a report religiously. Don't think the news of you marrying her has got out yet. Marie would have told me."

And Ben knows why.

"It was a very private wedding. Ah, Raina is at the house fixing things. With my parents away, the house will be locked up."

"Fine. I understand." But surprise lingers on Rob's features. "Raina Montgomery, eh…" And he grins. "I hope you'll bring her by to meet us, Ben. Maybe we could all go out for a meal; make it a Taylor Mining special occasion; the wives sure would love it."

Ben smiles, a lick of pride in his beautiful Raina swelling his blood. "I'm pretty sure that can be arranged."

Cliff

Cheyenne

By Tuesday afternoon, in the course of two days, he's crossed paths with Emma from one end of town to the other; he's tipped his hat each time, or muttered a civil greeting if required. Twice she was accompanied by her father and brief but polite conversation was called for. So much for keeping busy as a way of taking his mind off her. He calls a halt and sticks to his office. She's not likely to set foot there, particularly when he's in it.

Her father, however, decides to drop by.

"I'm leaving Cheyenne early in the morning," Preston Roberts announces.

"So soon, Mr Roberts?"

"Call me Preston, m' boy. Emmaline's mother will be keen to see for herself folks can come here and actually return."

Cliff grins. "Happens every day."

Preston chuckles; folds his arms. "Emmaline tells me she will stay here until this trial is over, possibly another three weeks. Would that be your estimation?"

"On paper. This case has a habit of detouring unexpectedly and often."

"I'm expecting Emmaline to be heading home as planned."

Cliff nods conversationally, wondering what Emma's plans might be. "Back to a warmer climate."

"Certainly. You originally hail from Chicago, I think you said. Never been there myself."

462

"My roots are there, family, business interests, life before Cheyenne..."

Preston's face lights up. "That so? Business interests. And yet you are a sheriff on the frontier. You know, Cliff, I understand that. A lot of people wouldn't."

"You turned your back on your family's expectations to become a sheriff?" Cliff asks casually.

"Not my family, Cliff, Emmaline's mother's family. The Pendletons."

"She mentioned her pedigree."

"There's no stopping those Pendletons," Preston says with a shake of the head. "Emmaline, God love her, takes after them. Ever visited the South, Cliff? – you might take a shine to it."

Not so subtle, but Cliff decides he definitely likes this man. He speaks a language that Cliff understands.

"I might," he says.

"Shame you and me never got to sit down over a good whiskey and talk properly. Swap stories. Discuss those business interests."

"Say, I have an hour to spare right now."

"Can't think of anything I'd like more, Cliff, but I managed to have Emmaline meet me soon. She's a hard one to pin down. And I can see you got your hands full. Don't know how you find your work, but never had a dull day in all my years a sheriff. I've seen Orlando grow from a wild cow town into what folks like to call civilized. I don't know about that exactly, but I guess we're more polite to one another than we used to be. Don't forget what I said about your liking the South. We're friendly and we'd be glad to see y'all. When you do come down, you should make New Orleans one of your stops. I'm betting you'll like New Orleans. She's quite a town."

"I've heard some interesting things about it, certainly."

"They'll all be true. Well, goodbye, Cliff." They shake hands in farewell. "And good luck with the trial."

"Glad to have met you, Preston."

"And you. I hope we meet again one day. And thank you again for taking good care of my Emmaline."

Ben

Home of Richard & Caroline Taylor
Omaha, Nebraska
Tuesday afternoon

As he stands in the hall, looking around at the old place, he experiences what it feels like to have the weight lifted from his shoulders. The house is spick and span, all valuables secured in his father's safe, the furniture draped with dust covers. All the windows and doors are locked and he has hired a man to come out and check the house every twenty-four hours until his parents return.

Raina joins him. She takes his hand and looks up at him with understanding eyes.

"Despite what you think, this is a lovely home. Your mother has made it so."

He grunts but her lively blue gaze reprimands him.

"Not like the citadel," she quips.

"No. I guess not."

"I'm so pleased that it's all still here."

"Luke and my mother did enough to secure the place…"

"They did. Now it is clean and well-secured and we can send your mother a telegram, if you like, telling her so. And, we will tell her that we have packed in our luggage the extra things she asked us to bring back to Cheyenne, as well."

He nods. "And you're definitely not annoyed that we stayed in a hotel?"

"I've told you no every day since we got here and registered at

464

the Millard. We're leaving tomorrow and you're still asking?" she says, rolling her eyes. "There is little point in staying in a house you are trying to clean and close up. And since you were working long hours, it was more convenient for you to be closer to the office anyway."

"You did an excellent job."

She found an army of cleaning women and organized them to scrub and dust the house from furthest corner of the attic to the bottom step of the front porch.

"I don't think the house has ever been this clean."

Her eyes sparkle with mischief as they peek out from beneath her thick silky lashes. "Likely that it always is, Ben, and you have never even bothered to notice."

That's one of the many things he loves about her – she has the prettiest way of not letting him get away with things. He gives a laugh and murmurs, "Thank you, for what you did."

"I am part of this family, am I not?"

"Oh, yes," he grins. "But I feel like I ruined your home and here you are building mine up."

"That's plain ridiculous. My father has Deanna, remember, and the brat they are expecting, poor little baby. I was in their way. My father was about to marry me off and be rid of me. You saved me."

"Listen to me, Raina, there is something. Something happened. I don't want to tell you, but I also don't want any secrets between us, ever."

"Nor do I," she says warily. "Ben…"

"It's nothing to be scared of. I… you remember when we spoke about getting you away from your father, we agreed that I would do whatever it took…"

"Yes, I remember."

Disturbed, he looks away.

Raina's soft hand steers his face back again.

"You can tell me anything," she says.

Sweet, sweet Raina. Second thoughts hound him.

"What am I doing?" he mutters.

"I am your wife, Ben. How can there be anything you can't share with me?"

One thing he's sure of – he doesn't want a marriage like the cold, inhibited, manipulative one his father perpetrated on his mother. He says, "Do you remember when we consummated our marriage?"

"Of course. In my room… it was amazing."

He smiles, remembering…

"So?" she prompts.

"What you didn't know was that your father was merely placating us downstairs in his study. When you'd gone upstairs to change, he tried to bribe me to leave you and never come back…"

She catches her breath.

"He said: if you leave now, leave Raina here now and go, I will have the marriage annulled before she knows what's happened to you. Rain, he said he would pay me a great deal of money."

"But… you remembered what we spoke about?"

"Doing whatever it takes, yes. We agreed, didn't we, Raina? We *agreed*."

She nods her head, intensity thick and dull in her normally dancing blue gaze.

"I defied your father, as I knew I must. I ran up the stairs to you, knowing what I had to do. Your father shouted, 'you will not consummate the marriage in this house' or something to that effect. But we did consummate it, and it was incredible. But it was the way it was because of what had to be done…"

She frowns. "Ben…"

"Raina, I knew your father would follow me eventually. He… he did and he saw us. He saw us making love."

Raina's eyes leap in shock. "Saw us," she murmurs. In her eyes he can see her recalling every detail of the event. "But I never saw him… what… I don't…"

"No, you didn't see him. But he watched us. Briefly… as he realized there was nothing he could do to stop us. That you belonged with me and he had no hold on you."

"Oh, God," she gasps and clutches her stomach. "I was… I… we…"

"Enjoyed ourselves thoroughly," he supplies.

"He saw all that…"

"He left before that... but what he didn't see he would've heard. Heard it, saw it, understood it."

"And you knew he was there?"

"I looked him straight in the eye and dared him to break us up. He would've realized it wasn't the first time we'd made love. I watched while he retreated, a broken and wiser man. That's why I have been so confident you are free of him."

"That's why you were so pale and weird afterwards..."

"Weird? Oh, yeah, I was a bit... pale afterwards... nothing to do with you. I love you, Raina."

Her eyes are almost burning, darting about. "I'm glad he saw. It's not as if he'd been discreet with Deanna. I hated being there with them. Not that Deanna was questionable; it was that my father was so keen to produce heirs – male heirs. So... so I hope with all my heart that they have a houseful of noisy, boisterous, obnoxious male brats!"

She takes off, wrenches open the front door and disappears, slamming it behind her.

He is left in silence, alone with the past that has finally caught up to them. They'll get through it. She had to know.

Surrounded by ghostly-looking furniture and the smell of recently waxed floors, he waits patiently beneath the hall lamp, the afternoon wearing on to the point when soon it will be time to light it. Eventually, after how long he doesn't know, the front door opens slightly and Raina slides inside. She's been crying, and she wipes her cheek impatiently with the back of her hand.

"You're still standing there," she says.

"Waiting for you. Counting the seconds till you returned."

"I think it's time we lock up and get ready to catch the train."

He breaks the seal between his shoes and the floor wax, goes to her and takes her in his arms. She's trembling.

"Does it change anything, Raina?"

"You... you certainly are a man of your word," she says in a shaky voice.

"Does it?" he whispers.

"I...I should fear you but..."

He cringes.

"...but the man I *should* fear is one who would hide it. I couldn't trust that man, but I know... I know..."

"Raina," he gulps when she can't finish. He raises her flushed face and looks squarely into her teary eyes.

"I feel as though I've lost something, Ben."

"Your innocence?"

"I... yes, I suppose it's that..."

"I'm sorry, Raina, I'm so sorry..."

"I thought being married and being with you meant I was grown up. I was wrong. I... think I just grew up then..."

He swallows hard. "Have I lost you, Raina?"

"After what you did to keep from losing me? That would be ironic, don't you think?"

He nods, miserable.

Until a smile forms on her lips and Raina-light begins to sparkle in her eyes. "I think you're supposed to say you'll make it up to me."

She almost laughs at his surprise.

"You chose to tell me," she continues, "you chose to tell the woman who chose you to be her husband. You must think of me as a woman. You do want me to be a woman and not a girl, don't you, Ben?"

"I just want you. Whichever way you come."

She smiles like she keeps the wisdom of the ages inside her. "Funny how we know so little about one another and are still surprised by it."

"Well, we have something that makes up for it, episodes of pure bliss to connect all those interesting surprises..."

"Pure bliss, are they?" she says, almost too womanly for him now.

"You know they are," he murmurs. He draws her close, bows his head and covers her throat with kisses.

"Making up?"

He reaches over and locks the door.

"Here?" she exclaims.

"And now," he says and scoops her into his arms.

"But the house is pristine," she insists as he carries her towards the stairs, "it's... it's in hibernation."

He laughs. "Good description."

"And the train..."

"We won't miss it."

"Ben, where are we going?"

"My old room, where else? Give it the one thing it always lacked... you, Raina."

"You can't be serious."

"I'm going to roll you, my white-breasted girl, in one of those dust sheets."

"You can't," she declares, but she starts to giggle.

"You will love it, I will love it, and this house will finally contain a memory worth having."

Luke

Cheyenne Depot
Wednesday, the day before the weddin'

"You look nervous," Jennifer remarks.

"And you're surprised?" he replies, adjusting his tie.

"It's only Frank and…"

"Are you kidding?"

"All right, all right…"

They watch while the train slowly puffs its way towards them.

"He's not like that, you know," she adds. "Think of how happy you're making me right now."

He doesn't make the effort to reply, one, because she is too excited to empathize, and two, the train engine hisses loudly and steam clouds rise all about them, while the whistle shrills.

And now he's so nervous he is making lists…

The car doors are thrown open. Passengers step down.

People surge in all directions.

Jennifer cranes her head this way and that. A few moments later, she declares, "There they are…"

A tall, well-dressed man, who seems barely older than them, waves; he becomes busy helping a brood of small children down from the train, followed by an elegantly dressed blonde.

"That's them," Jennifer says, clenching her hands. "Aren't they delightful?"

A porter is assigned to collect their luggage.

Then the whole tribe comes their way.

Jennifer receives a kiss on the cheek and a warm embrace from her brother. His wife Jeanne steps forward and does the same. The wriggling brood gathers around and seems to hug Jennifer all at the same time, arms of various lengths clinging to different parts of Jennifer's anatomy.

He's not sure what to make of all this… should he be moved by the love between them all or repelled by the cloying sweetness of it. This is Jennifer's world and he's gotta enter into it or be left outside where it's certain to get cold and lonely without her.

He chooses the first. How bad could it be?

"Oh, how wonderful to see you…" she's saying, her voice thick with emotion, "here, in Cheyenne…"

"We can hardly believe it ourselves," says Jeanne.

Any minute now his Jennifer is going to say…

"Let me introduce you to Luke…"

Frank Sullivan reaches across with his hand outstretched. "Frank Sullivan. Very pleased to meet you."

Luke gets a grip on the churn in his stomach and clutches the outstretched hand firmly. "Likewise."

"This is my wife, Jeanne…"

Jeanne also offers her hand; she's bright, pretty and alert. He suspects she owns a wicked sense of humor.

"Ma'am," he says. "I hope you had a pleasant journey."

"So very happy to meet you, Luke. The journey was uneventful and the children traveled well. What more could a mother ask?"

A mother of five… he grins. And she returns it.

"Let me introduce the children."

All five are immaculately turned out; cute from the greatest to the least; intelligent foreheads, bright eyes, strong limbs, good teeth…

They're not colts, you chucklehead.

"Boys, mind your manners. This is Conor, our eldest, he's ten. And Finn, who's eight nearly nine." The boys shake his hand politely. Jeanne continues, "Our eldest daughter, Ariel…"

"She's seven," the one called Conor butts in. "Davie is…"

"Thank you, Conor, I'm sure I can manage," Jeanne says with strained forbearance. "Davina is five. And our baby, Caroline."

"She's three, but you'd never know it because…"

"Conor, don't tell him about that," Ariel interrupts. "We agreed to make a good impression, remember?"

"Oh, Ari," Conor groans.

Jeanne gives Luke a big grin. "Children! *So* entertaining."

He smiles politely.

"That's fine, children, now stay close."

He doesn't think she'll have a problem, at least not with the two littlest girls. They look in awe of the place. The one who has some kind of affliction which would cause a bad impression if he knew about it, clings so tight to her mother's hand, Jeanne Sullivan can hardly move it.

As if she knows what he's thinking, Jeanne says, "Jennifer has told them so many stories…"

"We know a lot about this town," Conor says with a swaggering nod.

"Yeah. The cattle stampede," the other boy, Finn, pipes up.

"The guns."

"The scarlet fever epidemic."

"The gunfights in the streets."

"The bank robberies."

"With the guns."

"Bedtime was fun when AJ lived with us," says the little girl called Davina.

"AJ?" he murmurs.

"Auntie Jennifer," Ariel informs him.

"We call her AJ," Finn says while he looks around him.

"Aunties are old, anyhow," says Connor, pointing something out to his brother. "AJ's not old…"

Frank counts their luggage. "Right. Time to go. Everyone take their bag please. This is as good a time as any for a lesson in how to be responsible for your possessions."

The children appear to have their own luggage of varying sizes, even the baby… the smallest carpetbag Luke has ever seen.

"We have a wagon waiting," Jennifer says.

As one voice, they cry, "A wagon?"

"Why, yes," she says, with a wink.

"Oh boy, oh boy…" The young brothers start jumping around, muttering about getting to ride in a real 'wild west' wagon.

Luke says, "Let me help you with the heavier luggage, Frank."

"Just so you know," Jennifer whispers in his ear, "there is nothing wrong with little Caroline."

Her eyes are laughing as he looks into them.

Even though their hotel, the Inter Ocean, is only one block away from the depot, he takes them on a tour of Cheyenne in the wagon, the children and Jennifer and the luggage all piled into the back, and Frank and Jeanne up front with him.

As he begins to realize that Frank is a quietly-spoken feller, he relaxes. And he doesn't mind the intelligent observations Frank makes, or the pertinent questions regarding the growth of the town. Talking comes easier between them, and Jeanne is no shrinking violet when it comes to conversation. Meanwhile, he has one ear trained on Jennifer pointing out every feature of the town she can manage to five excited children.

When they pull up outside Jennifer's building, they all want to pile out and look inside.

"Seeing where Jennifer works and lives here in Cheyenne is very important to us," Frank explains.

"Ain't they tired?" Luke asks, watching the children whizzing from room to room.

Frank replies, "Not in the least, but we would be very much obliged if you could help us get them that way."

Frank

Inter Ocean Hotel
The Sullivans' Suite
16th Street, Cheyenne

Jeanne pulls off her gloves. "Frank, he's a darling. Tall... rugged. Those sparkly deep blue eyes. That *smile*. Oh, break your heart as soon as look at you. I begin to understand the cowboy allure."

"Allure? What are you saying exactly?"

"Only that I give Jennifer credit for knowing an attractive man when she sees one."

He shrugs out of his coat. "He seems like a *fine* man, which is more to point."

"He was nervous, the poor lamb."

"About meeting us? I hardly think..."

Jeanne raises her eyebrows at him.

"Well, what on earth could George have been saying to make him nervous about meeting a math professor? She's a doctor, so I can't imagine what else could bother him."

"I'll let you work it out, Frank. I have to see to the children."

A great deal of their daytime conversations ended with that sentence. He catches Jeanne's slender wrist and gently stops her.

"He loves George though."

She smiles, puts her arms around his neck. "You haven't got a thing to worry about." She kisses his lips softly and withdraws.

Of all things, the groom-to-be shows up ten minutes later.

474

"Luke…"

"Not intruding?"

"Certainly not." Frank opens the door wide and bids him enter.

"I thought you and I should talk."

"Is there something on your mind?"

"You wouldn't have anything to drink would you?"

"Ah…" It's barely lunchtime and he wants a drink? "Ah… should be something…" Frank finds the cabinet that contains one bottle each of whiskey and brandy. "Brandy?"

"Whatever you got. I ain't fussy."

Frank procures two glasses, seizes the brandy and pours. "You're not a drinker, are you?"

Luke gives a strained laugh. "No."

Frank hands him the glass and pours a brandy for himself. "A toast?"

"To Jennifer," Luke murmurs.

"Very good. To my sister."

They drink.

"Sit, won't you?"

"Jeanne takes care of the children by herself?"

"At home we have a full-time cook, although Jeanne herself is an excellent cook – I think they are conspiring to write a recipe book. And we have two women who come in twice a week to help with laundry and cleaning the house. Jeanne runs a tight ship. Very little escapes her notice. And considering so many things escape mine, I'm very grateful."

Luke smiles and then frowns at his brandy. "About what happened between Jennifer and me in San Francisco…"

"Regarding Dermot."

"Yes, it was about Dermot."

Frank sips his drink, not realizing until now how much he needed one. "I know that couldn't have been easy for either of you. Your reaction frightened her."

Luke looks up. "I'm sorry for that."

Frank sits forward. "Luke, you don't have to prove yourself to me."

"I think I do."

"No. My sister's devotion to you is proof enough. You broke through every barrier she had built around herself to protect herself from being hurt, and when they were all down and she got hurt, she picked herself up and tried again. And then again. You proved yourself to her and that's all that matters."

"I do love her."

"I guess that's all I really need to hear."

"And I will take care of her."

"Luke, I'm not her father..."

A flash of that disarming grin. "Then I should go all the way to Cape Cod to plead my case..."

Frank sighs, reluctantly amused. "No."

"Then it's you I should be talking to."

He frowns. "How much has George told you?"

"I reckon everything there is to tell. Listen, Frank, I love her and promise to take care of her. This is a difficult time for my family and friends. Jennifer knows this. She walked right back into the middle of it and if she hadn't I don't know where I would be right now. But we know that getting married now is the right step."

"Is she in any danger?"

He shakes his head. "She is one of the most respected people in this town. No one would dare harm her, even to get to me. And we have a lot of good people on our side."

"And when this difficult time is over – what then?"

"We still have to decide, but she will always be a doctor, for as long as she wants, that is her pledge to me."

"Hers to you?"

"She's a gifted woman. She fought hard for what she believes in and only she has the right to say if and when she's through with it."

"It won't be easy when children come along."

"I don't expect we'll be a conventional family."

Frank is beginning to see that; and, what George would be attracted to – the man puts up few barriers to living. Which is why George allowed hers to fall. The life she thought unattainable had become feasible. An extraordinary leap.

"Anything's possible," Frank murmurs with renewed gladness.

"That's right."
"I've been trying to tell George that for years."
"I think she gets it now."
Frank raises his glass. "Here's to that then."
Luke lifts his. "To being happy."

Luke

As he waits for Emmaline, he leans back against the wall beside the Tribune's doors and blows on his hands, annoyed with himself for leaving his gloves someplace he can't remember; the feller at the front desk inside said she was due back any time. The Tribune may be warm inside but Charlie Quaid makes standing on the cold, frosty street positively enticing. The thought of working for a man as high-strung as Quaid…

Emmaline comes into view, bobbing behind several people ahead of her on the sidewalk. He straightens up; Emmaline sees him, her eyes go wide, she stops dead in her tracks. Bewildered, he looks around to determine what she's reacting to.

Nothing. What – *him*?

Meanwhile, she's continued and reaches him.

"Good day, Luke," she says and is about to walk right by him.

"Wait up."

"Can't stop."

He halts her progress with a gentle hand on her arm. "I've been waiting to speak with you."

"What do you want?" she mutters, frowning at his hand.

He removes it. "Somethin' the matter? Have I grown an extra head?"

"No, the one you presently possess is quite big enough."

He blinks. And clears his throat. And attempts to figure out what she's thinking. Only one problem – that's never gonna happen. "Okay. Let's start again."

"Sorry, I'm busy," she says and attempts to sachet round him.

478

He swivels. "Jennifer asked me to give you a message."

She stops and looks exasperated. "She couldn't give it to me herself?"

"Well, she's busy with her brother right now and I said I'd deliver it on my way to..."

"I see."

"Emmaline, what is the matter with you?"

"It's cold and what's the message?"

He holds back a laugh of disbelief. "Emmaline..."

"What's the message?"

"There's a shindig at Amy's this evening. With the weddin' on tomorrow, the women decided to get together and..."

"I see," she interrupts again. "Well, I'm very busy..."

"Tress will be glad to see you."

"I'll do my best to come, but I can't promise. Thanks for your trouble. Goodbye."

She grabs the doorknob and with a final cursory glance at the streetscape lunges through the doorway of the Tribune and snaps the door firmly shut behind her.

He scratches the back of his neck. A lot of people have given him the cold shoulder over the years, but he never thought Emmaline would become one of them.

Emmaline

Emmaline reefs open the bottom drawer of her desk, stuffs her satchel inside, rams it shut and slumps in her chair. Some of the Sheriff's more salient words drift into her dark thoughts.

Emmaline, you can only become a victim if you allow it to happen.

He means the victim of personal abuse or harassment or mind games...

Jacob Hunter's victim.

What better way to destroy the competition, particularly if that competition is female, than to feed the public false information and create a scandal.

Hunter is out there, somewhere, she knows he is. Probably watched her with Luke; she imagines the pond scum jotting notes about everything he saw...

"Roberts, you look a little gray around the gills."

"Mr Quaid," she says, suddenly aware he's standing there.

"Something you need to get off your chest?"

"No. Why do you ask?"

"Like I said – gray," he says and walks away.

"Not gray," she sings to his back.

Sure enough, Jacob Hunter is loitering outside as she leaves for the day.

She starts walking. "No home to go to, Mr Hunter?"

He attaches himself to her side and keeps pace. "A very comfortable one, thanks for asking. You won't get rid of me, Roberts."

"That's interesting. I was just on my way to see Mac to ask his advice on what can be done about harassment."

Hunter chuckles. "Good idea, Roberts."

"Thank you, Mr Hunter. Unlike yourself, I have many of them."

"Ouch." He feigns a chest wound.

"Would you care to have supper with me, Mr Hunter? Nan Morris always has plenty on the table and welcomes guests, even you I should imagine."

From the corner of her eye, she spies Hunter's cocky expression slipping.

"You know the saying," she says, "if you can't beat 'em, join 'em.' "

"I know the saying, Roberts," he retorts.

"Scared of fraternizing with the opposition?"

"There's another saying, Roberts. Keep your friends close and your enemies closer."

"I've heard that, too. So, then, if we were friends we wouldn't have to be this close, now would we?"

Hunter laughs; actually, a genuine laugh.

"So," she says, restraining her tone, "supper?"

Before he can answer, Cliff and Mac swing around the corner and pull up short before all four of them run into one another.

While she does her best to remain poker-faced, lest Hunter discover for himself who it is she truly likes in this silly old town, Mac pushes back his hat and declares, "Well, here's a sight you don't see often... heck, never in all my recollection. Roberts and Hunter a-strollin' like pals down Main Street."

"Perfect timing," Hunter mutters. "Roberts was just on her way to see you, Mac."

Mac looks pleased. Jauntily, he says, "That so? What can I do ya for, Miss Roberts?"

"Well, er, you see..."

Hunter has the gall to start laughing at her.

"Somebody say something to amuse you, Hunter?" Cliff asks.

"This town is a barrel of laughs, Sheriff, you know that."

A glance at Cliff's face reveals that he's none too pleased, although the expression waxes and wanes like he, too, is trying to hide his feelings from Hunter.

She takes a deep breath. "It can wait till tomorrow, Mac. Mr Hunter, bless his heart, and I are on our way to supper. Wednesday is chicken fricassee aux champignons night. Simply ambrosial. Well, be seeing y'all. Have a pleasant evening."

Mac dips his hat, grinning. "Likewise."

She doesn't even look at Cliff, although she does notice Mac giving him a shove forward to move him along, and then another.

"You know, Roberts," Hunters says, chuckling, "it don't matter how ambrosial that chicken fricassee is."

"Oh?" she mutters, walking fast with Hunter keeping pace.

"I have supper plans of my own."

"How *will* I bear the loss…"

"Thanks anyway. Good night." He veers off to the right, crossing the street.

Dag-nab-it.

Too smart by half. She'll have to think of something else. Something so basic the smart aleck will fall for it. Protecting the secrecy of Luke and Jennifer's wedding is paramount and she does not intend to be the one who betrays it. Better not to turn up than do that. But the dismal thought of ditching the wedding because of Jacob Hunter gets her to thinking very hard.

Luke

Ethan slurs each word as he says, "Ain't that Ben?"

Luke pokes his head up and directs his eyes through the humming miasma of smoke and whiskey to the saloon door. "He made it."

Ethan makes some attempt to get to his feet.

Luke stops him. "Hang fire, pard. I'll fetch him."

The others laugh as Ethan drops back onto his chair.

As Luke gets up, Ethan's saying, "Glad he could make it. T'wouldn't've bin the same without 'im."

"T'wouldn't've?" John squawks. "Think Ethan just invented a new word."

Luke can't be sure what the other nose painters in the place make of his little shindig, bending the elbow with the boys before the big day, but a deeper mystery is how Ethan, full as a tick, spotted Ben.

As Luke comes his way, Ben lifts his brow in recognition. They grip hands and shake.

"You found us…" Luke grins. "Glad you're back."

"Good to *be* back. Spent the last hour with the folks; they told me where you were and that everything's set for tomorrow."

"All arranged. License, food… you name it. Time now for a quiet drink before…"

"Quiet? I could hear Ethan from outside."

"Yep, no one's more excited than Ethan."

"Look at them... You don't think Faraday and Ryan... Ryan... how's he holding up?"

"He's fine."

"As I was saying... you don't think Faraday and Ryan drinking in a saloon with all of us will raise some suspicion?"

"If they're not worried, I'm not worried."

"Fair enough. My father went to bed and left the women and those little girls to their wedding talk. Raina's with them. Amy and Signora are cooking like this is their last night on earth. Meanwhile the Severini boys are teaching the Sullivan boys how to play poker."

"Frank will be thrilled. Did you happen to notice Emmaline?"

"Don't think she was there."

Luke lets this pass. "And Omaha?"

"What is it Dan Hummer likes to say: mission accomplished..."

"Then you deserve a drink."

"Mm. I'm buying."

"Oh, no..."

"Oh, yes... fizzy and French."

Ben brushes past him and heads for the bar. Luke follows him.

"Champagne!" Ben exclaims, slapping down some serious money.

The barkeep says, "Sure. What's the occasion?"

"I just saved my legacy from the jaws of Loren Bodecker," Ben announces.

"Ain't you the lucky one," the barkeep says. "How many bottles?"

"Three to start."

With the barkeep gone to fetch the champagne, Luke exchanges glances with his cousin.

"Congratulations, Ben," he says sincerely.

His cousin smiles, and because it happens once in a blue moon it kinda means something. "C'mon, let's join the others. I want to meet your brand new brother-in-law. Warn him not to play poker with his kids anytime soon."

Cliff

Wedding Day

Thursday morning, the sun shines bright and the sky is bluer than yesterday to feed the notion that Spring will eventually come to Cheyenne.

After a morning's work ticks over into the afternoon, he leaves Mac in charge and heads off to Luke's. He finds him looking preoccupied and struggling with his tie.

"I can't believe I'm doing this."

"Let me fix it."

"You're calm."

"I'm not the one getting married."

"I can't believe I'm doing this."

"You said that."

"It's kinda nerve-wracking."

"So I've heard."

"Maybe if you said something profound…"

Cliff steps back and folds his arms. "Tonight, my friend, you get to be with Jennifer."

Luke blinks. Looks calmer. "Huh. That's deep."

"Mm. I thought so."

Emmaline

In the layout of the city of Cheyenne, Emmaline could not be sure if it was intended for most of the churches to be erected within a stone's throw of each other, but they are. In her opinion it gave Christian neighborliness a whole new meaning. The corners of Ferguson and 18th and 19th Streets on Sunday mornings amount to one of the busiest times and places in the town ever, with every kind of denomination clustered in this corner of Cheyenne, all a-prayin' and a-singin'.

St John the Baptist Catholic Church and the Congregational Church are east and west of each other but on the same block separated by only a few buildings on wide plots of land, including the parsonage.

This had better work. It won't be easy. This is Thursday, not Sunday, with only a handful of people coming and going over at the courthouse which dominates Ferguson and 19th, opposite St John's. Secretly, a wedding is coming together in the Congregational Church, but in the short time since she had arrived and glancing every so often down the block, she would not have suspected it, and neither would anyone else.

She knocks sharply on the door of Father Nugent's parish house. Opening the door is Mrs Payne, who bears the magnificently melodic Christian name Odelinda, and who comes in four times a week to bring cleanliness and order to the house, as well as ensuring their busy priest eats some nutritious home-cooked meals.

"Good morning, Miss Emmaline. How charming you look today. You'll be wanting Father Nugent. He's over in the church hearing Confession. A group of miners and their families came into town. You may catch him before he begins."

Confession. *Here we go again.*

She forces herself to slow down. Act natural. To listen for footfall other than her own. To keep her head straight while her eyes bend around corners. He is there; she knows he is because before she left the Tribune she spent a good five minutes examining the street from the front window and located him.

Jacob Hunter. The rat.

Time to nip him and his rattish ways in the bud.

Inside St John's, two dozen or more people warm several pews beside the Confessional. Oh, dear. At this rate, she'll miss the wedding. As a friend she desperately wants to attend; but her instinct as a reporter is just as strong – this will be an important story and (although some folks might not realize it yet) play a significant part in the trial. She just has to be present. No one will write it like her and no one will defend against gossip and scandal as resolutely. Besides, someone needs to teach Jacob Hunter a lesson he will not easily forget.

She takes a pew and catches her breath.

Face it, Emmie, you love those people.

She does love them. All of them. Some are dearer to her than others. Tressa and Adam. But it makes no difference. She will defend their liberty... their sweet land of liberty... and pursuit of happiness...

Behold, an idea – even better than the one she had – that sends sparks shooting from one side of her brain to the other.

Two of the children, little girls in plain wool dresses and calico bonnets, wander up to her, curious. Another idea...

She whispers to them, "I will give you a nickel each if you go put your heads outside the door and see if there is a young man standing about."

They nod in agreement and skip off.

She inhales a deep breath, hoping Hunter is so repulsed by religion that he has gone far, far away. The little girls are quick to return, giggling. And, dashing her hopes, they nod enthusiastically and hold out their hands.

"Are you sure?"

"We're sure," they whisper.

"What does he look like?"

"He has a blue coat."

"And brown hair and a round black hat."

"He's not old..."

"... but he's not as young as my brother over there."

Emmaline follows the sweet little hand and pointed finger to a spot where a boy about her brother Sam's age sits slumped and uninterested.

Satisfied, she hands them each a nickel. Thankfully, their parents are too busy praying on their knees to notice.

Just then Father Nugent emerges from the sacristy, his black cassock slightly visible beneath hem and cuffs of a crisp white alb; around his neck and flowing down over his chest is the purple stole he wears for confession. She gets to her feet at once. Father Nugent acknowledges her with a smile and a nod. She genuflects and goes forward to meet him.

"Emmaline, don't you look a picture today," he says in his hushed church voice.

"Thank you, Father. I'll be attending a function very shortly, but first... Father, I need a favor."

"Well, as you can see..." His hand sweeps in the direction of the waiting families.

"May I go first?"

He folds his arms. And raises an eyebrow.

"Father, I need your help."

Cliff

While Cliff straightens his own tie in front of the mirror, Luke stands by and asks, "Have you noticed Emmaline acting kinda odd lately?"

"More odd than normal?"

"Yep."

Cliff shrugs. He doesn't want to talk about Emma walking down 16th Street with Jacob Hunter.

Luke continues, "Didn't care to give me the time of day yesterday."

Meanwhile, she's giving Jacob Hunter time of day. And chicken fricassee…

"She even offered an insult."

"An insult; are you sure?"

"Kinda reminded me of one of K's. You don't realize how much you miss something…"

"I'm happy to insult you anytime."

"Emmaline?"

Cliff turns away from the mirror; folds his arms. "I ran into her yesterday as she was walking with Jacob Hunter."

"Don't get me started on Hunter. Stalks you night and day. Tip and I've had to devise some pretty ingenious strategies for putting him off the scent. What's Emmaline doing with him?"

"Shudder to think." But he *is* thinking. "You never told me about Hunter."

"Had it under control. Newspaper hounds. You just have to put them off the scent."

"Impressive. So, have you got a strategy to get to the church?"

"Won't need one."

"Why?"

"Because, Cliff, I'd say Jacob Hunter is tailing Emmaline."

They stare at one another wordlessly for several seconds.

Luke swallows hard. "You wanna go?"

Cliff clears his throat. "No."

"Look, Cliff…"

"No, I don't want to go chasing after that exasperating female!"

Luke's relief is obvious. "Then… are we late?"

"Have you ever known me to be late?"

Luke shakes his head. "You're weird that way."

"Would I let *you* be late?"

"Guess we're not late then."

"How d'you feel about your mother not making the wedding?"

"The telegram said she and Edith would be home when the weather warmed up."

"And that made Jennifer feel how good exactly?"

"When Frank and Jeanne and posse of ankle-biters showed up she forgot about my mother."

"They're a fine family."

"Frank is hardly older than you… and he has *five* children…"

"I know, pal. What can I say, except, Jeanne is obviously a very cooperative woman."

They set off for the church, trying to look casual if a little overdressed… and Luke saying, "Don't worry about Hunter. If he shows up sniffing around the church, Tip will know, and we'll just invite him to the weddin'."

"Invite him…"

"Alliance style. Tip knows what to do, trust me."

Emma invited Hunter for chicken fricassee aux champignons. *Keep your enemies closer…* Good girl.

Emmaline

"Good morning, my dear people."

"Good morning, Father."

"Excellent. Yes, you are all excellent people."

Some beam at him. The canny ones frown.

"So, gather round... yes, yes. Excellent. Bring the children in close. Good..."

One of the men says, "This is very unusual, Father..."

"It is. Indeed. Well, now. I have one question for you all. All you good, hard-working folk."

"Go ahead, Father. We're listening..."

"Excellent. Well, then. Er, the question... Here it is. This is Miss Emmaline Roberts – a woman you know, who through her way with the written word, does whatever she can to support the humble worker. Dear people, who would like to save her from the vicious jaws of one of The Bugle's scoundrel reporters...?"

The miner families look at one another. This much oratorical excitement is usually reserved for the pulpit. Father Nugent begins to countenance the persuasion of his own eloquence as he breaks out of his church voice and says, "The Bugle – who we know is no friend of the honest worker – has released a scoundrel dogged and determined to rain down scandalous disrepute upon this good Catholic woman and upon this church!"

Muttering breaks out among the families.

"So who's with me?" he cries.

There is the shortest and stillest of pauses...

Then two dozen hands are raised up to heaven.

Cliff

In dribs and drabs the guests gather at Cheyenne's Congregational Church, until the Keatons, Taylors, Benchleys, Sullivans, Faradays, and Duffy are all present, approximately twenty two people in all.

A significant gathering. But he can't see Emma anywhere. And he's beginning to worry about her fending off Jacob Hunter.

Better to concentrate on the wedding.

The bride is already present, as the circumstances warrant. Even though he'd once told Emma he had never noticed Jennifer's beautiful face, that is not possible for anyone; and today, it is impossible to ignore. She is glowing. And he'd be lying to himself if he said that he wasn't a tiny bit jealous of her happiness.

He didn't expect to be emotional. But he didn't expect when he was bringing Luke home on the train from North Platte that he'd be standing here either; he didn't even know then if they'd be alive in a week. From that moment to this, with everything that has happened, he should have realized his emotions would surface and want to take the lead. He could loosen the reins a little, give them a break. He's happy for his friends and they need to know it.

There is no organ to herald the impending nuptials and it makes for a refreshing change. Instead, as the Reverend appears and nods a greeting to the gathering, there is peaceful stillness and sunshine streaming through intensely colored stained-glass windows. Birds twitter in the intrepid oak outside. Nearby the clop of horse and buggy. Voices beyond that. The town in the distance. Layers of life present yet held at bay.

This peace is a fitting start to Luke and Jennifer's married life.

There had been precious little of it up until now and they were all due for some. It envelops everyone and everything in a sublime and radiant dignity. You can feel it doing you good.

And then it happens... a loud, *undignified* BANG! – and a crashing THUD! The rafters wobble overhead and it feels as though the stained glass will implode.

After the bone-wrenching shock and their involuntary cries, everyone turns towards the back of the church, only to have to endure the nerve-tearing squeak and screech of metal on metal.

Mutterings of 'oh dear' and 'what the deuce' ripple through the gathering.

The Reverend clears his throat and says, "Someone will need to inform Miss Roberts that Congregationalists don't bolt the doors of their churches, not for weddings anyway."

"That's some entrance," Luke mutters.

They swap glances.

Cliff sighs. "I'll go, Reverend."

"Thank you, Sheriff Ryan."

Deeply conscious of twenty pairs of eyes following him down the aisle of the church, Cliff locks his gaze on an image of Emma in the vestibule, reclining against the doors, eyes closed and breathing hard.

"Emma," he whispers as he reaches her.

Her eyes fly open. "Am I late?" she whispers back.

"Not... exactly."

She whimpers a little. "I'm sorry."

"Are you all right?"

"Cold... breathless... hurts... Just need... a moment... to catch... my breath... Go ahead... without me..."

He gives her a moment. "What happened?"

"Are you sure... you want to know?"

"Was it legal?"

"It involves Father Nugent, the Confessional and two dozen miners... a couple of little girls and a small but generous recompense."

"You've been busy."

"Mm."

"Are we…"

"Safe from the prying eyes and acid quill of Jacob Hunter? I believe so. Father Nugent is a brick. Hunter had a fair wait ahead of him but he's in the care of Mr and Mrs Rudowski. Noble people. And conveniently large. They once raised sheep back in the old country, they won't let him stray. He should be engaged in Confessional chit-chat with Father Nugent precisely in the middle of the wedding."

"That's good work, Roberts."

"Thank you. I… Then you're not…"

"About yesterday?"

"I was…"

"I know."

With her breathing almost back to normal, she straightens, leaving the doors to hold themselves up, adjusts her shawl and smoothes down her dress both of which are soft, pretty and show her figure perfectly in a very fetching shade of pale pink. Not a color he's ever seen her wear before. Rosy-cheeked, slightly fly-away, eyes sparkling, she's almost stopping his heart…

"You look lovely, Emma," he murmurs.

Her eyelashes flutter. "So do you… handsome, I mean."

"Emmaline…"

They raise their heads and separate at once… Tressa.

"Are you all right?" She holds out her hand.

Emma farewells him with guarded glance before she walks across and takes Tressa's hand. Cliff follows them as they walk arm in arm up the aisle and join the Keatons. He resumes his position beside Luke.

"Is she all right?" he whispers.

"Peach perfect, as always."

"D'you mind if I marry Jennifer now?"

"I believe it's safe to do so."

Luke gives him a searching look. "She didn't."

"She did."

"She's a keeper."

"Indeed."

Luke

His mind wanders back to the day he first saw Jennifer. In the Cheyenne Hotel with that old brown bag across her shoulders. His grief over Mart had obliterated all the color from the world; everything looked like it was painted black. Except her. She shone like a star, brilliant with light, a prism that revealed a world rich with color. He never wanted to stop looking at her. The desire to step into her world and remain was overwhelming. He had to fight it, and he did, for so long, through everything that happened. But the need to be with her not only never left him, it squeezed him into a different shape; he began to understand it as part of who he was. *She* was part of who he was. To live without her was to live half a life. To be incomplete somehow.

She wears a green gown that matches her eyes perfectly. Where did she find such a dress? Where did she get the glittering jewel in the side of her hair? And the creamy roses she carries in her bouquet?

She is his bride.

If he wasn't busy marrying her, he'd draw her.

He smiles at her… those soft-red lips smile back.

He'd never do her justice.

Could his hand make what his heart holds? Could a pencil stroke caress a page the way his lips caress her skin?

"Do you, Luke, take this woman, Jennifer Aisling Sullivan, to be your wife…"

He does. Nothing would ever change his answer, from now till forever… always yes.

He'll always be rich, always well, never bad, forever loved, honored and cherished, never forsaken, always truly hers.

And she always truly his.

"Do you, Jennifer, take this man, Luke Daniel Taylor, to be your husband, to have and to hold from this day forward..."

Her eyes glisten, gazing into his with so much feeling he forgets where they are; the words the Reverend is speaking and the emotion in her eyes are one and the same.

"...as long as you both shall live?"

"I do," she says.

"The ring, if you please, Mr Ryan..."

Emmaline

She watches the man of her dreams whom she can't have place a shining gold wedding band on the Reverend's service book. What would Ashcliff think if he knew she was technically prohibited to go into a church of another denomination and hear prayers from another's prayer book? Maybe he knew that by now. It certainly didn't bother *him*. And, after all, it is the same God. It gets her to thinking that it must be liberating to choose what religion you'd like to belong to, instead of being formed into it from infancy and forbidden to stray lest the promise of your eternity be hell.

Eternity. That's what the ring symbolizes.

The Reverend unleashes a prayer of blessing to which she tries her hardest not to listen. Because they are a small, intimate gathering the Reverend very kindly and purposefully positioned the bride and groom in such a way that their guests could see their faces, not their backs, so it's a remarkable thing for her to witness the look which passes between them; and it causes her to sigh. They look like they're in heaven. Their faces are radiant; their features soft with emotion.

"Luke, take the ring and repeat after me..."

Everyone in the church is smiling... after the torment of the past several days, it's like balm for what ails her. Yes, she is so pleased to be here.

"With this ring I thee wed..."

Her gaze inevitably falls on Ashcliff.

His person is like a magnet for her gaze.

The way he looked at her before made her a little weak-kneed;

his compliment was genuine, probably because for once she looked lady-like in her shell-pink silk and not like her normal appearance which Celie once dubbed 'tomboy in a dress'.

Emmie, stop staring at him or he'll see you…

Smart aleck. I'm looking at Jennifer now…

Mm, a woman not scared to go after her man.

I'm not scared and he's not my man!

She coughs… twice…

"By the power vested in me by God and the Territory of Wyoming, I now pronounce you husband and wife…"

…and feels a little light-headed.

"You may kiss the bride."

Still pleased to be here.

Cliff

John and Amy Keaton's House

Champagne flows. Children seem to be everywhere. Delicious food appears; a good deal of it has a decidedly Italian flavor.

Signora is in her element. She and Amy Keaton appear to get on famously since preparing food and having people consume it in vast quantities is something they clearly have in common; their food is devoured. And when it's time to cut the cake and make speeches, Ethan has to round up Tip and the Severini brothers from out back and a very boisterous game of poker.

The five Sullivan children sit politely on the floor in front of the cake, the little girls in beautiful dresses, the boys pulling at their starched collars; the one called Davina tugged on his coat earlier in order to tell him they all got special clothes for the day and that she was pretending she was an angel. Why she thought he would want to know is a mystery.

The speeches are made.

Considering wedding speeches are notorious for putting people to sleep, their speeches all turn out well. Fine sentiment combined with plenty of humor make them entertaining as well as heartfelt.

Including his as the best man.

The bride and groom deliver a relaxed and conversational reply to all the speeches that have gone before, and those who don't have tears in their eyes from the touching expressions of love and gratitude, are laughing at Luke's wisecracks which are mostly at Ethan's expense; he was giving as good as he'd got!

499

Together, Luke and Jennifer slice through Signora's layered melt-in-your-mouth concoction for a wedding cake, the joy on their faces lighting up the room. Luke catches his bride around the waist, kisses her and holds her close. What did Emma call them? – one of the great romances in this town's history. Here it is, right in front of his eyes.

Suddenly there is music. He looks about to see Alfredo with a squeezebox and Gianni plying a fiddle. It begins rowdily until their mother clips them over the ear. The dance hall melody miraculously turns into a mellow waltz, and everyone steps back to watch the bride and groom dance. He wonders if they've been secretly practicing because they're not half bad…

Meanwhile, the cooks take over the cake cutting.

As for dancing at his friends' wedding, he'd given it a great deal of thought. Even though Meg is matron of honor, he'd already arranged with Cam to dance with Meg; it was right and proper and they join in the dance with the happy couple.

There is only one appropriate choice of partner for him. He walks right up to her, smiles and says, "Duffy, would you do me the honor?"

Duffy grins a mile wide. "Knowing what a fine dancer you are, Cliff Ryan, the honor belongs to me…" And off they go.

Frank and Jeanne join in as well. Others soon follow.

This is not your average-sized dance floor, so it's small steps and good manners all round, resulting in more laughter. Signora blushes when Ethan sweeps her into the dance; she barely has time to put down the cake knife. Even Richard Taylor's mood has brightened, as Caroline coaxes him to dance with her. Ben and Raina have an invisible *Do Not Disturb* sign on their backs which is touchingly respected.

When Duffy declares she's not as young as she used to be, he fetches her a cup of punch and leaves her to tap her toes alongside the musicians. He stands back a bit himself and watches. The children run about between the guests, stuffing cake and other delicious treats into their mouths. The oldest daughter, Ariel, has taken a liking to baby Adam and sits in a cozy chair in the corner playing with him.

His heart feels very warm looking upon such a scene.

A sweet southern voice at his side says, "You dance very well."

"Off the record, my mother was strict about the social graces."

"Good for her," she says drolly, with gentle sarcasm.

He smiles at her. "Will you dance with me?"

"I didn't... No. Thank you."

"Ah, rejection, we know each other so well. Excuse me."

He notices Emma dance many times after that, with every other man in the room, in fact; every kind of waltz and polka. Even the little Sullivan girls get a turnabout, to their obvious delight.

Old friends Cam and Frank get together and talk for some time; when Jennifer, Meg and Jeanne join them the meeting comes to life. Luke affectionately dubs them 'the Blue Bellies of Boston' and invites Tressa to waltz with him; they chat quietly while they dance.

Then Ethan calls out, "It's a square dance, folks! Choose your partners. Gianni reckons he's got fire in those fiddle fingers, so hold on to your hats. I expect everyone born west of the Big Muddy to know what they're doing!"

The scramble to choose partners, while Gianni warms up his fiddle with strains of what's to come, causes some temporary mayhem. Before long, space is made in the center of the room and the couples square off: Ethan and Signora, Tip and Jennifer, Luke and Duffy, Ben and Raina. The pairing alone is entertaining.

Gianni starts up his fiddle in earnest... Alfredo claps the beat.

"Everybody bow... Now find those corners..." Ethan calls. And the dance has begun.

Jennifer and Raina need a little help but that only adds to the hilarity, and while Signora and Duffy are surprisingly good, the Taylor and the Benchley boys have the goods, as Ethan shouts bits and pieces of the call every so often while he dances.

When the dance is over and the excitement dies down, the music mellows for a spell with the gentle, romantic riffs of Alfredo's squeezebox. Jennifer hands him yet another glass of champagne.

"Didn't know you could square dance," he says.

"First time actually, you couldn't tell?"

"Not much," he grins.

"Mm, like to see you try it. So, how goes it with Miss Words?"

"Miss Words refused to dance with me."

"You asked her?"

"I did."

"Ask her again?"

"What do I look like to you? – the world's biggest sap?"

Luke comes up to them.

Cliff rolls his eyes. "Why do I get the feeling I'm about to be ambushed."

"Friendly warning: I'm coming back this way with Emmaline."

While Alfredo and Gianni are skillfully melting one tune into another, Luke reappears, this time dancing with Emma. It doesn't look natural and Emma looks confused. Luke bumps into them; it has as much finesse as a drunken cowboy in a saloon, but in the midst of all their apologizing, the bride and groom clear off and leave him alone with Emma.

"That was subtle," she says.

"You didn't suspect him?"

"Didn't have time. I was speaking with Caroline Taylor – off the record – and he drags me off."

"They seem to think we should dance – together."

"I've already danced enough for one day."

"Look, I know you think dancing together equates to some form of encouragement of me holding some false hope about us…"

"Good Lord, is that even a proper sentence? What champagne does to some people…"

"…but I'm over it. So you don't have to worry ever again."

She gives a muffled grunt. "Seeing how I know what 'it' is."

"So you do. I, on the other hand, had to find out the hard way."

"Well, ain't you sweet? Always such a gentleman."

"True to form! But you'll be back amid the charm and gentility of the Old South within a month and all will be well again."

Her cheeks suffuse with pink. "Old South… How quaint!"

"Your father seemed to think I'd like it."

"He did? What made him say a thing like that to a Yankee boy like you?"

"His enthusiasm was sincere but don't worry, I won't be paying you a visit or anything. So, would you care to dance?"

"No, thank you."

"Then…" He gives a slight bow and withdraws to a mahogany parlor sofa that's been pushed up against the wall furthest from the music. He's barely sat on the tapestry-style upholstery when she approaches him. He tries not to look at her.

"May we talk?" she asks, standing in front of him.

"Are we off the record?"

She gives an impatient sigh. "You'll be here in Cheyenne, right? You'll be running for re-election."

"I like this job well enough. In many ways it's a privilege. But maybe I'd like to convince Mac to have a run at it. There are other things to do in this world, occupations that would benefit from my experience here. I didn't begin my life as a sheriff and I don't intend to finish it as one, although according to you a sheriff is born with the badge permanently pinned to his pink baby chest with little else to do but wait till he grows into it."

"You talk as though you have lost the desire to do your job."

"For your information, it's a job I would prefer to do without a wife and family and since I want a family of my own someday, there you have it… and no, you may not quote me."

When she doesn't reply, he glances up at her. Her expression is extremely guarded. After a long moment she says, "You wouldn't give this future wife Emma by Jane Austen?"

Not what he expected. "I think you already know the answer."

"May I sit?"

"Of course," he says, pretending ambivalence to whatever she plans to say, even though his attention is so acute the room may as well be vacant.

She sits beside him on the sofa. There is only room for two. They are a perfect fit.

"There is something I think I should explain."

"I'm listening."

"What my father did, it will take me some time to recover. I know I should be all grown up about it and laugh it off, but I can't, not yet. His revelation took something from me. I've spoken with Father Nugent about it and he helped me understand myself. I'm sorry, though, that I can't make you understand."

She's hurting inside, he understands that. Although her parents are reconciling, a cause for celebration, the revelation had a sting in its tail. Deception. And that *really* smarts.

As if she reads his thoughts, she says, "They let me go on thinking something that wasn't true for ten years. Surely no one can expect me to forgive and forget in a few days. It's hardly fair." She looks at her hands. "All that being said, after the trial I need to go home, where all this truly belongs. You should remain here and be the person you are meant to be, and not go changing because of me. I want you to see that you and I would be a mistake. And I couldn't bear to be your mistake."

"My mistake! Emma, when you leave me and return to the land of warm seas and orange trees and I never see you again, you still wouldn't be even close to a mistake. Instead, I pity the poor future wife who picks up Emma by Jane Austen one day, a woman who for obvious reasons bears no resemblance to my grandmother's inscription, and who asks: Ashcliff, was there ever such a woman?"

She looks up, curious, as he expects.

"And I'll say, I asked her to dance once – at my best friends' wedding. And she said no."

"And what will future wife say?"

"She will say, 'Ashcliff, you and I dance all the time'. And that will be her reassurance and my consolation."

She lowers her eyes again. "She will call you Ashcliff?"

"She will."

"Why?"

"Because I won't be a sheriff."

"Why not?"

"Because that's not the life I want with her. She and I are destined for better things."

"How can you know that?"

"Because in my life I know what those betters things will be."

Things he needs to tell her about but knows she is not equipped to hear. Her father has seen to that. For all his good intentions, Preston spooked her.

He understands exactly how much as he studies her bowed head and observes the hands clasped white in her lap. Soon, he tells himself. When the shock and hurt wears off a bit. The two of them, together, would help her get over her disappointment; restore her in ways she couldn't begin to imagine, if she would only let it happen.

For now, she has achieved what she set out to do: garner some sympathy and understanding from him. The jilted lover wasn't for him anyhow. And he'd never win her that way.

So, he does what Jennifer advised him to do.

"Dance with me, Emma?"

"And shatter poor future wife?"

"A thousand dances with her won't even come close to just one with you."

He glimpses the beginning of a smile.

She says, "I'm sure I don't dance as well as she will."

He reaches across her lap for her hand. "Emma... you do."

She looks at him, her eyes so full of feeling it almost stops his heart. "Then I'm ready."

"No compassion for poor future wife?"

"None."

Later, Raina appears in front of him, without Ben.

"Raina, how are you?"

"I am exceedingly well, Mr Ryan. *You* look a little serious. Perhaps the news that a photographer has arrived, asking for you, might be pleasing."

"It might," he says. "Except that he was supposed to be here an hour ago."

"I don't think it matters," she says, putting her arm through his. They start walking towards the door. "Apart from the fact that nothing ever seems to faze you, Mr Ryan, I think everyone will look *very* merry in the photographs, which will make a pleasant change from how people usually look – the champagne's nearly all been drunk."

Ethan

"Time to go, Ethan."

"Already? Feels like we're just gettin' started."

"Been over four hours. Clive Aiken will be here anytime to take me and Jennifer…"

"You can say it – home."

"That doesn't sound right yet."

"You'll get used it to. We all will." He puts his hand on Luke's shoulder and gives it a shake. "For you Jennifer is home, wherever she is, and there ain't nothing wrong with that. In fact, you got two homes because you always got the one you had, you know that."

The boy just smiles wide with his big meaningful eyes.

"Aw, stop looking at me like that…"

Luke laughs. "How am I supposed to look at you?"

"You ain't gonna make another speech are you?"

"Nope. I said everything already. But what you just said… thank you."

"You learn a lot about what makes a home when you pick a lonesome Indian girl out of the dust thinking you'll take care of her and she ends up taking care of you."

The boy – although it's high time he stops thinking of Luke as one – swallows hard. "She's been helping me, Ethan."

"She loved you like you were her own kin. Never a day goes by when I don't hear her voice in my head and feel her love in my heart. And I thank God I found her before those turkey buzzards. She was the finest person I ever knew, but I reckon you went and found yourself someone just as beautiful."

"I reckon you're right. Dammit, Ethan, are you trying to make me cry?"

"How am I doin' so far?" he grins. But there's a lump in the back of his throat. "Look at us, a couple of grown men crying at a weddin'."

"Reckon we'll be bawling when Sara gets here."

"Yep," he sighs. "Shame she couldn't get herself here. She's gonna regret it." It'd been preying on his mind all day…

"She has to let go of the past sometime."

"Would've helped being here. Well, off you go, say your goodbyes."

Luke hugs him, hard.

Ethan returns it and when they part, Jennifer is beside him.

"Thank you, Ethan."

"Aw, you're welcome, darlin', but it's John and Amy you should be thanking."

"We will be," she says.

"You're gonna be happy, but if he gives you any trouble, you know where to come."

"And what if I give him trouble?"

"Bound to be good for him – and don't you forget that."

When he winks at her, she grins and kisses his cheek.

"Go on, the pair of you. We'll see you when we do."

If he thought it was good for Luke to put the weddin' off till Sara could get back here then he might've made a case, but considering everything that's happened and how Sara would likely take it, this is better. And looking at Jennifer's tender face, with her cheeks like roses and the smile that would melt ice, this is better than better. This is plain good.

He'll deal with Sara when the time comes.

"Here we go…"

And he makes the announcement that the bride and groom will be leaving.

Luke

John grips his hand and says, "You know me and Amy are proud of you. Always will be."

Amy hugs him. "We can't imagine our life without you, you know that don't you?"

They had to imagine – and live – a life without Mart and without K. Although he's been reluctant to admit it till now, he's felt their spirit around him all day long.

So much has changed since they'd been gone; he's changed, life has moved on from those confusing, frustrating days. The grief he'd suffered over their loss has changed with him. It travels his path, it does whatever he does, and today it got married, today it took the shape of love and joy. The loss needed to be justified and it was; he is living his life the way they would want him to, for the price they paid.

"Thank you, for everything."

"Go and be happy," Amy says. "You got the right, Luke. So be happy."

He has to believe she means it.

When Frank shakes his hand and wishes him well, when Jeanne kisses his cheek and the children gather round, that tired notion of gaining a family when you marry suddenly doesn't seem so tired; a few things in his heart are rearranging themselves to make some room for these likeable people who until a few days ago he had never met. They belonged to Jennifer and that meant something.

Unexpected, but kinda pleasant.

"That's a lotta family," he'd said to Jennifer after supper with them the night before last.

"You'll get used to it," she said. "Besides you never know when you might need them."

He didn't bring it up then but he reckoned she meant Dermot.

Dermot the Unknown.

The Unspoken... The Unresolved... who gives him an ache in his gut whenever his thoughts drift that way.

Davina pulls on his coat and interrupts his thoughts. He crouches down to make himself level with her.

"I had a good time," she says.

"I'm glad."

She nods and her curls dance. "Mama says you have the nicest blue eyes she's ever seen, and me and Caro and Ari think so, too."

They seem a little young to be noticing stuff like that, but then...

Girls start young.

Ethan's timeless advice to him when he was nine years old puts a grin on his face as the tiny Caro joins them and Davina takes her hand.

How young, Ethan?

Five, mabbe, six...They got you sized up, chewed up and spat out years before you even knowed they existed, that's how young. Luke was shocked; Ethan laughed. And more wisdom was added over the years... *Being female is a whole other country. They got language and customs and rules all their own. Helps if you make a study of them. You go bargin' in without givin' it some thought you might not get outa there alive...*

Caro asks, "Will you come visit us?"

"Sure."

"Don't forget to bring AJ," Davina says.

"I won't forget."

Conor and Finn jostle for position.

"When you come, we want you teach us about horses," Conor says.

"I think that can be arranged."

"And we'd like to stay on your ranch one time."

"That's enough, you two," says their mother.

"We'll work on it," he tells them. They grin and take turns shaking his hand.

Ariel waves at him shyly, as she stands beside her father.

"You did a fine job looking after Adam," he says.

She blushes. "He's very nice. Is he my cousin now?"

"You're second cousins, I guess."

"Ooh, never had one of those before. Did you hear that, Davie?"

He looks to Frank who's standing patiently.

"So you're still heading home tomorrow?" he asks.

"We are. The weather's not right for sight-seeing with five children. And you and Jennifer are tied up here with the trial."

"Maybe you could see your way out to the ranch for a holiday this summer."

"Sounds like excellent motivation for two young gentlemen."

"They'll learn a thing or two. Thanks for coming, Frank."

On he goes.

The Severini family. (*Grazie, Signora, alimento squisito, delizioso! Alfredo, Gianni, bravo, grazie!*)

And Tip. They hug hard and fast. (*noo nu puetsuku u punin ne, waha sia sumu tosa. ura, tami... See you again soon, Two Feathers One White; thank you, little brother.*)

Tressa, Ben and Raina, and Caroline. (*"Richard has gone upstairs to lie down."*) With them once more a united family, a sense of pride in them becomes emotion which almost overtakes him; especially when Tressa squeezes his hand and kisses his cheek.

Then Meg, with a wink... (*"The wedding cake was delicious."*)

...and Emmaline, who apologizes for her earlier odd behavior and her loud entrance at the church, and thanks him for inviting her. She might be quirky but she is certainly one of them and no apologies would ever be necessary.

Cam.

And Cliff...

Emmaline

The three of them – Ashcliff, Luke and Mr Faraday – stand in a closed huddle. If they're chatting about the flowers, the cake and the ceremony she'll eat her hat... her hair comb with the silk flowers that match her dress then, since she's not wearing a hat.

She bobs down so they can't see her, but close enough to them to overhear their conversation. Davina Sullivan is also within earshot; Emmaline calls her over in a loud whisper and when the little girl arrives, she asks her to talk about her favorite subject – angels. Little Davie Sullivan begins and doesn't stop.

Now for the men...

"See you Monday, I guess," Luke is saying.

"Unless voir dire takes a sticky turn on Saturday, testimony *should* begin on Monday," Mr Faraday offers. "But finding *this* jury will not be the proverbial piece of cake."

Luke mutters something she can't hear; it's probably what she's thinking – concurring with Mr Faraday about the jury. It is a real concern. One they have to consider carefully.

"But nothing for you to be concerned about," Ashcliff says firmly. Certainly, a groom should not be thinking about such things on the day of his wedding... on his wedding night.

"So angels can do all kinds of..."

"Good luck," Mr Faraday says.

Luke seems to have warmed up when it comes to Mr Faraday; he sounds genuine as he utters his thanks.

Ashcliff says, "Come on, you and your bride need to get out of here."

They break their huddle before Emmaline can get to her feet; she had to wear a tighter corset than normal for the pink gown. Mr Faraday steps back and almost falls over her. As he straightens up, apologizing to her and helping her upright, Emmaline does a double-take at the sight of Jennifer preparing to throw her bouquet of creamy white roses. The bouquet is launched and the darn thing is coming her way; she caught the bouquet at Celie's wedding and that was enough; folks bothered her for weeks after...*your turn next, Emmie Roberts.*

Quickly, she steps aside. Jennifer's roses land with a graceful *whoosh* in Mr Faraday's hands, right side up and not a petal out of place.

While everyone is laughing themselves stupid, Davina looks miffed.

"That's not fair. He's so tall..."

Emmaline lifts the little girl into her arms and together they look at Mr Faraday standing nonplussed with the bouquet in his hands.

"Boys aren't supposed to catch it," Davina explains to him.

Mr Faraday puts the bouquet straight into her star-shaped little hands.

"I got it, I got it!" Davina squeals, trying to show everyone.

Emmaline puts her on the floor and Davina runs off to show to her siblings.

"Really, Miss Roberts, was that necessary?"

Emmaline swallows a giggle and clears her throat. "Sorry, Mr Faraday. But may I say that was indeed a fine catch."

"No, you may not," he says and, with a dignified expression, walks away towards Meg, who is trying in vain to hide her amusement.

Emmaline's gaze runs into Ashcliff's; his eyes are shining, a grin moving this way and that on his face. He walks slowly by her, murmuring, "Wouldn't want to be a certain *someone* in the witness box next week."

Just minutes later, Luke leads his bride away while everyone is calling their goodbyes and well-wishes.

Down the hall and out the front door.

Tressa threads her arm through Emmaline's and walks her outside where it's now cold and dark.

Out on the street, Luke is handing Jennifer into the waiting buggy. He climbs in and sits close by her side. Light from a nearby street lamp casts a magical glow over them. They wave, and those on the sidewalk wave back. Bride and groom share a kiss as they are driven away.

Tressa sighs, "If I'd had a wedding like that..."

Emmaline studies her through the white clouds they breathe. "Yes, go on."

"It's cold out here, let's go back inside."

"So what was your wedding like?" Emmaline asks as they turn and start walking.

But Amy is standing alone on the garden path a few feet away, and Tressa stops, looks confused momentarily, and says, "I...I'll tell you some other time." She meets Amy on the path and the two walk into the house together.

Weddings!

And she had attended a fair few in recent times. The Roberts' family alone had had three up until this point in time. And she had dodged the bouquet at all of these weddings except Celie's. Each and every wedding had embodied hope and love, just as Luke and Jennifer's had done this very day. But who could blame her if she'd become a little marriage-shy, particularly after this latest development with the Sheriff and her mama?

You loved my wedding, Emmie, and you will love your own, when the time comes. Besides, you'll be singing a different tune by then.

What tune?

...Cliff

Saturday morning before voir dire

It's a cold, crisp morning and it's good to be out in it. The peaceful after-effects of the wedding still linger in the air he breathes. The trial is about to commence. The hour of evidence is coming. The day of justice is at hand. Waxing lyrical, in his own mind at least, he factors in a twenty minute bookstore detour on his way to the courthouse. Owner Freddy Hart has just opened his doors.

"Sheriff..."

"Freddy..."

"Miss Roberts has just beaten you." Freddy nods in the direction of the poetry books. "You two are my best customers."

Emma looks up, probably overhearing her name, and half smiles at him. She may not be as pleased to see him as he is to see her, but that could change if he plays his cards right.

"Morning," he says, casually crossing to her while quickly thinking of a reason to engage her. "Poetry?"

"You know I like poetry. What are you doing here? I thought you were..."

"I'm searching for a book..."

"Well, yes..."

"...to buy you as a matter of fact."

"Why would you do that?"

"If you could have any book in the whole store, which would it be?"

"I don't want you to go to all that trouble..."

"I want you to have something to remember me by when you go home. After all, you gave me books to remember you…"

She stares at him, a small frown across her eyes.

"I'm glad we crossed paths. I could have made a bad choice."

"Would it have mattered?"

He smiles. "Considering you probably read everything you lay your eyes on, probably not, but I'd prefer it to be meaningful. So," he says, looking around at the books, "which one?"

Finally she seems agreeable, and heads straight for a particular bookshelf. She lifts a book, two in fact, and brings them across, and as his heart beats strangely, she shows him.

Les Miserables. The extraordinary two-volume masterpiece of Frenchman Victor Hugo.

"Sure?"

"I'm sure." Her eyes are shining as though she's found treasure, and the right person to share it with.

He regards her with expectation falling all over itself.

"I feel sure you've read it," she adds.

He gives a distracted nod. And remembers how he felt when he first picked it up. He was fourteen years old; the words enveloped him; picked him up and took him away; reshaped him. This is his favorite work of literature…

"Then you know how I feel…"

"Yes," he says.

Her eyes are alight, like golden lamps.

"Listen," she says. With the second volume slipped under her arm, she opens volume one as though it holds no mysteries for her, only fabulous wealth. "The Author's Preface: *As long as there shall exist, by reason of law and custom, a social condemnation, which, in the face of civilization, artificially creates hells on earth…*"

And she reads (her gentle southern accent as beautiful a melody as he's ever heard) Hugo's powerful summation on the source of human suffering, his rationalization for having written one of the world's most important works of literature.

"*…so long as ignorance and misery remain on earth, books like this cannot be useless.*" She looks up finally. "It's wonderful. No matter how many times I read it."

And he could listen to her read it as often as she cared to. She is exactly as his grandmother described: intoxicated by the words; captivated by their power; heart and mind humming at the prospect of the endless discussions to be had.

He says, "*Part Three: Marius. Book One. Chapter Four. He may be useful.*"

In a heartbeat, she has located his reference. She reads with a question in her voice, "*Paris begins with the cockney and ends with the gamin...?*"

"*All monarchy is comprised in the cockney; all anarchy in the gamin.*"

She hands him the book and he takes it from her.

He reads lightly, since he knows it almost by heart, "*This pale child of the Paris suburbs lives, develops, and gets into and out of 'scrapes', amid suffering, a thoughtful witness of our social realities and our human problems. He thinks himself careless, but he is not. He looks on, ready to laugh; ready, also, for something else. Whoever ye are who call yourselves Prejudice, Abuse, Ignominy, Oppression, Iniquity, Despotism, Injustice, Fanaticism, Tyranny, beware of the gaping gamin.*"

"Perfectly done. I think you might love it even more than I," she says. "You seem to know it by heart."

"Victor Hugo is a hero of mine. And just now you looked like someone who'd found Aladdin's cave."

"I confess it's true," she laughs.

"Then this is the one."

"You don't have to buy it. Just to talk..." She stops herself from speaking what they both know to be true. "Well, if you insist."

He closes the book. "Even more now I know how much it means to you. You probably need a new copy anyhow."

"I... yes. Thank you."

He pays for the two volumes and tells Freddy it won't be necessary to wrap them.

"Anything else I can help you with, Sheriff? Miss Roberts? Always happy to advise a couple of book lovers like you two."

"Thank you, but I have everything I need," Emma tells him.

"Everything," he concurs and moves them away from Freddy and the cashier's desk to a table of books by the door.

"May I?" he asks, pointing to the pencil she has forgotten to remove from behind her ear.

"Oh…" With a blush in her cheeks, she offers him the pencil.

He opens the cover of the first volume and writes.

Thank you for being my Emma. I hope you find happiness and success in whatever you do and wherever you go. Live life to make the dreams of the world come true. God bless you, my sweet friend. James Ashcliff Ryan.

He closes the cover and hands the book to her. "Read it later?"

"I will."

"I won't get them back, will I?"

"No," she smiles.

As those eyes of gold gaze up at him and he is tempted to allow them to beguile him into thinking she doesn't have a devious bone in her sweet southern body, the desire to take her in his arms and kiss some sense into her begins its all too familiar struggle; however, since kissing her in a public place would not work in his favor, he glances into those sparkling eyes and ever so tenderly slides the pencil back behind her shell-pink ear.

At that moment a vivid recollection of dancing with her at the wedding flashes into his mind. Kind of shocked, he looks into her face and wonders if she with her bewitching ways put it there. But she was concentrating on the books, wasn't she?

As he slides deeper under her spell, he senses a change in her. Her natural sweetness has gained an edge to it, sharpened by…

By what? A certain recollection perhaps…

It was an exceptional dance; from the moment she placed her hand in his, nothing else was of any consequence. Their eyes got stuck on one another and didn't budge. They moved together with blissful unity. What began as the socially correct distance between two dancing partners had become barely two inches between them by the time they realized the music had stopped. Every cell in his body burned with the need to love her. His heartbeats bumped in his ears. At that moment, with her starry *kiss not me* eyes, her rose-tinged cheeks, her shallow breaths through parted lips, she was more his Emma than she'd ever been. And he knew she felt it.

Thank you for the dance, he murmured.

You're welcome, she murmured back.

They turned away at the same time and went in opposite directions, and didn't look at each other for quite some time.

So what began with him as a sensible, often ruthless but love-struck sheriff in pursuit of a difficult and fascinating young woman ended with him knowing he would never love another woman but her in his whole lifetime.

And Raina wondered why he looked 'a little serious'.

As he snaps out of his reverie, Emma appears to be surfacing from one of her own.

"Emma..."

"I have to go," she says quickly and leaves.

Testing his patience is a favorite pastime of hers; it is her right as the mistress of his heart, and his willing duty to oblige her.

Sunday morning

Church with the Severinis; just because he is guarding key witnesses doesn't mean he can't enjoy their company, and as usual he practices his Italian on the walk to and from St John's, the boys teaching him something spicy and their mother clipping them over the ear while trying not to laugh. Sometimes Signora, always primly dressed in black and wrapped in a huge black shawl, pays no attention to them at all; her thoughts drift elsewhere, to the upcoming trial perhaps, to the job they came here to do, to restoring the good name of Severini in memory of her husband.

The usual invitation to Sunday breakfast is extended at the gate, which this morning he declines.

Signora reaches up and pinches his cheek.

"Grazie," she says. "Grazie."

Didn't take long for her to forget he once was the Deputy US Marshal who arrested her son.

"Ciao, Signora."

Alfredo and Gianni snigger gleefully while Signora shoos them up the pathway, rebuking them in fast and furious Italian.

He heads back down 18th and intends to grab coffee and pie at Martha's before an unscheduled (and probably unnecessary) check on the prisoners. Mac's prison guards are highly regarded but the responsibility rests with him as Sheriff. Besides, he has a few hours to kill before a Sunday roast with Cam and Meg.

He comes across Emma, gazing up into the admirable oak tree on the corner near the Congregational Church. She is on her way home from Mass, but she always stays behind and chats with her fellow parishioners, which would be why she hasn't got very far. He imagines her and Nugent rejoicing over their success with Jacob Hunter.

Emma straightens up immediately upon seeing him.

He peers up into the tree. "Is there a kitten caught up there?"

"Not that I could see."

"Then what?"

"I have to go," she says hastily and sets off.

"Ah! I know… you're looking for signs of Spring."

"I like the tree, that's all…"

"Have breakfast with me?" he calls after her.

"No, thank you," she says over her shoulder.

"Coffee?" he calls even louder. "Pie at Martha's?"

"I have things to do."

"I'll bring my battered copy of Les Miserables and you can bring your new one; we'll break it in."

Abruptly, she stops and swings around. "Shhh! Stop shouting," she shouts in hushed overtones. "Have you no decorum?"

He quickly closes the gap between them. "What was that?"

"James Ashcliff Ryan, I swear…"

"My copy's a first edition."

"You read a first edition Hugo into batteredness?" she exclaims, her eyes flashing at him.

He changes his plans and starts them strolling in the direction of home…

"When was the work published – '62?"

"I believe so."

"Somewhat new compared to Emma by Jane Austen."

"Even so, by the time you have grandchildren…"

He laughs at her. "So, I should have kept my father's book on the shelf and bought another copy to read into batteredness."

"Too late now."

"I have no regrets. Nor did my father; he never liked Hugo."

"Thank you for what you wrote in *my* book. Cliff, I will be returning home because that is where I belong. Really, I can't stay here. I just can't. It was never planned that way. And I wish for you the same you wish for me, happiness and success. I mean it."

"I know," he says, keeping it light.

By now they have reached his gate. And they stop.

"Well, perhaps another time, when you are not so busy..."

He catches her looking up at his house; his books are an attribute decidedly in his favor.

"How many first editions do you have?" she asks.

"My father made a serious hobby of collecting first editions; did I neglect to tell you that?"

"Mm."

He opens his gate and walks through. "It's cold and you should keep moving, unless you want to come inside for coffee and books."

"Thank you, no. Nan Morris will have breakfast waiting. So, goodbye."

"I have eggs."

"I mean it, I'm saying goodbye."

"I think they're pretty fresh eggs..."

"Nan Morris keeps her own chickens."

"Oh." He closes the gate. "Does she have a cow?"

"Is she within the law to keep a cow?"

"After what happened in Chicago with Mrs O'Leary's, how can anyone think it a good idea?"

"I take your point."

"*Does* she have one?"

"I'm not divulging my landlady's business to the sheriff. You don't tell me things because I'm a reporter. Off the record is usually the first thing out of your mouth." She straightens her hat. "Good day." And walks off.

"Good day," he says, admiring the graceful swing of her hips, waiting to see if she turns around. After a bit, she flicks a glance over her shoulder. Satisfied, he crunches his way up the path to his door.

Once inside, he goes to his bookcase and lifts Emma by Jane Austen from its place. He opens the cover and runs his eyes over *Lita's* inscription. There is no guarantee written there in his grandmother's words that even if Ashcliff found his Emma he would get to keep her. He takes up the Tapirs next. *You might not know me in the tropics. I am different there.* Here in Cheyenne she is a warm body in a cold climate.

He rubs his eye.

There's a test coming. He's going to have to let her go.

Back to her mother and her twin sister. Back to her normal life and warm climate to discover for her that she truly loves him.

And he?

He needs to find out if he can fulfill his destiny.

Without her.

In any climate.

THE END OF VOLUME THREE

Taylor Family Tree

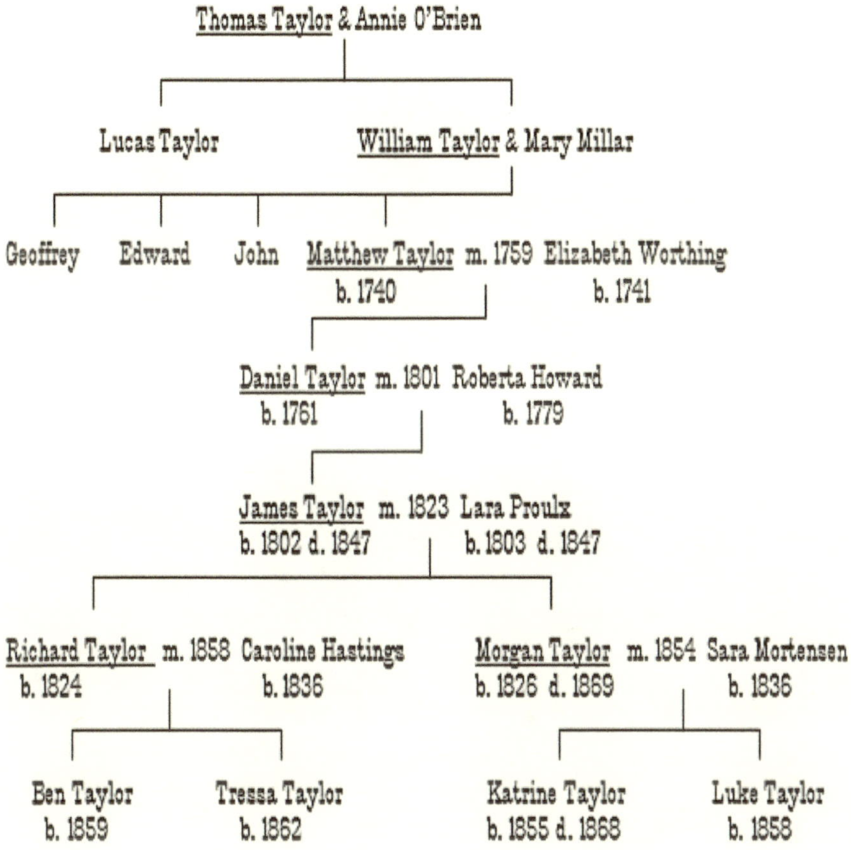

Thomas Taylor & Annie O'Brien

Lucas Taylor   William Taylor & Mary Millar

Geoffrey   Edward   John   Matthew Taylor   m. 1759   Elizabeth Worthing
b. 1740   b. 1741

Daniel Taylor   m. 1801   Roberta Howard
b. 1761   b. 1779

James Taylor   m. 1823   Lara Proulx
b. 1802 d. 1847   b. 1803 d. 1847

Richard Taylor   m. 1858   Caroline Hastings   Morgan Taylor   m. 1854   Sara Mortensen
b. 1824   b. 1836   b. 1826 d. 1869   b. 1836

Ben Taylor   Tressa Taylor   Katrine Taylor   Luke Taylor
b. 1859   b. 1862   b. 1855 d. 1868   b. 1858

The birthright we hold
We will not be slaves

THE LIBERTY & PROPERTY LEGENDS
A saga of The West and Gilded Age America

by
TERRI SEDMAK

America 1880's. Lives taken, justice sought. Love won and love lost.
Friendships forged and families fractured.
As terror grows, heroes rise.

HEARTLAND
On the Side of Angels

VOLUME ONE

WYOMING, 1883... Three families, one Alliance. A cold-blooded murder.
The conflict. The secrets. The passion. And the fight for justice.

ADVENTURE AND ROMANCE WILL NOT BE DENIED ANYONE
WHO HAS THE COURAGE TO BE FREE.

'...sweeping historical fiction. Heartland is meaningful, entertaining and high-spirited. Terri Sedmak paints a lucid picture in the course of her writing: stories are revealed through the characters... and readers are right there with them.' *PS News*

'I'm so impressed by the way Terri Sedmak is able to 'write a picture'. I feel as though I am in the same room/space as the characters. A creative, insightful and poetic writer.' *Keystone Creations*

'Recreations of 19th century America are evocative.' *Daily Telegraph*

'Heartland is a fast-paced and riveting read.' *Midwest Book Review*

THE LIBERTY & PROPERTY LEGENDS
A saga of The West and Gilded Age America

by
TERRI SEDMAK

America 1880's. Lives taken, justice sought. Love won and love lost.
Friendships forged and families fractured.
As terror grows, heroes rise.

EMPIRE ᶠᵒᴿ LIBERTY
Dangerous Lullaby

VOLUME TWO

WYOMING, 1885... THEIR DARKEST HOUR IS COMING...

In this fast-paced, character-rich second volume and sequel to Heartland, warmed
by humor and romance, we witness the best and worst of humanity. We are now
deep in the heart of The Liberty & Property Legends and there is no going back.

'This second instalment in The Liberty & Property Legends sees the
ghastly consequences of Ed Parsons' land grab, and the accompanying
murder, begin to spread. Ambitious reporter Emmaline Roberts arrives
in Cheyenne to investigate and is soon relying on the not-so-tender
mercies of Sheriff Cliff Ryan to stay alive. With the scope and intrigue
of a great soap, this story makes for compulsive reading.'
That's Life! Fast Fiction

'It's easy to get immersed in the vibrant history. As you are swept into
the lives of an engaging Cliff and a feisty Emmaline, you start caring for
the characters. Another emotional rollercoaster is assured with Empire
for Liberty, a second instalment in a six-part series. This Australian
author certainly knows how to paint a vivid picture!'
PS News

'This is one of the best fiction stories I have read in a long time,
regardless of genre. Empire for Liberty is a very clever second book.'
NSW Writers' Centre

www.ingramcontent.com/pod-product-compliance
Lightning Source LLC
Chambersburg PA
CBHW020822030726
47496CB00001B/49

* 9 7 8 1 9 2 5 0 8 6 1 9 5 *